PRAISE FOR *HOW LUCKY YOU ARE*

"A nuanced, heartfelt debut, HOW LUCKY YOU ARE artfully honors the importance of dear old friends. I can't wait to read more from Kristyn Kusek Lewis."

—Allie Larkin, author of *Stay* and *Why Can't I Be You*

"In this wise and compulsively readable debut, Lewis follows three thirtysomething female friends and tackles even the heaviest of subjects with a restrained and self-assured hand, avoiding sentimentality while displaying an impressive emotional range. I could smell the doughnut muffins, taste the margaritas, and feel each high and low right along with the delightful characters. If you've ever had a best friend or been a best friend, this is a book for you."

—Meg Mitchell Moore, author of *The Arrivals* and *So Far Away*

"Kristyn Kusek Lewis's HOW LUCKY YOU ARE is a moving, thoughtful story about what happens when friends become family and stay close despite all odds. It's an honest, empathetic novel of love, commitment, and female friendship with characters I didn't want to let go."

—Meredith Goldstein, author of *The Singles* and Love Letters columnist at the *Boston Globe*

"Charming and achingly real, Kristyn Kusek Lewis's HOW LUCKY YOU ARE is an endearing story about finding your way amid the many intricacies of friendship. I'm certain it will become a book club favorite."

—Sarah Jio, author of *The Violets of March* and *The Bungalow*

HOW LUCKY YOU ARE

HOW LUCKY YOU ARE

∞

Kristyn Kusek Lewis

five
spot

New York Boston

5 Spot
Hachette Book Group
237 Park Avenue
New York, NY 10017

Printed in the United States of America

5 Spot is an imprint of Grand Central Publishing.
The 5 Spot name and logo are trademarks of Hachette Book Group, Inc.

The publisher is not responsible for websites (or their content) that are not owned by the publisher.

ISBN 978-1-62090-502-9

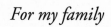

For my family

HOW LUCKY YOU ARE

CHAPTER ONE

I'm in the dining room, counting place settings, when the doorbell rings.

A happy, charming, ladylike clang, it's a sound only an old house could make, which mine is. I inherited it from my grandmother.

"That's probably Amy and Mike," I call to Kate, who's sitting in the kitchen. I put down the handful of silverware I was distributing and go to answer the door.

I love having people over. My house is a brownstone that I never could have afforded on my own, and while it's not the most extravagant home on the street or the best kept, there is something about it that makes people stop at the bottom of its terra-cotta steps, their mouths open in lustful, longing *ohhhhs*. Ivy creeps up the brick facade, nasturtium spills from the window boxes, stained-glass panels glimmer above the wide oak double doors.

To any passing stranger, it looks just like home.

I turn the brass doorknob and swing open the heavy door.

"Hell-lo-o!" I sing in three syllables, the way that I'm apt to do when greeting houseguests. Amy is my other closest friend. I hold my arms out for a hug and say hello to her husband as I wrap my arms around her. "It's so good to see you. Kate's already here."

As we walk back into the kitchen, I glimpse Kate sitting on one of the barstools at the center island, picking a piece of Roquefort off of the cheese plate I put together an hour ago. She hears us coming—Amy's voice is always two notches louder than it needs to be, and bubbly and eager, like when she was a cheerleader in high school—but instead of turning her head to acknowledge us and say hello, Kate waits, daintily licking a crumb from her finger. This is not unusual. My best friend is a bit of a princess. She's accustomed to having people come to her.

Amy walks beside me, telling me how Emma, her three-year-old, is going through a phase where she insists on dressing herself. "I've decided to just give in and let her do it," she says. "Today she went to school in purple tights, a Minnie Mouse nightgown, and the patent leather Mary Janes that I bought for her to wear with her Christmas dress." There's no quiet, small-talk easing in with Amy. Conversations with her are of the dive-right-in variety. When Kate and I first met Amy thirteen years ago, in the six feet of hallway that separated the door of our first postcollege apartment from hers, our eyes slid toward each other, silently asking, *Is she for real?* Unbelievably, she is. In all of the years that I've known Amy, I can't remember a single instance when she was surly, moody, or rude. It can get on your nerves. But I suppose that when I crave surly, moody, or rude, I have Kate, who's told me on more than one occasion that she and her husband secretly refer to Amy as "the golden retriever."

When we get to the kitchen, Amy stops midsentence, her face lighting up as if she's just stumbled into her own surprise party. "Kaaate!" she squeals. "No Brendan tonight?"

"Working," Kate says, smoothing her wool trousers with her hands as she stands to greet them. "Where else would he be?" She hugs Amy hello and halfheartedly holds up a palm to wave to her husband.

Mike nods back. While Kate and Amy get along fine—they are nothing alike but friends nonetheless, with me as the link between them—Kate and Mike are barely civil, meeting each other somewhere on the continuum between total indifference and outright contempt. "Why did Amy marry him?" Kate often says when his name comes up. After evenings like this one, when she actually has to share breathing space with him, she can be downright evil. On the phone the next day, she'll denigrate where he's from. (*What is it? Buffalo? Allentown? Some other horrendous place like that?*) It's actually Rochester, New York. Or she'll criticize his career. (*A family doctor? So he asks old people about their bowel movements and takes snot-faced toddlers' temperatures?*) I don't think that Kate has a right to be as cruel as she can be, but it's true that Mike's become kind of a drag. Whenever he's around, he sulks like he has some thrilling other life that he's missing out on, as if he might be out clubbing with Brazilian supermodels or chasing down Russian spies if only he didn't have to spend time with his wife and her friends. I don't particularly look forward to his company in the way that I used to, and to be honest, I've wondered how Amy puts up with it, though I'd never say anything to her. I mean, how do you tell one of your closest girlfriends—particularly one who tends to bounce through her days as if life's one big Broadway musical—that her husband's kind of a dud?

I hand Amy a glass of wine and ask Mike what he'd like to drink. "Oh, wait!" Amy says, pulling a small box of Crabtree & Evelyn soaps out of her bag and handing it to me. "I saw this the other day at the mall and thought you'd like it."

"Oh, Amy, you don't have to do this," I say, rolling my eyes and pulling her in for a hug. "Really, after all these years, aren't we way beyond hostess gifts?"

"Seriously, Amy," Kate says, twirling the stem of her wineglass between her thumb and forefinger, making the base skitter against the butcher-block countertop. "You're making me look bad."

I smirk at her over Amy's shoulder.

"Please, Kate," Amy says. "You've never had a bad-looking day in your life."

"I told her that she didn't need to bring anything, but she never listens," Mike barks from the corner of the kitchen. The sound of his voice is surprising and sharp. When we all turn to him, he shrugs his shoulders and glances around, shuffling in his leather bomber jacket and Redskins cap. Kate will say something about the jacket later—I can tell by the way that she raises her eyebrows at me. I turn away before Amy notices and open the refrigerator door, loading up my arms with salad greens, a jar of Dijon mustard, and the butter dish.

Amy clears her throat and starts to tell a story about something they heard on the radio on the way over—something about a pop singer's affair and surprise pregnancy. While I'm washing lettuce at the sink and listening to her talk, I glance at Kate, who's taking several healthy sips of her wine. My boyfriend's coworker and his girlfriend are joining our usual group for dinner tonight, and I hope Kate will behave herself.

"What are we having? It smells so good," Amy says as she walks to the stove. She picks up the wooden spoon next to the enamel pot to stir its contents.

"Beef bourguignon. Julia Child's recipe," I say. It had been the kind of pissed-off February weather that makes it perfectly clear that winter is nowhere near over. Plus, if I was going to feed seven people after working in my bakery all day, I needed something unfussy. "I've made this a million times. Mom used to make it for dinner parties when I was a kid. I'd stand on a chair next to the stove—in my *Dukes of Hazzard* nightgown, of course—and she'd taste a bit with her wooden spoon and then hold it out for me to try. 'Needs more pepper,' I'd say, feeling very important."

Amy laughs. "That's *so* cute. I can just see you, Waverly. The budding chef!"

I wink at her. "Well…" I turn back to my salad and listen to Amy ask Kate whether she ever watched *The Dukes* and whether she preferred Bo or Luke. What I neglected to mention about tonight's dinner is that I *also* chose to make beef bourguignon because stew meat is so cheap—and cheap is becoming increasingly important these days. To be honest, I should be serving ketchup sandwiches.

It seems like twice a week, I'll hear some analyst on NPR say that there are signs that the economy is finally picking up, but I have to say, this small-business owner isn't feeling an iota of those vibes. Maggie's, my bakery, sits smack in the middle of Maple Hill, Virginia. Less than ten miles from D.C., my hometown has a nearly perfect mix of urban and suburban living, with brownstones like mine surrounding the center of town, your typical family neighborhoods farther south, and supertony old farmhouse-style homes out toward what used to be the country but is now crazy D.C. sprawl. Because it's so close to the city, Maple Hill has always attracted transplants transferring here for government jobs, and before the economy tanked, houses were snatched up practically the minute a "For Sale" sign went up. That's not so much the case anymore—there are three foreclosures on my block alone—and over the past year or so, my business has started to suffer right along with everything else.

I'm someone who's prone to worry too much as it is—whenever Larry, my boyfriend, gets on a plane to visit his family back home in Minnesota, my latent Catholicism kicks right in and I start muttering Hail Marys—but this problem with my business is a whole other animal. Larry, Kate, and Amy know that I've suffered a little—who hasn't? But I haven't been *totally* honest about just how dire things are, particularly with Larry, who lives with me and shares my household bills. He doesn't know that I barely keep up on the payments for the home equity loan I used to fund my business. Or about the twenty-seven thousand dollars in credit card debt. Or the late rent payments on the bakery.

"Hey, Mike?" I turn toward him. He's examining the collage of junk on my fridge as if the appointment reminder from my dermatologist and a postcard picture of three women in old-fashioned swimsuits actually interest him. "Larry should be down any minute. Are you sure I can't get you a beer? Take your coat?"

"I'm fine," he says, shaking his head and shoving his hands in his pockets. I watch him wander off into the living room and breathe a secret sigh of relief. Finally, it's just the three of us.

"So, Kate!" Amy says, relieving the room of its five seconds of silence. "I haven't seen you in, what, two weeks? How's the campaign going?"

"You know, luncheon, meeting, luncheon, fund-raiser. Blah, blah, blah."

"Oh, Kate, you don't really mean that! It's all *so* exciting," Amy gushes, clasping her hands to her chest with the wistful enthusiasm of a Disney princess. "Just think, by this time next year, you could be living in the governor's mansion!"

"Yes, I know. Fantastic," Kate says evenly, motioning for Amy to bring her the wine bottle from the counter. "I can't wait to move to Richmond and spend my days watching hordes of fat tourists in new sneakers waddle by my front door. It will be heavenly."

"Oh, Kate, come on," I say, chopping the thyme I've gathered into a neat pile on the cutting board. Lately it seems like whenever anyone asks Kate about Brendan's run for governor, her response is just as it is tonight, sarcastic and unimpressed, like a teenager talking about some lame school dance. Her obvious bitterness belies the fact that even though the election is still nine months away, all of the newspapers are already running dreamy articles about Brendan's likely win and their impending Camelot-like reign over the state of Virginia.

You can't blame them, I think, glancing at Kate, who's fiddling with the gumball-sized diamond stud in her earlobe as she listens to Amy reminisce about the first time that she went on the White House tour after she moved to D.C. from North Carolina. Kate has a way of captivating people. I noticed it the minute we met, on our first day of ninth grade at Madeira, the private girls' school we both attended.

Kate had waltzed into our American history class a full twenty minutes late, her only explanation a simple nod of her head toward our prim, bespectacled teacher, an Alex P. Keaton type who talked with a lisp. It was the kind of gesture that a royal might give to her underlings while striding the halls of her palace, and it somehow, inexplicably, worked. She then flopped into the desk in front of mine, turned around in her seat, and offered her hand. It was manicured, I noticed. Even my mom didn't get manicures. "Hi, I'm Kate," she said, not even pretending to whisper, as if we were sitting on a park bench instead of in a classroom where a lesson was under way.

Kate is beautiful—the kind of beautiful that you don't know really exists until you see an old Grace Kelly film or visit Italy for the first time. I soon discovered that she also had a big mouth and a family name that let her get away with things. In short, she was everything we are supposed to want, especially as fourteen-year-olds. William Townsend, her father, had helmed the family business—a multinational shipping corporation—for decades. Her mother, Evelyn, was the daughter of a legendary Supreme Court justice revered by just about every right-leaning politician in Washington. The other girls at school envied Kate as much as they despised her, mimicking the way that she braided her hair and tied her mother's Hermès scarves onto a strap of the leather satchel she used for a book bag, all the while whispering about what a bitch she was. Men—our teachers, her father's colleagues, our classmates' fathers, passersby on the street—looked at Kate in such an unabashedly lustful way that it reminded me of those scenes in cartoons where the object of desire turns into a steak before the predator's googly, hungry eyes. My mom once said, as she watched Kate bound out of our house in a tennis skirt that just barely covered her ass, that she would grow up to be the kind of woman whom other women didn't want around their husbands.

I knew back then, and still know today, that our friendship is an improbable one. I had been able to attend Madeira only because of a financial aid package. My dad was a midlevel photographer for UPI, my mom worked in an insurance office, and though we were in Maple Hill, we lived in the kind of dim ranch-house neighborhood where everyone's front yards are blanketed with dead leaves year-round. Even if I had come from a family like Kate's, or like those of the politicians' daughters we went to school with, I just didn't look like the kind of girl she would cozy up to. I had my Polish grandmother's thickish build; I draped myself in loads of the burnout jewelry that my mother had collected while following bands with my father when they were dating; I couldn't—still can't—bother to deal with the mess of curls springing from my head like live wires. While Kate starred on the equestrian and tennis teams, I spent most of my time after school watching reruns of *What's Happening?* and reading the dirty sections of my mom's Judith Krantz novels while I waited for someone to come home from work.

Still, the two of us somehow clicked. There had been moments over the course of our teenaged friendship when I wondered about the very thing that I was certain the other girls around us said: Maybe Kate befriended me because I was such an underdog and posed no threat to her queen bee status. But as the years went by, those suspicions faded and our relationship deepened. If there was anything that initially drew Kate to me, it was that I was too clueless to care about who she was or where she came from. I know now, as you come to understand your close friends' insecurities without ever speaking them aloud, that Kate loves me because being with me means that she doesn't have to perform.

∞

We both ventured north for college—me to Bowdoin and Kate to Brown, a school so liberal that it was obvious she'd chosen it simply to spite her parents, who'd expected her to attend Yale like everyone else in her family. We met Amy when we were twenty-two, on the day that we moved into our first D.C. apartment. Housed in a dirty brick building in Adams Morgan, it was about what you would expect for a couple of recent college graduates—a dim hallway that smelled like cat food and takeout, a sticky galley kitchen, jewel box–sized bedrooms. I'd found it while Kate was in Spain for the summer, and the only person who was more horrified by it than Kate was Evelyn, her mother, who offered to cover my portion of the rent to put us up somewhere else. As much as Kate hated the place, there were few things she treasured more than defying her mother, so she agreed to slum it with me if I'd at least let her decorate, something I was more than happy to do.

Kate and I were in 4B. Amy lived across the hall with a roommate in 4A. Kate's then boyfriend (if you could you call him a boyfriend when she'd just met him four days earlier) had gathered a group of buddies to help us haul our stuff into the six hundred square feet we'd call home for the next four years. They were a rowdy group of fraternity brothers from Vanderbilt, all wearing worn baseball caps and embroidered ribbon belts. After moving day, we'd never see most of them again. Kate's beau was an aide for Trent Lott, who was about to become the Senate majority leader, and he spent most of his time at work. But even at twenty-two, Kate wasn't the kind of woman who waited around until somebody had time for her, so she dropped him within a couple of weeks for a bookstore owner who chatted her up at a cocktail party in the Hirshhorn Museum's sculpture garden.

We went out for beers with the guys after all of our stuff was loaded in, and on our way back to our apartment we encountered Amy in the hallway. Kate was fiddling with our new keys. "Hey, y'all." Amy smiled, approaching us. "I'm sorry to bother you, but my air-conditioning just broke and I can't seem to find the number for the super."

We invited her in and offered her a beer, which she initially refused, until we both opened our own, and Kate began to interrogate her—I knew that she was sizing Amy up to determine if she was worth getting to know. We learned that Amy had come to the city to work as a guidance counselor at a new charter school in southeast D.C., an area once deemed "the murder capital of the world." The administration had set her up with a roommate, another new teacher, but her boyfriend lived in the Maryland suburbs so she was almost never around. Amy was nervous about essentially living alone. Chapel Hill, North Carolina, was her hometown and the only place she'd ever lived. She'd spent the last four years in a sorority house at UNC, less than a two-mile drive from the house she grew up in.

She didn't need to worry about finding friends. Kate and I quickly discovered that Amy was an easy third for our group, and we started to live in the way that twenty-two-year-old girls live in a big city—meeting for happy hour, watching television on each other's sofas, discussing potential boyfriends, sharing each other's clothing, nursing our hangovers together.

In those early years, Kate and Amy were close. Not close in a confide-in-each-other kind of way but close in the sense that they spent time together when I wasn't around. One rainy Saturday night when I couldn't be convinced to go out—I never had the social stamina that they did and prized quiet nights alone in the apartment's kitchen—the two of them came home shortly before midnight, wobbling and desperate to tell me about the palm reader they'd been to see in Georgetown. We were twenty-four.

"You won't believe it! You won't believe it, Waverly!" Amy slurred, kneeling on the floor in front of the couch and gripping my legs with her clammy hands. "She said that I'm going to get engaged this year. *This year!*"

"It's true." Kate nodded emphatically. "I heard it from the other side of the curtain."

"She said that he'd be somebody I never would have dreamt for myself—a foreigner, she said. Right, Kate? That's the word she used, right?"

Kate was standing by the open refrigerator, digging a fork into my leftover container of lo mein. She'd already swiped two of the madeleine cookies from the cooling rack on the counter. I'd baked them while watching a VHS of *Annie Hall*.

"She said we'd have six babies," Amy said dreamily, letting her head fall into my lap.

"That's great, Ame," I said, patting her on the head. "And what about you, Kate?"

"Well," Kate said, flopping onto the other side of the couch and pushing my legs out of the way with her foot. "She said that I would also meet somebody this year—somebody well-known." She shrugged. "So what else is new? My mother has been telling me exactly what my future will hold—or *should* hold—for as long as I can remember. I've never listened to her, so why would I listen to some freak 'fortune-teller' on M Street?"

Back then, Kate was working at the *Washington Post* as a travel reporter. Her mother, naturally, viewed Kate's career as the kind of appropriate hobby that would keep her busy—and keep her meeting appropriate people—until her husband came along. Then she could retire, start lunching on the charity circuit, and get busy having kids. Kate had other plans. She'd always said that if there was one thing she was going to make sure of in her life, it was that she would not grow up to be her mother. She wanted a life where the conversation involved more than one-upping and name-dropping, and since our teens, she'd daydreamt aloud about being the kind of person with a thick, tattered, heavily stamped passport. Budapest on Tuesday, Santiago on Wednesday. An apartment in New York, a flat in Paris. There would be men, of course (there always were with Kate) but she didn't fantasize about a husband, per se, not in the white-picket-fence sense that Amy did. And kids? Kate was am-bivalent about the idea of children, I'm sure because she was such an afterthought to her own parents. She grew up in a home where children were something you did because you were supposed to, like joining Congressional Country Club or naming your springer spaniel after one of the founding fathers.

But when Brendan swooped into her life four years ago, every-thing changed. Suddenly, the round-the-world fantasies I'd heard her talk about for years were just little whims; "old daydreams," she'd say wistfully. After years of resisting a certain kind of life, she just settled into it like she was giving up. Brendan was raised in Charlottesville, prep-school and Harvard educated, and a moderate conservative. It was as if her parents had ordered him out of the Neiman Marcus catalog for her for Christmas.

When she told me that she was falling for him and thought she might marry him, and then proceeded to do just that barely a year after they'd been introduced, I wish that I could say that I was sur-prised, but I wasn't. I hate to sound like this, because I'm not the kind of person who believes you're supposed to settle down by a certain age, but I think that Kate heard the clock ticking. I'd been with Larry for six years. Amy had been married so long it was hard to remember her as single. Kate still had a trail of admirers that could circle a city block—and in my opinion, she always will—but I don't think she felt the same way. Brendan might not have been the man of her dreams, but marrying him gave her security at a time when I think she was starting to feel a little lonesome. And if I had to make a guess, the loneliness she'd experienced as a child was exactly what she'd always been running from in the first place.

There's another thing, too. As much as Kate talked about want-ing to flee her pedigree, it was hard for me to imagine that you'd give up that kind of privilege if it was what you'd known your whole life. When she stopped working six months into their marriage for the sake of Brendan's career? Okay, I found it a little ironic that she was stepping directly into the supportive wifely role that her mother had expected for her, but, again, it wasn't *that* surprising. As much as Kate hated her parents for basically overlooking the fact that she existed, she was quite comfortable with her station in life, and it probably felt natural to just make the easy choices and do what she'd always known. Plus, the thing with Kate—and it's actually something I admire, maybe even envy—is that she's so headstrong and sovereign in the way that she marches through every decision that you just don't question her, even if she is your best friend.

CHAPTER TWO

Larry's heavy footsteps pound the stairs behind the kitchen, shaking my collection of bud vases on the windowsill over the sink. *At last,* I think, peeking out of the kitchen door to check on Mike, who's sitting on the couch in the living room and thumbing halfheartedly through a coffee table book of *Rolling Stone* covers. Larry can keep Mike occupied.

"Hello! Hello!" Larry says, entering the kitchen. After ten years together and countless evenings like this, I still can't convince the man to put on a nice shirt for dinner. He's fresh from the shower—I can smell his Right Guard across the room—and his thick, wavy, wet hair has left a damp half-moon along the collar of his long-sleeved T-shirt.

"Lare, could you put on some shoes at least?" I say, pointing my knife at his bare feet. My boyfriend is one of those people who looks like where he's from. Just throw a flannel shirt on the guy and he could be an easy stand-in for the Brawny paper towel man. He moved here from Minnesota specifically to work at the Smithsonian and is now a curator at the National Museum of American History, where he oversees a massive collection of old campaign memorabilia and political artifacts. A lifelong history buff, he gets excited about an old World War Two poster in the way that I get wound up over buttercream.

"Baby, it's family here." He laughs, putting his beer bottle on the kitchen counter so that he can wrap Amy in a bear hug, his heavy arms folding around her shoulders and neck.

Larry is one of those rare people whom everybody seems to like. He tells ridiculous tales about growing up in Minnesota—ice-fishing mishaps, barroom brawls that led to best friendships—and when he does, he draws a crowd. Once, one night in Old Town, he got the whole bar singing "Skol Vikings," the Minnesota Vikings fight song, and this was during football season, in a roomful of rabid, beer-breathed Redskins fans. In short, everyone loves being around him, myself included...most of the time. The fact that I haven't shared my money problems with him (which, let's face it, since he's my roommate, are his problems, too) is wearing on me and, by extension, us. I've never kept secrets from him before, and I feel so guilty that I actually find myself looking for ways to avoid him. He's noticed, though neither of us has said anything about it. I tell myself that it's temporary, a rut, and that we'll push through it just like we have before, but deep down I know that's not true.

Larry lets go of Amy, ruffling her hair as he walks away as if she's his kid sister, and then he hugs Kate, calling her "Katie" even though she always asks him not to. Larry and Kate are just like siblings—outwardly mocking and secretly adoring of each other. When he finally makes his way to me, I'm stirring the pot on the stove. He wraps his arm around me and bends deeply to kiss me in the crook of my neck. He's six-two—big, but not NBA big—and strong in the best way, like he could haul a load of firewood if he needed to, but not like someone who pounds protein shakes at the gym. I am average—not the smallest girl in town but not the biggest either—and when Larry holds me, it's with every bit of him.

"What's the over/under on Dr. Feelgood cracking a smile tonight?" Larry whispers in my ear. He's talking about Mike, who's now gazing sleepily out my front window. I gently shove him off with my elbow.

"Go! Go get him a beer," I whisper. When I turn, I catch Amy watching me. At first, I fear that she heard Larry joke about Mike, but she's looking at me in the funniest, most longing way. She grins sheepishly and then claps her hands together and says, "So! What can I do to help? You can't just let me stand here and watch you work."

My dining room is too small for seven people. Kate lingers in the doorway between it and the kitchen and I know that she's waiting to choose a seat because she doesn't want to be near Mike, who seems to have at least loosened up enough to talk hockey with Larry and his coworker Kyle.

I squeeze past Amy's chair, holding the pot of stew over her head as I pass, and everyone nudges into their seats. "It smells incredible," she says, shifting dishes on the table to make room for the pot. Five years ago, after much prodding from Kate, Amy, and Larry, I quit my job as a high school English teacher to open Maggie's, which is named after my childhood dog. I know, the world has enough bakeries, coffee shops, and bars named after dogs. Yes, there's a black and white picture of her on the wall by the cash register. I won't apologize for it. She was a fantastic dog.

"So, a toast," Larry says, raising his glass when I finally sit down, easing in between Amy and Kate. "To Waverly, the hostess with the—"

"Oh God, Larry, stop before they are too nauseous to have an appetite," I interrupt. "Cheers, everyone." I raise my glass. "Let's eat."

"So," Kate says after everyone's plate has been filled, pointing her fork toward Kyle's new girlfriend, Rebecca. She's a petite woman with Gilda Radner hair who's a professor at American. "What is it that you teach?"

"Women's Studies." Her voice is surprisingly throaty, particularly for a woman with a figure skater's frame.

I glance around the table to make sure everyone has what they need and see Mike make a face. Kate knocks my foot with hers under the table. She's noticed, too.

"Interesting!" Amy says, nodding her head emphatically while she finishes chewing. "So, give me an example of one of your classes," she says after she's swallowed.

"Well, I also work out of the English department, so right now I'm teaching a course on women's autobiography. We read Carolyn Heilbrun, Annie Dillard, Maxine Hong Kingston. Do you know them?"

"No, I'm sorry." Amy laughs self-deprecatingly. "Since I had my daughter, I'm lucky if I read a book a year."

Mike shakes his head.

"What?" Amy says teasingly.

Mike rolls his eyes, and it's not in an amused way. He looks genuinely peeved.

"Do you have something you'd like to say, Mike?" Kate says.

Shit, here we go. The fact that she's getting a little drunk doesn't bode well for the rest of us.

"Mike just knows how little I read," Amy says, laughing to lighten the mood. It's obvious that she's trying to placate him. "I mean, to be honest, my sister gave me a *People* magazine subscription for my birthday and I can't even finish one issue before another one arrives in the mail."

Mike puts his fork down and shakes his head at Amy. "No, Amy." He laughs sarcastically. "Believe it or not, I actually wasn't reacting to you. I just don't understand the point of a 'Women's Studies' department." He makes little quotation marks with his fingers as he says it. "I mean, if equality's the issue, shouldn't there then be a 'Men's Studies' department, too?"

"Oh, Mike," Kate says. "That's the same flimsy argument that my barely postpubescent classmates at Brown used fifteen years ago."

"Come on," Mike says, sputtering sauce. "You think Brendan, the Republican superhero, is into 'Women's Studies'?" He makes the little quotation marks again despite the fork in his hand, which is close enough to Larry's face that he has to jerk his head to avoid getting hit by a forkful of beef. Here goes my relaxing Friday night dinner party. I see the way that Mike is glaring at Kate, feel the way that Kate has sat up in her chair—almost as if it's in case she needs to pounce across the table at him—and I suddenly remember a movie scene I once saw of a dinner party gone bad where the ominous sound of an escalating roller coaster was piped in over the actors' voices—boom, click, boom, click, boom, click. It's exactly what I'm feeling in my chest.

"My husband's masculinity isn't threatened by strong women," Kate says, taking another swig of her wine.

I look over at Amy. Her eyes are pinned to her plate.

I put my hand over Kate's arm. "I'm sorry," I say to the table. "How about we, uh, change the subject?" I have the kind of complexion that's always rosy, like I've just come out of the cold, but now I can feel that I'm flushed down to my collarbone.

"No, no, it's fine," Rebecca says, unruffled. "I get this reaction from men a lot. It's not a big deal. Some men just don't comprehend the usefulness of a women's studies curriculum in the twenty-first century."

"Exactly," Mike says, banging his fist on the table and making the wineglasses shake. The sound makes me jump, and I look across the table at Larry, whose eyebrows have now shot into his hairline. "I mean, what do you think about all of this?" Mike says to Kyle.

"I'm sorry. What's the question?" Kyle says, looking up from his nearly empty plate. You can tell what his politics are just by looking at him. He's intellectual looking in a contrived way, wearing wire-rimmed glasses and a wool turtleneck sweater. He looks like someone who meditates. A tea drinker.

"What do you think of your girlfriend's job?" Mike says, slow and loud, like an ignorant person speaking to a foreigner.

"Well," Kyle says, carefully resting his fork on the table and then folding his hands at his chest like a yogi. "I think it's fascinating. I've learned a lot from Rebecca about feminist theory and what it's like to be a woman in the modern world."

"Kyle just read *The Feminine Mystique*," Rebecca says.

"Really?" I say, hoping that I can steer the conversation away from Mike and Kate. "Larry, maybe you should take a cue from your coworker." Aside from the history journals he reads for work, Larry never reads anything heavier than the sports page, the Sunday comics, and paperback thrillers, but I'm trying to lighten the mood. I smile at him as I hand him my glass—he's stood to man the refills—and hope that he can tell by the way that I'm looking at him that I'd like some help.

Seconds later, I can tell it's of no use.

"Oh, c'mon!" Mike groans. "Hey, Kate, I guess you can count these folks out of your husband's constituency. No way they're voting for Brendan!"

Kate shakes her head toward the ceiling. "*You are so—,*" she starts.

"Well, I think it's all very interesting," Amy interjects, finally speaking. I've had one eye on her—she's been swirling her fork in figure eights around her plate. "I read *The Feminine Mystique* in college and I loved it." She smiles at Rebecca.

"Oh, give me a break, Ame," Mike says, laughing. "You can barely remember to pick up the dry cleaning, much less whatever you studied in college." He looks at Rebecca. "My wife's just trying to impress you," he says.

Amy takes a deep breath and shakes her head. "Please, don't mind my husband," she says. "He has strong opinions."

"Whatever," he says, scooping a forkful of food into his mouth.

The room falls silent and Amy looks at me from across the table. "I'm sorry," she mouths, and I notice the tears in her eyes. The old radiator under the window hisses and cracks. Larry clears his throat. "Who wants seconds?" he says.

I look over again at Amy as Larry and Kyle begin to tell the table about how one of Tony Hawk's skateboards has joined the museum's permanent sports collection. She is subtly gnawing on her bottom lip and I can tell as she nods and smiles and listens to Kyle that her mind is entirely somewhere else. Mike's behavior tonight is nothing I haven't seen before, but he seems a little more explosive than usual, and he's *never* acted this way in front of people outside of our small circle.

I know that Amy must be mortified, but I'm having a hard time feeling sympathetic—this is not how I'd planned tonight to go, and there's no one who's more humiliated than me. Kate must sense this, because she squeezes my wrist under the table and mutters, "What an asshole," under her breath. I tap her foot with mine in acknowledgment, then stand up to get dessert out of the kitchen.

CHAPTER THREE

Saturday morning, five a.m. Emmylou Harris is on the stereo, coffee is brewing, and my staff—a motley crew of college students, artists, recent immigrants, and felons—won't start trickling in for another hour. This time alone, when the only noise in the bakery is my music and the whir of the industrial-sized mixer, is my favorite time of the day. I do my best thinking before the sun comes up, feeling like I can solve the world's problems while I sift flour through a sieve that I make with my fingers or knead bread dough until it's warm and pillowy under my palms. It's not that I'm a morning person exactly, but there's something about knowing that most people are still in bed when I see the sunrise each day that makes me feel industrious and optimistic, like I'm getting a head start. Of course, the feeling all goes to shit the minute the bakery opens and things start hopping, but this early time is mine and mine alone, and it's sacred.

My mom cooked dinner every night after her ten-hour days in the insurance office where she worked. They weren't elaborate meals, but they were homemade: spaghetti and sauce, tuna casserole, baked chicken. I complained about the menu, whining that I wished we could be like Kate, whose parents were always out in the evenings, and just pick up Chinese or a pizza. My mother never gave in. Instead, she'd toss one of her rotating Liz Claiborne blazers onto one of the kitchen chairs, roll up her sleeves while she walked to the refrigerator, and say, "Waverly, you know I have to cook. It clears the noise of the day from my head."

It took the worst day of my life to understand what she meant. I was nineteen and midway through my sophomore year in college. My roommate, Nancy, and I were headed out to dinner, the door to our dorm room just slamming behind us, when our phone rang. She ran back into the room to get it, saying that it might be Christopher, her boyfriend, who was coming to visit from Massachusetts that weekend. I'd rolled my eyes. One of their marathon phone sessions had ended just a few minutes before, I was starving, and it was pizza night in the cafeteria—the one opportunity I had each week to eat something edible on campus.

But the call was for me. It was the Virginia State Police, calling to inform me that a drunk driver on the Beltway had hit my parents' car. Both of them were in intensive care. My father died the next morning, three hours after I arrived at the hospital after driving all night—despite Kate's and Nancy's insistence that I shouldn't be on the road by myself. My mother died the next day. When I said good-bye to my father, he squeezed my hand, acknowledging that he heard me, but my mother's spinal injuries were so severe that I could tell from the moment I first saw her in the hospital bed that she had already left her body. I sat next to her, examining her for hours before she was taken off of her ventilator, noticing the chipped polish on her fingers, the broken blood vessels around her eyes, and tried to remember the last thing we'd talked about. Years later, I still can't recall what it was.

I took a leave of absence for the rest of the semester and spent most of the next two months in my parents' kitchen, cooking. Babci, my Polish maternal grandmother, moved in with me and did the dishes. Because my parents had both been only children like me, she was now my last living relative. Sometimes she rolled up her sleeves to cook with me. Other times she came into the kitchen and offered gentle suggestions ("that cheese will slice easier if you freeze it for a little while…toss those berries with some flour and they won't clump together when you bake the muffins"). Before she walked out of the room, she'd kiss my cheek, her lips leaving a smudge of Max Factor red on my face.

Kate came home from Providence every weekend and sat at the kitchen table with me, talking if I felt like talking, reading aloud from the books and magazines that she brought when I didn't, and eating the banquet of food that Babci would end up giving away or throwing out because there was enough, as they say, to feed an army. I must've been the only grieving person who's ever given food to her neighbors instead of the other way around. I went through every yellowed, splattered recipe card in my mother's file at least once, discovering along the way that the choreography of chopping and mixing and measuring was a kind of religious ritual, as practiced and soothing as prayer. The particularities of the way that I pinched a piecrust or seasoned a roasted chicken were because I'd learned them standing next to my mother, who'd learned from her mother, who'd learned from hers. I made my father's famed gumbo in the middle of the night, then ate a bowl of it on the kitchen floor as the sun started to come up. I made my mother's mushroom soup, my grandmother's pot roast, the carrot cake that my mother made from an old *New York Times* recipe every year as a birthday gift to herself. It was the only way that I knew how to hold on to them.

Now it's hard for me to fathom that I'd ever considered another career. Sometimes one of my former students will come into Maggie's and I'll get a pang of nostalgia for my old job—the hollow thump of the eraser against the blackboard, the moment each day when you're standing in your empty classroom and can hear your students coming down the hall, roaring like an approaching wave—but cooking is what I was meant to do. It's the one constant in my life, the thing I can always go back to, the place where there are no disasters that I can't fix.

Every day, the hours roll out with an easy, dependable rhythm I've come to rely on. At ten to seven, three of my regulars, all retired engineers from the Naval Research Lab, huddle outside the front door waiting for me to unlock it. By eight, the bakery is humming with the commuters who don't bother to look up from their phones as they order. At ten, it's the young moms with strollers who've been up for hours and need a caffeine fix. Then the lunch crowd, then the teenagers when school gets out at three, and then, finally, the coffee break stragglers who wander inside in the late afternoon, dazed from staring at computer screens all day.

Unfortunately, the money is not as predictable as the clientele. Those of us who sell coffee out of cups that don't feature a certain megachain's logo are struggling, and as much as I understand that trips to the local bakery are the kind of thing that quickly gets cut when a family tightens its budget, I still want to throw something at the television every time I see a personal finance expert advising people to watch their "latte factors." Catering jobs—bridal showers, corporate luncheons—have always supplied the little extra that kept me in the comfort zone after I paid my eight employees, bought my supplies, wrote the building's landlord a check, and paid my utilities. Now those gigs are necessities that I rely on to make my numbers each month. Last year, in an effort to find some extra cash, I created a little market in one corner of the shop where I sell gifty-foody things like artisanal honey and tea tins and Barefoot Contessa cookbooks, but it turns out—shocker—that selling an eight-dollar jar of Stonewall Kitchen jelly a couple of times a week doesn't ex-actly wear out my cash register (and, frankly, just gives me more crap to dust). Things haven't been so bad that I've had to stop tak-ing a salary, but I'm close. Very, very close.

I've started to brainstorm new business ideas: a dinner delivery service, a cookbook. But as they say, it takes money to make money—not to mention time. And with fifteen-hour days in the shop and no extra cash to devote to new projects, I don't have either. I'm stuck. Screwed, really. My accountant is the only one who knows how fast I'm sinking. And, lucky for me, he reminds me on a nearly daily basis.

This morning, I need to make lemon-coconut cupcakes for a bridal shower. After knotting my hair back with one of the elastics I usually wear on my wrist and drying my hands on my favorite orange apron, I scoop sugar and butter into the mixer and switch the speed to high. I still can't get over the dinner party last night. As hard as I try to forget it, my mind keeps sliding back to the scene Mike made at the table. Kate was right—what an asshole. How does Amy live with him? By the time she was putting on her coat to leave, I wanted to throttle her. Mike had continued to be less than charming—he'd snickered loudly when Kyle mentioned that he was taking Rebecca to an Ani DiFranco concert on Sunday, huffed when Kate answered Rebecca's questions about the campaign—and Amy just sat silently beside him, grinning placidly like a heavily sedated 1960s housewife. I cannot understand why she just lets him get away with acting the way he does, and why she doesn't make more of an effort to make him stop. Amy may be a sweetheart, but she's not a shrinking-violet, damsel-in-distress kind of girl. When she lived across the hall from me, I heard their occasional fights. It was always just garden-variety stuff—he forgot to call when he said he would, or she made plans for the weekend without checking in—but she wasn't shy about expressing herself when she was upset with him. Now it's as if she's blind to his behavior, like Mike's one of those horrible geometric posters that they sell in crappy mall stores that can look like two different images depending on your perception, and she just can't see the picture that the rest of us so clearly do.

Larry insists that Kyle and Rebecca aren't insulted. "Seriously, Wave, I'm sure that Rebecca gets that all the time—she did not care," he'd reassured me after everyone left. "And it's not as if anyone else was shocked. It's obvious that Mike's a dick before he even opens his mouth."

I crack an egg on the side of a mixing bowl and watch it disappear into the creamed sugar and butter. I wonder whether it would be too much to send Rebecca something as an apology. A dozen raspberry thumbprint cookies. Twin loaves of zucchini and banana bread. Maybe an old-fashioned chocolate cake? I didn't believe Larry when he said that it wasn't a big deal. Everyone had scurried home right after dessert, even Kate. That never happens at my house.

I walk across the kitchen to grab a spatula. Larry's right about Mike—he's a jerk—and I shouldn't waste time fretting over him, but I just can't blow it off. Larry insists that my need to understand things like this, to unfold them and figure out *why*, is something intrinsically female, like talking on the phone for sport. "Don't worry about it, babe; forget it," he'd said last night. "You take things too seriously." If I keep brooding, he'll tell me to go for a run or have a beer. He's right, of course. I could benefit from learning how to let things go. But Mike is Amy's husband and that somehow makes him family. He'll be in her life forever, which means he'll be in mine, too.

The whole thing is so strange. Mike has never been the most gregarious person in the room, but he's been friendly and pleasant to be around, easy with a "How's everything going?" and a "Nice to see you." Back when he and Amy started dating, we all insisted that they were perfect for each other, and we meant it. They wanted the same things: family dinners at the kitchen table, a swing set in the backyard. She and Mike even look alike—both lithe and athletically built, both dark haired and freckled. Together, they resemble the kind of vanilla, All-American, scrubbed-up couple you see on a billboard for a cosmetic dentistry practice or a jewelry chain.

When he proposed, bending down on one knee after they'd gone for a run on the C&O Canal trail, I couldn't have been more excited for them. Their wedding, a down-homey pig picking in Chapel Hill, was one of those rare matrimonial events where the wedding guests truly seemed to revel in the couple's bright future, not just the free food and alcohol. I remember thinking, watching them skip down the aisle together after the ceremony, that their relationship was exactly what I wanted. I wholeheartedly approved. Since then, Mike and I have been around each other enough that I shouldn't dread conversations with him because of the way we fumble to find something to say to each other. But we do. At one point last night when I was getting the tiramisu ready and he came into the kitchen to throw away his empty beer bottle, it was like I was talking to a stranger, but I've known Mike for ten years—and not just as my close friend's boyfriend, but as *my* friend, too.

For example, there was one Sunday afternoon, years ago, when we were still living in the apartments. Mike and Amy were in the throes of their newfound romance. I was single and, frankly, feeling sorry for myself. I apparently hadn't done a great job with the "I'm independent; I don't need a boyfriend" speech I'd given Mike when he asked if I was dating someone because Mike—this *very same* Mike—set down the bowl of chili he was eating while we watched the Redskins game and declared that he was going to set me up with one of his fellow residents.

The following Friday, the four of us went on a double date. The guy—*what was his name again? Rob? Bob?*—was far from my type, and I knew I wasn't his. I could tell as soon as I spied him from Amy's bedroom window, where I watched him walk up the cracked cement pathway toward the front door of our apartment building. He looked like a Brooks Brothers ad—khakis, respectable brown loafers, the same light blue oxford shirt that nearly every man in

Washington wears at least twice a week. Meanwhile, I had on this atrocious patterned skirt that I'd bought from a street vendor during a weekend in New York that I thought was cool and bohemian at the time but later realized was a kind of gaudy throwaway that looked like a loan from Mrs. Roper's closet.

So the guy wasn't for me. In fact, oddly, it was Mike who made an impression that night. He carried the dinner conversation in the most engaging way, making all of us feel at ease. I remember watching Amy as he spoke, noticing the way that she rested her hand on his forearm and squeezed it when he said something particularly funny or smart. When Mike started rattling off my accomplishments to try to impress Rob/Bob—"She was summa cum laude at Bowdoin!" "She finished the Marine Corps Marathon in three and a half hours!" "You haven't eaten a brownie until you've had one of Waverly's!"—I had been a little startled that he knew so much about me, and I remember being so flattered that I pined for him just the tiniest bit, and wished it was my hand on his arm instead of Amy's.

I add shredded coconut to the mixing bowl and fold it into the batter. I wish I could figure out how to broach the subject with Amy in a gentle way, which should be easy, as close as we are. ("What are you going to say, Waverly? 'Your husband's an ass'? 'No one can stand to be around him anymore'?" Kate says when we talk about it.) Save for the usual "he's driving me crazy" kind of stuff that you bitch about with your girlfriends, Amy is as bright and cheerful as she's ever been, but I just think it has to be a lie. How could she not be miserable, living with him? But then again, I think, pulling out the cupcake tins, maybe I shouldn't judge. Lately I'm not exactly someone who can speak with confidence about the importance of being honest about your relationship. I mean, as much as it annoys me that Amy ignores her husband's terrible behavior, I'm also a person who swiped a couple of twenties out of her boyfriend's wallet this morning because I needed gas and didn't want to put it on my credit card.

Six hours later, the morning rush over, my manager Randy and I are standing at the front counter when Kate swoops in, immaculate in a camel cape and navy pantsuit. Sometimes she looks like a caricature of herself, like a movie star playing the role of the political wife. I wipe the sweat from my hairline with the inside of my forearm and then reach for the silver coffee thermos in Kate's hand. It's been a steady Saturday morning despite the cold drizzle outside, which has brightened my mood a little bit.

"Where are you headed all dolled up on a Saturday morning?" I say. I know she mentioned a campaign event last night but I can't remember what. These days, they all run together.

"Ooh-la-la," Randy says. "Love the getup today, Kate." Randy's been my manager for a couple of years now. He's in his early thirties and his look screams "Apple Store employee" to me—skinny corduroys, hipster sneakers, bedhead haircut, white headphone wire eternally hanging out of his back pants pocket. He won me over during our first (and only) interview when he told me that he'd started baking in high school as a way to cope with the merciless bullying he endured on a daily basis. It also helped that he brought the most amazing cheddar and apple pie I'd ever tasted to the interview. His palate's a lot like mine; we'd both rather eat homey comfort food (chocolate cake, bacon anything) over intricately designed, architecturally assembled fancy food. When we're coming up with recipes and get stuck, our jokey solution is to say, "Bacon it" or "Butter it." In other words, add more of one or the other—or sometimes both. Most times, it actually works.

"I have a campaign contributors' luncheon," Kate whines. "Another Saturday, another speech."

"At least you get a free meal out of it, right?" I fill the thermos while Randy opens the bakery case and reaches for a blueberry scone, Kate's regular order.

She raises her eyebrows. "Yeah, great. If it wasn't for you, I'd eat nothing but rubbery, hotel ballroom chicken." She takes a sip of her coffee. "Speaking of which, thanks for last night."

I send Randy back to the kitchen. "Ugh. What do you think?" I whisper after he's left. "Was it a disaster?" I bite my lip, wincing and waiting for the punch, but Kate's distracted, glaring at two older women who are edging closer to her as they wonder loudly whether the spinach and bacon quiche in the bakery case looks better than the ham and Gruyère. She shudders like a horse shooing away a fly and shuffles closer to the counter.

Our future First Lady, a woman of the people, I think.

"So," Kate says, turning back to me. "Last night. What the fuck was that all about?"

One of the women stops talking, looks up at Kate, and then makes a face at her friend.

"Kate, language," I whisper. *Once a teacher, always a teacher.* "I'm really embarrassed," I say. I pull out the rag that I keep in my apron pocket and start wiping at invisible spots on the counter. Randy jokes that I use it like a security blanket, which is probably true, and now my employees all call it my "wooby." "Do you think I ought to do something for Rebecca?" I ask. "Larry doesn't think it's necessary, but it was bad, wasn't it?"

"Well." Kate shrugs. "It wasn't the kind of party that would make me want to run back to your house again next Friday night."

I stop wiping and sigh. "Thanks."

Kate rolls her eyes. "Let me finish! It was no reflection on you. It was Mike." She cracks a smile. "What a piece of shit that guy is. He's always been a piece of shit."

I glance at the older women crowded behind Kate. They seem to be busy inspecting the fruit salad. "I don't know," I say. "To be honest, it's not me that I'm worried about. It's Amy. I just don't know how she deals with him. Do you think she sees it? What happened to him? And why doesn't she ever say anything about it? It's starting to piss me off."

"I'll tell you what happened," Kate says, now pouring a stream of sugar from a glass canister into her coffee. "The life they chose is what happened. I mean, house in a cul-de-sac, minivan in the driveway, and potluck dinners with the neighbors where the conversation revolves around *American Idol*?" She makes a face like she's talking about the contents of a dumpster. "I love Amy—you know I do—but that kind of life would make me an asshole, too."

"Kate, come on. I know that you and Amy have different tastes, but be nice."

"I'll say." Kate chuckles. She starts to say more but then stops herself, waving the thought away. "Anyway, there's no excuse for how he acted. He was a dick last night, no question about it. A total dick."

"But he wasn't always."

"Waverly, you give people too much credit. I mean, listen," she says, leaning closer to the counter. "I know that my husband isn't perfect—hell, trying to talk to him about something other than the campaign is like, I don't know, trying to talk to him about my period—but if you ask me, Amy settled. She wanted the fucking fairy tale. The white picket fence, the doctor husband, the kid, the whole thing. And she got it. It's just too bad that Prince Charming turned out to be such a fucking dud."

Say how you really feel, Kate. Whenever she talks like this, my mother's voice starts ringing in my ears: "Mean-spirited people are just jealous people."

"By the way," Kate says. "Did you notice that Mike was still wearing that same bomber jacket he's probably had since 1994? I mean, a *bomber jacket*?"

"Wait a second!" one of the elderly customers says, taking off her red-framed reading glasses and stepping closer to Kate. "You're Brendan Berkshire's wife!"

Kate glances at me, raising her right eyebrow in the same subtle way that she used to in high school when her mother would peek her head into Kate's room while we were pretending to study to remind Kate about a Daughters of the American Revolution luncheon. Then she turns to the two women and her face softens. She smiles wide, her veneered Chiclet teeth gleaming. It's like watching a magic act, a transformation with the flip of a cape, the snap of a finger.

"Why, yes. I'm afraid I am," she says, extending her hand. I notice how Kate expertly folds her fingers around the woman's palm, letting go just as soon as they make contact. It's a warm and practiced gesture—not intrusive, not cold, just right. "How nice to meet you. May I ask your name?"

"I am Ruby Sampson," the woman declares, looking up at Kate. "And this is my friend Roberta Jenkins."

"Ms. Sampson and Ms. Jenkins, I am delighted to meet you," Kate says. "Now, I can't help but mention that I overheard you two talking. I have to tell you, both types of quiche are wonderful, but I prefer the ham and Gruyère."

"Then that's what we'll have," the woman says to me, keeping her eyes on Kate. She's drinking her in, taking in the flawless hairstyle, the glowing complexion, the tasteful pearls. I watch Kate pretend not to notice like I have so many times before. Sometimes it's as if she can't get down the block without people stopping to gawk at her. It's like she lives inside of a shampoo commercial.

After the women walk off with their plates, chattering about their brush with the future First Lady of Virginia ("She's even more stunning in person!"), Kate rolls her eyes. "All in a day's work," she says. "Speaking of, I better run. Brendan's staff acts like I've been off sleeping with the enemy when I'm late."

"Okay," I say. "See you."

She turns to leave and then stops herself. "Are you going to say something to Amy about Mike?"

I shrug.

"Because you could, you know. It wouldn't be out of line at this point. He ruined your dinner."

I shake my head. "I don't know. We'll see."

"I'm just saying." She flips her cape over her shoulder, a dramatic gesture that she can actually pull off. If *Town & Country* ever decided to run a comic strip, she'd be the perfect superhero. She waves as she exits, and the wind rushes in when she pushes the door open. It's cold and clean and a part of me wishes that I could follow Kate out. My customers are in sweats and heavy sweaters, their hair unbrushed, lazy Saturday, the week peeling off of them. Oh, to sit and read the morning paper. To look up over a cup of coffee and say to the person across the table, "So what do you want to do today?" To not dodge calls from your landlord, to not fret over the stack of overdue credit card bills on your desk, to not be a broke thief who steals from your boyfriend—your boyfriend who is blissfully unaware that any of this is going on and would want to help you if you could just abandon your pride and tell him.

I watch Kate zoom out of her parking space in front of the bakery. I understand that she's exhausted—I really do—but she's also about to be greeted by applause, probably a standing ovation. I would *so* trade places with her today, maybe just to see the look on her face when I showed her the dwindling numbers on my spreadsheets.

I glance at the clock—nine more hours. I need to finish the cupcake order, call my suppliers about next week's deliveries, check over the menus for next week's specials, look over the staff schedule, and—let's not forget—attend to the customers who are actually here.

"Waverly!" a voice yells behind me, snapping me away from my to-dos. It's Javier, one of the dishwashers. "*¡No agua caliente!*" *No hot water.* Jesus Christ. Perfect.

"No *agua*? Okay." *Fuck.* I stuff my rag into my pocket. "I'll be right there."

CHAPTER FOUR

Back when I was teaching, Sunday afternoons were reserved for grading papers. To make it less of a chore, I often took my work to the Dubliner, an Irish pub on Capitol Hill, where I'd mark them up against the backdrop of other customers screaming, "Bad call!" and "How could he miss that?" to the Redskins game on the television in the corner.

On one particular Sunday during my third year of teaching I discovered that I could tune out the broadcast football game but not the sound of someone rapping his knuckles in absentminded rhythm against the oak bar. I kept trying to ignore it—focusing on my work and bites of the corned beef sandwich I'd ordered—but the noise just seemed to get louder and more insistent. It was driving me insane, not least of all because I couldn't figure out what song it was—*"Honky Tonk Woman?" No, wait…"Copacabana?"* I apparently got so lost in trying to figure it out that I didn't immediately notice when the guy finally stopped. I looked down the bar and our eyes met. He turned up his palms and shrugged sheepishly.

"'Looking out My Back Door,'" he said across the bar.

I wrinkled my brow.

"The song." He tapped his knuckles against the bar a couple of times. "'Looking out My Back Door.' CCR. Creedence Clearwater Revival?"

"Oh, right," I said, wondering how he knew I'd been paying attention.

"You were nodding your head along with the rhythm," he said before I could ask. "You know the song, right?" He started to sing. "Doo, doo, doo, looking out my…" His voice trailed off.

It was a quiet afternoon in the pub. In fact, we were the only two people sitting at the bar aside from a tweedy middle-aged couple at the other end who were busy examining a city guidebook.

He stood up and walked over, then pulled out the stool next to me. He swung one leg around it, sitting down like a cowboy mounting a horse.

He leaned forward and rested his forearms on the bar, his pint in one hand. "Sorry about that." He smiled. He had a nice smile. Wavy hair that could stand to be cut. Reddish stubble. He was scruffy, almost like he'd had a rough night the night before, but it was a good kind of shabby. Most of the men in Washington were so neatly pressed. "Can I buy you a drink to make up for interrupting whatever it is you're working on?" He pointed down to the paper I was grading.

"Um." I looked at my glass. It was still three-quarters full.

"I'll buy your lunch." He pointed to my plate.

"Oh, you don't have to do that," I said. I should have been working harder to get him to leave—the stack of papers I needed to grade before seven a.m. the next day was several inches thick—but I found myself enjoying the distraction.

"Nope, I insist," he said, taking a sip of his thick, dark beer. When he pulled his glass away, it left a foamy mustache on the stubble above his lip. "So what are you working on?" He pointed at my work.

"Grading papers. I teach high school English." I tugged at the worn long-sleeved T-shirt I was wearing, a relic from the back of my closet, and wished, as I often did, that I was more like Kate and Amy, the kind of women who actually looked in the mirror before they left the house. My cosmetics of choice were Chap Stick (the black one) and a tube of mascara that I used on special occasions. I'd never had a haircut at the kind of salon that required an actual appointment. I didn't own a hair dryer. I tucked my feet beneath my barstool to hide my mud-stained running shoes.

"Ah," he said. "So Stephen Barton is a fan of corned beef?"

"What?" I had no idea why he knew the name of one of my sophomores until I looked down and realized that my sandwich had been dripping all over the poor kid's essay about *A Farewell to Arms*. "Oh, fuck!" I reached for the napkin in my lap to swipe at the brown splats on the paper and knocked my beer over in the process, sending a pool of Guinness splashing over the carefully typed essay. I leapt for the stack of other students' papers, snatching them just before the puddle washed out three classes' worth of homework.

"Well." I looked over at the guy and laughed. "I guess Steve's getting an A."

He laughed back. He had a genuine laugh, the kind that you could tell was often employed. I smoothed my hair, wishing that I'd bothered to wash it that morning.

"So what's your name?" I said, putting out my hand. I wasn't accustomed to introducing myself to strangers, but he seemed harmless enough.

"I'm Larry," he said. His handshake was firm—always a good sign of a good man, according to my father. "And yours?"

"Waverly."

"Cool name," he said.

"Thanks. It's British. My mom was a bit of an anglophile."

We talked easily and at length. It got dark outside, and then it started to rain, and before I knew it, we had exchanged numbers and he was paying a cabdriver to get me home safely.

Over the next few weeks, we quickly became buddies. When the school day ended, I'd take the Metro to the museum and he'd give me the "Larry Tackett tour of American history." While the memory is still sweetly vivid, I have to confess that I was always way more excited about seeing the museum's pop culture holdings—Archie Bunker's chair, the prosthetic breasts that Dustin Hoffman wore for *Tootsie*—than I was about the patriotic relics that Larry is so enamored with. On the weekends, we wandered through the farmers' stands at Eastern Market, where I introduced him to broccoli rabe and jicama. We saw obscure bands at the 9:30 Club, where he taught me more than I ever needed to know about Swedish garage rock. We shared more pints and late nights at the Dubliner. Three weeks in, he finally kissed me as we stood on the sidewalk outside the bar.

One Sunday, I took him out to Maple Hill to meet Babci. He sat in the room that's now our living room, looking like an elephant balanced on her bitsy chintz chair, and told her stories I hadn't heard yet about his family back in Minnesota. Six brothers and sisters, all older, seventeen nieces and nephews, parents who ran the hardware store that had been in his family for three generations. Babci's smile emerged from between her chubby cheeks, like a knife cutting through bread dough. Her eyes slid toward me. I fell in love with him that day.

She died the next year. As difficult as it was to say good-bye to her, she was ready. She'd told me as much. Her life had been full and difficult—she left Warsaw during World War Two with my grandfather, who, despite being Catholic, was a Nazi target because he was educated—actually, a professor—and therefore considered a threat. She'd witnessed his death after a long battle with emphysema, had endured the death of my mother, her one and only child. She told me to move into her house and to make it my own—and gave me her blessing to have Larry move in, too. So that's what I did. I was twenty-six.

When Babci died, I officially became an orphan, with no living blood relatives. Larry, with his family large enough to fill a movie theater, became mine. Our early days of living together are some of my favorite memories. I'd get home from teaching in the afternoon, cook something wonderful for dinner, and then we'd have these long, decadent weeknight dates, perched on the stools at the kitchen island and talking late into the night. In the morning, he brought coffee up to me while I showered. On Saturdays, we played our music loud and barbecued in the courtyard out back. We played house.

I wish that I'd appreciated that time together while we had it. Now I leave too early in the morning for him to bring me coffee. At night, we both often work late.

This year marks our ten-year anniversary, and referencing my "boyfriend" in daily conversation is starting to feel like something I should have outgrown by now, like using the word *awesome* (which I do) or shopping at Old Navy (which I also do). I've made an art out of fending off the "When are you guys going to finally get married?" question with a shrug and a wave of my hand and a lame joke about a ring being wasted on me when it would just get covered in batter every day, but the truth is that I'm thirty-five, and as hard as I try not to be that kind of woman, I can't help my eyes from slipping toward the left ring fingers of my customers when they pay for their coffees, can't help but gaze at the ponytailed young moms juggling their diaper bags when they come in after preschool pick-ups, can't help but wish—just a little bit—that that was me.

So why isn't it? Good question. Larry is my best friend. We finish each other's sentences and support each other during hard times and do everything that any romantic comedy would tell you that successful couples are supposed to do. We talk about making it official, and those talks always end when I change the subject, sometimes throwing in a "Why rock the boat when things are fine as they are?" for good measure. While all six of his brothers and sisters are married, and his mother makes no secret of her wish that we would follow suit, Larry is frankly ambivalent about the whole thing—he says that if I want to do it, he will, but he doesn't feel like we need a license from the Virginia court system to build a life together. And that's the thing—we've *already* built a life together, and it's a good life. But is it perfect? Is this *it*, in both the *it* and *It* senses of the word? And shouldn't I know the answer to that question already, in the way that both Kate and Amy say that they "knew" about Brendan and Mike within days of meeting them?

I can no longer fool myself into believing that we're simply a cool, modern couple who don't need to follow the conventional rules to be fully committed, and the worst part about all of it is that I know that I'm the one holding us back. But if I tell Larry that I want to get married, I will probably also need to tell him about the true extent of my money problems, and who knows how he'll react to the fact that I've been keeping secrets from him for the first time in our very long, very honest, and very open relationship.

I suppose that if I saw a therapist, she would tell me that I'm afraid of commitment, or that the loss of my parents makes me afraid of loving somebody that much again because I might some-day lose him, too. There's a good reason why I've never seen a therapist. I don't need to pay someone to tell me what I already know.

CHAPTER FIVE

On Sunday morning, Amy meets me at Fort Hunt Park for a jog. I've decided not to bring up Mike's behavior from the other night. I'm just not in the mood. After losing hot water at the bakery yesterday, my day got *even more* exciting: We became short staffed when one of my employees cut himself slicing tomatoes and had to leave to get stitches, the mother of the bride of the lemon-coconut-cupcake bridal shower flipped out when I delivered the cupcakes, telling me that she'd ordered plain lemon—no coconut—even though I had an email record of her order, and just when I was about to turn the "Open" sign on the front door to "Closed," the toddler accompanying our last customer of the day vomited all over the floor in front of the cash register. It seems to be a rule of my business that the last customer of the day is always, without fail, the most high maintenance. Anyway, my point is that when I arrive in the parking lot and pull in next to Amy's minivan, I am still exhausted from the day before, and bringing up the whole Mike thing isn't anything I want to deal with right now. In fact, I hope that Amy will just be Amy and do all of the talking during our run. I need to zone out.

She's stretching when I meet her at the trail where we typically start, and singing to herself. "Hey!" She smiles when she sees me. "You won't believe what song I heard on the radio on the way over here!"

"What?"

"I'll give you a hint: '*I'm the king of the world!*'" she bellows.

"Oh, geez. Don't remind me." Back when we were living in the apartments, the neighbors who lived above us incessantly played "My Heart Will Go On," that Celine Dion song from *Titanic*. Being twenty-two, we proceeded to do the mature thing and respond by blasting the most irritating songs that we could think of—everything from "The Macarena" to "Cotton-Eyed Joe."

"Are you ready?" she says, jumping up and down to keep herself warm. Or maybe just because she's Amy and is prone to spontaneous jumping.

I nod and we start to trudge along. Once upon a time, Amy and I were both dedicated runners—our weekends often revolved around local road races and we ran the Marine Corps Marathon together twice—but now our jogs are more about chatting than anything else.

"So how's work?" Amy says.

"Ugh, don't ask," I say, the freezing air stinging the back of my throat. It's much colder than I'd realized.

"Oh no!" Amy stops midstride. She always hyperreacts to anything remotely negative. Well, anything except her husband, apparently.

"No, no, it's nothing," I say. "Just one of those days."

We keep plodding along, the run starting to feel good as the minutes pass by, like it always does. Amy begins telling me about the house her sister is renovating in North Carolina. Amy's older sisters are southern supermommies, and whenever Amy talks about them, the stories always involve either pregnancy (I can never remember how many children each has, but it always feels like one of them is about to push out another one) or whatever Junior League/ college sorority/ church event they're currently planning.

I'm half paying attention—I'm just too brain-dead to give more than that—but I notice that the house reno Amy's describing—a sunroom, a butler's pantry—sounds like more than a little upgrade.

"So what does Celia's husband do, anyway, that they can afford all of this?"

"Oh," Amy says. "Something financial. He's some sort of accountant, I think. To be honest, I don't really know. But Celia and Todd are just about the most frugal people I know. They're like the kind of people who wash and reuse Ziploc bags. They probably have bags and bags of cash buried in their backyard."

"How many kids do they have now?"

"Four boys! And one on the way!" Amy says. "I'm *sooo* excited. She finally relented and found out the gender like we've begged her to do every time. It's a girl! I keep referring to her as Baby Amy!" She laughs at her own joke, but I'm still focused on the money part of the conversation.

"He must do some serious accounting work if they can afford for her to stay home with five kids *and* renovate a house."

"I guess."

I can tell from her succinct response that I've been as nosy as I can be. It just kills me to hear about people whose lifestyles require way more cash than mine (I mean, five kids on one income?) who don't seem to have any problem funding it. And I've met Amy's sister Celia. She looks so much like Amy—the same thick, mahogany-colored hair, the same richly freckled skin—but has a totally different aesthetic. She looks like a highlighted, manicured, fashiony-handbag-carrying woman who isn't afraid to spend some money, no matter what Amy says about her Ziploc-bag-washing habits. Meanwhile, I have no one but myself to take care of, I live in an inherited home with no mortgage to pay, and I'm at the point where I can't afford the T-shirt sale at Target. It makes me feel so far behind, like such a loser.

"Are you excited about our Palm Beach trip?" Amy says. It's no fault of hers, of course, but given what I'm thinking about, the question stings.

Every February for the past nine years, Amy, Kate, and I have spent a weekend in Palm Beach at Kate's family's house there. The first time we went, for Kate's twenty-sixth birthday, she trotted us all over town. We followed her to the International Polo Club, where we gawked at the impossibly handsome Argentinean players as if we were cavewomen seeing modern man for the first time. She took us to the boutiques on Worth Avenue, where Amy and I inevitably ended up slumped in seats outside of the dressing rooms while Kate tried on clothing with price tags the size of what most of us might expect to pay for a new car. As we've gotten older—and, frankly, lazier—the trip has assumed a luxuriously slothful routine: We spend all day drinking shameful quantities of margaritas by the pool, nap in the chaise lounges surrounding it, and change out of our swimsuits only when it becomes absolutely necessary to leave the house for more provisions. The trip is next week.

I know that I shouldn't be dropping everything to jaunt off to Florida any more than I should be running out to buy myself a diamond necklace, but last fall, Kate went ahead and bought all of our tickets, saying in her typically nonchalant way that it was an early Christmas present and that she'd paid for the trip with miles anyway, so we shouldn't think too much of it. I told her at the time that I really should skip this year because it's such a bad time for me to be away from work, but she just looked at me like I was speaking in tongues. "*You* can't be away from work, Waverly? Do you think *I* can really be away from the campaign? This is tradition. You have to go." There were a million things I wanted to say in response but I didn't because part of me agreed with her—it was tradition. Amy didn't even skip the year that Emma was born. And, hell, a couple of days away might give me a little perspective.

We turn uphill, and Amy, who never has difficulty talking no matter how challenging our runs get, is telling me how worried she is about being away from Emma. "Mike is such a good dad, though, that I know she'll be fine," she says.

I bite my tongue.

"The other night after we got home, Wave, it was so sweet: Emma was still awake—the sitter said she couldn't sleep—and Mike went into her room and read to her for over an hour. He took warm milk to her and everything. I swear he loves that kid more than he's ever loved anything."

"So he recovered from the dinner conversation, then?" I blurt out.

"What?" She pulls a tissue out of the waistband of her running tights to blow her nose as we jog.

"He was just a little…wound up," I say, wishing I didn't feel the need to be so diplomatic. *Just say it, Waverly,* I think. *He was a jerk. He insulted my guests. I'm pissed at you for not acknowledging it. I don't believe that you don't see what everyone else who meets him sees.*

"Oh, you know how Mike can be when he doesn't agree with something," she says nonchalantly, then blows her nose again.

No way! Does she really think I'm buying this?

"I can't wait to feel that Florida sun," she says, changing the subject. "It's going to be so nice to get out of this weather." Before I know it, she's launched into a monologue about the beach, the new bathing suit she ordered online, and the sunscreen she needs to remember to buy, and I've lost my opportunity to steer the conversation back toward Mike. I look at my watch. We've been moving for only ten minutes but it feels like it's been an hour. I'm too tired to run, too tired to listen to Amy talk about nothing, too tired for my own thoughts. I set my eyes on the horizon and keep pushing forward. It feels nearly impossible.

CHAPTER SIX

I was seventeen the first time I came to the Palm Beach house, for Easter with Kate's family, though I suppose that implies that we actually spent any time with her parents. The only time we were actually in the same room with them was at the Sunday brunch her mother threw for sixty of Palm Beach's finest. I've been to the house almost every year since, but the shock of seeing such luxury never wears off. Unlike Kate and Brendan's home in Maple Hill—a rambling farmhouse that looks expensively rustic in that Kennebunkport, Ralph Lauren way—the beach house is an ornate Mediterranean-style place that spreads itself out along the coast like a cat stretching in a pool of sunlight. Calling it a "beach house" is an understatement in and of itself, but like all good WASPs, Kate was raised to trivialize her trappings. Her five-carat antique engagement ring is "a hand-me-down from Brendan's grandmother," the Gauguin in her foyer is "a little something my mother fell in love with on vacation," and the beach house, all twenty thousand square feet of it, is "our beach getaway."

No, it isn't just a beach house, I think, lying on my stomach on a chair in the courtyard and watching the hibiscus planted around the perimeter softly flutter in the afternoon breeze. This place deserves a loftier word. *Estate.* Or *mansion*, obviously. No, it's a *manse*, I think, repeating the word to myself. *Manse. Manse.* It sounds stranger each time I say it.

I flip over, take another sip of my second margarita of the day, and glance over at Kate, who's immersed in the latest issue of *Vanity Fair*. Amy's scanning the paperback she bought at the airport, thumbing halfheartedly through the pages. She looks over at me and tosses it onto the Spanish tile. "I can't concentrate," she says, fiddling with the strap of her gingham tankini. "I'm dying to call home to check on Emma."

"Then do it," I say, turning onto my side and propping myself up on my elbow. "I called the bakery before we were out of baggage claim. This one"—I point my chin toward Kate—"this one's phone rings so much that you'd think she was running an escort service."

"I heard that," Kate mutters, flipping pages.

Amy picks up her phone and looks at the screen.

"What time is it?" I say, pressing my fingers into my thighs to see if I've really gotten as much sun as it feels like. White spots appear under my fingertips.

"Four thirty." Amy flops back onto her chair and looks up at the cloudless sky. "Mike said he was going to take Emma into the city—to the zoo, if it wasn't too cold. To the children's museum, otherwise." She sighs. "I don't know why it's so hard to be away from her this year. I mean, it's not like I've never done this before." She glances at me and chews nervously at her lip. "Anyway, I'm sure everything's fine. Emma is the apple of his eye. He's probably more careful with her than I am. If there's one thing you can say about Mike Rutherford, it's that he's a good father."

I hear Kate huff behind me. This is the first time his name's come up.

"I'm not going to call," she declares. "I'll wait till later, after he's put her to bed. That will be better. He'll have the day behind him; I won't be interrupting them." She glances over at me again and smiles apologetically. I can see my reflection in her sunglasses. *Ugh, a bakery owner in a bathing suit,* I think. She shakes her hair off of her face and readjusts her sunglasses. "Sorry," she says. "I'll shut up now."

Please do, I think. I normally enjoy Amy's stories about Emma—and there is no shortage of them—but it's not as if she's never been away from the child before. I mean, hell, she's with her father. And it's just three days.

She puts her phone down on the small glass table between us and shoves it toward me, as if distancing herself will ease the temptation to call. "Come swim with me."

I turn back onto my stomach, hooking my finger under one of the leg holes of my trusty black one-piece and pulling it down over my behind. "I'm too tired." I squint up at her. "Ask Kate."

"Ask me what?" Kate says, putting down her magazine and looking at us over the top of her oversized sunglasses.

"Get in the water with me?"

Kate shrugs. "Yeah, okay." She tosses her magazine aside and takes off her wide-brimmed straw hat, then places it carefully on her chair, as if it it's one of the Fabergé eggs her mother's decorator arranged on a shelf in the powder room.

I watch as they glide down the tiled steps into the water, the sky a perfect cerulean blue behind them. They could be an ad for a beach resort—Kate, in her white bikini, for a sexy exclusive island, and Amy, with her high ponytail, for a family-friendly, sandcastle-building-contest kind of place. Once waist deep, they both walk in slow circles, combing their fingers along the surface as they get used to the temperature.

I close my eyes and try to rest. I want so badly to empty my head, to officially relax and forget reality for a few days. But wouldn't you know, when I checked my voicemail after we landed, my one and only message was from my accountant. While Amy and Kate were excitedly stripping off their coats and turning their faces toward the sun, I was listening to a somber message telling me that it's imperative that I freeze my salary for a while.

Who would have thought that my former career as a public school teacher would make for a lavish life compared to the one I have working at my dream job? I was a good teacher—maybe not teacher-of-the-year good, but good enough that when June rolled around, I always found a letter or two on my desk from the sweet students who felt compelled to tell me that my class was their favorite. Every once in a while, I dig the letters out and read them to remind myself that my adult life has not been a complete catastrophe. I wonder what the chances would be of my old boss taking me back? I'm sure that my landlord would be thrilled to rent the bakery space out to a Panera or a Starbucks.

I turn over again—I just can't get comfortable—and try to distract myself from my self-flagellation by listening to Amy and Kate chat.

"So it must be nice to get away from the campaign for a few days?" Amy says.

Kate readjusts the messy bun on top of her head, the muscles in her slender arms flexing as she does it. "You have no idea," she says, a little too harshly. She sounds vaguely condescending, as if it would actually be impossible under any circumstance for Amy to understand. Sometimes, watching them, I feel the way that a mother must feel watching two of her children interact, hoping and praying that they will just get along. As different as Kate and Amy are, it shouldn't surprise me that the closeness they'd once shared was short-lived. It especially shouldn't surprise me now. They exist in such dramatically different galaxies, though equally seamless perfect worlds. Gorgeous Wife Kate. Adorable Mommy Amy. And then there's me...broke, unmarried, childless baker. I force myself to bury the thought before I go further.

"So it's tough being away from Emma?" I hear Kate ask.

Even with the sun's glare marring my vision, I can see Amy's face light up. The question's obviously surprised her as much as it does me. Kate isn't interested in hearing about people's kids any more than she's interested in clipping coupons.

I watch Amy get riled up all over again, telling Kate how much she wants to call home. Larry has occasionally asked me what the two of them talk about when the three of us get together. "Nothing of consequence" is what I usually say. They connect on the things that don't have much to do with either of their lives—celebrity gossip, movies they've seen, the news. He met them just when their close-ish friendship was fizzling out, so he has a hard time believing that they've ever been good friends at all. More than once, he's asked me why they even bother to keep in such good touch. "Because they have a history," I say. "And because I make them." Someday, I hope they'll find their way back to each other.

They initially started to drift apart when Amy got engaged. Kate made no secret of her disapproval of Mike. She thought that he wasn't good enough for Amy, she said, but I think that the real problem was that Mike stood up to Kate like no other man—or woman, frankly—that I'd ever witnessed. When they were in the same room, Kate physically tensed up, her aggression as obvious as a cat's when its hair stands up on its back. It didn't help that when Mike wasn't around, Amy was usually talking about how wonderful he was and the happy future they were planning.

Amy's bachelorette party sealed my suspicions that Kate might actually be jealous of the stable family life that Amy had ahead of her—the kind that Kate had never experienced. We were in New Orleans, it was nearly five o'clock in the morning, and we'd just returned home from the bars and settled into our shared queen bed in our hotel room when I figured it out. "Wave, is that what you want?" she slurred, her back to me.

"What?"

"Do you want the kind of life Amy's about to have with him?"

"You mean to get married and have kids?" There had been a stretch of time during our evening in the French Quarter when Amy told the group—most of them friends from her UNC sorority—about how they hoped to get started on children right away.

"Yeah, to settle like that. To be so...so..." She sighed. "So *ordinary*."

I knew from all of the time I'd spent at Kate's house that *ordinary* was the adjective that her mother most often employed when she criticized something.

"I don't know," I said honestly. Larry and I were newly dating. I couldn't picture getting married any more than I could see myself becoming a Vegas showgirl.

"Well." Kate sighed. "I think Amy's going to be dead from boredom before her thirtieth birthday. It's too bad. She's so much fun without him."

I thought for a moment about asking Kate straightaway if she was jealous. It was the kind of question that I knew would set her off—Kate Berkshire didn't envy anyone—and the timing wasn't exactly perfect. It was one of the few (brief) moments when she wasn't dating somebody. But before I could get up the nerve to actually open my mouth and spit out the words, I heard her begin to softly snore beside me.

I shield my eyes from the sun with my hands and watch them. The blue backdrop of the sky above them and the water beneath them makes them look like they're floating in midair. Amy is still talking—about how applying to preschool these days is like going through college admissions. Kate picks at her manicure, entirely somewhere else. When she looks up, she catches my eye. "Can you grab my phone?" she mouths.

I roll my eyes and get up to fetch it.

Later that night, we sit on the patio off of the kitchen in a different set of chaise lounges, these ones upholstered in some sort of sumptuous cottony fabric that feels like the best combination of cashmere and an old worn-in T-shirt. Amy and I are both still in our swimsuits. On a table centered between us lies the detritus of our dinner—chips, dips, and cold fried chicken that I picked up at Publix.

"Tell me again why we only do this once a year?" I say, looking out at the ocean beyond the terra-cotta railing, taking in the reflection of the moon over the water. The Atlantic glistens like it's been sprinkled with thousands and thousands of diamonds. The air smells clean and sweet, like just breathing in the breeze could add ten years to your life. I am finally, finally loosening up a little bit, thanks to the four margaritas I've consumed since arriving here and the glass of champagne that I'm now working on.

"I'd love to spend more time here, but I'm working all of the time," Kate says, dragging a potato chip through a plastic container of onion dip.

"Work, work, work," I mock, pulling my cover-up—Larry's monstrous "Cherry Blossom 10K" T-shirt—over my knees. We're all feeling our alcohol but I'm frankly getting tired of hearing Kate complain about her charmed life, particularly since I got the voice-mail from my accountant about my salary.

"Jesus, I'm sorry," she snaps. She slumps forward dramatically and puts her head in her hands.

I look at Amy and raise my eyebrows. She shrugs back.

When Kate announced that she was going to quit her job at the *Post* almost right after she got married (because it was nothing if not an announcement—she'd never even mentioned to me that she was considering it), I was floored. Kate had always loved her job—I mean, hell, I can't imagine many people wouldn't like the cushiness of being a travel reporter. She wrote stories about wine tastings in Argentina, long weekends in Nashville, summer bargains in Europe. I teased her that she went on vacation for a living, but I knew she took her work seriously, and I suspected that it was because it was one of the few things in her life that she'd done on her own merit. Her name had helped her get her foot in the door, of course, but she'd worked hard to prove that she wasn't just a pretty face looking for something to do in between social calls. And she was good at it—she was promoted three times in two years.

But she said that she had started to resent the running around now that she had Brendan in her life. With the long hours that he worked at his law firm, she wanted to be with him when he was off, not in a hotel room by herself in another time zone. She said that she would continue to do some freelance articles, and to her credit she did write a few, but that eventually trickled off, and until Brendan decided to go into politics, she mostly busied herself with spin classes, trips out to Middleburg to ride the horses at her parents' farm, and spa treatments.

Her mother tried to get her involved with one of her many causes: the American Red Cross, Friends of the National Zoo, the Smithsonian Institution, the Junior League of Washington. It took only two or three luncheons, surrounded by women who talked about table linens as if they were a matter of national security, for Kate to confirm that while she would happily write checks for charities, she wasn't about to befriend groups of women whose aim was to be exactly like her mother. It was precisely what she'd always tried to avoid.

I have to admit that when Brendan announced his candidacy, I was most excited about the fact that Kate would now have legitimate reasons to whine about being stressed and busy. She finally had something to do. Trust me, there's nothing worse than venting to your best friend about your grueling day and then hearing her try to commiserate with you by recounting the horrible way that her facialist kept her waiting. She called her father, he wrote a check, and the campaign was off and running. She was behind Brendan all the way, pushing him squarely into it with both hands—if you ask me, because it gave her a purpose, too.

"Listen, I know that I bitch about the campaign all of the time,"

Kate says now, looking forlornly down at her toes. "But you don't understand. It's not just the hours, which are longer than you could *ever* imagine. Even you"—she nods toward me—"with the god-awful hours that you work." I try to picture Kate operating the espresso machine at the bakery or sweeping up after a group of kids who'd come in for after-school snacks. One hour of assembling sandwiches alongside some of my college-aged employees would send her running and screaming back to the grind of personal assistants and private jets.

"It's not just having to be 'on' all of the time," Kate rails. "I'm used to that. I've been doing it my whole life. You know my parents."

I nod. This is definitely true.

"Or dealing with all of these idiots on Brendan's staff who think that they're more important than me just because I'm 'the wife.'" She makes little quotation marks in the air with her fingers. "You wouldn't believe it. Some of these people on staff, even the young women who should know better, treat me like I'm some bubble-headed society whore whose only ambition is to decorate the governor's mansion and wear pretty ball gowns. Earlier in the campaign, they'd tried to butter me up, calling me *Ms. Berkshire* instead of Kate, constantly asking if I was hungry or if I'd like any coffee, wondering if they could do 'anything, anything at all' for me. Once they realized that I don't follow the code of symbiotic Washington relationships, they stopped. Now they're all business, with none of the bootlicking pretense: 'Make sure you're here on time.' 'Here's the speech you need to read.' 'We need you to circulate at more of the events—you know, shake more hands, be with the people.' They treat me like a child. Even Brendan acts that way." Her voice trails off. She picks up her wineglass, rests it on her chest, and tilts it toward her mouth to take a sip. "He's just...I don't know."

I watch and wait for her to say something else. I've seen Kate through every boyfriend she's ever had—the prom kings, the lacrosse stars, the tortured-artist phase that she went through at Brown, the cardiologist whom she dated afterward to prove that she was over it, the nationally ranked tennis player who was too self-absorbed even for her. Kate dumped every single one of them, ridding herself of them as easily as if she was throwing away an empty milk carton. She never admitted to any specific problem in any of these relationships—they just ended. She sees things in black and white; they either work or they don't, and her marriage to Brendan *works*. She complains about him all day long, but Kate is about as likely to reveal true relationship problems as she is to go on the news to talk about having hemorrhoids.

"Okay, here's the thing," she says, sitting up again. She wobbles and grabs the sides of her chair to steady herself, gripping them as if she's floating on a raft in the ocean before us. "I always knew that this would be the path we'd go down. It's not a surprise. He told me on the night that I met him that he was going to run for governor."

I remember Kate calling me from the lobby of the Willard Hotel that evening. Larry and I were sitting on the couch, my feet in his lap, drinking beer and watching *Three Amigos!* on cable. She was at a family friend's wedding and Brendan was a groomsman. "I'm ditching my date," she'd whispered into the phone. "There's just *something* about this guy." This was true of course, given the way things worked out, but it wasn't something I believed at the time—it was what she *always* said. It was the kind of thing you could say when you could have whomever you wanted, when the "something" you'd noticed about the guy was how he fell in love with you the minute he saw you.

Kate takes another gulp of her drink, burps, and keeps talking. "I told Brendan to go for it. Hell, I fantasized about it. *Governor and Mrs. Brendan Berkshire.*" She points her finger into her open mouth as if she's going to make herself vomit. "I just didn't realize..." She shakes her head. "Sometimes it feels like I wouldn't recognize him if he wasn't standing behind a podium."

"The perfect couple," Amy says, to no one in particular. When I turn to look at her, she's gazing pensively out toward the ocean. Given her personality, you would think that she would be a bottle-rocket, bouncing-off-the-walls kind of drunk, but alcohol actually tends to mellow her out.

"What?" Kate says.

"Oh." Amy turns to her. "I said 'the perfect couple.' You guys just always seem so perfect. Like JFK and—"

"Don't even say Jackie," Kate snaps. "That marriage was hardly perfect."

"Have you talked to Brendan about this?" I jump in to save Amy.

Kate looks at me as if I'd just suggested that she run off with one of my dishwashers.

"And say what? *Pay attention to me?*" she whines. "All I'm saying is that I wish that we had some more time for us. Like there used to be. He's like my father, always at work." She grimaces as if she's just tasted something rotten. "I guess I pictured that this would be more of a partnership and that I'd be involved in a way that doesn't make me feel like I'm on Brendan's payroll. I mean, sure, at these campaign events, we walk onstage together holding hands, looking very much like a team, but the truth is that I'm a minor player in this whole thing. Brendan hardly acknowledges me. Hell, when I want to talk to him, I have to go through Stephanie." She tilts her head back, sighs, and rubs her shoulder with one hand. "God, I need a massage."

"Who's Stephanie?" Amy says, her voice careful.

"His horse-faced assistant. I swear he spends more time with her than he does with me. Most of our communication these days either happens through her or the notes he leaves for me at home on the rare occasions that he's actually there. I hate those fucking notes. They remind me of the ones from my mother that welcomed me home from school when I was growing up—*Won't be home until late. Finish your homework. Order dinner.* As if instructions printed on a piece of her personalized cardstock were an equal substitute for actual parenting." She pulls the wine bottle out of the silver bucket on the table between our chairs, finds it empty, sighs, and drops it on the ground next to her. I watch it roll across the patio. "And now he says he wants to have kids."

I'm not sure I've heard her right.

"*What?*" I blurt.

"Kids?" Amy gasps.

If there is one unwavering truth about Kate, it's that she does not want children.

"I don't know how he thinks that's going to happen given how rarely we even sleep in the same bed. Does he think he can just send a sperm sample through his assistant?"

"Whoa, whoa, whoa," I say. "Hold on. Explain all this, Kate. Kids? I thought Brendan was on board with you not wanting them."

"That's what he said." She shoves her hair behind her ears and looks up at the sky. "I don't know. I guess he started mentioning it about a year ago. Around the time the campaign really got rolling." She raises her eyebrows. "That's probably not a coincidence."

"A year ago? Why didn't you mention anything?" I ask.

"Because I'm not having children!" she says. "There's nothing to talk about."

"But he wants them?" Amy ventures.

Kate shrugs. "I think he thinks he needs them."

"Oh, but people don't really have kids because it's good for their jobs," Amy says.

Kate snorts. "You are *so* not from Washington. I totally think that, actually. He started dropping small hints at first—stories about some of the staffers' kids—and then his brothers' wives both got pregnant... The next thing I know, he's sending me texts about it. I mean, *texts.*"

"What?" I say.

"Yeah, jokey little messages about having a little Kate or Brendan. And then we'd be at a campaign stop and he'd see a pregnant woman in the audience and lean over to whisper to me about how adorable I'd be with a belly."

"I can't believe this," I say. "You've never mentioned anything."

"There's nothing to mention," she says again. "I'm not having kids."

"But Brendan wants them?" Amy repeats, a little too sympathetically.

Kate shoots her a look. Then her eyes rest on me, and her face softens in a way that reveals that the issue is not so cut-and-dried.

"We'll figure it out," she says, her tone implying that the topic's closed for discussion.

"Things will get easier," I say, knowing it's a lame sentiment, but it's the best I can come up with given my shock and my alcohol consumption. "You've said that this is the most intense time in the campaign, right?"

"It's *always* intense, Waverly," she growls. "He's not running for class president."

"But he's basically won, right?" Amy offers. "And once the campaign's over, then the stress level won't be so high? So maybe things will get better?"

Kate vigorously shakes her head, sucking in her breath as she does it. She looks just like her mother. "No, Amy, he'll be *governor*. Of *Virginia*. It's not a small job."

"Well, I remember how stressful it was for us when Mike was finishing up his residency," Amy says. "He'd have these thirty-hour shifts, and when he'd finally get off work, he was such a zombie that it wasn't like we could actually do anything. It was a really tough time for us, but we got through it." She nods emphatically. "You will, too, Kate. It's just temporary."

Kate chuckles. "Yes, you're right, Amy."

I jump in before she can say more. I can't stand the patronizing tone of her voice, and she obviously just wants to complain. I'm tired of listening to it. A part of me is tempted to tell her about what I'm dealing with—that much reality would surely shut her up. "Well, no relationship is perfect," I say definitively, clapping my hands together. "Larry and I have our issues."

"Please, like what?" Kate says.

"Oh, you know, the typical stuff," I say. "He's a huge slob."

"Well, that sounds serious," Kate says, rolling her eyes. "I think you should kick him out."

"No, it's really bad," I say. "He leaves plates of food on his night-stand, mail goes unopened for weeks. I feel like I'm constantly nagging him, and the last thing I ever wanted was to be was a nag. It's not like me. Sometimes it feels more like we're roommates. We go weeks without having sex." I leave out the part about this be-ing a hugely contentious issue for us right now. You would think that with all of the stress that I'm under at work that sex might be a good antidote, but I'm not remotely interested. When I get home at night, the last thing I want is one more person needing some-thing from me. Larry, naturally, doesn't understand—how could he, given that he has no idea what's going on?—which makes me feel even worse. "Last week, I was working late on my laptop in the kitchen when he came in with that look in his eye. I gave him the least sexy excuse I could think of—digestive issues—blaming the chili that I'd eaten for lunch," I say.

"I understand that," Kate says. "Here's the funny thing about Brendan: We are almost never alone in the house together, but now? With this kid thing? Whenever he's actually home, he's trying to get me into bed. And there's nothing romantic about it—I'm telling you, it's just a means to an end with him, another competi-tion he has to win."

I have to laugh. I can't help myself.

"It's true!" Kate says. "I do it, of course. I have needs. And it's rarely more than once every couple of weeks. He keeps needling me about going off my birth control pills. Little does he know, I got an IUD six months ago."

"Kate, that's awful!" I say. I look over at Amy, who's just shaking her head.

"What?" Kate shrugs. "I'm not going to risk getting pregnant. I should really just get a hysterectomy. He probably wouldn't even notice when I went into surgery." She looks down at her lap. She's far drunker than I thought—otherwise she'd never be so candid. "It's pathetic. I'm the wife figure in his campaign and the incubator for his offspring. That pretty much sums up how he sees me."

"Oh, Kate," I say, putting my hand to my heart. I can tell she's really hurting. She never admits this kind of vulnerability.

"Sometimes, in the middle of the night while he sleeps, I'll rest my hand on his shoulder blade or hook my foot over his, and it actually feels strange to touch him. Even in his sleep, he squirms away," she says. I can tell by her downcast eyes that she's avoiding looking at me. "Anyway," she says, matter-of-factly. "I have to remember that it's just the job. It has nothing to do with me." She turns to Amy. "What about you? How's your marriage?"

Uh-oh. I know this can't be headed in a good direction.

Amy shifts in her seat. "Oh, I don't know." She laughs and looks down at her lap. "I don't know; we have the usual disagreements. We're just normal, I guess."

Kate smirks at me. "So what's the deal with him, anyway?" she says, grinning in the self-satisfied way that a high school bully might right before throwing a punch.

Fuck. Kate!

Amy shrugs again. "The deal?"

"Yeah, the deal. He seems a little, uh, *off* these days." She says *off* like it's a code word for something else, which it is, of course—*asshole, son of a bitch.* "Like the incident at Waverly's last week. What was that all about?"

My heart jumps. "Kate, really, come on," I say. "Amy, don't listen to her. It's nothing." I still wanted to talk to Amy about Mike, but not like this.

Kate laughs. "It's just a question, Waverly. Right, Amy?"

Amy looks at me. She looks tired, her eyes glazed over from all of the alcohol.

"Waverly, I'm so sorry," she says, her face crumpling like a paper bag. "All week long, I wanted to apologize, and when we went running the other day and you asked me about it, I just was so embarrassed that I blew it off. I should have said something then." She looks so sad and worn down that I suddenly feel guilty for wanting an apology at all.

"It's fine, Amy." I wave my hand at her. "Really, it's no biggie." There are tears in her eyes. I've known Amy long enough to know that disappointing someone is her biggest fear. "I promise, it's over."

"But what's his *problem?*" Kate slurs. "He's really become kind of a prick."

"Kate!" I cry. "Stop."

"It's okay, it's okay," Amy says. Her face is crimson. "He's just— he gets overwhelmed with work." She fiddles with the tiny gold pendant she wears around her neck, a round disk with an engraved *E* for *Emma.*

I shoot a look at Kate, whose nose is so deep in her wineglass that it looks like she's trying to climb into it to get the last sip. "Well, I never liked him anyway," she mumbles.

Oh God.

"You don't exactly make it a secret," Amy says flatly.

Kate shrugs.

I don't know what to do—I could just sit back and let the two of them hash it out, but I know that Kate will bulldoze right over Amy, especially since she's drunk. I decide to change the subject entirely. "You know what—let's not talk about the men anymore.

They're not here and this is our weekend—they should be out of sight, out of mind, right? Kate, I would *much* rather hear what you were telling me on the plane about the neighbors next door. Something about him running some sort of prostitution ring?"

"Oh, yeah!" Kate's face lights up at the prospect of good gossip. "You won't believe this."

Kate starts to ramble, but my eyes are locked on Amy. It's almost too dark to make out her face, but when she shifts in her seat and the patio light flashes across her like a lightning burst, I can tell that she's upset. Kate was rude, but it's not as if her distaste for Mike is any big secret, so it strikes me as odd that Amy looks as distressed as she does, and I wonder if something else is going on with her.

The next morning, I'm sure that something's really wrong. I'm lying in the king-sized bed in one of the several bedrooms that make up the guest wing of the house, my head pounding from the alcohol the night before. I'm trying to will myself to get up and walk across the plush carpet to the marble bathroom to brush the rotten taste out of my mouth. The bedroom that I'm in looks like it's straight out of *Dynasty*—mauve and pink silks, gilded furniture, a brassy chandelier over the bed that's about the size of a carousel. Kate's mother apparently hasn't bothered to redecorate these rooms since the eighties.

I'm lying there in the quiet, mindlessly counting the crystal droplets on the chandelier above me, when I suddenly start to hear something. At first I think it's a bird chirping outside, but then I realize that it's somebody crying—Amy. I sit up and press my ear to the wall behind my bed—her bedroom is right next door. These aren't soft little cries. They're full, from-the-belly sobs. I jump out of bed and pull on my sweatpants and rush into the hall. I knock softly on the heavy wood door.

"Just a minute," I hear Amy say.

She opens the door in her lavender nightgown. Her cheeks are slightly sunburnt from the day before and her eyes are puffy, of course. There's no way she can get around the fact that she's been crying.

"Are you okay?" I say, reaching out to touch her arm.

"Fine." She forces a smile and then, just as quickly, looks away from me.

"Are you sure? It sounded like you were crying pretty hard."

"I just miss Emma," she says, grinning again. "I don't know why it's so hard on me this year. I know it's silly..."

"No, it's not silly at all," I lie. I actually think it's completely odd—and I don't buy her story for a second. I may not be a mother, but I know Amy, and she's not the kind of woman who would get this worked up over being away from her child for a few days.

"Are you sure it doesn't have something to do with last night?" I say.

"Last night? Oh, no." She laughs unconvincingly. "That was just Kate being..."

"Kate," I finish for her.

"Yeah," she says.

"Are you sure everything's all right, Amy?" I say again. What I heard was full-on breakdown crying. It sounded like she was flipping out.

"Yeah, yeah," she says. "I'm really fine. In fact, I'm actually pretty hungry. Are you?" She raises an eyebrow at me and forces another smile. "Any chance you feel like cooking?"

The rest of the weekend is downright weird. Kate's huffy and agitated. She buries herself in her magazines and goes out shopping, leaving Amy and me back at the house, where we mostly lounge by the pool. On Saturday night, her birthday, we give her the double-chocolate birthday cake that I had shipped down from the bakery, and Amy presents her with a gift—pretty monogrammed cocktail napkins that I'm sure she fretted over. Kate's gracious enough, but the celebration lasts all of twenty minutes before she says she wants to take a long bath and go to bed.

Moodiness isn't all that unusual for Kate, but it is strange for Amy, who continues to be a black-and-white version of her usual self all weekend. She insists that she's fine—she is just hungover, or she's tired, or she's had too much sun—all lame excuses that I don't believe for a minute. Every time I ask her about missing home or if she's talked to Mike, a shadow falls over her face. "I'm fine, Waverly, really," she says.

By the time we're on our plane back on Sunday, I can't wait to get home, no matter the problems that will greet me as soon as we touch down in D.C. I'm not returning home relaxed, with color in my cheeks and the residual scent of suntan lotion on my skin. Instead, I feel edgy and tired. Kate is softly snoring in the seat across the aisle from me. Amy is in the window seat to my right, dog-earing recipes in *Cooking Light*. On the way to the airport earlier, the three of us kept saying that we were sad to leave, but it was bullshit and we all knew it.

"Hey." Amy taps my arm and points at a page in the magazine. "What's *crema mexicana*?"

"It's kind of like sour cream, but thinner."

Amy isn't fine, no matter how many times she says it. I'm as sure of that as I am of my own name. Something is up, and the more that I think about the way she reacted when Kate asked her about Mike, and the more I think about how Amy and Mike interact when I've seen them lately, I start to wonder: What if he's cheating on her? I can't imagine why any woman would fall for him, but maybe he's channeling all of his long-lost charm to someone else and that's the reason why he acts the way he does around us. Maybe someone at work—I know that Mike's partner is an elderly man, but maybe there's a young nurse in the office...or even a patient? A lot of women swoon over a white coat. The more that I think about it, the more plausible it seems, and by the time the pilot announces that we're beginning to make our approach into Dulles, I'm convinced. As the flight attendants walk up and down the aisles, collecting trash, Kate finally stirs. I check to make sure Amy's still busy with her magazine and then I reach across the aisle and poke Kate. "Need to talk to you," I mouth, turning in my seat so that Amy can't see me.

Kate furrows her brow, annoyed.

"Have a theory," I mouth and glance toward Amy.

Kate sighs deeply, rolling her eyes, and turns her back to me.

CHAPTER SEVEN

After we get our bags, Amy and I say good-bye to Kate and head to my car, wheeling our suitcases behind us. It's just dusk and it's nearly sleeting outside, and I'm dying to get home, put on my ratty sweats, and avoid reality for the last few hours before work tomorrow. I've missed Larry, and it's a welcome feeling. I want to settle in with him on the couch. And I want scrambled eggs. I'm obviously the expert in our kitchen, but Larry is undeniably the king of eggs. It's his thing. I try to remember whether we have a carton in the fridge.

In the car, Amy asks me if I have a big week coming up, and my stomach drops when I think of the meeting I'm having with my accountant tomorrow to talk about freezing my salary.

"Just the usual stuff," I lie. She is so excited to see Emma that she's the most animated that I've seen her all weekend. She talks the whole way to her house—a forty-minute trip because of the traffic that never lets up in this part of the world, even on a rainy Sunday night—and when we pull into her driveway, she asks me to come inside and say hello.

"Oh, no, it's okay. I'm sure they're dying to see you. I don't want to interfere." I am so desperate to get home that the seven-mile drive between our houses already feels like it will take days.

"Oh, come on. Just a minute?" she says, gathering up her things. "Just for a minute," she says again, this time definitively.

I reluctantly turn the key to shut off the ignition and we run in the rain up her front walk. It's odd that she wants me to come in so badly when she hasn't seen her family all weekend, but she's so keyed up I guess she assumes it would be fun for me to say hello, too.

When Amy opens the door, Emma tackles her before she's over the threshold. She drops her purse and keys on the floor and hugs Emma close.

"Oh my goodness, you smell so good," she says, burying her nose in Emma's neck. "I missed you so much!" Living here has washed most of the drawl out of Amy's voice, but you can hear it when she's baby talking to Emma.

"Mommy, I have something for you," Emma says when they let go. She grabs Amy's wrist with both hands and pulls her toward the living room.

"Wait, now, hold on a second, honey. Say hello to Aunt Waverly. She came in to see you." *I should have left the car running,* I think. *Then I could have had a quicker escape.*

"Hi!" She smiles up at me and waves quickly. "Come on, Mom. Come on!" she says, yanking Amy's wrist again.

Amy rolls her eyes at me. "Come on in for a second."

"No, it's okay, Amy. Really..."

"Waverly, just for a second," she says, letting Emma pull her through the arched entryway to the living room.

Mike is on the sofa reading the paper. A basketball game is blaring on the television. Several of Emma's stuffed animals are lined up on the floor, with a plastic tea set arranged carefully in front of them.

"Hey," Mike says halfheartedly, looking at Amy over the top of the paper. He gives her a once-over.

What a welcome, I think.

"Hi!" Amy smiles at him.

"Waverly, hey," he says to me, with somehow even less enthusiasm.

"Waverly just came in for a minute to say hello, Mike," she says. I can tell she's disappointed with the way he's acting, and it makes me want to get out of here faster. I wonder if he saw his mistress this weekend. I wonder if he's had the gall to bring her around Emma.

She tugs on Amy's arm again. "Mommy, I have to show you!" she whines.

"Okay," she says, running her hand over Emma's hair. Mike's looking at her expectantly, his eyebrows raised, like, "Well, what are you waiting for?" *Welcome home, Amy,* I think again. *I missed you so much. It's so nice to see you. How was your trip?*

"Mommy," Emma pleads, shaking Amy's arm.

"Okay, baby, okay." I follow behind the two of them as Emma leads us to the kitchen.

"Close your eyes," Emma instructs. Amy squeezes them tight, scrunching up her face. "You, too, Aunt Waverly!"

I do as I'm told.

"Okay, now! Look!"

Emma holds over her head a piece of pink construction paper on which she's painted a red house, several orange hearts, and a yellow sun in the top right corner.

"I made it for you," she says, beaming at her mother.

"Oh, thank you, honey! It's beautiful! I love it," Amy says, bending down to kiss her.

I look at the thick finger-painted images. Hearts. A house. During college, I took an Intro to Psych class where we did a section about art therapy. The professor was an elderly man with horrible eczema who spent most of the quarter enjoying the fruits of his tenure by reading *The Nation* at his desk while we watched videos of troubled kids drawing pictures about what they were feeling. I look at Emma's picture and wish I'd retained something from that class. Amy's obviously an incredible mom, but now I wonder what that little girl's experienced with a dad like Mike, no matter what Amy says about him being a great father. Kids can sense things.

"Did you and your daddy have a good time?" Amy pulls Emma toward her for another hug.

"Uh-huh," Emma nods. She has red stains around her lips. Fruit punch.

"What did you do?"

I feel Mike walk up behind us. He stands next to me and leans on the kitchen counter. I scoot over a step to put some distance between us. *I'm on to you,* I think.

"We went to the park...umm...we went to the children's museum," Emma says, ticking off the places on her fingers. She pauses for a moment, looking up at the ceiling with her head cocked to the side and her hands on her hips. A three-year-old's thinking pose.

"We went out for pizza," Mike offers.

"Yeah, pizza!" Emma yells, jumping up and down.

"Well, that sounds great," Amy says. "I missed you sooo much!" She pulls Emma in closer. "It's soooo good to be home!"

"Did you miss Daddy?" Emma says.

Amy glances up at Mike. "I did, I missed you both very much," she says, cupping Emma's face in her hands.

I notice that Mike doesn't even look at Amy. His eyes are locked on Emma. *Asshole.*

"Mommy! Now you hug Daddy!" Emma says excitedly, jumping up and down.

Amy glances at me, then stands and gives her husband, the father of her child, the most awkward, formal, un-Amy-like hug I've ever seen her give anyone. It's the robotic kind of hug you'd give to a distant cousin you rarely see. Is it possible that Amy actually knows or at least suspects something?

I watch her walk to the refrigerator and slide Emma's masterpiece under a magnet that says, "Martha Stewart Doesn't Live Here." *Yeah, right.*

"Did you eat?" she asks Mike.

"We did," he says. "There's leftover pizza in the fridge if you want it."

"Waverly, do you want some pizza? We haven't eaten since this morning. You must be starving."

I am actually ravenous—so hungry that I could eat the cardboard box it came in, much less the pizza—but I have to escape this crazy house before I witness any more of this. I feel awful for Amy—I'm going to have to think long and hard about how I'm going to bring it up—but right now, I just need to get home. My relationship with Larry is beginning to seem over-the-top wonderful to me now. I make a mental note to remind myself of this when I actually see him.

"No, no. I'm fine. I should really—," I start.

"Did you have a good time?" Mike interrupts. He hops up onto the kitchen counter.

"Yeah, we did," Amy answers. Emma's playing with her alphabet magnets on the fridge. "It was about what you would expect, a lot of time lying by the pool. You would have hated it." She forces a laugh. "I know how restless you get just lying around."

"Did you go out at all?" He drums his fingers along the countertop. I start to rattle my keys in my hand, trying to subtly signal that I need to go.

"No, not really. We walked around town a little bit late Saturday afternoon, but we mostly hung around the house. Was everything okay here? No problems with her?"

"Everything was fine. We had a good time," he says. "Last night, she came into our room in the middle of the night. Had a nightmare."

"Our room?" Amy says. She looks confused. *Whoa.*

"Yeah, you know, our bedroom?" Mike says.

"Oh, yeah," she laughs. "Sorry. I am *really* tired." She looks at me and shakes her head at herself. She's blushing. "Wow. I'm out of it."

"I have to go do some bills," Mike says, out of nowhere. He leaves the room without saying good-bye to me.

"So, I'm going to go," I say, trying to be casual.

"Okay," Amy says. "Are you sure you don't want to take some pizza with you?"

"No. No, thanks." I rattle my keys.

"Emma, say good-bye to Waverly."

"Bye-bye," she sings.

At the door, I give Amy a hug. "I'll call you tomorrow," I say.

"Sounds great. It was so fun!" she says.

I nod back. *Not really.*

"Okay, see you," I say, and then turn to run to my car.

An hour later, I am sitting on the couch with a plate of scrambled eggs and toast in my lap. Larry pushes the Sunday paper aside to put a cup of chamomile tea on the coffee table for me and then sits down. He has had a do-nothing weekend—grabbed a burrito lunch with a buddy, finished the book he was reading—and the house reflects it. Four pairs of his shoes and a sweatshirt dot the living room floor, and it annoys me more than it should but I don't say anything. I am happy to be home and I don't want to fuck it up by nagging him.

"Good eggs," I say, placing a forkful onto a piece of toast and taking a bite. He somehow always gets the salt and pepper ratio exactly right.

"Thanks," he says, shifting closer on the couch and stretching an arm behind me to rub my back. "So tell me why the trip was weird."

When I'd walked in and dropped my suitcase by the stairs, he'd asked, "How did things go in the Sunshine State?"

"Not so sunny," I'd replied.

"It was just weird," I tell him now. "Mostly because of Amy." I tell him about the sullen mood and the crying. I leave out Kate's crankiness, which isn't exactly breaking news, and forgo telling him about Brendan wanting kids, which has the potential to lead to a talk about our future as parents. We both want kids, but like everything else concerning our relationship, it's something we act like we'll just 'get around to,' as if I'm twenty-five instead of thirty-five and we have all the time in the world.

"I developed a theory on the plane," I say.

"What's that?" He reaches to wipe a toast crumb off of the corner of my lip.

"I think Mike's cheating on her."

"Really?" He looks skeptical.

"Yeah, you don't think it's plausible?"

"I don't know. He's not exactly Casanova. I can't picture how he would meet someone."

"I know, but think about it: He's a decent-looking guy, he's a doctor, and he *used to* have a normal personality. It would explain why he's such an ass to Amy and why he seems so tortured when he's with us."

"Yeah." Larry shrugs. "I guess I always assumed he was just kind of a miserable person. He's been like this for years. Do you think he's had a girlfriend all that time?"

"Who knows? Maybe he's had lots of them. I don't know, but the more I think about it, the more it all makes sense."

"I can see where you're going with this, but I hope it's not true," Larry says.

"Yeah," I say. "I wonder if Amy knows."

"Wouldn't she tell you if she did?"

"I don't know," I say, polishing off my toast. I reach to put the plate on the coffee table and get my tea. "People can be funny about that kind of thing, you know? Maybe they're trying to work through it. Maybe she's embarrassed. Or maybe she's in denial." I drum my fingers against my mug. "I mean, Emma's young. Amy might be trying to work it out to keep their family together. I need to figure out the right way to approach her."

"For sure," Larry says. "Wish I had some advice for you."

"Yeah." We sit there quietly for a few minutes and Larry puts my feet in his lap and starts rubbing them. He's been handsy since I walked in the door. I know he wants to have sex, and I know that I also should, but...I sit up and cross my legs underneath me and put his hand in mine. Now would be the perfect time to tell him about the meeting with my accountant tomorrow. To just tell the truth. "So what did you do last night?" I say instead.

"You know, actually, it was weird," he says. "I wanted to watch this new HBO series about Teddy Roosevelt, but when I went to turn on the TV, the cable was dead. Then, when I called the 800 number, they told me that our service had been cut off because our bill was overdue."

Fuck.

Fuck, fuck, fuck.

Larry and I split the bills and the cable is one that's my responsibility. I've been meaning to switch the bill to another credit card since the one I usually use to pay it has been near my limit for more than a month now. Had I bothered to open the mail, I probably would have caught this, but I've been letting myself just throw the bills into my bag when I get them out of the mailbox. I keep telling myself I'm going to go through them when I get a break at work, but I don't exactly get a break at work, so...*fuck.*

"I went ahead and paid it," he says. "They said your credit card was denied?"

"Shit, I'm sorry," I say. "I don't know how that happened. Maybe the card that I use to pay it expired or something. I'll have to check."

"It's no biggie," he says, and reaches again to pull me toward him. "Come here. I missed you."

"I missed you, too," I say.

He starts to kiss me and I kiss back, giving in. As his lips start to move down my neck, I reach my hands around him and under his shirt and try to relax, but my head is spinning. I tell myself that everything's going to be okay. I'll meet with my accountant tomorrow, figure some things out, and I'll tell Larry everything this week. I will, I tell myself again. I really, really will.

CHAPTER EIGHT

This coming September marks my fifth anniversary as a bakery owner. Whenever the subject comes up, Larry says that I should throw a party—do *something* to mark the occasion—but I keep waving him off. Celebrating doesn't feel right at all. I can't imagine clinking glasses of champagne and giving a thank-you toast to a staff that I can barely support.

It's ironic, isn't it? I've often thought that the very essence of my business is to help people celebrate. There are so many milestone "say cheese for the camera" moments that center around the food—and, specifically, the cake. What would a family photo album be if not for the picture of the bride and groom cutting one, or the one-year-old in her high chair blowing out her first candle? These sweet, celebratory moments are my currency, if not, at the moment, my personal reality. And God, wouldn't I love something to celebrate?

Before Maggie's became Maggie's, the building had been a bar. When I was a kid, my mother and I used to pass it on our way to the grocery store on Saturday mornings. The facade was covered with what looked like cheap lumber from an abandoned construction project. There was one window, so high up that it was impossible to see inside, with a neon Miller Lite sign that blinked fitfully like somebody's nervous tic. In the passenger seat of Mom's VW bug, I'd wondered what went on in a place like that. I never could have predicted that it'd become my second home someday.

Larry had actually found it. He'd circled the ad in the back of the *Maple Hill News & Record*—"Restaurant Space for Lease, Full Commercial Kitchen, 64 Ford Street"—and left it for me on top of the fraying backpack I used to tote my stuff to and from work. The idea of opening a bakery was something I had toyed with for a while, mentioning it now and then in a wistful way. But I was always baking, so every time I plied Larry, Kate, and Amy with whatever I'd made that week—pumpkin muffins, lemon bars, chocolate chip cookies with sea salt—they prodded me to think seriously about it. In time, the wispy clouds of my daydreams started to take form, and the idea became so solidly obvious that it was impossible to ignore.

I'd have to give up my job, and though I loved being a teacher, I knew deep down that I wasn't passionate about it in the way that I should be. I'd majored in English because I'd always liked to read and writing assignments came easily to me, but in my last year of college, I didn't really know what I wanted to do with my life. I was still coping with the loss of my parents, and thinking about my future in any way, much less embarking on a career path like so many of my classmates, wasn't something that I had the energy for. Babci advised me to just pick something "that paid a decent salary and would help make the world a little better," and added that whatever I chose, I didn't have to do forever. All of my fellow English majors were either going to grad school (no thanks) or law school (being from D.C., I'd met enough lawyers to know better) or becoming teachers. So that's what I did.

On a Tuesday afternoon, I left school right after my last class and Larry and I went to meet the owner of the restaurant space. The bar was nasty, with a gluey linoleum floor, decades of tobacco stains around the ceiling fans, air thick with the syrupy scent of spilled beer. But the kitchen was in decent shape—probably from disuse, as far as my inexperienced eye could judge—and the eight hundred square feet of space out front was more than enough for a few tables, a display case, and a cash register. A week later, after several long discussions with Larry and the girls, I handed over a check for the deposit and first month's rent and took out a home equity loan on the brownstone to help fund my start-up costs. The next day, I told my boss that I wouldn't be returning after summer break.

I never, ever, ever could have opened Maggie's without Larry and the girls. Larry, who'd become a semi-expert on construction from working in his parents' hardware store, helped me find the contractors who tore out the bar and replaced the covered-up storefront with floor-to-ceiling windows. Kate helped me run the numbers, sometimes literally holding my hand when I stared, stunned, at what it was going to cost to outfit a bakery, buy supplies, hire a staff, and contract with suppliers. Amy pulled paint chips at the hardware store, enthusiastically corroborated my furniture choices, and applauded my menu ideas.

In the weeks leading up to the opening, I worked around the clock, stopping only long enough to doze off, have an anxiety-driven nightmare (I give the entire town food poisoning; someone discovers a pubic hair in her apricot torte), and wake up frantic, ready to get back to work. Larry, as sweetly faithful as the dog I was naming the place after, helped me scrub the floors before he went to work in the morning and returned at the end of the day, a change of clothes under his arm, to help me work. One night we were wiring light fixtures, doing the work ourselves so that I could save some money. At some point well after two a.m., I was standing at the bottom of the ladder that Larry was perched on, shooting questions up into the air: "Do you think that charging for coffee refills is cheap? Will that piss people off?" "Are you sure that I shouldn't offer more than a cup of fruit salad with the lunch sandwiches?" "What about people to bus the tables—do you really think that when we're cooking and ringing people up and doing dishes, we'll have time to make sure that the front is always cleaned up, too? I don't want to have the kind of place with sticky tables and crumbs on the floor…"

Larry looked down at me, squinting in a certain way, and stepped off of the ladder. "Hold on a second," he said, wiping sweat from his hairline. He was wearing a faded T-shirt over an old long-sleeved thermal one. His jeans were splattered with the pale blue-gray that we'd painted the walls a week earlier. He walked to the boom box we kept in the corner, in the space where I planned to install the stereo I'd splurged on, and fiddled with the dial until he found the blues station out of D.C. Then he came back to me, peeled my hand off of one of the rungs of the ladder, and pulled me toward him to dance. I surrendered my weary head to his chest, closed my eyes, and let him lead. There was still sawdust on the floor and only two of the light fixtures worked. Muddy Waters sang through the empty space: "You can't lose what you ain't never had."

The song is stuck in my head as I sit across the desk from Gary, my accountant, and wait for him to wrap up a call so that we can start our meeting. He's holding a Styrofoam Dunkin' Donuts cup, and maybe I'm oversensitive, but it annoys me that he didn't think to buy his coffee from me today. His phone call is taking forever, and he keeps shrugging and rolling his eyes and mouthing that he's "so, so sorry" between sips of his drink. His desk is OCD orderly. The neat stacks of paper look like they were arranged with a ruler.

I press my palms against the seat of my chair. My hands are clammy, leaving faint damp marks on the burgundy leather. I keep telling myself that I'm not nervous.

My thoughts drift back to my opening-night party. It was two years before Amy had Emma and became a stay-at-home mom, and she actually took the day off work to help me. The two of us, along with Kate and three college students who'd answered my Craigslist post, spent the day sweeping the floors, straightening the framed photographs on the walls (most of them ones my dad had taken), and arranging platters of food with the kind of precision that I imagine someone might have used when preparing a still life for Paul Cézanne. At six o'clock, having changed into an emerald green dress that Kate helped me pick out at a little boutique in Georgetown, I opened the doors and greeted my guests: neighbors, the other storeowners on the block, childhood friends, old pals of my parents, former coworkers. Each time one of them complimented what I'd done to the place or told me how good the food tasted, I got the most delicious, heart-swelling confirmation that I'd been right to take this risk.

I didn't have a liquor license but we got champagne anyway, reasoning that I wasn't *officially* opening until the following day so this was sort of a private party. It was so worth it. Larry knew how nervous I was about everything going right, so he stuck close to my side, refilling my glass whenever it went half-empty. Kate circulated among the crowd, whispering pointedly into my new employees' ears whenever she noticed a stray glass on a table or a near-empty tray of food. Amy kept the music loud and dragged Mike out to dance, even though I hadn't pictured it being a dancing kind of party. I can still remember how their laughter rose above the noise of the crowd, and how he twirled her around and around until it seemed she might spin right up to the ceiling if she let go of his hand.

At the end of the night, it was just the five of us—Larry and me, Kate, and Amy and Mike. The last bottle of champagne was popped and passed around. When I look back at it now, the scene seems so unlikely, so barely familiar, that it's like when you watch a rerun on TV that you *think* you've seen but aren't totally sure. Mike kept walking back to the buffet table for more snacks, each time telling me again how much he loved the artichoke and feta crostini. Kate and Amy danced in the corner, the two of them drunk enough to put their fading friendship aside. They kept calling me over, but I was happy where I was, sitting on Larry's lap, his arms tight around my waist. He kept smiling up at me, saying wordlessly that I had "done good," which is exactly what he said later, and that he was proud of me. I was proud of me, too. Just look at how happy everyone was, in this place that I'd created, with my father's photographs on the walls, my mother's recipe box in the kitchen.

It occurs to me now that the five of us have never been together in a room like that again.

So much has changed.

Gary finally ends his call. "So," he says, swiveling in his chair and clasping his hands together on his desk. He's a prominently balding redhead with a mustache to match. He kind of reminds me of Ron Howard, which somehow makes him less intimidating. "We have a lot to talk about."

I just nod. I fear that if I open my mouth, something pleading and awful will come out. Something like, *Help me*.

Gary clears his throat and continues. "I've spent a lot of hours this past week looking over your financials. As I mentioned on the phone, there isn't enough cash coming in for you to continue without taking some serious cuts. And as we've talked about recently, there just plain isn't much left to cut."

During one of our recent phone calls, proving just how little he knows about food, he suggested I switch to a "cheaper cheese" for all of the products that require it, as if I could just slip sliced American into my goat cheese tart. Months and months ago, I'd started adding menu items that were a little easier on my budget—more rice and pasta salads at lunch, fewer chocolate desserts because the cocoa I prefer isn't cheap—but there were only so many sacrifices I could make before I worried I'd start compromising my work.

"Waverly, I've been over and over it, and there's just no other solution that I can come up with other than that you need to stop taking a salary."

I nod again. I hate the pitying way that he's looking at me. It reminds me of the way people look at me when I tell them how my parents died.

"So the next question is whether you think you can handle that, and for how long. I think that if we cut your salary, you'll have just enough coming in to pay for everything else that the business requires—your rent, your supplies, and your employees' salaries, though we may need to keep talking about cutting your staff."

"You know how I feel about that," I say. Gary and I talked about it months ago. I've had to let people go before—the younger kids can just be unreliable, and there have been a few serious cases, too, like the addict who was a whiz in the kitchen (probably because of all of the amphetamines) and stole money out of the cash register. But it's a whole different thing to have to cut someone loose because you can't afford to pay him or her. Plus, I already have what feels like a skeleton crew. I need every hand that I've got.

"Waverly, we're unfortunately in a situation where your business is at stake. You're going to have to do things that are uncomfortable."

I throw my head back and laugh. Gary is the only person who knows exactly what's going on with my money—the maxed credit cards, the dwindling emergency savings account that hasn't seen a new deposit in nearly a year because I keep drawing from it, and scariest of all, the fact that I barely have enough after I pay my business expenses to pay my home equity loan and the personal bills that Larry doesn't cover. He knows I'm already *quite* uncomfortable—sharks-circling-me-in-deep-water uncomfortable. "Gary, I don't need tough love right now."

He nods.

"What's your opinion?" I say. "How long do you think I'll have to stop paying myself?" My salary goes directly to paying down my overdue bills. I can't hold off on those payments.

"I wish I could give you an answer. As long as it takes. Your credit is already stretched. You're really not in a position to even qualify for a loan now should you need one." He shrugs matter-of-factly and stares blankly at me. I often wish he would work on his bedside manner. Accountants should have offices like therapists—a comfortable couch, a handy box of tissues, New Age-y spa music in the background. Gary has a Dilbert calendar on the wall behind his desk. The fluorescent overhead lights hum like a swarm of angry bees. "So let's stop paying your salary. Use that money to pay for your business expenses, to try to pay off some of the credit card debt and other personal expenses, and to make sure that you stay caught up on the home equity loan payments."

"Because it's just that easy? I make sixty thousand dollars a year, Gary. I know it's not nothing, but it's hardly enough to pay for my business *and* my personal stuff. Not with all of my debt."

"I know. But this is the situation we're in now."

His use of *we* is probably meant to make me feel better, but it doesn't—he's hardly a passenger in my sinking ship.

"Gary, you're like the know-it-all older brother I never had."

His shoulders drop. "Waverly, I know this is hard."

"You have no idea."

"We'll just do the best we can."

"Yes, *I* will," I say, emphasizing the *I*.

"Let's see how it goes over the next few weeks and we'll stay in touch."

"Yup," I say, standing. I loiter there for a minute, waiting for…what? I just wish there was something else that Gary could do. He looks up at me expectantly.

"We'll figure this out," he says, and then his phone rings, leaving me no choice but to go deal with my life.

After I leave his office, I race back to the bakery to get ready for the lunch rush. Jeannette is my primary helper in the kitchen today, which is highly unfortunate. She's a dumpling-cheeked singer-songwriter who performs moody love songs in area clubs and has a tattoo of Billie Holiday on her forearm. She's been with me for almost four years now. While she is by far my most conscientious employee—always arrives early, is phenomenally popular among the regular customers—she is slow, slow, slow. When she decorates a cake, the finished product is magazine-cover perfect but it takes her three times as long as it takes Randy, who is my other main cook when he's not fulfilling his managerial duties. I quickly wash my hands and survey the kitchen to see what needs to be done. Jeannette is making chicken salad wraps. I watch out of the corner of my eye, cursing her sluggish precision.

I walk out to the display case in front of the store to make sure that the various salads and quiches are ready to go. I have an emotional hangover from my meeting and I can't concentrate. I flit around, arranging and rearranging platters of cookies and brownies, checking the supply of sodas and bottled water in the drink case, and watching to make sure that Donovan and Bryant, my other two employees, aren't ignoring the handful of customers who've come for late morning coffees or early lunches.

I wish that I could be more like Jeannette, who is even-keeled and mild and content, almost certainly from her daily marijuana consumption, but still. I am more like my mother, who could subsist for days on Alka-Seltzer and Tab when she worried about something.

I remember hearing my parents fight about money. It's not that we were poverty-stricken—we were an ordinary middle-class family occasionally stretched thin by normal life circumstances—but it was obvious to me from an early age that my parents were both carpe diem types who believed that when you came into a little extra money—a bonus check, a tax refund—there was no better way to celebrate it than to spend it. They also neglected to ever really teach me anything about money. I didn't have an allowance, and they never advised me about what I should do with the money I made at my summer jobs waiting tables. I don't blame them, exactly, for leaving me to fend for myself. Actually, that's not true—I *do* blame them a little bit. I wish I'd had the kind of parents who'd sat me down on a Sunday afternoon and taught me how to balance a checkbook, or explained the difference between a stock and a bond.

I'm fortunately not the kind of person who enjoys shopping for sport. I couldn't really care less about having the designer something-or-others that Kate gets worked up about. I know that this mess of mine has nothing to do with splurging. My problem, I'm realizing more and more, is that I'm good at ignoring things like bills that make me uncomfortable and subsequently bad at managing my money, which is a horrible, dangerous combination.

When my parents died, I was not in a position to handle all of the details about their finances. I just wasn't psychologically able to sit in a lawyer's office and talk about my parents' assets as if what was left for me was some sort of sweepstakes prize I should feel good about. Babci stepped in and dealt with the life insurance payout and the will, and after I finished college, we sold the house and used the proceeds to pay off my college loans and to start a little money market account for my savings.

There wasn't exactly a windfall left over, despite what some people thought. Kate and I had one of our few legitimate fights—one that escalated beyond our usual bickering—because of this misconception. It was right after I decided to open the bakery, and we were sitting on the floor in my living room, looking over one of the many spreadsheets that she'd helped me put together to determine my start-up costs. I suddenly got overwhelmed by the size of it all and moaned to Kate that I was starting to second-guess whether it was something I could really do.

"But wait a second," she said, an excited gleam in her eye. "What about the money you got from your parents?"

"What money?" I'd said.

"From their estate…After the accident…" We hadn't really talked about their death since it happened. She was being uncharacteristically careful with her words.

"There isn't anything, really. Just some savings that I'm trying not to completely obliterate by doing this."

"What do you mean there isn't anything?"

"My parents didn't leave me with much," I said. I shuffled the spreadsheets on the floor. I didn't want to talk about this.

"What do you mean they didn't leave you with much?" She was incredulous all of a sudden. Our different stations in life were something we rarely discussed. With someone as rich as Kate, it wasn't necessary to speak about it aloud, but suddenly it seemed like she was doing just that.

"Not all of us are the children of moguls, Kate," I snapped.

"Waverly, come on," she said, pissed off at my comment. "Surely there's something."

"Actually, there's not," I said.

"That doesn't make any sense."

"It's the truth."

"But it doesn't make any sense," she pushed. "Were they totally irresponsible with their money? I mean, I know they didn't make much, but…"

I blew up then: "Kate, what can I say? Some of us have parents who make the Forbes list and some of us have parents who love us."

She didn't say a word. She got up, grabbed her keys, and walked out. Three days later, she was the one to break down and call first. She pretended like nothing had ever happened and I was relieved to follow suit. A couple of years later, after one of her alcohol-fueled birthday dinners, she repeated my line to me, laughing. When I winced, she laughed and told me to get over it—she'd been a thoughtless asshole, too.

I am happy to have grown up in a family where money wasn't the goal, the Shangri-la I was supposed to strive for. Our budget family hiking trips and beach motel vacations are some of my favorite memories. I never thought to wish that we had more, even especially when I got to my fancy high school and saw firsthand how money could affect people. Don't get me wrong—I wouldn't have frowned upon finding a brand-new BMW convertible in the driveway on my sixteenth birthday like several of my classmates did, and it would have been nice to have been able to chime in after Christmas break when everyone compared notes on their Caribbean getaways. But ninety percent of the time, I am happy that my parents didn't teach me to focus on money. Except for now, of course, when not having any is making it the focus of my life.

CHAPTER NINE

When I arrive at Kate's house the next night for dinner, I don't bother to knock. "Helloooo?" I call out as I push open the heavy oak door, my voice echoing in the cavernous foyer. My eyes fall on the portrait of Brendan's great-grandfather in foxhunting garb on the far wall. He stares back at me, a mocking half smile on his face that reminds me of Brendan when he does his "let's make this one good for the camera" pose, which is something Kate pointed out to me a few months ago when we were examining a picture from a campaign rally in the paper. I've always wondered why Kate picked this particular portrait for the entryway when I know that her taste runs more modern. When we lived together, she had a Rothko hanging over her bed. It always scared the shit out of me to have something so priceless in our crappy, no-security two-bedroom.

"Waverly!" Brendan comes around the corner. I'm surprised to see him. It's been at least a month. He is far too pretty to be my type, but he really is *that* good-looking—thick black hair, bright green eyes, a Hollywood smile. He gives me a hug and gently claps my back a couple of times. He smells like tweed and firewood. It's a combination that works.

I follow him down the hallway to the kitchen. Kate's kitchen: such a dream—and such a waste. She has a professional-grade La Cornue stove, impeccable Carrara marble countertops, and a wall-sized refrigerator that I know holds little more than some over-priced yuppie condiments, wine, Pellegrino, and Kate and Brendan's house beverage, Diet Coke. Aside from the occasional grilled cheese sandwich, Kate does not cook. Case in point: the bag of Thai takeout that she's opening as I walk in.

"So what do you two have planned for girls' night?" Brendan says overenthusiastically. He is all politician. Kate looks nauseated by him.

"I don't know," I say. "Probably just shoot the shit, huh, Kate?"

"I'm so fucking tired from this day that I honestly don't care. I'm just ready to relax."

"Kate was in Roanoke today." Brendan smiles. "She gave a *great* speech to a local high school."

I know this already. Kate called me from the plane afterward and whined about how most of her teenaged audience was slumped down in their seats and texting during her talk. The teachers stood lined against the walls, their faces slack and vacant, like losers at a school dance. Kate said that she spoke for exactly eight minutes about the success of public education in Virginia, glancing throughout at the wristwatch she kept on the podium, anticipating the end of the speech with as much impatience as the kids who sat sprawled out before her.

"How would *you* know it was great speech?" Kate barks to Brendan.

Brendan doesn't acknowledge that he's heard her. His eyes don't even move in her direction. "Waverly, did you know that Roanoke County has been named one of the top ten places in the U.S. for jobs by *Money* magazine?"

"No, I didn't—," I start.

"Oh God. Here we go," Kate interrupts. "Brendan, Waverly doesn't need to hear your Virginia factoid of the day. Jesus, is it even possible for you to not speak in sound bites?"

"Wow, someone's in a good mood," I gasp.

Brendan laughs—it's a mocking laugh. There's nothing good-hearted about it.

"You sure you want me here, Kate?" I say.

She rolls her eyes. "I'm fine," she says. "Just a really, *really* long day."

"On that note"—Brendan claps his hands together and flashes me his photogenic smile—"I'm going to head out. You girls have a good time." He gives me another squeeze and before he can circle around the massive island to get to Kate, she puts her hands out and tells him not to wake her when he comes in later.

"You know, I might just stay at the apartment," he says. Kate's parents have an apartment in D.C. that Brendan sometimes uses as a crash pad after strategy meetings.

"Fine, whatever," Kate says.

I wait to say anything until I hear the door slam behind him. "What was that about?"

"What?" She slides a foil container of basil rolls across the counter toward me.

"You weren't very nice to him." I say it teasingly so that I don't piss her off. More.

"Are you kidding me?" she says.

"I'm just saying…"

"You have no idea what you're talking about. Let me tell you about the day I've had."

She starts to go over the details, many of which are the same complaints I already heard on the phone earlier: how the private plane they flew down to Roanoke was late leaving town for no discernible reason, how the disrespectful young staffers who accompanied her spent most of the flight crunching loudly on Doritos and gossiping about other politicians' aides, how the only person who paid attention to the truly boring speech that Brendan's team wrote for her was a creepy fish-eyed history teacher who asked for her autograph…

Kate and Brendan's Chesapeake Bay retriever pads into the

kitchen. "Reagan!" I coo, leaning down to scratch his ears. Brendan had the dog—and obviously named him—before he met Kate. "Hey, boo-boo!"

"Are you listening to me?" Kate says.

"Of course I am."

She raises her eyebrows.

What I really want to say to her is that I am exhausted by her constant complaining and that I came here tonight hoping to forget about my own set of problems, which are actual, *real* problems, and far more *irritating*—a word I'm sick of hearing Kate say—than the torture of having to share a private plane ride with some twentysomethings who don't feel inclined to kiss your ass.

Instead, I say, "It just sounds like you're not having much fun, Kate. Do you even enjoy this whole thing?"

"I don't know—and it's not like that matters anyway. Come on. Let's go into the living room." I grab my container of curry and follow her down the hall.

Kate's house is showroom beautiful, but it's cozy. Like me, she appreciates creature comforts—soft throws tossed casually over the furniture, scented candles, background music. Of course, Kate's stuff isn't a miscellaneous collection of sentimental hand-me-downs, flea market finds, and IKEA purchases like mine. Rather, she spots a one-of-a-kind piece in an antique shop and has it shipped to her house.

I sink into an oversized chair in the living room and kick off my shoes before I cross my feet on the ottoman. The dog noses his head under my arm, looking for more scratches. A fire crackles beneath the oak mantel.

"I need a vacation," Kate says as she digs into her pad thai.

"We just got back from Florida a few days ago!" I laugh.

"You call that a vacation?" She raises her eyebrows at me.

"It was weird, right?" I've been dying to talk to her about Amy and Mike.

"It was completely bizarre. I felt tense the whole time we were there."

"I think you really upset Amy."

"Well, I'm sorry, Waverly, but *somebody* had to say something."

"That might be true, but you could've been more tactful."

"Well…" She shrugs and stabs her fork into her takeout container. "Is yours hot enough? I could put it in the microwave."

"It's fine," I say, swallowing before I launch into my theory. "You know what I think? I think that Mike's having an affair." I outline my reasons, and when I finish she is surprisingly thoughtful.

"I think you could be right," she says. "Honestly, with the way that things have been going with Brendan and me lately, I can completely understand why people stray. Marriage is tough. You're smart not to do it."

Kate's never needled me about not getting married like Amy occasionally does. She's asked me, in her characteristic, straightforward way, whether I'm scared to do it, and I've told her that I am. Still, I don't think she entirely gets how much I crave the certainty that I need to move forward. She doesn't understand that I'd very much like to marry Larry, if only I could convince myself that a forever partnership with him has no chance of fizzling out.

"Lately I find myself fantasizing a lot about my life before Brendan," she says. "This morning on the plane I closed my eyes and pretended like I was headed off on one of my old travel assignments. Belize. Reykjavik. Remember the art history professor I met during that Napa trip? He had this fabulous apartment in the Presidio…"

"Yeah," I lie. When Kate was single, she collected men like baseball cards. I don't remember all of them. "I know that you don't really have the time, but maybe you could take on a freelance assignment? You know, to scratch the itch."

"No, not with the campaign," she says forlornly before tilting her head back to deposit a huge forkful of noodles into her mouth. She chews for a moment and then continues. "It's ironic, isn't it?

This morning, while I was sitting on the plane, I remembered how much I looked forward to changing my name once I got married. No more, 'Oh, are you *that* Townsend?' when I introduced myself to somebody new. No more waiters handing my credit card back to me with an expectant gleam in their eyes."

I wince. *Us poor, lowly food service folk... always begging for tips,* I think.

"I couldn't wait for anonymity, and now, here I am, giving speeches behind podiums bearing my last name. Not to mention that being on the campaign trail is so fucking boring," she continues. "Today, when I was giving that speech, I wasn't even thinking about what I was saying. I've said the same words so many times, to so many different groups of people, that it no longer even occurs to me to stop to consider what the sounds coming out of my mouth even mean. It's like acting. It's... it's..." She grasps for the words. "It's *soulless*. I just fake a smile and emphasize the words I'm supposed to like I'm hitting the right notes in a song: *the education you DESERVE! YOU are our biggest investment!*"

"Does Brendan know how you feel?"

She laughs. "Tonight was the first time in a week that Brendan and I have been together in this house, and he had only been home for maybe ten minutes before you got here and he turned around and left again. It's lucky you got here when you did—he had that baby-making gleam in his eyes. You gave me a good excuse."

I laugh. "So you're really sure, huh? No kids?"

She just stares at me. It was a stupid question.

"Anyway," she says. "He just found out today that he's going to be on *Meet the Press* next Sunday, so I probably won't see him for days."

"Really? That's exciting!" I say. "Isn't it?"

"Yes, totally," she says. "It's wonderful for him to get that kind of national attention. But just like everything else about this campaign, I feel like it's one of those things that we should be celebrating together but aren't. I feel like I don't know him anymore. I wonder how much I even still fit into the plan. Or, more accurately, if the plan is something I even want. So much of my life now resembles what I couldn't wait to get away from when I was younger—the protocols, the public image, the feeling that the rest of the world was free to just *be*. Remember how *I* used to be?"

I nod emphatically. "Oh, yeah."

"Crazy," she says.

"Something like that," I say. It's not like Kate was in danger of ending up in a *Girls Gone Wild* video; she just was so much more free-spirited, so loosened up, with so much joie de vivre. Some days, in the height of her brief but storied travel-reporting career, I didn't even know what country she was in, much less what time zone. And when she came home, she was full of stories. Kate's depth was most evident then, in the way that she talked about the people she met, the cultural traditions she witnessed, the beauty of discovering a place she'd never known or understood. I miss that part of her. It's obvious now that she does, too. I've of course known that the campaign's been wearing on her, but I didn't for a minute suspect that it was making her question her choices so deeply. I know that it's selfish, but I'm kind of relieved to see that I'm not the only one second-guessing my decisions.

"The thing is, I have no one to blame but myself," she says. "When Brendan announced that he was ready to make this move, it was like...I don't know...it was like coming upon the drink of water at the end of a long, long, trip through the desert. I'd been unemployed for a while and it was a relief to finally have something to do. Now every time I come across his picture in the paper, I have to turn the page or stuff the paper in my bag as quickly as I can...so I don't have to see his goddamn smiling face."

"That's not good."

"No."

"So what are you going to do?" I say.

"What do you mean?"

"Well, you're obviously miserable and you're obviously craving something that's your own, something personally fulfilling. What are you going to do about it?"

Kate laughs. "That's the difference between you and me, Waverly. There's nothing I *can* do—I don't have the choices that you have, being on your own. You have nobody to worry about except yourself. Your life is so much simpler. You don't know how lucky you are."

I don't know whether to laugh or to hurl my dish of food at her head. "Yeah, being a struggling small-business owner is one big party. It's *simple*, all right. That's exactly the word I'd use to describe it."

Kate sighs. "I guess what I mean is that the stakes are different. Your bakery is great. Obviously. I'm there almost every day. I know you work hard to make it what it is, but it's not like running for governor."

"I can't believe you just said that."

"What? Isn't it true?"

"It's two totally different things!" I shriek. "It's like comparing being a police officer to being a surgeon. Each has its own set of challenges and pressures—and believe me, my job has plenty of pressure."

"Yeah, but…" She shakes her head.

"But what?"

"It's just different. You know, forget I said anything." She's backpedaling now. She knows I'm pissed off.

"Do you want to know pressure, Kate?" I say.

"Waverly, come on. I didn't mean to make you angry."

"I'm about *this close* to losing my business. How's that for pressure?"

"Oh, come on. You are not." She shakes her head. "Every time I go in there, it's packed."

"You don't know what you're talking about," I say, silently cursing the way that my voice is cracking as I speak. I can feel the tears welling up in my eyes.

"Okay, okay!" she says. I can tell that she's surprised by my reaction. "So tell me, then. What's going on?"

I take a deep breath. I could tell Kate about the overdue bills, the salary freeze, the potential layoffs...But looking at her across the room, in her cashmere loungewear—because Kate's the kind of person who owns pajamas you have to dry-clean—I know that it's pointless. She could never understand what it's like to be me right now, and I don't want her pity.

"It's nothing," I say, pressing my thumbs to my temples and pausing to take a deep breath. "I'll figure it out."

"Are you sure?" she says.

"Yes, I'm positive. I just had a long day. It's been stressful after being gone all weekend."

"I understand what that's like," she says.

I close my eyes, centering myself. I wish that I had the energy to tell her that every time she tries to commiserate with me—to play the "who's more stressed?" game—I want to slap her across the face.

Instead, I clear my throat. "So Amy and Mike," I say, knowing unequivocally that I'm changing the subject so that I can stop thinking about my own problems. "What do you think we should do about that?"

CHAPTER TEN

I am standing at the worktable behind the front counter in the bakery, adding heart-shaped candies to a tray of Valentine's cupcakes, when Amy and Emma walk in. "Well, hey!" I say, putting down my spatula. I haven't seen her in the week that's passed since our trip and I haven't bothered to call. I could say that it's because I've been busy, but I've actually been avoiding her. I haven't decided if or how to confront her about Mike.

Kate said the other night that I should definitely share my suspicions with Amy. Her interest in Amy's life would have surprised me if I believed that her primary concern was Amy's well-being, but I know better. She was more excited by my speculation than worried about its implications. It's not that I think that Kate *wants* Amy and Mike to break up—she's not so mean-spirited that she would wish a divorce on anyone, especially someone with a kid—but I think she'd welcome the opportunity to definitively extricate Mike from all of our lives.

Emma is dawdling, dragging her Dora backpack behind her. "Emma, come on," Amy says. "Let's go say hi to Aunt Waverly."

"Just come from picking her up at school?" I say.

"Yeah, and some errands—dry cleaner, grocery store, post office…my glamorous life." She laughs, smiling. "I've been craving one of those cheddar biscuits," she says, pointing to them in the bakery case. "We can only stay for a minute. I have groceries in the car. Emma, say hello to Aunt Waverly."

Emma smiles coyly up at me and sways shyly from side to side.

"Can she have a cookie?" I mouth. Amy nods yes.

"Look what I have for you, little Emma," I say, reaching into the glass jar on the counter. I wrap a napkin around the cookie and reach over the counter to hand it to her. She grins back up at me. She has her father's big brown eyes.

"Say thank you," Amy says, playfully tousling Emma's hair. "So how's it been since we got back?" she says to me. "Wish we were still in Florida?"

"Yeah, you know." I walk over to the stereo to turn down "Purple Rain." It's the lazy hour between lunch and the coffee-break / after-school crowd. Besides two gray-haired men sharing the paper at a table by the window and a college student hammering away at her laptop, Amy and Emma are my only customers. "It's always good to see that this place won't fall apart without me, even though I like to think I'm indispensable."

I decide not to mention that I discovered that a hundred dollars had disappeared from the cash register while I was gone, and that Randy and I spent most of the week doing detective work before firing the person who did it, a mousy high school senior who was working for free because her dad, one of my regulars, said she was thinking about culinary school and wanted some experience.

"I have something for you!" Amy says, beaming. She opens her giant bag and digs around the coupon book and sippy cup and container of Wet Ones that's threatening to spill onto the floor. "Ah! Here it is," she says. She pulls out a little vial of perfume. "It's orange blossom. I saw it in a little shop that opened up near the house a few days ago." She winks. On the trip down to Florida, I'd noticed a perfume article in Kate's *Vogue* and mentioned that I loved the scent.

"Amy, that's so thoughtful!" I say. *And so typically Amy,* I think. I reach over the counter to give her a hug. "Thank you."

"It's nothing," she says. "I hope you like it. I have to confess, I've spritzed it on myself a few times since I bought it."

"Well, thank you," I say, and put the perfume aside so that I can pick a biscuit out of the case for her. "Do you want me to warm this up?" I hold it up for her to see.

"No, no, it's fine just like that," she says, pulling off Emma's mittens so that she can better manage her cookie. "I don't want to interrupt you," she says, pointing at my tray of half-frosted cupcakes. "We're just going to sit over here and eat our treats. You keep doing what you need to do."

"Amy, you can keep talking to me," I say. "I'm just frosting cupcakes. It's not like it's advanced calculus."

"Yes, but Valentine's Day is in three days. You must have a ton to accomplish before then."

"I wouldn't mind a little more, actually," I say.

"What's that?" Amy says.

"Nothing," I reply. Early this morning, when I was apparently still too sleepy to know better, I made the masochistic decision to spend the first hour of the workday comparing this week's sales to the last five years' during the same time period. Despite the usual orders for chocolate cakes and heart-shaped cookies, my sales aren't close to what they've been in previous Februarys. There hasn't been a single catering order for a Valentine's party (or an anti-Valentine's party, like the one I did three years ago when I was asked to design a cake that featured Cupid shooting himself in the head with his own arrow), and the extra merchandise that I'd ordered for the store—balloons, boxes of chocolates, saucy greeting cards—isn't selling like I hoped. I just pray that the actual holiday will bring in the last-minute rush of boyfriends and husbands that I used to be able to rely on, and probably took for granted.

I watch as Amy leads Emma to one of the mosaic-topped café tables in the center of the room and it reminds me of the Saturday before the bakery opened when Amy and Kate helped me tile and glaze the tops. I'd been such a lunatic in the weeks leading up to the bakery's opening that it was silly to add an unnecessary project to my mountain of to-dos, as Kate—never one to make something that she could just buy—needlessly reminded me throughout the day. But now, each time I notice one of the tables, I think of how the three of us spent the day laughing and daydreaming in this once-empty space. It was one of the rare moments of calm I'd had during that period.

The funny thing is, with the way that things are going these days, I actually feel justified that my anxious alter ego kept second-guessing my decision to open a bakery in the first place. *Is it stupid to give up a regular paycheck?* I'd wondered. Yeah, maybe it was, now that I don't have a paycheck, period. *Did Maple Hill really care about whether or not I could make a good scone?* Maybe not. *Was it too risky to use my home as collateral to fund the start-up of my business?* It's hard to let my brain even go there. I *can't* go there. And I can't believe that it's fucking cupcakes and chicken salad sandwiches that might determine my fate.

I watch Amy tug Emma's coat off. My friends may have their relationship troubles, but I can't help but envy their grown-up lives. It sometimes seems like they are following the instructions in some secret, celestial manual that never found its way into my hands. Amy and Kate have always seemed to know what they need to do next, as if making the decision to get married or leave a job or have a child is as simple as following one of those old dance-step footprint posters. Just the other night, Kate said that she was going to talk to Brendan about taking a few weeks off from the campaign, just to get some rest and reboot before the primary in June, as if it's just that easy to take a break. And then I realized: For her, it is. She can just change course. No repercussions. Or none like mine, anyway.

Amy turns and catches me staring at her.

"So it sucks to come back to this cold weather," I say.

"Ugh, definitely." She rolls her eyes and turns back to Emma.

Usually, when she comes into the bakery, she doesn't bother to sit. We always stand at the counter gabbing away, and we'd normally be deep into her fifth or sixth anecdote by now. I wonder why she's bothered to come in if she doesn't want to talk to me.

"So how did Mike do playing single parent while you were gone?" I say, hoping this might get her going. Amy enjoys talking about Emma over anything else.

"Hmmm?" She looks at me as if she didn't hear me.

She heard me.

Just then, the bell over the door clangs and a crowd of teenaged girls spills in, their giggles and shouts rousing the room from its midafternoon slumber. They all wear the same warm-up suits, bright blue with "Maple Hill Varsity Basketball" printed on the backs of their jackets. I glance at Emma, who's scrambled out of her seat. She is mesmerized, staring at the girls and absentmindedly swinging her right foot around her left leg like a drunken ballerina. She licks cookie crumbs off of one palm.

"Aw, she's so cute," one girl says, noticing Emma and elbowing the dark-haired girl standing next to her.

"Awww! Hi!" the girl says, waving to Emma, who rushes to Amy and buries her face in the crook of her elbow.

I take their orders. Biscuits and cookies, slices of cake and bagels with cream cheese. One girl asks shyly for one of the cupcakes I've just finished frosting. Their voices thread over each other's.

"But what about their point guard?"

"Did you know that he said no when she asked him to the dance, and then said yes to that freshman?"

"I hope Coach Brewer isn't in one of her shitty moods. I really don't want to run suicides today."

"I would die if that happened to me! I mean, di-ie!"

"Do you have a game today?" I ask a gangly redhead as I hand her a Diet Coke. You can tell that she's going to be a knockout by the time she hits her twenties.

"Yeah, we're playing the best team in our division," she says, stuffing her change into a Hello Kitty coin purse.

"Good luck!" I smile. The girls barrel out just as quickly as they entered, waving good-bye to Emma on their way.

"Say bye-bye, Emma," Amy directs, holding Emma's arm up to help her wave.

"Bye-bye!" Emma calls out after them, brave now that they're leaving.

The door closes behind the last girl. Through the window, I watch them shuffle out toward the street, all of their mouths seeming to move at once as they look both ways before jogging across, some of them arm in arm, one tugging on the back of her friend's jacket, another racing ahead.

"Ah, to be young," I say.

"Yeah," Amy says.

I look over at her. She is entirely somewhere else, but whatever memory she's sunk into doesn't look like it's a good one. The corners of her mouth droop and she's hunched into herself like she's trying to keep warm. Emma wanders across the bakery, talking to herself in a singsongy voice.

Enough's enough, I think. I wipe my hands on the rag in my apron—my wooby—and walk around the counter.

"Hey," I say, sitting across from Amy. She doesn't notice that I'm there until I scoot my seat up close to the table.

"Oh, hey," she says. "God, I spaced out for a second." She turns to check on Emma, who's climbing into one of the booths against the far wall. "Honey, be careful," she calls out. Her eyes look glassy, I notice now that we're closer.

"So, do you and Mike have big plans for Valentine's Day?" Amy adores Valentine's Day, what with all of the pink and the flowers and the sugar sweetness. Before Mike came along, she used to give Kate and me big heart-shaped boxes of chocolate each year. She decorated the door of her apartment building like she still lived in a dorm.

"Valentine's Day. Hmmm," she says, as if she's just considering it for the first time, which I know she can't possibly be. "Yeah, I'm sure we'll do something. I haven't really thought about it, to be honest. I guess with being away and all, it just slipped past me." She twists around in her seat to check on Emma. Again.

I know that she's lying to me. Nothing "slips past" Amy. She is a color-coded-calendar kind of a girl.

"Ame, what's going on?"

"Huh?" She turns back to me, acting, once again, like she hasn't heard me.

"Are you okay?"

"I'm fine," she says, smiling wide, her cheeks blooming pink as she shakes her head at me. "I'm just tired. I tossed and turned all night for some reason." She pushes her hair behind her ears and scratches her nose.

I watch her for a moment and I think of Kate, who told me, in her delicate way, to "stop being such a pussy and just ask her already." I clear my throat. "Listen," I say, my hand escaping into my apron to fiddle with the fraying edge of my rag. "I don't want to be nosy," I say, "but you don't seem like yourself lately."

Amy doesn't say anything. She looks at the table where my other hand rests; my mother's opal ring on my left middle finger, the orange sports watch that I've had since college. I notice that she's nibbled just the tiniest corner off of her biscuit. "Want something else?" I point at it.

"Oh, no," she says. "I guess I wasn't as hungry as I thought. I'll save it for later." She looks back down at the tile tabletop, tracing her finger around a red triangle of broken pottery. "Mike and I have been fighting a lot lately," she says quietly. Her eyes stay frozen on the table.

"Do you want to talk about it?" I reach across the table and squeeze her hand. "Amy, you kind of look like you're carrying the weight of the world on your shoulders."

"It's just—" She bites her lip. She looks over at Emma and I follow her gaze. Emma is lying on her back on one side of a booth, making shapes with her hands at the ceiling. "We got in a horrible fight last night and I didn't sleep at all."

"Do you want to tell me what it was about?" I tread carefully.

"Ugh." She shakes her head.

"Ame, come on. You know you can talk to me about anything."

"I know," Amy says. "I know." With the way that she says it, it's hard to tell whether she's trying to reassure me or convince herself. "It was just a silly fight. I don't know why I'm letting it get to me. I was telling him how I'd missed him while we were gone, and that turned into me telling him that I wished we spent more time together. We never really do anything datey anymore, not since Emma." She looks over at her daughter again and I wonder if she keeps checking on her just to avoid looking at me.

"Does Mike agree with you?"

"Agree with me about what?" She looks confused.

"Does he agree that you could use some more time together?"

"Um." She takes a deep breath. "He just…he doesn't want to talk about it. A typical guy, you know?" She forces a laugh. When I don't return it, her smile straightens and she keeps talking. "He feels overwhelmed with work, he was exhausted from being alone with Emma all weekend, and then I came in complaining. It got overblown." Her eyes flit around the room, dancing everywhere but in my direction.

"Yeah, but Amy, if you're upset, you're upset. You shouldn't make excuses for him."

"I know, you're right," Amy says, nodding a little too emphatically, like she's trying to convince herself.

Neither of us says anything for a minute. I'm not convinced she agrees with me.

"Listen, I don't mean to snoop," I start. "And I hope this doesn't offend you." I swallow, pausing. "But Mike does seem different lately."

Amy nods again. "I understand what you're saying. He's been a little stressed-out...work, you know. With everything that's happening with health care, being a family doctor isn't exactly a Norman Rockwell scenario."

It's not that I don't believe her, but if she's trying to tell me that work stress gives you license to act the way that Mike does, than I should be a tantrum-throwing, hotel-room-wrecking Hollywood nightmare by now.

"Are *you* handling everything okay, though?" I ask.

"Of course. We're fine."

My ears perk up. I can't help but notice that even though I asked about how *she's* doing, she's answered by telling me how *they're* doing. I suppose it's the kind of slip that any coupled person could make—and after all, we are talking about her relationship—but it's ironic, and it reignites my suspicions that she's not being honest with me.

"It's just a rough patch. Things get busy with work and kids and everything," she says again, glancing over at Emma. "Honey, come over here, please," she calls to her.

"Well, if more time together is what you want, then what do you think is preventing it, exactly? I mean...is Mike gone a lot? Does he ever work late?" I say. I'm quickly discovering that there isn't a subtle way to ask, "Do you think your husband is cheating on you?"

"What do you mean?" Amy says. She looks at me quizzically.

"I don't know..." I grasp for words. "I really...I don't know." Is it the right time to bring up any of this in the first place? At any moment, I might have to jump up to answer the phone or help a customer. Emma's just a few feet away... "I just hate to see you looking so miserable."

Amy gasps. "Have I really seemed that miserable?"

"Well..." I shrug. "I'm sorry, but yeah, I've been a little worried."

"Waverly, really?" Amy teases and cocks her head to the side, as if I'm putting her on. "Come on. I'm fine."

I suck in my lips and raise my eyebrows at her.

She shakes her head and starts sweeping crumbs off of the table into one cupped hand, then dumps the contents into her napkin and folds it up. "Everything's okay," she says. "It's just a rough patch. Nothing for you to be concerned about." She stands up. "Emma, come on, honey, we have to go."

She turns to me. "I'm sorry, groceries in the car. I totally forgot."

"Yeah, of course. Call me later." I feel instantly guilty, like I've crossed a line that I shouldn't have.

"I will," she says, but it's a breezy kind of promise, even a little passive-aggressive.

I watch them leave, Amy helping Emma with her coat as they walk because she's apparently in such a hurry that she can't stop to do it. Kate and I bicker plenty—like an old married couple, Larry says—but I've never had any sort of confrontation with Amy. This tiniest, most benign little scuffle feels awful and foreboding, like some current between us has changed.

My father always warned me not to give people advice unless they ask for it, and I worry whether I've gone too far, even though I barely criticized Mike. It's alarming to see Amy tense. I've seen her upset before, of course, lots of times. But there is never anything covert about her feelings—happy or sad, you see it in the genuine, transparent way that you see in a child. And when she talks about a problem she's having, it's always in this buoyant way, as if she already knows the solution and is just giving it a voice for her own sake, not because she needs your help. Now, seeing how obviously reluctant she is to admit that something is wrong, it's jarring.

Strange, I think, pushing up from the table and walking back to my cupcakes, how you can't really talk openly to your friends about their relationships once they get married. I remember that when Amy and Mike started dating, every little detail was fair game. I can tell you everything about how they met: She and Kate and I were at an Independence Day party on the roof deck of a law firm on K Street. I was standing with Amy at the buffet table, each of us shoving pigs-in-a-blanket into our mouths, when she turned, accidentally bumped into Mike, and spilled her plastic cup of white wine down the front of his golf shirt. Humiliated, she rushed to fix it, patting him down with the crumpled cocktail napkin in her hand. He laughed, got her another drink, and then another, and then several hours later, having talked about everything from their childhood pets to their favorite college courses, they stood together, hand in hand, and watched the fireworks erupt over the Washington Monument.

As they got to know each other in the ensuing months, we discussed everything about him, from his reluctance to say much about his family to his reluctance to go down on her. I know that he put on a whole candles-and-roses production to prepare for the first time they had sex. I know that Amy saved the stubs from their first movie date.

But as soon as they got married, those conversations stopped. Same thing with Kate. When I first met Brendan, I thought he was a nice-enough guy but ultimately the same kind of cocky, self-important pain in the ass that we'd grown up around. She says as much, but I would never, *ever* think to chime in. You just don't do that. I'd be just as pissed if they criticized Larry.

The thing is, though, now that those dishy girl-talk conversations have come to an end, I've also stopped learning anything worthwhile about my friends' spouses. If Amy and I have grown to know each other so well over the years that she's like a favorite worn photograph, admired so often that I can re-create every last detail from memory, Mike is a faint pencil drawing, one-dimensional and thinly known to me. I don't like it, how such a big part of her life is such a mystery. And somehow, in some way, the silence that's growing between us feels like the loudest alarm.

CHAPTER ELEVEN

I can hear the music before I even get out of the car. *Shit.* After ten years together, I know that when Larry blares music at night it almost always means that he is feeling celebratory. I am not in the mood for celebratory. I am in the mood for my sweatpants, a massive bowl of the chipotle macaroni and cheese that I swiped from work, and an extra-large glass of something with a very high alcohol content. I don't want to hear about Larry's fantastic day; I don't want him to grab me and twirl me around the kitchen in the way that he's apt to do when he's feeling especially euphoric. I don't even want to speak. I huff up the steps and fumble with my bags— my purse, the mac and cheese—to get the key in the door, then turn the knob and kick the door open with my foot.

I drop my purse on the kitchen floor. "Hoochie Coochie Man" is blasting throughout the house. *Good God.* Muddy Waters. Not this. Not tonight.

It is not fair for me to be this way. Not tonight. Not on Valentine's Day. While Larry is not exactly a Valentine's guy (is *any* man a Valentine's guy?), he has historically been supremely understanding about it being one of the busiest days of the year in my business. He is accepting of the fact that I will always work late on February 14 and is probably secretly relieved that the very last thing that I want to see when I get home at the end of this particular day is anything indicative of romance. In fact, the very best thing he can do, which is precisely what he's done the past several years, is to act like it's any other day. Last year when I got off work, we drank a couple of beers and watched old *Cosby Show* reruns. It was perfect.

But I'm not even in the mood for that. Even though we were slammed all day with people elbowing their way into the bakery for last-minute Valentine's sweets, and even though my guess is that we did better than last year, the unrelenting albatross around my neck is that I know it's just a drop in the bucket. I need 365 days of Valentine's shoppers to pay off my debts.

"Larry!" I scream, walking to the living room. Muddy's voice booms off of the walls. "*Larry!*"

I scream his name as I stomp up the stairs, pulling off my jacket and letting it fall behind me as I ascend.

When I push open the door to our bedroom, he's lying on the bed, his arms crossed over his face. "Larry?"

"Hey." He pulls his arms from his face and props himself up on his forearms. He does not look celebratory. Not even a little bit.

"The music's loud," I say. "What are you doing?"

He purses his lips for a moment before he looks at me. I gulp. *Did he find one of the overdue bills?*

He clears his throat. "Something bad happened at work."

The words don't register at first. "What do you mean?" I sit down next to him. Bad things don't happen at Larry's job.

"Well," he says. "They're cutting people from our department."

"What?" *No!* "Cutting people?" I put my hand to my chest.

His eyes meet mine for a moment and then he looks away. "It's bad."

Larry Tackett is, above almost everything, a patriot. My boyfriend is the kind of person who gets teary the moment he hears the opening bars to "The Star Spangled Banner." When we watch the annual State of the Union address and the guy announces the president with the customary "Ladies and gentlemen, the president of the United States!" Larry stands in the living room, beer in hand, and bellows joyfully right along with him, whether or not our current commander in chief got his vote. Last summer, when we went to a Nationals baseball game, I thought he was going to throttle the three guys in front of us who not only talked loudly about their predictions for the game during the national anthem but also neglected to take off their caps while the ten-year-old music prodigy from Anacostia sang.

He moved to D.C. specifically to work at the National Museum of American History. When he was eleven, his family had taken a rare family vacation to D.C., and Larry says he'll never forget the awe he felt when they toured the museum and he saw the top hat that Abraham Lincoln wore to Ford's Theatre, or the desk microphone that FDR used to give his famous "fireside chats" during the Depression and World War Two. After grad school, he got an internship at the museum, which led to his current job as a curator. Ninety-nine percent of the holdings he takes care of aren't even on display. He seeks out new items to add to his department's collection, works with other curators to create exhibitions, and generally gets to dork out on a daily basis over things that he realizes many people couldn't care less about. When we first met, he told me about how he was the kind of kid who collected odds and ends that he kept in a shoebox under his bed—an old piece of rock that he found in the woods that he was convinced was an ancient arrowhead, random plastic toys that held special significance, an oddly shaped screw found in the back of his parents' hardware store. "My job is like the big-kid version of that," I remember him telling me. "It's the greatest job in the world."

I look at him now, with his eyes closed and his lips pursed in an anxious way I've never witnessed before. "What happened?" I say, as sweetly as I can, given the volume of the music—and the way I feel my blood pressure ratcheting up with every passing second.

"The head curator pulled us together for a meeting and said that he heard from one of his higher-ups that furloughs are probably going to happen in the near future." Curators at the Smithsonian are federal employees, and furloughs—involuntary, unpaid leaves—have been a possibility for a while given the horrendous state of the federal budget.

"Fuck." *Fuck.*

"What's worse is that because of budget cuts, we might have to reduce the department altogether, which means I could be out of a job."

"But you've been with them forever!" I shriek. "They wouldn't cut you. Aren't there other people who'd be more likely? People who are more junior?" I don't want to freak out, but if Larry can't pay his half of our bills... *Fuck.*

"I wish that were the case. But with layoffs, they typically cut people who have higher salaries because they can be replaced with cheaper employees. I don't know..." He scratches his chin and starts to gnaw at his cuticles. Larry is never nervous. It's unsettling to see him like this. "I haven't published any papers in a while." He says it so quietly that it's as if he's talking to himself. "Though I did just bring in those paper ballots from Grover Cleveland's election."

"I can't imagine that you would be one of the people they cut." My mind is reeling now. Way back when we first moved in together, we decided that since Larry wouldn't have to pay rent, he'd pay most of our homeowner's insurance and utilities. Then, when I opened Maggie's, he started to chip in even more. He even helps me pay my exorbitant self-employed health insurance plan. He shares the cost of groceries, gas... there are our cell phone bills, auto insurance. My heart starts to pound, thinking about all of the ways his income keeps us afloat. "They can't cut you, Larry. They just can't." My voice quivers. "If they furloughed you, how long would you go unpaid?"

"As of now, they're talking about two weeks, which isn't much, I know, but I'm worried about the bigger picture. You start with two-week furloughs and then what happens? I mean, if federal employees' jobs need to be cut, I have to believe that a curator at the Smithsonian is going to be far more disposable than someone working in Homeland Security, Health and Human Services…anywhere, really."

"What about another job somewhere? Do you think you should look around, just to be safe?" I'm the one chewing my nails now.

"I have a friend in the history department at Maryland that I could call, I guess, but my options are limited with just a master's. I don't really want to go back to school for a Ph.D." I can tell that the idea depresses him. He has his dream job.

"When will you know whether they're cutting people in your department?"

"Next few weeks, I think."

He looks up at the ceiling. I pull my knees to my chest and wrap my arms around my legs.

"Thank God for the bakery," he says. "If anything happens, at least we'll have that to keep us going until I find something else. I know it's not ideal, but at least it's something."

I clench my jaw and let my head fall to my knees. I squeeze my arms tighter around my legs, curling myself into a ball, wishing I could disappear.

"It's going to be okay," I say into my knees, not believing a word of it.

He doesn't say anything, and I realize that for the first time in all of our years together, I am the one doing the reassuring instead of the other way around. Larry is actually worried, and there's nothing scarier than that.

CHAPTER TWELVE

Y ou're here, thank God," Kate says, giving me a quick hug hello. She's wearing a trim black suit with a silver ribbon pinned to the lapel.

"What's the ribbon for?" I point at it.

"What? Oh," Kate says, looking down at her lapel. "You know, I don't have any idea. Someone from the campaign put it on me this morning. Listen, I really appreciate you coming to this."

"Of course," I say. "I've never been to a campaign luncheon before. This is exciting for me."

Kate laughs. "Yeah, I'm sure it will be just as memorable as when Larry got you tickets to see that singer-songwriter you love." She snaps her fingers, trying to think of his name. "You know, the one who looks like an organic farmer."

"Ray LaMontagne." Larry had taken me to his show for my birthday the year before.

"Right, him. It'll be *just* like that," she jokes. "Seriously, though, thanks for coming."

"Yeah, yeah. Stop thanking me," I say. I look around the crowded room, searching the overwhelmingly white male crowd for one particular female face. "Is Amy here yet?"

"Haven't seen her," Kate says, studying her BlackBerry.

"Hmph, that's weird. She's never late for anything." I haven't talked to her since her visit to the bakery. Worse, she hasn't returned the messages I've left on her home and cell phones. It's been almost a week.

"Huh?" Kate says, her thumbs furiously typing out a text message.

"Nothing," I say.

The ballroom of the local Hilton looks like every other hotel ballroom I've ever been in—for wedding receptions, the junior and senior proms, and the local restaurant association meeting that I drag myself to each year, wondering the whole way through how it is that a *restaurant* association finds it reasonable to stage their annual meeting in anything other than a restaurant. Everything from the carpet to the damask wallpaper is a drab peachy-beige that reminds me of silly putty.

I could be at one of the bland teacher's conferences I used to go to if not for one conspicuous difference: the throng of Berkshire fans crowding into the room and twisting around each other to get to their seats. They move swiftly and deliberately, like mice in a maze, and their excitement is so palpable that you would think that the small wooden podium decorated with campaign bunting at the end of the room is the elaborate set for a U2 concert. Behind it, a banner tacked to the wall reads, "BERKSHIRE: What's right for Virginia."

"I just need to go...," Kate starts while walking away, her eyes still locked on her BlackBerry.

"Yeah, yeah, go do your thing." I look down at the number on my ticket, squeeze past some suits to get to my table, and sit down. I scan the crowd again for Amy, noticing that most of the women are wearing pantyhose. *Women still actually wear pantyhose?* I fiddle with the sleeve of my black button-down from the Gap, the go-to in the back of my closet for the rare occasion when I need something more formal than my usual T-shirt and jeans, and say a silent prayer of thanks for the long tablecloth that conceals the clogs that I'm wearing because I forgot to bring something dressier when I packed my stuff for work at four thirty this morning.

I don't recognize a soul, which is strange considering that I've lived in Maple Hill my entire life and a decent chunk of the town's population passes through the bakery each week. I crane my neck to get a better look at the tables at the front of the room. Surely Evelyn is here. Kate likes to joke that her mother would attend the opening of an envelope. But there is no sign of her at the large round table placed in front of the podium—just a couple of older men who look like money and a woman with a stiff bob in that particular shade of not-quite-blond and not-quite-gray that so many older women prefer.

News crews from all three of the D.C. affiliates are setting up their cameras to the right of the stage along with the cable channels. I watch as the cameramen joke with a couple of the photographers, who are easy to pinpoint in their jeans and wrinkled button-downs. I think of Dad, my favorite photographer, who wore the same uniform. He was the only father in the neighborhood who didn't go to work in a tie and who carried a bag bigger than any of the moms did because he lugged his equipment *everywhere*. A lifelong political junkie, he loved covering Washington, and his job at UPI meant that his photos were regularly published in many of the major newspapers and newsweeklies. He should be here right now. He would've gotten such a kick out of photographing Kate in this environment. I check my watch. *Where is Amy?*

It still isn't entirely clear why Kate has asked us to come. The Virginia Medical Society is responsible for putting this thing together, according to the invitation, and most of the attendees are members who've donated to the campaign. I wonder why Kate didn't invite Mike along with Amy; as a doctor, he must certainly be a member of the state medical society. Now that she's not here, I'm wondering whether the slight pissed her off. In any case, it's

Brendan's first major event in Maple Hill, and I'm actually excited about getting to finally see him in action.

Three paunchy, middle-aged men in nearly identical gray suits appear across the table from me and pull out their chairs, followed shortly thereafter by a woman who immediately reminds me of the piano teacher I had growing up because she's wearing those glasses that look like they're fitted with magnifying lenses. As they sit, they introduce themselves as members of the local Rotary club. "Have you seen him speak before?" the woman asks, her eyes dancing like she's a thirteen-year-old talking about Justin Bieber.

"Um, no. Well, not officially," I say, recalling all the times that Brendan has stepped up on his proverbial soapbox in my kitchen after a few bourbons. Those nights usually end with Kate dragging him out of the house by his ear. "I'm a friend of the Berkshires'," I say to the woman and reach for the goblet of ice water above my place setting. "Kate and I grew up together."

As if on cue, one of the men elbows the guy next to him. He leans toward me, cupping his hand to his mouth like a bad comedian, and says in a stage whisper, "I was just saying to these two that Berkshire has had my vote since he announced his candidacy—the real reason that I wrote a check to be here was to get a good look at the wife!"

The three burst into jolly laughter and the woman shrugs, a resigned "boys will be boys" grin on her face.

I muster a polite nod and check my watch again. Five past twelve. Brendan is running late. Kate had warned me that I'd better settle in if he got up to the podium and said that he hadn't prepared any remarks and was going to talk "off the cuff." "It may as well be code for 'longwinded jerk-off about how fucking fantastic I am,'" she'd said on the phone the night before. I pull my seat out and half stand to get a better look at the entrance. Amy is never, ever late for anything. Something is definitely up.

Suddenly, the lights dim and a very tall, lanky woman approaches the podium, asking everyone to please take their seats. She has a draggy voice, the kind that sounds perpetually congested. It must be Stephanie, Brendan's assistant, whom Kate is always bitching about.

My phone buzzes and I jump for it. But when I pull my phone out of my pocket and look at the caller ID, I'm dismayed to see that it's not Amy, but a restricted number, which I know means only one thing: It's my bank. I consider whether to answer, the phone buzzing in my hand like an insect, my thumb poised over the buttons. The adult thing to do would be to answer the call—own up and deal with it. I send it straight to voicemail.

The sound system clicks on and the room fills with microphone feedback, making the crowd groan. Then, after a beat, Brendan's campaign theme song starts—Sting's "Brand New Day." I remember Kate complaining about it back when his team chose it. I'd agreed with her then that they couldn't have picked a whiter song.

A spotlight appears on a set of double doors to the left of the stage and Brendan strolls out, dapper in one of his custom-made suits. Were it not for the campaign paraphernalia, anyone passing by the ballroom could have easily mistaken his entrance for some local department store fashion show, or one of those cheesy win-a-bachelor charity auctions. *And now we have the modern-day WASP,* I imagine the emcee would say. *He's got it all—an Ivy League diploma, a family line stretching all the way back to Jamestown, and a worldview that can't see beyond the borders of his mirror!*

The crowd jumps to their feet. As they applaud wildly, Brendan waves with both hands above his head, a wide, almost cartoonish, smile on his face. I stand and clap along while I take in the pandemonium around me. Brendan is taking his time, shaking the hands of the well-wishers at the front tables. *He really was born for this,* I think, watching the ease with which he works the crowd, speaking a sentence or two to each person he passes and laughing heartily at whatever comes out of their mouths.

Once he reaches the podium, he lets the cheers ride out for several more seconds. Then he raises his palms to quiet the applause, shaking his head with a sheepish, "aw, shucks, you're too kind" smirk on his face. Everyone obediently takes their seats. I check my watch again and turn to the door. If she isn't here by now, Amy definitely isn't showing up. Maybe Emma's sick? I glance toward the corner of the room where Brendan's staff is gathered. Kate stands next to the woman who is presumably Stephanie with her arms crossed high on her chest. She has a placid grin on her face. I recognize it as her "I know you're watching me but I'm pretending not to notice" look.

Brendan starts to speak. He is typically more cocky than confident, even a little standoffish, but here he looks as comfortable as a concert pianist at a baby grand. His eyes glint against the flash of the cameras, an expression that he perfected over the past six months, I know, because Kate told me that his staffers had gently approached him about the "issue" (not "problem") and "handled" (not "fixed") it with training sessions and a highly paid specialist. As he speaks, I watch his hands: He points into the crowd ("*You* have the power to change Virginia!"), he raises his palms toward the sky ("Together, we will *lift up* the commonwealth!"), and he clenches his fists ("I *believe* in the people of Virginia!"). After twenty minutes—just enough time for a plate of chicken breast and boiled vegetables—he winds down, thanking the crowd for their support. Then he points to the end of the room where Kate is standing: "And to my wonderful, loving, and supportive wife, Kate," he says. I hear a few *awwws* from the women in the audience. "Thank you for taking this journey with me." Kate presses her hands together in a prayer at her chest and finally smiles, tilting her head coquettishly. I have to bite my lip to keep from laughing out loud. It must've been something to be in the meeting with the staffer who told her that *that* was the choreography she'd need to perfect.

After Brendan leaves the podium, the crowd starts to disperse, many of them clutching the "Berkshire for Governor" bumper stickers that were piled next to the bread basket in the center of each table. I make my way to the back of the room, hoping to check in with Kate and say hello to Brendan before I leave, but the news crews have already cornered them.

Once outside, I check my phone. No call from Amy. I dial her cell and it goes straight to voicemail. "Hey! This is Amy!" the recording chirps. "Leave a message and have a great day!"

"Hi, it's Waverly," I say after the beep. "I just left the luncheon. Did you forget? Hope everything's okay over there. Call me."

I dial the home phone. Voicemail again.

"Amy, it's Waverly. Just wondering where you were today. Hope Emma didn't get sick or something. Anyway, call me."

I punch the presets on the car stereo as I drive back to work—some earnest poet on NPR talking about his muse, Fugazi on the college station, Jim Croce singing "Operator" on the soft-rock station that I listen to more often that I will ever admit, always sucked in by an old Hall & Oates or Lionel Richie song.

I can't distract myself. Amy is nothing if not a well-mannered southerner. Her signature joke that she used to always tell at happy hours was "Why don't southern girls have orgies? Too many thank-you notes."

I brake at a red light and glance at the car in the turn lane next to me. The woman behind the wheel yawns wide and rubs her eyes. Dry cleaning hangs in her backseat. She mutters something as she looks at herself in her rearview mirror.

An unnecessarily rowdy car-dealership commercial comes on the radio and I finally just punch it off. I scratch at the spongy tube of the steering wheel with my fingernails. Before I can talk myself out of it, I turn on my right blinker and wave to the driver next to me, pointing to ask if I can sneak into her lane. When the light changes, I merge and mouth "thank you," then turn onto the street that will take me to Amy's house.

CHAPTER THIRTEEN

The drive takes me past a blurred series of manicured shrubs and brick fences flanking the entrances of big-builder subdivisions. I recite the name of each development as I pass—Trotter's Ridge, Woodward Stables—and remember what the land looked like back when this part of town was actually a bunch of horse farms. Oak Hill, Amy's neighborhood, is a cookie-cutter subdivision, with houses squeezed close together and, despite its name, hardly a hill or tree to speak of. Her house on Green Leaf Court is identical to two of the homes across the street, though hers is painted a sunny yellow, with purple and pink pansies lining the front walk. I ring the doorbell, remembering the Valentine's Day–themed wreath on the door from the year before. I used to think that Amy's penchant for holiday wreaths was ridiculous—the word Kate once used was *geriatric*—but ever since I became a bakery owner and found that I could bump up sales by getting creative with green food coloring around St. Patrick's Day, or by sticking tiny American flags in everything that comes out of the oven during the week leading up to the Fourth of July, I've come to appreciate it. I shuffle on the concrete stoop and then peer into one of the long windows that frame the door, cupping my hands around my eyes to get a better look inside.

Amy finally appears around the corner, dressed in yoga pants and a UNC sweatshirt. Her hair is piled sloppily on top of her head with a giant clip. Is she *limping*? She waves and smiles weakly as she reaches to unlock the door. "Hey." She runs a hand across her forehead, smoothing her hair back. She looks like she's just woken up from a nap. I can hear the squeaky sounds of Emma's cartoons on the television in the background.

"Hey, did I wake you? I'm sorry for just popping by. Are you...sick or something?"

"No, no, it's fine," she says, opening the door wider. She smiles again, but it's the kind of mandatory smile that you give to your coworkers on a Monday morning. I instantly regret showing up unannounced. Amy scratches at the back of her head. "Come in, come in." She waves with her hand. "Sorry, the house is a mess."

"Are you sure?" I say. "You look a little..."

"I know, I look like crap. I'll explain everything. Come on, come in," she insists. "I left Emma in the kitchen and I have a pot boiling on the stove."

I step inside. "It smells good in here. What are you cooking? Marinara?"

"Prego," Amy says. She laughs—a forced laugh that ends as quickly as it began. "Will you forgive me? And give me your marinara recipe for next time? I'm making baked ziti for dinner." She leads me into the living room and I notice, walking behind her, that she is stepping as tentatively as if on hot asphalt. The house is a wreck, with Candy Land pieces, Legos, and crayons strewn across the living room floor. A pile of laundry is half-folded on the couch. This is bizarre. Amy's house is normally spotless, even *too* clean in that scent-of-Windex-in-the-air kind of way.

"Ame, what happened?" I say, scrutinizing her walk. "Are you limping?"

"Ugh, I'm *such* a klutz." Amy laughs again, not looking back as she walks ahead into the kitchen. "You won't believe it. I was carrying a load of laundry downstairs this morning and I tripped. I fell halfway down the stairs and landed on my hip."

"Oh my God. Are you okay?"

"Yeah, yeah, I'm fine," she says, walking to the stove. "I'll probably have a big ugly bruise, but no biggie."

"Is that why you didn't come to the luncheon?" I look around the kitchen. Shit's everywhere.

"The luncheon!" Amy smacks her forehead with her hand. "Oh my goodness, I totally forgot!" She shakes her head. "I've been such an airhead lately. I can't believe I did that."

I study her face. She keeps talking.

"I've just been so caught up with everything around here, and then after I fell this morning…Shoot, I'll have to call Kate."

Emma appears from around the corner, carrying an armful of wooden puzzle pieces.

"Emma, say hello to Aunt Waverly."

"Hiiii, Emma," I tease.

She curls her little fingers into a bashful, tiny wave and then runs into the living room, giggling.

"Sit down. Do you want something to drink?" Amy says, gesturing toward the kitchen table. "Or something to eat? Did you have anything at the luncheon?"

"No, I'm fine. I ate."

"What did they have? Was it good?"

"Nothing special. Chicken."

"How about a soda at least? Or some water? I even have seltzer— would that be better?"

She's babbling. More than normal.

"Okay, I'll have a glass of water," I say, pulling out one of the stools beside the kitchen counter. I wipe away a few crumbs before sitting down—that morning's toast, or maybe Emma's lunchtime PB and J. "Amy, why don't you sit with me? That limp looks bad."

"I'm fine, Waverly, really." She shakes her head, filling a glass of water from the spigot on the outside of the refrigerator and then handing it to me.

She walks to the stove and dips a fork into the pot of pasta, fishing out a piece of ziti and blowing on it before she takes a bite to see if it's done. "I just can't believe that I forgot the luncheon."

"Yeah, it's not like you," I say, trying to get a reaction.

"So how was Brendan's speech?" she says, apparently deciding to ignore me. "Did Kate talk, too?"

I recount the major details—how Brendan looked onstage, the crowds of people and the news crews, Kate's gesture of wifely support at the end—but I want to be talking about her and Mike, and it's nagging at me like a ringing in my ears. It is disconcerting to see Amy so disheveled at two o'clock in the afternoon, and her limp looks bad, way worse than she is making it out to be. She shuffles around the kitchen with her hand on her hip, and I can tell by the way that her shoulders rise and fall that she's stopping to take deep breaths whenever she turns away from me.

"I'm sorry I missed it," she says. "Was Kate upset? I hope she's not mad." She goes to lift the pot of pasta off of the stove, winces, and then sets it back down.

I jump up from my stool. "Ame, let me get that for you."

"Waverly, no, it's fine," she says, lifting it again.

I put my hands over Amy's. "Come on, put it down, I'll get it."

"I'm fine!" Amy snaps.

I let go and step back. Amy laughs, trying to cover for herself.

"I'm fine, really." Her voice softens. "You're worse than my mother would be. Now, go sit down."

I take another step back, watching as Amy lifts the pot and dumps the ziti into a colander in the sink. *What the hell is going on?* "Did you tell Mike that you fell?"

Amy makes a face, her mouth an awkward squiggle. "No, should

I have?" she says. "Waverly, why are you so worried about this? I'm not that badly hurt. You're acting weird." She turns back toward the stove.

I'm the one acting strange?

All of a sudden, there's a crash in the living room. "Mommy!" Emma yells, her voice warbling.

"I'm coming," Amy says, dropping her dish towel and shuffling as fast as she can past me into the living room. I follow.

"What is it, honey?" Amy kneels down to where Emma's standing in the center of the room, bawling. Legos and blocks are strewn around her.

"I was making a castle and the whole thing fell down!" she wails.

"Oh, honey, it's okay," Amy says. "You can make another one."

She reaches to put her arms around Emma to console her, and that's when I see it: On Amy's lower back, between the waistband of her pants and where her sweatshirt has inched up, is a long purplish black mark crossing over the bumps of her spine. It looks like a stain on her skin, like grape juice through newsprint. Dried blood is crusted along one edge.

"My God, Amy, what is that?" I say.

"What?" Amy says, whipping around.

"On your back!" I step toward her and reach to pull up her sweatshirt.

She stands before I can and straightens her top.

"It's just from where I fell," she says brusquely. "I know it looks awful. I couldn't believe it when I saw it this morning." She turns back toward Emma. "Honey, are you okay?"

"Amy, are *you* okay?" I reach out and put my hand on her shoulder. "You really did that just carrying laundry down the stairs?"

"Yeah, I know! It looks bad, doesn't it?" she says. She begins picking up toys and piling them into a red plastic bin. *Why is she acting like this? Avoiding me in her own home?*

"Ame?" I try again. I glance at Emma, who is now happily stacking alphabet blocks on the coffee table.

"Yeah?" Amy says, still picking up the toys.

"Are you *sure* you're okay?" I don't know what else to say, but that mark...the way she's acting...

"Waverly, what is *with* you?" she says, not looking up at me. "I'm fine. I just fell down the stairs. If something was broken, I wouldn't be able to move." She tosses a handful of crayons into the bin. "When Mike gets home, I'll have him take a look at it."

I watch her. Something isn't right about this. There is no way that a fall down the stairs caused that thing on her back. I am sure of it. "But how did it cut your skin?"

Amy sighs, her back still toward me, and shakes her head. "I don't know. The cheap carpets we had put in, maybe?" She places the plastic bin in a corner of the room and starts collecting Cheerios off the floor.

I nod and watch her tidy up. The bitter tone of voice isn't like her, the flaking on the luncheon isn't like her either, and normally, when you're a guest in Amy's house, you have her undivided attention. Even if you just swing by for a minute, she forces you to sit down and plies you with snacks, and she *never* makes you feel in the way, not like she is doing now.

She keeps cleaning, limping around the living room. I would try to help, but it is obvious that Amy doesn't want me pitching in, or doing anything, really.

"So, I'm, um, going to go," I say after a few awkward minutes. I wait a beat for her to beg me to stay, the way that she usually would.

"Okay." She turns toward me. "Thanks for stopping by."

I nod. When our eyes meet, Amy looks away. I start toward the front hall and Amy follows behind.

"If you talk to Kate, tell her sorry about the luncheon," Amy says as she opens the door. "And I'll send her an email later."

"Okay." I play with my keys as I stall for a moment and squint at Amy. One last look.

"Jesus, Waverly." Amy sighs. "How many times do I have to say it? *I. Am. Fine.* I promise. I'll call you after Mike gets home and let you know what he says." She reaches to give me a hug.

"Okay." I carefully wrap an arm around her, as if she's a feeble-boned old woman. "Promise?"

Amy groans. "Yes, I promise." She fakes a smile again and I turn away. I don't want to see it.

An hour later, back at the bakery, I sit at the old wooden desk in my small office behind the kitchen. I try to concentrate on the numbers on my computer screen. Payroll. My least favorite part of my job, especially lately, when there's hardly enough in the pot to go around.

I bite into the toffee cookie that I snagged from one of the cooling racks on my way in and stare at the screen, drumming my fingers on my mouse pad. This is useless.

A single thought hangs over my head like the banner that was draped behind Brendan at the luncheon. When it first occurred to me, pulling out of Amy's neighborhood, I slammed on the brakes, making a woman who was walking her dog on the sidewalk jump like I was about to careen into her. I keep trying to ignore it but it's like trying to ignore the barrel of a gun being pressed between your shoulder blades.

I sit up, my spine cracking, and take a deep breath. I swipe the crumbs from my fingertips and log on to Google. Into the search field, I type, "how to tell if a friend is being abused." I click on the first search result. *There is no way, right? It really couldn't be this.*

"Warning Signs of Abuse" reads the heading in big, block letters. My eyes scan the list of bulleted items underneath, and each line makes my throat tighten like somebody is closing their hands around my neck.

> *A victim might seem uncharacteristically anxious, worried, or depressed. She or he may exhibit symptoms of low self-esteem and may withdraw from usual social activities. Fear toward the victim's partner may be evident. The partner may seem unusually jealous or critical, even controlling.*

And then:

> *The victim may have repeated injuries, the explanations for which might seem odd, even far-fetched.*

I press my hands to my lips and shut my eyes. *No, no, no, no, no, no, no.* It can't be this bad, can it?

I hop up and close the office door, then pick up the phone and dial Kate's cell.

"Hey! So what did you think?" Kate answers. It sounds like she's outside, the whir of the wind making it hard to hear her.

"Hi." I gulp. "Kate, I need to talk to you."

"Okaaaay, so we'll talk about the speech later," she says, her voice flat. "Actually, can you hold on?"

She always does this. It drives me crazy.

"Why did you bother to answer the phone if you can't talk?" I shout into the receiver, but instead of a response I get the sandpapery rustling of Kate putting her hand over the phone.

Oh God, Kate, come on, I think, wishing I'd called Larry instead. I realize that she's talking to Brendan. "Yes, I'll see you at home later," she says. "Oh, you won't? Oh. Well, okay, then. I'll just see you later, then. No, it's okay. It's fine. I'll just see you later."

Kate sighs. "Sorry, I'm in the parking lot. Just leaving the campaign office. Finally heading home and can take off these fucking shoes. You wouldn't believe all of the press they made us do after that thing. I had no idea that there were so many newspapers in the state of Virginia. And blogs, local news stations, radio shows...it's amazing that people actually care so much about this crap. Anyway, I really need a glass of wine. Do you want to join me? Leave early. You never do."

"Kate, I need to talk to you." I hear the ding-ding-ding of Kate's open car door, then hear her slamming it shut.

"Okay, what is it? Is something wrong?" The ignition starts. "I'm sorry that I wasn't able to talk to you at the luncheon. It was shitty of me to make you sit through that and not even spend any time with you."

"Kate, this has nothing to do with you." I wonder for a second whether I should just bag this entire conversation and call Larry.

"Okay, well, what is it, then?"

"It's Amy."

"What about her? Did she end up coming? I couldn't get a good look at your table from where I was standing. I'm sorry about that, by the way. I would have put you in the front but there were VIPs, and—"

"Kate, just listen to me, okay?"

When she doesn't respond, I can't tell whether she's actually obeying for once or if she's become distracted by her BlackBerry or a hangnail or a stray hair underneath her brow that she's spotted in her overhead mirror. With Kate, it could be anything. "She didn't show up," I say.

"What?" Kate crows. "Why wouldn't she show up?"

"I went by her house afterward."

"Wait, you went by her house just because she didn't come today?" She laughs.

"I know. But she's been acting strange lately, and then she didn't call. I just had this feeling that something might be wrong."

"Slightly paranoid of you."

I hold the phone out from my ear and take a deep breath before I continue. "Just listen, okay? So I get there and she was a mess. Dressed like she had just woken up, the house looked like it had exploded, she was acting weird, and she was limping."

"Did she fall or something?"

"She said she fell down the stairs, but I saw these marks on her back, Kate. And they didn't look like something from a fall."

"But she's okay?" she says impatiently. "I don't understand where you're going with this."

"Kate, it just seems weird!" I shriek. "You know how Amy is, always put together and happy. She was totally the opposite today."

"So, what? People can't have bad days?"

"No, no, it's not that. It's just that Amy hasn't acted bitchy or withdrawn in the fifteen years we've known her. Now all of a sudden she's moody. She has an injury that certainly doesn't look like it came from a little fall down the stairs. Her husband's turned into an absolute nightmare." I tick off each statement with my fingers. "I don't know. Something's up."

"What are you saying?" I can hear her changing radio stations.

It's harder to say it out loud than it is to think it. I close my eyes and whisper into the phone, "Do you think that it's possible that Mike is hitting her?"

"Mike?" Kate gasps. "Hitting Amy?" She laughs. "No, I don't think so."

"Kate, I'm being serious."

"Waverly, I really don't think so," Kate says, lowering her voice into the patronizing tone she uses when she's being a know-it-all. "She probably actually fell down the stairs—that can be painful if you do it the right way. Trust me, I did it several times during college. Mike's a jerk, but beating her? No way. No fucking way."

"Do you really think so?" I lean back in my chair and look up at the exposed pipes on the ceiling. "Maybe I am jumping to conclusions."

"Waverly, you're letting your imagination get the best of you. Let it go. We'd know if something was really going on."

"How?" I honestly want to know.

"We just would. Hell, you knew she was pregnant before she told us." It was true. I dreamt about it three weeks before Amy finally fessed up that the reason she'd stopped drinking wasn't her new allergy medication.

"Okay, but you could look at it the other way, too. I mean, if I had a hunch about that and I have a hunch about this..."

"No, no way. Think about who you're talking about. They're far too normal for that kind of thing. Amy sends out all of those 'happy family' emails with pictures of Emma nearly every other day." It's true. I've started to just skim through the slideshows—Emma at the zoo, Emma at the botanical garden, Emma on the swings at the playground—because the Hallmark-perfect pictures began to depress me when I realized that my own life could be summed up with a photo of me, sweaty and flour dusted, hunched over a stack of unpaid bills.

"They're at home in that house together every night," Kate says. "Plus, it's Amy. Do you really think that if something was happening, she wouldn't tell us? She's transparent about everything. And she's so close to her family. She'd be in North Carolina by now."

"I guess." Maybe I am overreacting.

"I think you need a drink more than I do."

I don't say anything.

"Come on. Why don't you come over? We'll go for a walk or something. That will clear your head."

"I don't think so." I have to finish payroll, among a zillion other things. And maybe, if I'm lucky, find some time to actually cook.

"Okay, suit yourself. But seriously, I don't think we have anything to worry about. So stop worrying."

"Okay."

"I just don't think—"

I'm tired of hearing her voice. "I know, Kate." I feel worse than before I called. Spent and exhausted, like I've just walked away from a fight.

Later that night, I climb into bed next to Larry, who's reading one of his Harlan Coben paperbacks. "Lare?" I say, turning toward him. He smells like Listerine and the pasta pesto I served for dinner.

"Hmm?" He drops his book to his chest.

"Do you really think I'm crazy for thinking this?"

"Crazy? I've always thought you were a little crazy." He lifts his head from the pillow to kiss my forehead.

I jerk away. "Larry, come on." He'd had the same reaction as Kate when I came home from work and told him the story. "You know, I'm starting to feel like a little kid who can't get anyone to believe that there's a monster under her bed. Why doesn't anyone believe that this could be plausible? Am I really so deluded?"

"No, babe," he says, laughing. "I just don't think Mike is the wife-beating type." Larry pulls at me, trying to kiss me again.

I sit up, ignoring the defeated look on his face as he drops his hands to his sides, and look down at him, his head propped up on two pillows. *How can he be so lighthearted all of the time?* I think, hating him for a moment. *It's like he thinks he lives in one of his beloved comic strips.*

He cuffs his hands around my arms and pulls me back toward him. I give in and flop down next to him, knowing that if I don't, it's going to become something we'll have to talk about. "I'm sorry, you're right," he says, weaving his fingers into my hair. "It's not funny. But I wouldn't joke about it unless I really didn't think that there was anything to worry about. We know them too well. It would be more obvious."

"How do you know that, though? I mean, you never really know what's going on with people. You've seen the stories on the news. It's always the respected pastor who ends up killing his family or the beloved teacher who ends up being a pedophile, or some soccer mom disappears and then they discover that her husband buried her beneath the doghouse in the backyard. It's always the last place on earth that you would expect it."

"That's true, I suppose. But still."

"But what?"

"Hon, come on," he says, squeezing me so close that I can feel the dampness beneath the armpit of his undershirt. I wiggle away. "You're just fixating on this for some reason. It's like that time that you thought you had a brain tumor because you had those horrible headaches, and then you remembered that you'd given up caffeine a few days earlier."

I don't say anything. If he isn't going to take me seriously, why should I bother? It isn't a good habit and it isn't something I'm proud of, but I've discovered over the course of our relationship, and especially the past year, that I excel at giving him the silent treatment.

"I'm serious, babe," he says more carefully, now that he realizes I'm angry. "I think you're getting worked up over nothing."

I reach over him and pick up his book where he's rested it on the mattress. "Here, go back to your reading."

He takes the book from me. "You're pissed now?"

"I'm fine," I lie. "I guess if you and Kate think it's ludicrous, then it must be." *Could it be?*

He sighs, looking at me sideways. "Is sarcasm really necessary?"

"Larry, just forget it. I'm fine. I'm tired." I turn over and close my eyes, knowing that he's waiting for me to say more. Finally, I hear him pick up his book and flip the pages to find his place.

Thirty seconds of fretting with my eyes squeezed shut is all it takes to convince me that it's useless to try to sleep. I reach for the red notebook on my nightstand. It's mostly filled with notes for the bakery; there are ideas for new menu items, flavor combinations that I think up while washing my hair or driving to work, recipes copied from my mother's musty cookbooks, and—from before I got too poor to eat out—notes on really good and really bad restaurant meals. I browse through the pages, looking for inspiration for the spring menu. "*Ginger peach shortcake?*" I've scrawled across one page. "*Orzo salad: kalamata olives, artichokes, thyme,*" reads another. After a few minutes, I realize that this is useless. Everything sounds as bland and uninspiring as dry toast.

Larry turns to me. "What's going on with you?"

"Are you kidding?" I say.

"No, I'm not."

"Well, like I told you two minutes ago, I think one of my best friends is being abused by her husband. Let's start with that."

"No," Larry says, sitting up. "I'm not asking about Amy; I'm asking about *you*. There's been serious distance between us lately, Wave. We both know it. Every time I try to touch you, you pull away from me."

"That's not true," I say, thumbing the edge of my notebook.

"You know it's true," he says, snatching it out of my hands. "Look at me, Waverly."

"Don't talk to me like I'm a child!" I say, turning away from him.

"Waverly, come on, look at me," he says, almost pleading. I didn't think it was possible for me to feel worse about the way I've been treating him, but now, hearing his voice… "What is going on with you?" he begs.

"I just have a lot on my mind," I say.

"Talk to me about it."

"I have talked to you," I lie. "Work's crazy right now, but it's nothing out of the ordinary. And this thing with Amy—it's really worrying me. Anyway, you have your own stuff to think about right now, with work and all."

He studies me for a moment, and I know he's weighing whether to push further.

"I'm sorry if I haven't been completely myself lately," I say. "I know I haven't been as attentive as I should be." I mean it—I really do—but I know that I'm only saying it right now to appease him. The last thing I want to talk about is our relationship.

He nods. "Thanks," he says. He reaches out for me.

I lie down next to him, reluctantly. He doesn't deserve this, but I can't bring myself to give any more tonight, not when I can't stop thinking about Amy. All I can see is that mark on her back and the possibility that maybe, *maybe*, I know far more than I'm supposed to about where it came from. I close my eyes, knowing that Larry will leave me alone if he thinks I'm falling asleep.

He turns over and reaches to shut off his lamp. After a few minutes, I sit up in the dark, find my notebook, and grab a pen off of the mess of stuff on my nightstand.

"Where are you going?" Larry calls as I step out of bed.

"Don't worry about it. Go to sleep," I say.

In the living room, I turn on Babci's Tiffany lamp and sit cross-legged on the couch. I haven't kept a "real" journal—a deep-thoughts, hopes-and-dreams kind of diary—since…well, ever. But I put the date on the corner of a new page and start to write.

CHAPTER FOURTEEN

Later that week at work, I'm sprinkling hunks of feta cheese onto a roasted vegetable salad and happily listening to Jeannette tell me about her recent Internet-dating adventure. It feels so good to be laughing after my last few days have been consumed with worrying about Amy. Yesterday, when I asked her on the phone if she was feeling better, she insisted that she was completely back to normal. When I probed further by asking whether Mike thought that the wound looked as bad as I did, she said that he said it was no big deal, and then quickly—I think, suspiciously—changed the subject to a story about an annoying neighbor she'd encountered at a three-year-old's birthday party that morning.

"So I was under the impression that he was a painter—you know, an art-class, has-shown-in-galleries, looks-up-to-Leonardo-da-Vinci kind of painter," Jeannette says. "But when I get to the bar, I discover that he's a *house* painter." She uses the spatula she's holding to mimic painting a wall, and Randy, who's dicing onions across the kitchen, collapses into hysterics.

"Remember *The Karate Kid*?" he says. "'Up, dowwwwn! Up, dowwwwwn!'"

"Wait, it gets better," Jeannette says. "He was dressed like a house painter, too."

"What, like paint splattered?" I say.

"To say the least," Jeannette says. "Unfortunately, the splatters were not an homage to eighties fashion. He was wearing a full painter's uniform: white carpenter pants, white T-shirt, paint under his fingernails."

"Nooooo!" Randy moans.

"He came to our date straight from painting a dentist's office across town. I don't think he'd even bothered to wash up beforehand. There were little dots of paint on his cheeks and forehead."

"Was he wearing one of those paper hats they give you for free at the paint store?" I laugh.

Jeannette giggles. "No, thank God. You know, it's not that I have any problem with house painters. It would be nice to date someone who could do some work around the house, actually. But I just assumed that when he said he was a painter..."

"He was an artist," I finish her thought.

"Well, it could have been worse," Randy jokes. "He could have been dressed like the little Dutch boy on the paint can."

I look up just as Larry turns the corner from the front of the shop into the kitchen. It's been weeks since he's popped in for a visit and I'm surprised to see him—particularly on a weekday, when he should be at work, in the city, thirty minutes away. I check the old metal schoolhouse clock on the wall that I bought on eBay—11:25. I know I should be pleased to see him, but things have been flowing nicely all morning and it's about to be our busiest time of day. I'm not in the mood to stop working to chat.

"Hey, Larry," Jeannette and Randy sing in unison.

When he reaches me, he bends sideways from his waist to plant a kiss on my cheek.

"What are you doing here?" I say, mixing the salad with my hands. I look up and see Donovan, a twentysomething with dreams of becoming a professional skateboarder, practically spinning a heavy tray of mini quiches with one hand. "Donovan! Buddy!" I yell. "We worked on those all damn morning! Could you be more careful?"

I shake my head. I don't like to reprimand my staff—it's not my job to play den mother, as far as I'm concerned—but I haven't slept all week and I know that it's wearing on my mood.

"That salad looks good," Larry says, nearly resting his head on my shoulder from where he stands looking over me.

I roll my shoulder, worming away from him. "Larry, stop," I say, looking up at the clock again. "You know how crazy it gets in here around lunchtime."

He takes a step back and considers me, his head cocking to the side.

I stop, sigh, and wipe my hands on my wooby. "What is it?" I say wearily.

"Uh, just thought it would be nice to stop by and say hello," he says, clearly disappointed by the way I've greeted him. I can't really blame him.

The past few days have not exactly been idyllic. I am admittedly obsessing about Amy's injury, and every time I bring it up, I feel like Larry brushes me off. He keeps saying, as he *always* says, that I worry too much, and it's starting to make me feel like he just doesn't take me seriously. In fact, I think it's a little demeaning. Of course, instead of doing the mature thing and actually telling him this, I hold it in, and my irritation has percolated to the point that I've now decided that he's just unsupportive, period. I know logically that this is not true—Larry is actually incredibly supportive—but his reaction (or *non*reaction) to this whole Amy thing is pissing me off. For the past forty-eight hours, I've effectively ignored him. Last night, I busied myself ironing the pile of clothes that's been waiting patiently in a basket in the back of my closet since before Thanksgiving. The night before, I spent two hours combing through back issues of food magazines I've been meaning to read. I know that it's irrational for me to blame Larry for our problems when I'm the one who won't communicate. And given his new issues at work, I shouldn't fault him for not putting my problems first, especially when he plain *doesn't know* about the stress I'm under. I just wish he would…I don't know what I wish. I just wish he wasn't here right now.

"Hey? Waverly?" Larry waves a hand in front of my face. "Where did you go?"

"Oh, sorry," I say. I begin drizzling vinaigrette over the salad and then move it to the "ready table" for Donovan to take out to the bakery case in the front of the store.

Out of the corner of my eye, I can see Larry shuffling his feet, waiting for me to stop and acknowledge him. I feel the tiniest pang of guilt for acting like a thirteen-year-old. I know that I should talk to him about what's wrong, but I can't. *I just can't.* It is so unfair to him, but it feels physically impossible to play the doting girlfriend right now. I head to one of the refrigerators and pull out a tray of bacon to start frying for sandwiches.

"So, you're busy," he says pointedly from across the room, shoving his hands into his pockets.

"Yeah," I say. "What are you doing here anyway? Shouldn't you be at work?"

Larry laughs. "Nice, Waverly," he says sarcastically.

"What?" I say, feigning innocence. *He could ask me how Amy is doing,* I think. *He could offer to help me figure out how to deal with her. He could try asking me about how things are going at* my *job. Why is he just* standing *there?*

"Since you asked, everything at work is fine," he says flatly. "I had a dentist appointment this morning. I thought it might be nice to stop here afterward and grab some lunch."

"Looking for free food?" I say.

"Waverly, what the—?" He looks over at Jeannette, who is quietly sprinkling pecan pieces over a tray of carrot-cake cupcakes— and not missing a word of this, I'm sure. Most of my employees know Larry practically as well as they know me, but I don't need them all witnessing our spat.

I start toward the griddle to begin frying bacon, and just then, because things couldn't possibly get any better, Randy pops his head in to the kitchen from the front of the bakery. "Uhhhh, Wave? You have a visitor," he says. His tone of voice and the expression on his face can mean only one thing: My landlord is here. *Fuck.* My rent was due more than three weeks ago and he's been calling incessantly. Of course, nobody knows this but me—not my employees, and certainly not Larry, who's loitering beside me and apparently not in a hurry to get anywhere.

Before I can think of a reason to rush everyone out of the kitchen, Alec, my landlord, saunters into the room, dipping his finger into the bowl of frosting next to Jeannette's cupcakes as he passes by. There is nothing I like about this person. He became my landlord last year, precisely one month after he graduated from Virginia Tech, when his grandfather, the sweet Irishman who was my landlord, made the unfortunate decision to gift him the building. Alec has the kind of brash, bigheaded attitude that only a twenty-two-year-old can have. From what I've seen, he spends most of his time either at the gym or listening to Howard Stern. The bumper sticker on the back of his bright blue souped-up pickup truck is one of those absurd "Calvin pissing" stickers. He doesn't even *need* my money—I know for a fact that his grandfather paid off the mortgage years ago. My best guess is that my rent goes toward cases of beer and lap dances.

"Waverly Brown!" he announces to the room when he sees me. *Oh God, I hate this prick.* He's wearing a Hokies sweatshirt and matching sweatpants, one leg of which he has pushed up to his knee, a look I'm apparently too old to understand. "What's up?" he says to Larry. He's never met Alec but he's heard me describe him enough that I'm sure he knows who this is.

"So you know why I'm here," Alec says, much louder than necessary.

"I do," I say. "Let's just go back to my office..." I motion with my head for him to come with me. I really don't want to write a check in front of my staff and Larry, and God knows what Alec's capable of saying.

"Oh, sure," Alec jokes. "Make me wait a little *longer* for your check, Waverly. Have you not been getting my messages?"

I ignore him as I walk back to the converted closet that is my office. I got his messages, which I confess I have a tendency to delete before I listen to them in full. Can you blame me when he leaves them at all hours of the day and night, with one of his idiot friends and/or thumping house music blaring in the background?

"Um, *Wave-er-ly*!" I hear Alec shout teasingly from the kitchen. "Don't forget the late fee, okay? And last month's late fee, too. You forgot it last time."

I clutch my pen tighter. It kills me to have to write his name on the payee line.

"Here," I say after I walk back out and hand him his money. Jeannette is busy at work, or pretending to be. Larry, unfortunately, is standing in the same spot where I left him, watching all of this.

"You can't keep paying me so late," Alec barks, punctuating every word with a hand gesture.

"I know, Alec."

"It's gotta stop, man. It's not cool," he says.

"I know."

"Do you?" he says. He puts his hands out to his sides and raises his palms to the air. He's trying to either intimidate me or show off his pecs or both. I know for a fact that the kid grew up in the Watergate building, where the neighbors were Bob and Liddy Dole, so I don't know how he thinks he's getting away with the street-tough act.

A platter of tomato and mozzarella salad catches his eye. "What's that?" he says, pointing at it.

"Caprese salad."

"I want some," he says.

"You want to pay for it?" I say.

He laughs, wipes his mouth, and holds the check up to eye level. "Really?"

I sigh. "Donovan?" I say as he passes by me with a broom. "Put that down and get Alec here a pint of the Caprese, please."

"Thank you." Alec smiles, winking at me.

I walk back toward Larry, ignoring Alec when he shouts, "On time next month!" as he leaves.

"Your rent was late?" Larry says. I appreciate the discreet volume of his voice but can't bear to look at the concerned expression on his face, so I turn back to my food prep.

"I've got it under control," I mutter, knowing that what I've just said couldn't be further from the truth. I bite the inside of my cheek to keep from bursting into tears.

Last night, before I left the bakery, I spent two hours going over my financial stuff. Despite the decent Valentine's sales, I don't have enough to cover my business expenses, the rent for the bakery, and my house loan payment. Now that I've handed Alec a check, I'm going to have to default on the house loan. There's no way around it.

"Waverly, are you sure you're all right?" he says, placing a hand on my shoulder.

"Larry!" I snap. "Shouldn't you be at work, making sure *your* job is safe, instead of worrying about mine? I mean, the longer you're gone, the more they might realize how much they don't need you."

He steps back. "Wow."

I glance at Jeannette and Donovan as they hurry out of the kitchen.

"What is going on with you, Wave?" Larry says.

I suppose that I could tell him now—about everything that's happening with work and my money, about how I wish he could share my concern about my girlfriend, about how irritated I am by the fact that he can't just read my mind and anticipate what I need from him so that I wouldn't have to actually ask for help. I want him to be my boyfriend, though I know it's my fault for not letting him be.

I swallow hard. "I'm fine," I say. "I just spaced out on the rent this month. I went to Florida, then everything with Amy...I just forgot. Am I not allowed to forget something every once in a while?"

He just shakes his head. He's had it with me, I can tell.

"You going to be home later?" he says as he starts for the door.

"No, I have dinner with the girls," I reply.

"Right," he said, twirling his keys in one hand. "Okay, then."

The minute he's gone, remorse floods over me. I want to sort this out, but there is so much I have to confess and so much that I'm worried he won't understand. I know that he is just the innocent bystander to all of my crap, and it's not fair for me to treat him like this. I peek out into the front of the store and watch him and Donovan exchange a casual "See ya, man." I say good-bye under my breath.

CHAPTER FIFTEEN

Y ou would not believe this fucking day," Kate says. She throws her bag down onto the vinyl banquette and slides in next to me.

"I'll take that for you," Amy says after Kate wiggles out of her blazer. I watch her reach across the table for Kate's jacket and then neatly fold and place it on top of her things. We haven't been waiting for more than ten minutes, but I am as relieved to see Kate as if Amy was some tedious, onion-breathed stranger I'd just met at a cocktail party.

I've been listening to Amy tell me about her day. Well, listening is probably a strong word, because I couldn't tell you what she told me if you paid me. My mind keeps flashing back to being at her house. This is the first time we've seen each other since, and neither of us has said a word about it. In fact, Amy seems to be overcompensating to make up for the odd mood she displayed during my visit. When we met in the parking lot, she gripped me like we were long-lost siblings reuniting on daytime TV. Then, inside the restaurant, she nodded at the table the hostess had chosen for us as if it had views of the Manhattan skyline. Amy's enthusiasm has always seemed genuine, but now I don't know. I'm starting to wonder more and more about the distant, sullen woman I discovered at her house.

"So you had a bad day?" Amy says sympathetically to Kate, pushing her bottom lip out. I slide a menu across the table.

Kate reaches for it and exhales loudly, her cheeks puffing up like she's blowing out candles on a cake. "Oh, it's nothing, it's nothing," she finally says, shaking her head like she's shaking off the day. "I told myself on the drive over here that I wasn't going to complain."

A laugh escapes through my mouthful of bread.

"Waverly, come on." Kate scowls wearily. She raises her hand to get a waiter's attention. "The service has always sucked here," she says, waving her finger in the air. "I don't know why you two insist that we keep coming back."

Finelli's is a neighborhood Italian place in an old cinderblock building a few miles from the bakery. It has been a fixture in Maple Hill since the 1950s and is wedged into a nondescript corner between the Best Buy and Target that have sprung up on either side of it. The walls are wood paneled, there are predictable red-and-white checkered tablecloths on the tables, and the elderly waitstaff appears to have worked here since opening day. Our waiter shuffles over to our table, glowering at us as he pulls a notepad out of his waistband and waits for Kate to look over the menu.

"I guess just the house red," she says after scanning it, shaking her head as if it's written in Sanskrit. "I've never seen any of these wines before," she says, adding under her breath, "Hardly surprising." The waiter raises his eyebrows and writes the order on his pad, as slowly as if he's just learning his letters. My parents and I started coming here for Sunday night family dinners when I was in middle school, and then Kate began to tag along after I met her. She pretends to hate it, but I've never once seen her leave anything on her plate.

"So I haven't seen you since Florida," she says, turning to Amy.

"I know!" Amy says, touching Kate's forearm. "I hope you got my email about Brendan's lunch. I'm so sorry I missed it."

"Did you send me an email?" Kate furrows her brow. "I don't remember."

"Waverly said that there was a huge turnout," Amy says.

Kate shrugs. "I guess."

I reach for the cruet of olive oil on the table and pour a pool of it onto my bread plate.

"So guess what happened today," Kate says, pulling her hair into a ponytail and then letting it fall. "As I said, it was nuts, but it's for a good reason, actually. Brendan's been getting a lot of good feedback since *Meet the Press* the other Sunday."

"Oh, yeah!" Amy squeals, putting her hand to her forehead. "Kate, I'm so sorry! I totally forgot to watch it! How was it?"

Kate looks across the table at her like she's a child who's just interrupted two adults talking. I want to kick her under the table to tell her to give Amy a break, but I don't want to hit the wrong foot. It's one thing for her to treat me like this, but when she does it to Amy, I take it personally. She knows damn well that Amy is just being nice, and I especially don't want to see Kate's mean-girl act when I'm convinced that Amy's cheerfulness is a cover-up for something awful.

"Well, like I said." She clears her throat. "He did really well."

It was true. When Larry and I watched, I'd actually forgotten that the guy on the screen was the same Brendan I know. He'd convinced me at the luncheon that he could give a good speech, but the interview proved to me that he actually knows his stuff. He even seemed like he cared about it.

"The point is," Kate says, pausing for a moment as our waiter sets her glass on the table, "it's huge for him to get this kind of national attention during his first major campaign, especially when the race is pretty much his."

"We need another minute." I smile at the waiter, who rolls his eyes and shuffles away.

"What's the story on the guy who's going to run against him?" Amy says.

Kate sighs. "Well, there's still the primary," she explains, seeming annoyed that she has to. "Brendan's the Republican nominee—no one is running against him in the primary. There are two Democrats who still need to fight it out, but one is almost definitely going to be the one who's going to run against Brendan."

"Right," Amy says. "So who's the guy? I've seen his picture in the paper—short, skinny, bald. That guy, right?"

"John Tookin." I say his name like it's a punch line. "He's a nut job. As Larry says, he makes Ross Perot look as steady as that pilot who landed the plane on the Hudson."

"Ugh." Kate makes a face like she's just bitten down on a lemon. "Tookin's a moron. He's way too liberal for Virginia."

"So what does all of this mean? Is Brendan freaking out?" I say.

"Well, actually." Kate runs her index finger along the rim of her wineglass. She leans in and lowers her voice. "It probably means that Brendan's going to start thinking about something bigger after the governorship."

"Bigger?" Amy leans into the table. "What could be bigger?"

I lean in, too.

"They're talking about the presidency," Kate says. She tosses it out like it's nothing; like Brendan is a carpet salesman and she's just said that he's thinking about transferring to the Omaha office. She reaches for the bread basket.

"Wait, *president*?" Amy says, handing it to her. "You mean, like...*oh my God.*"

My eyes may as well have just popped out of my head on cartoon springs. I am far too shocked to try to pretend to be excited about this. If there is one thing I know about Kate, it is that she doesn't want to be the First Lady of the United States any more than she wants to pick up trash on the side of the interstate. It is one thing for her to be the First Lady of Virginia, a position that is prestigious but not all that visible, but quite another for her to pretend to be interested enough in our country's welfare that she'd devote her entire life to it.

Kate shrugs. "It's the next step."

"Have you talked about this before? I mean, that's huge," I say. "Like the biggest job on earth."

I can tell by the way she's looking at me that she knows exactly what I'm thinking. "What's there to talk about?" she huffs. She bites into her roll like she's an animal taking off the head of her prey. "He's going to do it no matter what I think," she says through her full mouth.

Amy looks at me, her mouth a perfect *O*. This is one of those moments that happen very occasionally when I realize that Amy still sometimes gets starry-eyed over Kate. I guess I know Kate too well to be awed by any of it. In fact, when I see Berkshire paraphernalia around town—signs in storefront windows, bumper stickers on cars in the Safeway parking lot—it takes a moment for it to register that those things refer to *my* Brendan and Kate, the same people whose dog I watch when they're on vacation.

But, Jesus, First Lady? Kate? My mind flashes back to the last Inauguration Day, watching the Obamas walk down Pennsylvania Avenue. I can't visualize my best friend doing that any more than I can imagine myself. I picture her in the private residence later that night, whining to Brendan: *Goddammit! My fucking feet are killing me! Why the hell did you make me do that?* Or on the cover of *Parade* magazine, a headline running across her photo about...what? What would her cause be? She's always been full of opinions, but I've never known her to feel passionately about any social cause, period.

Our food arrives and I dig into my manicotti, my imagination wandering toward five years from now: Kate, helming the East Wing, and me...what? Teaching again? Working in someone else's restaurant?

Although, I reason, maybe if the bakery flops she can get me a job as the president's personal pastry chef.

But I know Kate. I know her better than Brendan does. There is no way that she can go through with a presidential campaign, I think, sliding the shaker of red pepper flakes across the table toward her because I know she wants it.

"You haven't really said anything," she says, taking it from me.

"What?" I sit up taller and fake a grin.

"You look a little"—she narrows her eyes at me—"peeved."

"I don't know." I shrug. "I guess I'm just wondering whether you and Brendan have really talked about this. And how does his whole 'wanting kids' thing fit into it?"

"You're kidding, right?" She slurps up a forkful of linguine with clam sauce. "Of course we've talked about it. This was always part of the plan," she says. "Waverly, it's just the natural way things are going to go with his career. It's like getting a promotion; that's all."

"Have you lost your mind?" I blurt. "Your husband will be the leader of the free world. You will be the fucking First Lady of the United States of America. Think about it: Nancy Reagan, Barbara Bush, Hillary Clint—"

"Stop right there," Kate says, putting her hand out and nearly knocking over Amy's wineglass in the process. Amy reaches and grabs it with both hands before it topples over. "Why are you acting like this?" Kate whines. "I thought you'd be excited for me."

I take a deep breath and soften my voice. "Kate, of course I want to be excited about this, but think about it: You'd lose any shred of privacy you have left, and I know how much you hate the attention now." Despite what she says, I actually think that she doesn't mind it so much. How could she? Her press, so far, has never been anything but positive. "Can you imagine what it would be like? The magazine articles, the talk on the cable news channels, the criticism."

"I can handle it, Waverly. I've handled it my whole life."

She has a point.

"Not like this, though," I say. "This is different. You know how harsh the press can be. They'd dig into everything—your past, Brendan's past, your marriage."

"Our closets are skeleton-free." Kate puts down her fork. "And my marriage is fine."

I raise my eyebrows.

"What?" she says through gritted teeth.

"Our last conversation didn't make it sound like everything in your marriage is fine."

"Oh God. Really, Waverly? The stuff I said at my house the other night? Or in Florida, after a gallon of margaritas? The kid thing, not that it's any of your business, is a nonissue. It's not happening. Brendan and I are two people in the midst of a major political campaign. I'd say that we're doing better than most," Kate says. "Frankly, it's something that you know nothing about."

I shake my head. I don't want to fight with her, too, not with everything going on with Amy and me hardly speaking to Larry. "Listen, I just want you to be happy," I say. "I remember how you used to talk growing up—you didn't want the charity circuit, the party pictures in the *Washingtonian*, the mentions in 'Reliable Source.' You wanted to run off to Spain and marry a bullfighter."

"Hey, what can I say? I wanted an Ernest Hemingway novel, I got C-SPAN." She laughs.

"Well, it would be exciting, that's for sure," Amy chimes in, obviously trying to put an end to our squabbling. "I mean, Christmas at the White House, the Easter Egg Hunt. I *love* the Easter Egg Hunt."

"Yeah, it would be something," Kate says. She looks at me for a fleeting moment, but I can't read her expression. Shit, now I've blown it with her, too.

"So is this guy ever going to come check on us?" she says. "I need another glass of wine."

CHAPTER SIXTEEN

After dinner, Kate rushes off, explaining that she has to get up early to go to Charlottesville for a fund-raising barbecue. "Do you want to stay and have one more drink?" Amy asks.

I check my watch. After our tiff at the bakery, Larry certainly won't be eager to see me. "Sure, why not?"

We move to the back corner of the restaurant, sliding our tin containers of leftovers onto the heavily lacquered mahogany bar. A guy with a thin red mustache sits a few seats over, drinking an Amstel and talking to the bartender about the basketball game they're airing.

We order a wine for Amy and a water for me. I'd love another pinot but I can't afford it, even after ordering the $9.99 special dinner. I sip my water. Amy fluffs her hair, checking out her reflection in the mirror behind the bar.

"So that's some big news about Kate," I start. I don't quite know what to say to Amy, and I haven't decided whether I should bring up the incident at her house again. The websites I've been reading suggest being direct yet supportive. Lately I feel like I'm failing at both.

"I can't believe it," Amy says. "I know that Brendan has high aspirations but it's just so surreal."

"I know." I reach for a cocktail napkin and wipe up a wet spot on the bar. Force of habit. "I worry about them."

"The kid thing threw me for a loop," she says. "But it sounds like Kate has everything under control."

"Yup, that's Kate, always in control."

"She can handle anything, it seems."

I detect a sort of weary sarcasm in her voice, so I jump at the opportunity to find out where it's coming from. "How are things going with Mike?" I say. "The last time we really talked, at the bakery, you said that things had been kind of distant?"

"Waverly, things are so much better." She reaches out and touches my arm for emphasis. "We went out to dinner last night, the three of us. I can't remember the last time we did that. I really can't believe it," Amy says. "It feels like we're dating again."

She seems to mean it, and I immediately feel a pang of guilt for the scenarios I've concocted in my head over the past few weeks. What is wrong with me? First, I decide that Amy is being cheated on. Next, her husband's beating her. And tonight, I can't be happy for Kate. I'm obviously the problem, and all of my judgy BS must have something to do with the fact that my life is the one that's in shambles. I make an executive decision: I will just take what Amy and Kate give me at face value. No more worrying about them. No more imaginary disaster scenarios. They are competent grown women who are obviously handling their lives better than I can manage my own.

I need to concentrate on solving my *own* problems instead of distracting myself by inventing them for my friends. Jesus, if I actually told Amy about what's been going on in my head over the past week, she'd probably commit me immediately.

"It's good to see you happy," I say.

Amy smiles a half smile. "Yeah." She starts to say something and then stops.

"What?" I ask.

"Never mind."

"No, tell me," I say.

"It's just the other day at the house. I was kind of a bitch. I'm sorry about that."

"Oh, don't worry about it," I say, relieved that she's clearing the air. "It's no big deal." We're like a couple making up after our first fight, all awkward and overapologetic, but at least it feels like things are normal again. Amy looks over at the basketball game on the television. Maybe I should just tell her, I think, watching her mutter encouragement to the players dribbling down the court on the screen. If I confess what I've been thinking, I can officially move on and never think of it again.

"I have to tell you something." I smile sheepishly. I can't believe I'm going to admit this. The voice in the back of my head—the rational one that apparently hasn't been affected by the glass of wine I've consumed—tells me to keep my mouth shut.

"What?"

"Oh God, never mind." *Idiot! What are you thinking?*

Amy laughs. "Just tell me. You have to now." She's still looking at the television. "Come on," she whispers to the screen.

"You won't believe what I thought." I wince.

Amy looks at me and cocks her head like a puppy.

"I'm embarrassed to even tell you," I say, putting my hands to my face. "It's so stupid."

"Waverly!" Amy says. "Just tell me!"

"Promise me you won't get angry."

Amy smirks. "Come on," she says. "Out with it."

I purse my lips and consider her. I'm backed into a corner now. "Actually, it's kind of funny," I say, knowing that it isn't at all but that saying so might soften what I am about to admit. "After I came over that day and saw that you were limping, I thought that maybe…"

Amy takes a sip of her wine. I reach across the bar for my water and follow suit.

"Oh, I can't tell you! It's so insane!" I backtrack. "Please just change the subject."

"Dammit to hell, Waverly, come on," Amy says, grinning.

I lean toward her, keeping my eyes pinned on her lap because I certainly can't look at her face when I tell her this. "I thought that maybe Mike had done that to you, to your back," I say, spitting it out as quickly as I can. "I mean, how stupid is that?"

Amy straightens up. "That is kind of crazy," she sputters, then raises her glass to her mouth again.

"Oh no," I say. Her mouth has formed a thin line. Her eyebrows have developed corners. "I've offended you. I know that it was so stupid. I never should have even said anything. I'm embarrassed now." I want to crawl under the bar, to press my cheek against the dusty, sticky, crumb-covered floor until I disappear into it.

"It's okay," Amy says.

I can tell that it isn't. "Oh God, Amy. I'm so sorry. I know that Mike would never—"

"No, it's—" She sucks in her bottom lip.

I pinch a handful of my hair and start to chew on it.

"Waverly, it's okay," Amy says. "Actually . . ."

When her eyes meet mine, she doesn't have to say another word. I stop chewing. My eyes widen.

Amy nods.

"Wait," I say. "Amy?"

She mouths, "You were right."

"Amy?" I lean into her. "What are you saying?"

"I'm saying that you saw what you think you saw," she says. She reaches across the bar for a cocktail napkin and dabs at her eyes. "It really started just after Emma was born, but it's okay now."

She looks over her shoulder at the bartender, who is still engrossed in sports talk with the other customer, and then she leans her elbow onto the bar, puts her head in her hand, and starts talking.

The first five years of their marriage were good. Sometimes even idyllic, like when he would surprise her with a phone call on a Friday afternoon, tell her to be ready by seven, and then whisk her off to a picnic on the National Mall. Sometimes things weren't so good, particularly during his residency at Georgetown, when he would come home so exhausted that he could barely kiss her hello before collapsing into bed. But the occasional rough patch didn't worry her. She'd witnessed her parents' fights growing up and knew that no marriage was without its battle scars. Arguments were bound to happen. It didn't mean that he didn't love her.

Mike had always been inordinately thoughtful, the kind of husband who not only remembered that she preferred tulips to roses but actually bought them for her. And, okay, sometimes this devotion could border on the extreme. More than once, back when she worked, she'd had to turn off her phone because he sometimes called repeatedly when he couldn't immediately reach her, and the background noise of an incessantly ringing phone was not conducive to helping her teenaged students work through whatever college admissions problems or romance crises they were having. He could also be too heavily invested in what she wore—the first time they were invited to Kate's parents' legendary Christmas party, he'd made her return the first dress she bought for the occasion, stating that it was too revealing, when, for the record, it was a navy dress from Talbots, a store hardly known for its scandalous style. These sorts of things were frustrating, she says to me, hardly meeting my eyes as she talks, but they happened infrequently enough that she didn't let them worry her. Then she got pregnant, and everything changed. "His attentiveness seemed to go into overdrive," she says. "And then"—she turns to see whether anyone can overhear us—"it became something more."

At first, she loved the way that he coddled her. He tucked a pillow under her knees while she read *Fit Pregnancy* on the couch in the evenings after work. When she woke up nauseous, he brought her a stack of saltines and a glass of ginger ale. As she tells me this, I remember it, and how she'd told me about what a good dad Mike would be if he treated their baby half as well as he treated her.

By the end of her first trimester, she says, all of his attention was starting to make her feel smothered, like he didn't trust that she was capable of carrying their child without his presiding over her every move. At doctors' appointments, he'd stand over the nurse's shoulder while she was weighed and had her blood pressure checked, meticulously recording the numbers in a notebook that he kept in his back pants pocket. By the fifth month, he'd convinced Amy to keep a food diary to make sure that she was getting all of the nutrients that the baby needed. Every day, she wrote down everything that she ate, along with the amounts and the time at which she'd eaten. It was a fastidious request, for sure, but she found herself not questioning him, dutifully filling in the information at the kitchen counter. "After all," she says, "he's the one with the medical degree. I wanted to do everything I could to have a healthy baby. At night, when he pored over the journal and remarked on the fact that I'd only had one serving of fruit, or that I could have had a glass of milk with breakfast, I just nodded quietly, trying to be a team player and reminding myself that he only had my best interests at heart."

But there was one Saturday afternoon during her eighth month when she splurged on a Big Mac and he flipped out. She'd seen him get really angry before—they'd had those atrocious, once-a-year-or-so throw downs that every marriage endures—but he'd never been like this. "I told myself that we were both just anxious about this major life change that we were about to undergo," she says. "Plus, Mike had every reason to worry about becoming a parent. His own father had disappeared shortly after he was born and his mother only calls when she needs money. And Mike can be such a perfectionist. When he makes a mistake at work, it hangs over him for days, as if one tiny error could derail his entire career. But," she says, tears welling in her eyes, "things just got worse after Emma arrived. I started to feel like I was living with a stranger. He had definitely shifted into some darker place, and each day it seemed like he sank deeper, moving further and further away from me."

Emma didn't sleep for more than ninety minutes at a stretch for the first several months of her life. At night, Amy would pace the halls, deliriously sleep deprived and weeping while she rocked and shushed the baby and Mike screamed from their bed, "Can't you get her to sleep? Are you so stupid that you can't figure out how to comfort your own child?"

Her only solace, she says, was that he reserved this vitriol for her and spared their daughter. To both of them, Emma was perfection. He ran to her when he got home at night, barely glancing at Amy while he swooped up Emma into his arms. "Of course, when I was pregnant, I'd imagined this differently. I thought he would walk in the door at the end of the day and wrap us both in a family embrace, like on *Donna Reed*," she says. "But he never announced his arrival with words. There was no 'Honey, I'm home,' no 'Hey, how was your day?', just the angry, banging sounds of the door slamming behind him, his briefcase being thrown on the floor. I stood in the threshold of the doorway between the kitchen and the laundry room feeling totally invisible as he talked to Emma in goopy baby talk: 'Did your mother feed you well today? Are you sure? Did you spend enough time on your tummy? At least an hour, I hope? Are you a happy baby?' He made me feel as if I was some unqualified babysitter, not the mother of his child."

Each day, she says, it chipped away at her, making her feel smaller and less competent, a flimsy whisper of the person she used to be. She'd never believed in the stereotype of the harried falling-apart mother, and now she feared that it was exactly what she was becoming. "Eventually, he just stopped talking to me altogether, save for the times when he was criticizing me. 'I can barely look at you,' he'd say while I was getting dressed. 'If I'd known that you were going to be one of those women who packs on the baby weight...'"

The whole thing was baffling, and finally, one day while Emma was napping, she decided it was time to face the problem head-on, with or without his help. She went to the guest-room closet, dug her psych books from college out of a box on a shelf, and began to comb through them.

An hour later, deep in a chapter about postpartum depression, she discovered the treasure that she'd been looking for: While it was rare, new fathers could also suffer from the condition, and unlike mothers, whose depression typically manifested in the way you would expect, dads were more likely to become irritable, impatient, and even aggressive. Reading, she felt a ringing in her ears, a tingling in her gut. This was it. It had to be. "And in the same way that women with postpartum depression get through it, I thought that this would pass for Mike, too. I told myself that it was temporary, like a bad flu. So later that night, after I put Emma to bed, I sat down on the couch next to him and told him what I thought. He was quiet for a long time," she tells me, still avoiding my gaze. "I kept squeezing his hand and telling him that I was going to help him get through it. Waverly..."

"What is it?" I say, so stunned by what she's said that I'm hardly able to get the words out.

"That was the first time he hit me."

I close my eyes and take a deep breath. "Amy, this has been going on since Emma was a *baby*?"

"Three years," she says. "It's strange, but my *very* first thought the first time he did it wasn't why he had done it or how he could have done it. What I wondered before anything else was whether the slaps would leave a mark."

They did, she says, along with the bruises that came later, sporadic and without warning. The one on her hip where he kicked her after she forgot to call his mother on her birthday. The marks on her upper arm from where he'd grabbed her one Saturday while she was cleaning out the freezer in the garage and didn't hear Emma crying when she woke up from her nap.

I can feel tears running down my cheeks but I'm too shocked to even wipe them away. "I can't believe this," I say. I've never felt the kind of outrage that prohibits your brain from forming a single coherent thought. My mind is a vast, foggy expanse of gray.

"Waverly." Amy looks into my eyes. Hers are deep and brown, her best feature, but right now they remind me of the mechanical, lifeless kind in the creepy vintage dolls that my grandmother displayed on top of the dresser in her guest room. I used to flip them in my hands, up and down, watching the lids flick open and closed. "I'm fine. I really am," she says. "It's over now."

"What do you mean?"

"It's been a while, first of all. When it started, you know...I was in shock. I never expected this to happen to me any more than I expected to wake up one morning to find unicorns grazing in my backyard, but it *had* happened, and it was almost as if it had spawned this entirely new person inside of me. I didn't know who I was anymore, or what I believed, or how I should act. I felt crazy, which is a word that I'd stricken from my vocabulary when I'd taken enough psychology courses to know better. On the one hand, I knew that I should leave—intellectually, I got it. I kept thinking about the students I'd counseled who'd dealt with this: Jocelyn, one of the first teenagers I ever worked with, whose mother came to my office one afternoon with her eye swollen shut and a busted lip. And this kid Brad, whose father beat the shit out of him every

time the varsity football team lost. I'd sat behind my desk with my
hand on a stack of informational pamphlets from support groups
and told them that there was a way out, that they deserved better
than this from the people who were supposed to love them. But..."

"What?" I say.

"It's different. Once you're in it," she says.

"But Amy—," I start.

"No, no," she says. "Listen: Mike has agreed to start seeing a
counselor. We had a big talk just last week, after we got back from
Florida. I've found someone who seems really great." She nods.
"Really."

"But Amy, he hit you." I correct myself: "He *hits* you."

"You don't know what he's been through," she says. "It's a disease."

"Why didn't you say anything sooner?"

"That's the million-dollar question, isn't it?" She shakes her
head. "It just wasn't right. I can't explain it. The thing is, I always
knew that he would come around again. I always had faith that we
would work it out, and I was sure that if I said anything, people
would try to convince me otherwise."

Wait, did she just say that she knew that he would *come around
again*? Were those really the words I'd just heard? I slap my hand
down on the bar. "But, Amy—"

She cuts me off: "Wave, I know. Believe me, I do. But Mike's
getting help and we're really working as a team. I know that I've
mentioned that Mike had a less than idyllic childhood, but believe
me when I tell you that none of us can even begin to imagine what
it was like. His mother had this endless stream of boyfriends when
he was growing up. Several of them hit her, and Mike, too. His
mother packed them up every few months, moving them to a new
town whenever she lost a job or a boyfriend. None of us can fathom
what he went through."

"But, Amy, that might be a reason, but it's not an excuse. What about *you*?"

"I'm fine," Amy says again. "I really am. You don't have to worry. Listen, Mike and I are talking about this. I knew we were right for each other from the beginning because we've both always wanted a family more than anything in the world. While other boys grow up dreaming of becoming professional athletes, Mike grew up wanting to have a family. It's still our dream. This is just a rough patch."

She sounds like she's been brainwashed. This is not the confident, kindhearted former guidance counselor I've talked to almost every day for more than a decade. It's ludicrous that she wants to help a man who treats her like something he wants to destroy— and already obviously is. I clear my throat. "Amy, I know that you know your relationship with Mike better than anyone else in the world," I say. I know that my tone of voice makes me sound like I'm trying to talk her off of a ledge, but fuck it. I am.

Amy nods.

"And I know that you love him."

"I do."

"But are you really listening to yourself?" I reach out and touch Amy's leg. "Physical violence is—"

"He's my *husband*." She blurts it before I can finish, like she's lobbing a tennis ball back over a net.

"Amy, I think you should think about this. You might not be safe there."

"What, you think I should leave him?" she says.

I nod so hard that my whole torso wobbles.

"Just run off *Thelma and Louise*–style?" Amy laughs.

She *laughs*. I'm even more alarmed that she's not taking this seriously. "Well, yeah, Ame."

She shakes her head. "It's just hard for you to understand. You've never been through it, and I'm sorry, but you're not married and you don't have kids. Those things create a bond that you can't fathom. I would never just leave him. We're a family."

It takes a moment for me to choose what I'm going to say before I say it. I can't believe that she's justifying this horror by telling me that I don't get it because I'm single. It stings, but, more than that, it's more evidence that I need to be extremely careful with what I say, because Amy is quite obviously so deeply involved in this that she can't see what's happened to her. "Amy, I may not be married or have children," I say cautiously. "But I do know that it's not okay for anyone to put their hands on you, whether it's a stranger or a family member or whomever."

"Waverly, listen." She shakes her head. "I have dealt with this situation lots of times as a counselor, and I know how to deal with it now. We are getting him professional help. There is absolutely nothing for you to worry about." Her words are careful and clipped, like a robot's.

"Amy, people always say that once somebody is an abuser, he's always an abuser."

She rolls her eyes. "That might work for after-school specials and *Dateline*, but I'm telling you, that's not how it is in the real world. Don't forget what I used to do for a living. Mike is serious about getting help."

"Amy, we're not talking about helping him come back from a broken leg or something!" I really can't believe what I'm hearing.

"But he's sick, Waverly. He really is. This is a disease, just like having cancer or...or...." She looks up at the ceiling as she searches for another analogy. "Or being an alcoholic. Would you tell me to leave him if he was going through chemo? If he'd just gone into rehab?"

"Amy, this isn't the same thing," I plead.

"Listen to me: I am fine. Really."

I just stare at her. I am dumbfounded.

"Have you told your family?" I ask. That will get her. She tells them everything. If she hasn't at least told her sisters, then I'll know just how poorly she's handling this.

"No, I haven't," she says, resigned. She knows exactly what I'm doing. "Waverly, I told you because I know you can trust me. My family would never understand. I'm telling you because I know you can believe in me. I know that you have faith in me."

I feel like I'm being manipulated. I wish I could remember one single, helpful thing I'd read on those websites. They'd said not to give unsolicited advice and not to badmouth the abuser...but what am I supposed to do? "Amy, you know I'll always support you, but this is different. I mean, have you thought about what could happen if he—I don't know—has a relapse? What if things go back to the way they were? Or get even worse?"

Amy just shakes her head. "Waverly, with all due respect, you're not in my house. You don't understand."

I want to scream. I want to yell to the bartender to call 911, do something! But I can't.

"I know my husband and I know our commitment to this," she says. "Maybe I shouldn't have said anything."

"No, no, Amy. I just want to be sure that you're okay," I say. The last thing that I want is for her to feel like she shouldn't have said anything—then she never will again. "I'm so glad that you told me. Just imagine what it's like to hear it from my perspective. You'd immediately be protective, too. I trust you, though. I know that you can handle yourself." I'm lying, of course, but it's the only thing to do until I figure out how to deal with this correctly.

"I really am fine. There's nothing for you to worry about." She reaches around to the back of her barstool for her purse and pulls out her wallet. I don't want her to leave now. I'm not convinced that she'll ever speak to me about this again, and most of all, I now know what she's going home to.

"Will you promise me that you'll talk to me about this?" I put my hand on her wrist. "That you'll be open with me about what's going on?"

"Of course." Amy smiles at the bartender while she hands him her card. I watch her dig into her purse, pull out a lip gloss, and start to unscrew the cap.

"Amy," I say again. I can taste my dinner in the back of my throat. My chest aches from heartburn.

She swivels her stool so that we are sitting knee to knee. "Waverly," she says pointedly, my name sounding like a declaration. "For the last time, I'm fine. I've never been so sure about anything in my life."

CHAPTER SEVENTEEN

I sit in my car in the restaurant parking lot and watch Amy's tail-lights disappear down the road. I have a horrible foreboding sense of doom, like I've just watched her get on a plane that I know is about to crash. I fiddle with the falling-apart rabbit-foot key chain I've kept on my key ring since I was seventeen and wonder whether I ought to follow her home. But what would I do, stand watch from the front curb and search the windows for shadows? *Well, yes,* half of me screams. *Obviously! And you'll call the police while you're at it!* The other half of me, the deep-down part that knows that this is a situation I can't fix, turns the key in the ignition and starts to drive home.

Amy.

Amy, who never forgets a birthday, who always ends phone calls with "Love you," who signs her emails with a ribbon of *X*s and *O*s. Sweet Amy, who is always giving little gifts that she picks up just because she is thinking of you—a bag of candy, a small tube of hand cream, daisies from her backyard. Amy, who from the time we met and long before, has single-mindedly cast all of her hopes and her dreams on a white picket fence and a family. How could he do this to *her*?

When I get home, I slam the back door behind me and throw my bag on the counter beside the fridge. I can hear Larry in the shower upstairs, singing "Ophelia" along with The Band on the shower radio he's suctioned to the tile. I stand there, listening to the growly, familiar tone of his singing voice, and consider going straight upstairs to tell him. Instead, I get a glass of water and go to the living room.

I lie on the couch, cradling my head on a needlepoint pillow that my mother made when she was pregnant with me. God, I wish I could call her. She'd know exactly what to do. Amy's voice rings in my ears: "It really started just after Emma was born." Three years. How could this have just slipped by?

I turn into the couch and close my eyes, searching my memories of Amy and Mike as if I'm digging through the old card-catalog files at the library. There have been dinner parties, baby showers, birthdays, holiday parties, happy hours. There were the nights that I took dinner to them just after Emma was born, when we'd stand over her bassinet and marvel over the cooing sounds she made while she slept. There were Saturday barbecues in their backyard, where Mike stood at the grill flipping burgers while Amy led all of the neighborhood kids in games of tag and kick-the-can. There were so many opportunities for me to have noticed.

And I hadn't.

Maybe it would have been easier if the four of us spent more time together. The few times we tried, back when Larry and I first got together, it quickly became obvious that double dates weren't going to work. Mike and Larry couldn't connect, so the evenings became too composed and strained, with the two men moving food around their plates while Amy and I overcompensated, talking too much to fill the silence.

Now when Mike comes to the house with Amy, I don't bother to ask how work is going or whether he is up to anything new. He's met my questions with one-word answers too many times over the past few years, so I just give him a beer as soon as I can get one into his hands, to keep him occupied. I should've paid closer attention. I try to remember the last time I saw him touch Amy, and whether the memory could have—should have—told me any-thing.

There has to be some way I could have known.

I suppose I've always assumed that if something like this were to happen to a friend, the signs would be more obvious: long shirts in the summertime, sunglasses to hide a black eye. Amy has been less herself in the past few months, but three *years*? What must have she been going through all this time?

I guess I've always assumed that if a friend were being abused—the word *abuse* sounds so hard, so formal and final—she would im-mediately leave. I wouldn't have to fish for signs because any friend of mine would be smart enough to get the hell out as fast as possi-ble. Then again, I'm realizing now, I probably also assumed that it wasn't possible for a friend of mine to fall into something like this. Things like this just don't happen to people I know.

But now, here it is.

Doesn't Amy understand that you're just supposed to leave? My eyes bore into the ceiling. They burn from lack of sleep and from the tears I'm fighting back.

Isn't this one of those simple rules you learn just by being born fe-male? I think. When somebody leers at you at a stoplight, you focus on the car in front of you or fiddle with the radio. When you live alone, you record an outgoing message on your voicemail that says that "we're" not home. And when a man hits you, you leave. You do whatever is necessary to get away—escape in the cover of night, empty the bank account, walk through the woods if you have to. *You just go.*

Was it something about our friendship that kept Amy from say-ing something? It couldn't be, I think, because one of the unspoken truths of our relationship is that I am the friend whom Amy always calls first. I was the first person Amy called when Mike proposed and when she announced that she was pregnant. But Amy hasn't ever really confided in me, has she? She isn't like Kate, who veneers over every problem with her practiced, got-it-together comportment, but she also never really appears to be bothered by anything.

In years and years, Amy has always just been fine, as still and untroubled as bathwater. I have envied the ease of her life. Maybe that's the red flag I should have noticed.

Larry comes down the stairs and into the room. He's wearing a Maggie's T-shirt. "Hey," he says, in a way that tells me he's still angry about our fight at the bakery earlier today. He sits down next to me. He smells like Irish Spring.

"How was dinner?" he says, reaching for the remote.

My face crumples as soon as our eyes meet.

I bend my head down into his chest, gripping his upper arms with both hands as if I might otherwise sink into a black hole in the floor. I start to sob and watch my tears fall onto his bent legs. "Amy," I finally gulp out against the phlegm and saliva that have built up in my throat.

"Amy?" Larry says, stroking my back. "What about her?"

"I was right," I say. Larry's hand stops moving on my back. I close my eyes.

"Oh my God," he says. He cups my chin and gently guides my head up to look at him.

"Are you sure?"

"She told me everything." I flop back on the couch and press my fingers to my eye sockets as if I can push away the thought of it.

"Wait—what are you saying? Mike hit her? That's where those bruises came from? Where is she now? Where's Emma? Does she need to come stay here? What did she say?"

"She doesn't plan on leaving." I say through my hands over my face.

"What?" Larry says. "What do you mean she's not leaving?"

"She says he's agreed to see a counselor. It's been going on for three years."

"*Three fucking years?*" His outrage makes me feel better. I'm not the only one.

I nod, wipe my nose.

"We should go over there right now. Or call the police. Something."

"We can't do that, Larry." I sit up again. The room is spinning.

"Why not?" He stands up from the couch and paces for a moment, runs his hand through his hair. "Three years?" he says again. "Does anyone else know?"

I shake my head. "You wouldn't believe how casual she was when she told me. It was as if we were talking about them getting in a fight over, I don't know, whose turn it was to finish the dishes. It was crazy."

"Jesus." He sits next to me on the couch. "How bad has it been?"

How bad?

I look at his face, so close and familiar. The patch of red stubble on his cheekbone that he always manages to miss with his razor, his eyes the color of sea glass. *How bad has it been? Is there a degree of better or worse?* "Did you really just ask me how bad it is?" I say. "*He hit her.*" Each word pops from my mouth with the definitiveness of a book being dropped on the floor. "That's how bad it is."

"Waverly, I didn't mean…" He inches closer and puts his hand on my knee.

"I know," I say. I push his hand away.

"I'm sorry," he says.

"I know."

At two thirty that morning, staring at the spiny shadows on the ceiling from the trees outside our bedroom window, I finally resign myself to the fact that I'm not going to sleep. I pull myself out of bed, grab my journal, and slowly hopscotch over the piles of clothes on the floor, cursing Larry for leaving his things everywhere.

Downstairs in the kitchen, I turn on the light over the sink, get my leftovers from dinner out of the refrigerator, and grab a fork from the drawer. After a few bites of cold pasta, I pull a stool up to the island, sit down, and start writing. It's just stream-of-consciousness ramblings about what Amy's told me. I hope that by getting it down on paper, I can stop obsessing over the details and get some sleep, but it doesn't work. Each thought breeds ten new ones: Has he hit her in front of Emma? Have the neighbors heard anything? Could he have—God forbid—hit Emma? Ten minutes later, I flip open my laptop and click to the domestic violence prevention website that I'd visited before. There has to be some way to convince Amy that counseling isn't going to be enough. I scroll through the site's homepage and my eyes snag on certain words as I read: *intimidation, assault, battery. Oh, Amy,* I think. *What have you been through?*

After a while, wanting a distraction, I check my email, but there is only a forwarded joke from Larry's mother and an automated message from my bank reminding me—as if I need the reminder—that my home equity loan payment was due two days ago. I'll deal with it first thing in the morning. I close my email and click back to my web browser and, almost as a reflex, over to the *Washington Post* website. And then—

It takes a minute for the words on the screen to register. My eyes scan over the headline again: ALLEGED AFFAIR COULD RUIN BERKSHIRE BID.

Wait a second.

I tentatively click on the link, knowing that I'm not going to like whatever is about to load on the next screen. Then there it is, in big emergency-red letters: BREAKING: FRONT-RUNNER IN VIRGINIA'S GOVERNOR RACE CAUGHT IN SEX SCANDAL.

Oh no.

Brendan, no.

I keep reading:

According to an unnamed source, Brendan Berkshire, the Repub-
lican contender for the Virginia governorship, is reportedly in-
volved in an extramarital affair with a member of his campaign
staff. His wife, Kate Berkshire, is the daughter of tycoon William
Townsend and the granddaughter of deceased Supreme Court
Justice Roger Todd.

The candidate was photographed leaving the Dupont Circle
apartment of his coordinating assistant early Wednesday morn-
ing. The woman, Stephanie Hanson, is a twenty-six-year-old
former college basketball star. According to the source, the affair
has been under way for at least six months. "These late-night
trysts are nothing new," says the source, who also stated that Berk-
shire's wife appears to be "either totally in the dark or in complete
denial."

Berkshire, widely believed to be a shoo-in for the state office,
is a former attorney at Fitzgerald Sanders, the Washington law
firm. He has no prior political experience. Pundits inside the
Beltway have speculated that the success of his campaign is due
in large part to donations from his wife's family and their long-
standing Washington connections. No statements have been is-
sued by the campaign regarding the allegations or the photos,
which have not yet been released to the public.

I slam the screen shut like I am turning away from an accident on
the highway. The only sound in the kitchen is the clock over the
kitchen sink. Noticing it, I can't help but think that it sounds like
a ticking time bomb.

CHAPTER EIGHTEEN

By noon the following day, I start to consider calling Kate's mother. I fiddle with my phone in the pocket of my apron. I'm checking it every few minutes, when I'm not leaving Kate another message. It kills me that I didn't go straight to her house this morning, but I have to work. Sarah, the owner of the jewelry shop next door, hooked me up with a last-minute catering job. My oldest friend is going through the worst tragedy of her life and I'm stuck making deviled eggs for a local Realtors' conference. I can't believe what the past twenty-four hours has taught me about my two best friends. My *perfect* friends.

This morning, I had Larry drive by Kate's house on his way to the Metro station. When he called from the car, he said it was mayhem, the worst version of what we could have expected. News trucks were lined up along both sides of Kate's street with reporters loitering in the spaces in between. "You would think that Lindsay Lohan is in there," he'd said. I could hear the muffled sound of a crowd outside his car. It sounded like he was calling from the stands at a football game.

My phone buzzes. Another text from Amy: *I can't believe this. Do you think it's true? Is Kate okay?* I look at the words on the display and think that if I'd only told Kate about what Amy had confessed the night before, Kate might be texting me with the same words about Amy.

I'm hiding out in my office when I should be cooking. In addition to the damn eggs, I need to make two hundred turkey sandwiches and several dozen brownies. My eyes fall on the picture on my computer's desktop: Larry at the beach the previous summer in the unraveling Minnesota Twins cap that I've threatened to throw away but secretly love on him. We were at Rehoboth with his parents and his brother's family. In the photo, Larry's leaning on his knee, with his foot propped up on the mountain of sand that we'd piled on top of one of his nephews. Nathan, the boy, is laughing hysterically in the photo, his mouth open so wide that you can see his molars. I remember how later that night, over crab cakes, Larry's mother asked us whether we'd "thought any more about a wedding," as if she didn't bring it up nearly every time she communicated with me. She was looking directly at me when she'd said it, and I purposely took a big crocodile bite out of my corn on the cob so that I could avoid answering—and wait to hear what Larry would say, since he normally avoids this subject with his family, all of whom believe that marriage is something you do well before your thirtieth birthday. "We're cool, Ma," I remember Larry saying.

I look at him smiling through the screen, noticing the slight gap between his two front teeth that makes him look boyishly mischievous, up to no good. God, I love him. I hope he knows that. I remember the conversation that the girls and I had in Florida, and how I'd complained about Larry's sloppiness. How inane that must've sounded to them, like bitching about a hangnail to an amputee. Compared to Kate and Amy…we're fine. We are. I need to remember that.

I walk out to the kitchen and pull a handful of tarragon from the pile on the worktable and start chopping.

"Fuck!" I drop the knife and put my finger to my mouth.

"You okay?" Randy calls from the counter out front.

"Fine, just sliced my finger."

I walk back to my office to grab a Band-Aid out of the stash in my desk and dial Kate again.

"Hello, you've reached the voicemail of Kate Berkshire…" I know the recording by heart—every nuance, every pause. It is Kate's "formal" voice, something I've teased her about ever since I first heard it on her college answering machine. It sounds like the vaguely sultry voice on a hotel's television welcome screen (*to sign up for one of our luxury spa services, please dial the front desk…*).

I cradle the phone on my shoulder while I wrap the Band-Aid around my finger and wait for the beep. "Hey, Kate, it's me. Listen, I know—well, I don't know at all what you're going through, but please call me back. Or send me a text—just do *something* to tell me you're okay. I'm not worried about you—I know you can handle this—but I just want to talk to you. Okay? Call me." I am lying, of course, but I know Kate well enough to know that coddling isn't what she needs. Sympathy just looks like pity to her.

I think back to the dinner party I had just weeks ago. Everything had been fine.

Actually, no, I catch myself. It hadn't really been at all, had it? It had appeared that way, as if we'd all been actors blocking out scenes on a stage. We'd stood in the kitchen drinking wine and talking about…what? The usual stuff. Nothing memorable. Where had Brendan actually been that night? What had Amy dealt with when she got home? Mike had been so angry…

My phone rings. "Kate!" I yelp, not bothering to check the caller ID first.

"No, Waverly. It's Gary."

My stomach drops. I emailed him yesterday afternoon to tell him that I wasn't going to be able to make this month's house loan payment. "Hi, Gary," I say.

"I got your email," he says.

I don't say anything. What's left to explain?

"So here's the deal," he says. "Under the terms of your loan, you have 150 days to make up for missed payments before the bank can start foreclosure proceedings."

I slump into my chair. *Foreclosure.* Babci's house. My home.

"Listen, I'm not going to lecture you," he says. "But I wouldn't be doing my job if I didn't tell you how serious this is. You cannot miss another loan payment, Waverly. Under any circumstances."

"I know," I say. "But *foreclosure*?" I can barely get the word out. "After just *one* missed payment?" I hadn't actually looked back at the loan paperwork to discern exactly what the consequences might be. I assumed there would be some sort of fee or warning, but foreclosure? After one misstep?

"We could argue against it if your credit was intact and you had no history of defaulting to other creditors," he says, tactfully omitting that neither scenario applies to me. "But let's just assume we're not going to get to that point because you're going to get caught up before we even face the risk."

"Right," I say. "Okay."

"Stay in touch," he says. "I'm here to help."

I hang up and put my head on my desk. When Babci left her house to me, it was about so much more than brick and mortar. Her home—my home—is the only remaining tie I have to my family. The knowledge that I've now risked losing it fills me with a shame I've never felt before. My grandmother and grandfather put everything they had into that house. Their legacy permeates every inch of it: the paint colors they chose for the walls that still remain in most of the rooms, the dent that my grandfather put in the banister carrying up the new king-sized bed that Babci finally convinced him to get, the dogwoods that they planted out back that bloom faithfully each year. *How could I?*

"Hey, Wave?" Randy calls, knocking from the other side of the door.

"One second, Randy," I call, wiping my eyes.

"I think you should come see this," he says. He speaks carefully, his tone like the time that he accidentally left the refrigerator door cracked overnight and everything in it spoiled.

I stand and open the door. "What? Is something wrong?"

"The press conference is starting," Randy says.

"Oh, no." I can only imagine. "Okay. Turn the stereo off."

Last year, I'd finally relented and put a small television in an inconspicuous corner of the bakery. Customers kept asking for it, and I compromised by keeping it muted with the closed captioning turned on, with my music playing over whatever high-speed chase or celebrity's rehab stint the news channels deemed to be break- ing news. I walk out to the front of the store and lean against the countertop. One of my favorite regulars, a retiree named Mona, gets up and stands beside me. She squeezes my wrist. Mona knows Kate through my stories and always asks about her. She's one of those women of a certain age who frequents yoga classes and poetry readings and is full of stories about her Reiki workshop or the new bulgur salad recipe she's found.

"Randy, turn it up just a little." I glance over at him. There are four other customers in the room—two couples I've never seen before— and I'm grateful that there aren't other regulars here who would be as interested in my reaction to the press conference as the event itself. I look up at the television screen and wonder if Kate will be there.

"And now, Brendan Berkshire is about to speak," whispers the anchorman over the shot of Brendan approaching a podium in front of his campaign office, a brick storefront just a few blocks from here. It's a bright windy day and he squints hard against the sun as he looks out at the crowd beyond the podium and adjusts his microphone. But then...what is it? I lean forward slightly to get a better look. Something is off. Wait a second—

"Does he have a black eye?" says a woman at one of the tables.

"I think he does," says the man at the other, laughing.

"Please," Mona says gently. "We want to hear what he says."

I look closer at the screen. The spot under Brendan's eye is caked with orangey makeup, like a thirteen-year-old girl applied it, and there is a very definite, slightly swollen bruise underneath.

"I want to start by apologizing to my fellow Virginians," Brendan says. The camera pans out to show the usual crowd of suits standing behind him. Two particular women are very conspicuously missing.

"I have disappointed my campaign team, the people who have worked so hard for what they believe is right for the future of our state. I have disappointed you, the public. But, most of all, I have disappointed my family. Kate, I love you and I hope that you can forgive me. My wife is the most important person in the world to me, and I'm so sorry to have let her down."

"Asshole," Mona says under her breath. I couldn't agree more. I white-knuckle the counter behind me for fear that if I let go, I might rip the television set off of the wall and throw it through the front window.

"To the rest of my family, my parents, my parents-in-law, I'm so sorry."

Because you cheated or because you just lost your meal ticket? I think of Kate's mother, who has surely already told Kate to get over it for the sake of appearances, and of her father, who's almost certainly placed calls to his legal team and his bankers just in case she doesn't.

"It's an unfortunate fact that I have been unfaithful to my wife. By now, you've all seen the pictures," he says. He purses his lips and bows his head slightly, a contrite expression that looks a little Clintonesque. Knowing Brendan, he probably checked Clinton's impeachment trial testimony on YouTube before the press conference to study the facial expressions. "I want to tell you that I know that what I did was wrong and so does the other person involved in this thing. But I also want to tell you that this was not, um, a long-term relationship. It was just a couple of isolated incidents. The stress of a campaign...it's hard to describe. And people start to forget who they are. It's easy to get swept up by the whole thing, to feel entitled, to forget what life is really about. To forget what you really stand for." He stops and looks up, taking a moment to glance around at his audience, and then he looks directly at the camera. "But I now know, more than ever, what's really important. Family. Values. *Doing what's right.* I think that this experience, while it's horrible and it's something that I take complete responsibility for, is going to help me remember where my priorities should be. And if you'll forgive me, I'd like to prove to you that I have my priorities straight. Family, values, *doing what's right.* For my family and for you, the people of Virginia."

"Oh, give me a break," says someone in the room. I keep my eyes glued to the television screen. Where is Kate watching this? Is Kate watching this?

"I don't know yet what the future holds for me and my family," he says. "I can tell you that I'm so, so sorry, and I'll do whatever it takes to win you back. I believe in the power of Virginia. Always have, always will. If you can believe in me again, I'd like to prove it to you. Thank you." He nods quickly and then turns from the podium and off of the screen, leaving the reporters collected in front of him clamoring like zoo animals watching their caretaker walk away with a handful of food.

"Well, that was a command performance," Mona says, patting my arm.

"He has a black eye!" Randy says. "She hit him! Don't you think she hit him?"

I turn, pointedly glaring at him to remind him that he's talking about his boss's best friend, but he's probably right. Kate can get riled up over having to wait too long for a table at a restaurant. I can only imagine how this would set her off.

"Excuse me." I touch Mona's arm and walk back to my office. Just as I'm sitting down at my desk, my phone rings. Finally.

But it's Amy. "Hey, any word?"

"Still nothing."

"Did you see it just now?"

"Yeah."

"Poor Kate."

"I know."

"And, um. Kind of ironic, huh?"

"What?"

"His eye."

Oh God. It hadn't occurred to me until now. Kate hitting Brendan. Amy's situation.

"Do you really think Kate hit him? They're already talking about it on TV."

"I...Amy, I don't know." I rub my eyes. This is all too much. I want to pretend that none of this is happening. Amy and Kate need me now more than ever, but I just want to go home and lock the door, to pull down the shades and hide out where everything is...well, it's not perfect, but it's stable, isn't it? I take a deep breath. "How are you doing?"

"Me?" Amy asks. "I'm fine. Why?"

Why? Because you told me last night that your husband's been beating you for three years; that's why. "Amy, I'm not going to lie to you. I don't feel good about it, what you're doing."

"I know that you think I should leave," she says. "That's why I never said anything. Don't take that personally, Waverly. I'm sorry. I just...I know what I'm doing, okay? My God, you must feel like you're the next to fall, huh? First me, then Kate."

"Well." I take another deep breath, and just in the nick of time, my other line clicks in. "Let me take that. It might be Kate."

"Okay, call me back."

"So can you believe this shit?" Kate says, skipping hello.

My stomach flips at the sound of her voice. "*Finally!* Are you okay? Where have you been?"

"Here at home, trying to avoid both my mother and the media. Not to mention my husband."

"Did you get my messages? I'm dying to get over there. Oh, Kate. What happened?"

She laughs. "Well, my husband fucked his assistant. That's what happened."

"Oh, Kate."

"Yep. What a guy. It's a perfect Washington story. A reporter told me. Called me in the middle of the night. I could still hear him talking when I threw the phone across the room."

"Oh, no. Oh, Kate."

"Gotta love this town.

"I mean, it's not like I should be surprised," she continues. "Did you see what I did to him? His eye? I don't know what got into me, Waverly. I've never done anything like that before."

"So you did hit him?"

"Well, I didn't exactly *hit* him. I threw a shoe at him." She laughs. "And then I pushed him over and kicked him—hard—where it counts."

"Oh, Kate." It's hard to imagine Kate physically harming someone, like picturing a swan in a dogfight.

"He just rolled over. Like the spineless piece of shit that he is. And then he left. Off to work as usual."

"What are you going to do, Kate?"

"Oh, I'm leaving him. Or I guess, more accurately, I'm kicking him out."

"You're sure? That quickly?"

"Yes, I'm sure," she says. "He's done. There's no 'three strikes, you're out' with me."

It's surprising that she can be so certain, so soon. "I'm dying to get over there, Kate."

"I don't think you could even get to the house, Wave. And I don't want you to end up on TV."

"Is there anything I can do?"

"Nope, got it covered. Has anyone tried to call you yet? Any reporters?"

"No, nothing." I know they will inevitably show up at some point. Soon after Brendan announced his candidacy, a newspaper reporter came into the bakery to interview me about Kate. She wanted to know everything from the names of her college boyfriends to the name of her hairdresser.

"They'll be there, so be ready," says Kate.

"What should I tell them?"

"Just 'no comment.' I'll answer all of their questions myself. I'm going to release a statement, probably tomorrow morning."

"Are you going to say anything about the shoe?"

"Why should I?"

"Amy says they're already talking about it on the news."

"Well, fuck them! It's not as if I wasn't provoked. I'm the victim here."

"Right." She is, isn't she? This is different from Amy and Mike, undoubtedly. You can't even compare the two. But still . . .

"I'll call you later. I'm fine, so don't worry."

"Okay." I wait a beat, considering. "Hey, Kate?"

"What?"

"I love you."

She groans. "I'm fine, Waverly," she says. "And I love you, too."

I leave the catering job around ten o'clock that night and call Kate from the car to tell her that I'm on my way over. She tries to convince me that it's unnecessary, and when I pull onto her street I discover that she was justified in telling me that it would be difficult to get into her house. It is still media mayhem. I park way down the street and then cut across the lawn. I think I'm being crafty, but before I make it to Kate's driveway two reporters stop me, both of them grinning in a way that's not so much friendly as pleased with themselves for spotting me, their assumed bait. I shake my head and hurry past them, not even bothering to stop, and slip into the house, entering through the side door with the key that I use when I watch the dog.

"Kate?" I call. She'd said on the phone that nobody was there with her. She sent everyone home. "My housekeeper reads a *lot* of tabloids," she said. "This might be too tempting for her."

"I'm upstairs," she yells.

When I get to her bedroom, she's sitting in the middle of the floor in a pale peach nightshirt. There's a glass decanter of whiskey on the floor next to her. Her face is mottled. She's been crying. "Want some?" she says. "I've been taking swigs all day but, I swear, I don't even feel it."

She actually seems quite pulled together. The room, however, is not. "Sorry about the mess," she says, laughing. "I just, you know…" She shrugs and laughs again. Brendan's clothes are strewn everywhere—shirts and ties, boxer shorts, balled-up black socks. "Look at all of these loafers," she laughs, picking up a white suede buck and tossing it across the room. "There are enough shoes here to outfit the entire Nantucket Yacht Club. I hate these stupid shoes. *Always* hated these stupid shoes."

I sit down next to her on the Persian rug and put the bag of food that I brought with me in front of her. I doubt she's eaten today. I packed a grilled cheese, a turkey club, a few of her favorite scones, chocolates—all of the things I know she loves most. "Tell me what happened," I say, unwrapping the grilled cheese for her and handing her a piece.

She considers it and hands it back to me. "Thanks, but I can't."

"It's okay," I say, placing it on a napkin in front of her, just in case she changes her mind. Let's not forget that I'm a person who eats her way through tragedy.

"Evelyn called a little while ago," she sulks, as she typically does

when talking about her mother. "She's so predictable: 'Put on a
brave face, Katherine,'" she mimics her saying. "'People like us
don't air our dirty laundry. Certainly there's a way to move past
this.'" In the way that some people are great conversationalists and
others are quietly insightful, Evelyn's trademark characteristic is the
steely way that she can turn the other cheek. She is as effusive as the
ice sculptures she has made for her annual Christmas ball.

"How could he do this to me?" she says. "I mean, putting aside
the most obvious thing—that he's my husband—think about the
money that my family invested in him, the career I gave up for
him. My *life*," she moans. "All of this," she says, waving her hands
around the room. "All of this was apparently nothing to him. I've
been sitting here all day long, thinking about how carefully I'd decorated this room when we moved here. Isn't that weird? But I've
been thinking about how, for example, I chose the sheets because
they're the same ones that we slept on during our honeymoon, and
how I'd found this rug in this great little shop in Savannah when
we were there for a long weekend." She rubs her hands over the
pattern. "This all feels so artificial now, like our bedroom is the set
of a bedroom on a soap opera's soundstage. This was all just a huge
fucking act to him."

"Oh, Kate, no. He loved you. He still loves you." I'm not sure I
believe it—I don't quite know what to believe—but it feels like the
right thing to say to spare her any more heartache.

"He wanted to bring *kids* into this?" she says, incredulous. "Can
you imagine? If I'd agreed?" She gulps.

"I can't...," I start. I can't imagine. *What was he thinking?*

"Do you know that when he came in here this morning, after
supposedly working all night at the apartment, he *didn't even know*
that it had come out? I was the one who told him. His team is in
touch with him every ten seconds. They call him when someone
on staff sneezes and yet they hadn't told him that this had broken.
It's suspicious to me. I wonder if he'd turned his phone off because

he was with her. Anyhow, he walked in, saw that I'd trashed the room...you should have seen the look on his face, Waverly. He begged me to try to understand. Can you believe that?"

I shake my head.

"I just don't know how I fell for this," she says, straightening her shoulders. "We grew up in this town. Just like French women know how to dress, or Italian women know how to cook, we are D.C. girls—we know how to deal with these vultures who will do anything for the right connection. I mean, I was barely out of puberty when men started taking me out to dinner to try to get closer to the 'empire.' They all thought that they were so original for waiting until the third course before asking about my father. I thought that Brendan was different," she says. "I feel like I've been totally duped."

She gets up and peers out of the window to look at the news crews. "I wonder how long they'll stay. They showed up less than an hour after the reporter called and told me. Four o'clock this morning. I swear, I don't know how they sense it...they're like ants at a picnic." I've already decided not to tell her about the three reporters who came into to the bakery today, each more vicious than the last.

Kate sits down at the writing desk under the window. "Stephanie. I can't believe that she's what he wanted, with her stringy hair and schlumpy pantsuits. She's probably not even the first one. I should've known. It's not as if men in D.C. aren't known for this. My own father has occasionally, quietly, been known for this."

This is news to me, but I don't say anything. I don't want to interrupt her. She needs to get all of this out.

"Stephanie is always with Brendan, but I never suspected anything because it's her job. I have to call James. I can't believe he didn't say anything to me. Surely, he knew."

"James?"

"Brendan's body man. He's responsible for taking care of Brendan's basic needs throughout the day—holding his cell phone, ordering his lunch. Stephanie's job is to make sure that he gets to wherever he needs to be…apparently in more ways than one. But James practically sleeps at Brendan's side, practically wipes his ass for him, so there's no way he couldn't have known about this." She looks at her watch. "We're right on time for the eleven o'clock news. Let's see what they're saying." She walks across the room, picks up a remote off the nightstand, and turns on the television in the armoire in the corner.

"Kate, no, let's not—," I plead. "You don't need to see this crap."

"Waverly, I can handle it," she says, sitting down next to me on the floor. "My husband—the one who's spent a good part of the last year trying to convince me to bear his children—is sleeping with someone else. What could they say to make it worse?"

I want to grab her hand, pat her back, something, but I know that it will just anger her if I try.

"Brendan must've thought that I would play along if he ever got caught," she says, her eyes locked on the television screen, waiting for the broadcast to start. "He never would have risked this otherwise. And you know what occurred to me earlier today? I think he may have been pushing for kids because it would have made it harder for me to leave if this ever got out."

"Oh, Kate, I don't know—," I start.

"Come on, I'm the bank account!" she interrupts. "He needs me. But I don't know what made him think that I would be the kind of sweet, muzzled wife who'd stand by her man, no matter what. Have they started comparing me to the other ones yet? To Hillary and Jenny Sanford? Silda Spitzer? I should call Jenny Sanford. Mark didn't stand a chance after what he put her through. She handled her situation perfectly."

"I haven't watched the news," I say. "Just the press conference."

"Breaking news today," the newscaster's voice rolls into the room like a cloud of smoke. "Brendan Berkshire, the candidate for the Virginia governor's office, admits to an affair. These pictures, obtained overnight by WUSA news, show the candidate kissing his assistant at her Dupont Circle residence."

"Have you seen these?" Kate says. "These are great."

I'd seen the photos online earlier in the day. Brendan, in grainy black and white, is kissing his assistant in the dim vestibule of her apartment building. His palms cup the sides of her face. His wedding ring is conspicuous.

The newscast cuts into footage of Kate speaking to a group of women. "Oh Lord," she groans. "That's from a few weeks ago. Some women entrepreneurs' thing." She points at the screen. "See that scarf I'm wearing? Ferragamo? He bought it for me when we went to Italy when we were dating.

"God, in the entryway of her building?" she says to me, watching the report. Her speech has become watery.

"Oh, Kate. I know."

"Did he actually think he'd get away with this?" She's looking at me like she legitimately wants an answer. I just shake my head.

"He said this morning that he loves me. Did you hear that in the press conference? That's what he kept saying when he came in this morning and I confronted him: *I love you, Kate.* He doesn't love me. He loves the idea of me, just like everyone else." She looks at me and laughs. "He ruined us," she says. "He didn't think he could, but he did. He ruined us." There are tears in her eyes. "You are so lucky. You know that, right? You are so, so lucky not to have my life."

I shift closer to her and pull her into a hug. Whatever my problems right now, I agree with her.

CHAPTER NINETEEN

When I finally get home, it's well past midnight. I'm surprised when Larry meets me at the back door.

"Rough day?" he says, wrapping his arms around me.

"Yeah." I rest my head on his chest and close my eyes. "What are you doing up?"

"Waiting up for you." He kisses the top of my head. "You want to take a bath? I'll get it going for you. Are you hungry?"

"I should go to bed. It's so late," I say, my voice muffled by his shirt. "But maybe a bath." Despite the grueling workday and the obvious emotional hangover, I know I'll never fall asleep if I try now. There's too much on my mind.

"I'll run the water for you," he says, smoothing his hand over the top of my head. "Go fix yourself a drink."

I hug Larry closer, joining my hands together behind his back. "Okay."

I stretch my leg out of the water to turn the faucet off with my foot. I breathe the steamy air in and out, in and out, wishing that the thick fog could cleanse me of every single thought in my head. Sweat drips from my forehead. Larry has run the water extra hot, which is how I prefer it. I hook one leg over the ledge of the old clawfoot tub, the same bathtub that my grandmother filled with

Mr. Bubble when I slept over here as a child. The tiles on the wall are a color that inspired my dad to deem this the "mint ice cream bathroom." My mind flashes to the conversation I had with Gary earlier today. I tilt my head back and shake my glass of Baileys, as if the sound of the ice cubes rattling the quiet could shake the thought away. *Foreclosure.* The threat looms over everything now.

I think of Kate. This summer will mark her and Brendan's third anniversary. Their wedding was a five-hundred-person affair on the back lawn of a private home on the banks of the Chesapeake. Tuxedoed cocktail waiters offered glasses of champagne in crystal flutes, a six-course dinner was prepared by Evelyn's longtime caterer, and members of the National Symphony played a string version of "Someone to Watch over Me" for Kate and Brendan's first dance. In short, it was Evelyn's gig, and nothing at all like the intimate ceremony that Kate had fantasized aloud about having on the roof of a boutique hotel that she'd discovered while on assignment in Buenos Aires. Kate wanted calla lilies and Evelyn wanted peonies. Kate wanted a city wedding; Evelyn insisted on the country. My take on the whole thing was that since Kate already seemed perfectly happy marrying someone who represented the lifestyle she'd always said she wanted to run from, then why should the actual wedding day be any different? Just by dating Brendan, she'd already buried much of the freewheeling, adventuresome spirit that had once been her compass. At the time, I didn't give much thought to it. In some ways, I guess I figured it would go against the laws of nature for her to live any other way.

On the day of the ceremony, with the sea air softly blowing and the sky bluer than blue, Kate looked radiant as she walked on her father's arm toward the pergola where I stood with the rest of the wedding party. Kate wore her grandmother's gown, refitted into a more modern design by a sought-after designer I'd never heard of.

Amy and I wore custom-made bridesmaids dresses, sea-foam green raw silk sheaths that did nothing for us.

I stood behind Kate during the ceremony, her slender bare back to me. As she and Brendan began exchanging their vows, I twisted the gold band on my thumb that Kate was about to slip onto Brendan's left ring finger. Evelyn would have loved a stand-in for maid of honor—one of Kate's blueblood cousins, perhaps. Instead, I stood in the sun, my upper arms pressed tight to my sides to hide the half-moons of perspiration that had appeared under my armpits, and watched Brendan stare at his almost wife with a reverence that soothed me somehow. He looked like he couldn't believe he'd gotten so lucky. As the bride's best friend, I was comforted to see that he knew it. They'd barely dated a year. I hardly knew him.

During dinner, Amy, Mike, Larry, and I were seated with Brendan's two brothers and their wives. They looked well bred and robust, like all of those years spent in the fresh air on their horse farms had paid off. The brothers were strong jawed, with clefts in their chins deep enough to slip quarters into. Their wives both had the same Ivory scrubbed look—hardly any makeup, with identical chin-length blond bobs and discreet pearl earrings. The women asked me a thousand questions about Kate: What was she like growing up? *Even mouthier.* She's so thin—does she ever eat? *You should see the girl around a meatball sub.* Did I think that Brendan could ever convince her to move to Charlottesville? *Anything could happen, now that she's gone this far.*

We dug into our dinners—roasted duck and a prissy mélange of spring vegetables—and the conversation drifted toward...what else do people talk about at weddings? Marriage. Larry and I quietly chewed our food and sipped our drinks while one of Brendan's brother's wives explained how she met her husband through a boarding school friend and the other gushed about her Mustique honeymoon.

"So what about you guys?" the shorter brother of the two asked, waving toward us with his drink.

Larry and I looked at each other and laughed, a nervous huh-huh-huh that meant, *So are you going to take this one or am I?*

"Yeah, what about you two?" Amy said, grinning and raising her eyebrows at me. It was her first time out since Emma was born.

"Well," I said, clearing my throat before the moment could get awkward. "We've lived together for seven years and we're pretty content. We're still relatively young. What's the rush?"

"We have the rest of our lives," Larry boomed with conviction. He put his arm around me and crossed his legs, resting one of his scuffed loafers on the knee closest to me.

"I wish I could have convinced this one of that," one of the brothers said, nudging his wife. She rolled her eyes.

"But marriage is so wonderful," Amy gushed. She gazed dreamily at Mike. This was the first wedding I'd attended with her outside of her own and she was every bit as oversentimental as I'd expected.

"It *is* different than just dating," Mike said, glancing at her. "There's something about getting that ring on your finger that just changes things," he said to the rest of the table. I remember this now as one of my last glimpses of the old Mike, before it became impossible for him to socially interact without offending someone. But then I realize—no—Emma was a newborn, so things had already changed between them. He was deceiving all of us, including Amy.

Later that night, after the cake cutting, Larry and I danced on the platform that had been constructed by the water's edge. I looked up at him. "Why do you think it is that married people are always pushing other people to get married, too?"

"Misery loves company," he joked. "It's like being a vegetarian. Or living in New York. People want you to suffer as much as they do, and when you don't appear to want to, they feel the need to convince you, and probably themselves, about why their way is so superior."

I laughed into his shoulder. I could smell the dry-cleaning chemicals that had been used to launder his suit.

"You're happy, right?" I said, squinting up at him.

He squeezed me closer. "Of course," he said into my ear. "Aren't you?"

"I am," I said. And it was true.

I still so clearly remember watching Amy and Kate at the wedding that night, huddled together and inspecting Kate's shiny new ring with a kind of wonder that would have made you think that it had been chipped off of the actual Hope Diamond. And I remember the little pang of jealousy I felt when Kate returned from her honeymoon in France and she and Amy compared the details of their trips—rose petals on the bed, champagne at breakfast.

It's not that I can't have those things without a wedding ring. I mean, really, I don't even like all of that smarmy, rose-petal stuff. I am simply tired of being in limbo. We need to either decide that we're going to get married or not, and I know, I think, that we should. But marriage scares the fuck out of me. Especially tonight, given what I've just learned about my two best friends and their relationships, which I thought were perfect. Kate seemed to have such an easy life. Amy seemed to have exactly what she wanted.

I am so disoriented that I feel like someone has removed my brain from my skull and is shaking it inside a cocktail shaker. I need some clarity, some relief. I down my drink.

"Hey, Lare?" I yell through the steam. "Larry!" I yell louder.

I hear him come up the stairs, taking them two by two. "Yeah? Everything okay?"

"Come in here a sec." I hug my knees to my chest.

"Yeah? What is it, babe?" He pushes my pile of clothes aside and sits down on the matted bathmat by the tub.

"Marriage," I say solemnly.

He raises his eyebrows at me.

"Commitment," I say.

He looks around the room. "Are we playing Password?" he jokes. "Are those clues? Am I supposed to guess what you're thinking?"

I take a deep breath. "Why do you think we haven't gotten married?" I say.

He twists his mouth to one side and nods. "Today's got you thinking about it?"

I nod.

"I'll go down to city hall tomorrow," he says, like always. "If it's what you want."

I shake my head at him. "Uh-uh," I say. "Do *you* want to marry me?"

"I still feel the way I always have." He sticks his finger in the tub and draws a figure eight in the bubbles. "I'm happy how we are."

"We always say that, though. Are we really? Are we *really* happy? And if we are, then why haven't we started talking about the next step, like kids?"

"Why not?" he shrugs. "I'm happy. I'd love to have kids with you, married or not," he says. I know that he's being honest. Larry's easygoing nature is so innate that it almost has a religious quality. "The question is," he says, running his finger along my damp shoulder, "are you happy like this? Because if you're questioning it this much, you must not be."

I shake my head. "No, no." I grab his hand.

"This does seem to come up every six months or so."

I tilt my head in acknowledgment. "This has nothing to do with how much I love you," I say. "I don't know—I think it's just this day. I keep thinking that the problems we have are nothing compared to what other people suffer through, so what are we waiting for?" I stare perplexed at the bathwater, as if the bubbles might magically part and reveal the answer I need. "I think about Amy, so sure about Mike, and Kate, so sure about Brendan. And look what's happened to them. I thought their lives were so flawless when, really, they're a wreck."

"Right," he says. "But then look at our parents, with the decades of marriage that they racked up. And all of my siblings, all happily married."

"But how are they so happily married?" I say. "How do they know it's a sure thing? I mean, is it better to do it our way, where we know we have an out?"

"Do you need an out?"

"No, I just...I don't know how to feel sure. One hundred percent, undeniably sure." I glance at him. "After ten years, shouldn't I be sure?"

"I think that when you start needing to feel sure, you get into trouble."

"What do you mean?"

"Everything's a leap of faith, Wave. Everything. You can plan all you want and wait for confirmation that what you're doing is the right thing, but you know better than anyone that things just happen. Life can get turned upside down in an instant."

I remember one of my grandmother's favorite quotes—the one that she had taped inside the door of one of the kitchen cabinets: "Expect the best, plan for the worst, and prepare to be surprised."

On the day after my parents' funeral, she forced me out of bed and made me take a long walk with her. My legs felt like they'd been weighted down with sandbags. I couldn't say a word. All the while, my grandmother, this woman who'd just lost her only child, pointed toward the trees and noted the colors of the leaves, a bluebird on a branch, the fiery orange mums in a neighbor's front yard. She could just press on, no matter the situation, whereas I can spend three hours agonizing over what to have for lunch. Or ten years trying to decide whether to marry a wonderful man. A wonderful man who might leave me when he discovers that I've been keeping secrets from him.

"I'm not going anywhere," Larry says.

Even if..., I think. I should tell him about the money stuff right now. He has to know. This is our home. *Say it*, I think. *Just say it.* I smile weakly. "I'm sorry about this. I just—"

"I know," he interrupts.

"I don't want you to misconstrue that how I feel about this has anything to do with how I feel about you. I love you," I say. "I can't imagine my life without you." *Tell him.*

"I know," he says.

"You do?" I say. *Tell him now and get it over with. This day can't get worse, after all.*

"I do," he says. "And I really think that you'll feel better about all of this after a good night's sleep." He stands up and pulls a towel off of the rack. "Come on. You're pruning up."

I step out of the tub, holding Larry's hand for balance, and stand on the mat, naked, while he towels me off. I close my eyes. *Tomorrow. I'll tell him tomorrow.*

"Hey," he says, brushing my hair away from my forehead. "I love you." He wraps the towel around me, tucking it in at my chest.

"I love you, too," I say. I press my hand to his heart. "I'm just going to brush my teeth and stuff."

"Okay," he says. "I'll go lock up."

I've always pictured my life as so messy compared to everyone else's seemingly dollhouse-perfect ones. I'm an orphan. *Is there a word more pity inducing than* orphan? I spend most days running around in a dirty T-shirt, flour in my hair, trying to maintain my fledgling business. I drive a rusted old Subaru. I live in a home that was given to me through no accomplishment of my own. I have this flimsy, cardboard box of a life—a not quite grown-up life, really—but now, after today, after everything I've learned about Kate and Amy, I almost feel like I should be thankful. God, they always seemed to know *exactly* what they were doing. I aspired to be as certain, to have my shit together like they did.

Larry knocks lightly on the door. "Come to bed," he says when I open it. I shuffle behind him into our bedroom. A glass of water sits on my bedside table. After I get in, he kneels down next to me as if he is about to pray.

"This is hard for you," he says.

I nod.

"Anything you need, you just tell me," he says.

A tear escapes down the side of my face and he rubs it away.

"I'm never going to leave you," he says.

I nod. *He doesn't know.*

"Okay, get some sleep." He kisses my forehead and then circles around to his side of the bed and turns out the light. I nestle myself against his side, the way that I always do. He is, when you get right down to it, the thing that I know best, and what should comfort me in the dark.

I lie there, listening to Larry's soft snoring, a sound that's so familiar to me that I hardly notice it half the time. The amount of time that we've been together is long enough to become a doctor. Or have several children. I don't necessarily believe in the idea that you can ever *completely* know a person, and I know how that sounds, coming from me—the dishonest, lesser half in my relationship—but I do think that ten years is long enough to develop a true, down-to-the-roots understanding. And this is what I know about Larry: He is a good man. He is solid and upstanding. He loves me despite the fact that I am who I am. And as scared as I am to reveal the worst parts of me—that I'm broke, that I've now put our house at risk, and that I've lied to him for so long—I know at my core that he will still love me, despite it all. He may still leave me, but he will always love me.

We have had down years, I tell myself. The adjustment to living together was wonderful but difficult, in all of the usual ways. I hate things about him. He can't ever remember a birthday. He doesn't stand up to his mother, who mostly stays out of our lives but occasionally gets pushy about our choices. He never takes me out on dates. He also has his list of grievances. I was never around in the bakery's first year. When I was, I was not the fun, up-for-whatever girlfriend I'd been before. I was too tired. Preoccupied. Both.

I rarely touch him just because I want to. He asks me—actually *asks* me—to hug him more often. And I don't. I forget.

Do you know what I would give to hug one of my parents? Do you know what I'd give up for ten seconds of that?

I realize that taking each other for granted after being together a long time is hardly unusual. But shouldn't it be? Shouldn't we be more demonstrative now that we've developed a history, when our life together has not just been long, but wide? Full of dreams realized and disappointments, deaths and births, monotony and unexpected joy? Shouldn't we look at each other and marvel? Just look at what we've done! Just look at how we've held up, despite everything!

I am so sorry.

It shouldn't be this difficult to say.

CHAPTER TWENTY

It's ten a.m., and Randy and I are just starting to concentrate on today's lunch dishes. Nearly three-quarters of the tables in the bakery are full, and most of my customers are busy jamming away on their laptops. There's a steady, productive hum in the air, like all of us are collectively on our second cup of coffee after ten hours of sleep. I have spent the morning tick-tick-ticking things off my list at a steady pace, and I feel efficient and capable, which is nice for a change. A week has gone by since my friends' bombshells dropped, and while I'm constantly plagued by my worry for them, and the fact that I need to come up with the money to get caught up on my loan, I have to confess that it feels good to be focusing on myself.

A few hours ago, we got a massive order of early spring strawberries, and we've been brainstorming menu ideas ever since—shortcakes, smoothies, strawberry pies, strawberry salads. I'm telling Randy about this strawberry vinaigrette I used to make—it had poppy seeds and red onion—while I make a cappuccino for a sweaty, spandexed customer who's come in postworkout. I've just finished pouring the foam when I hear the bell over the door. I look up and my stomach drops. Brendan is here.

He smiles and gives me a little salute, which is weird, but I suppose anything he did right now would seem odd. When you're embroiled in a national scandal because you cheated on your wife, how are you supposed to greet her best friend when you stop in to her place of business? Do you smile and wave like it's just your average Tuesday and you've come in because you have a hankering for a scone? Brendan apparently doesn't know the answer to this question either, because for the first time since I've known him, he appears unsure of himself. He steps carefully toward the counter, walking unsteadily, as if his body and brain are engaged in a tug-of-war over which direction to move. I notice that the bruise under his eye has faded to yellow. I don't quite know how to act. I'd like to throw this cappuccino at him. Instead, I hand it to the customer and then wait for Brendan to approach me.

"What can I do for you?" I say, businesslike, as if I've never met him. I am not going to give him anything extra.

People in the bakery are staring. A woman at a nearby table folds her hand over her mouth and leans to whisper to her friend. They giggle, not taking their eyes off of him. He is either so keenly aware of this that he can ignore it or so accustomed to it that he doesn't notice. "Hi, Waverly," he says, smiling sheepishly. "Can I talk to you?" His voice drips with empathy, as if I'm the one he's wronged.

"Go ahead, shoot," I say, opening the cash register to pretend to count the change.

"Uh." He leans on the counter. "This is awkward."

I close the register and fold my hands at my waist. "It's about to get really busy in here with the lunch rush, Brendan. What can I do for you?"

"Of course, of course," he says, not sincerely. "Listen, I need you to talk to Kate for me."

"Talk to Kate for you?" *Are you kidding me?*

"Waverly, I miss her so much." The way that he says this—the feeble crack in his voice, the pinched expression on his face like he has horrible stomach cramps—is almost enough to make me feel sorry for him. But I know Brendan well enough to know that there isn't anything about the way he acts that isn't premeditated. Now I just need to figure out what he really wants from me.

"Waverly, she won't answer my calls. I don't know what to do if I can't talk to her." He's whispering and glancing behind his back, as if anyone within five feet of him *wouldn't* be listening.

"Brendan, you actually expect her to talk to you?"

"She's my wife, Waverly." He puts his hand to his heart. "She's the love of my life."

I roll my eyes. "Sure didn't treat her that way, Brendan." I check my watch—I really do need to get to work before the lunch rush, but more than that, I want him to know how uninterested I am in helping him.

"Waverly, please," he says, putting both palms on the counter and leaning toward me.

I take a step back.

"I don't know who I am without her," he says.

"That's hilarious," I say, laughing. "You really expect me to believe that you came in here to get my help because you legitimately want to repair your marriage? That you're well-intentioned? Do you really think that I don't know the real reason why you need Kate?"

"The real reason...?" He shakes his head like he doesn't know what I'm talking about. *Man, he's really good,* I think.

"I could see the dollar signs in your eyes from a mile away," I say, pointing toward the front of the store. I turn away from him to clean the coffee grounds on the counter around the espresso machine.

"Waverly!" His voice is sharp and quick, a stab.

I whip around.

"*You don't understand what this is like for me!*" he shouts. The room suddenly goes quiet.

He is shaking his fists at his sides like a two-year-old on the verge of a major meltdown. "She has to come back to me, Waverly! She won't talk to me! What am I supposed to do if she won't even return my calls? I mean, *she won't even return my calls!*"

Everyone in the bakery is watching him now.

"I can't even get into the house! Do you know that she changed the locks, Waverly? I can't even get into my own house! I don't have anything without her! I have nothing! *Nothing! Nothing! Nothing!*" He punches at the air, his fists punctuating each repetition. "*Nothing! Nothing! Nothing!*" He keeps saying it. "*Nothing! Nothing! Nothing!*"

"Brendan! Brendan! Come on," I say sternly, leaning over the counter to try to calm him. "Brendan, take it easy!"

His hands drop to his sides and he looks at me, weaving a little, like he might fall to the floor. He exhales loudly, trying to catch his breath. "Sorry," he mutters.

I just nod.

"*Holy shit!*" someone whispers.

He shakes his head and makes a sound that is almost like laughing, but then I realize…he's crying, I think? It's a hysterical sort of sobbing, ugly and twisted, and just as I'm about to turn to get Randy to help me, Brendan collects himself. "I'm so sorry to have bothered you," he ekes out, his hands shaking as he clasps them together. He can't look me in the eye. "I'm so, so sorry, Waverly. You have no idea how sorry…" When his eyes meet mine, I can tell that he's sincere. I notice the dark circles, the pallor of his skin.

And then, just like that, he's gone.

After the door closes behind him, the room erupts. People are laughing, screeching, calling their friends. I race back to the office to call Kate. This might be the strangest thing I've ever experienced.

And then it gets weirder: By the time lunch is over, Brendan's episode in the bakery is running in a seemingly endless loop on all of the cable news stations. In the midst of everything happening, I didn't notice that one of my customers was recording the whole thing on his phone's video cam. What's especially unfortunate—especially for Brendan—is that this particular customer just happens to be a blogger for Politico, the country's major political website, and his post of his eyewitness account of Brendan's—what do you even call it? freak-out? breakdown?—has gone viral.

"It's so bizarre to see the store on TV," Randy says to me, walking up behind me as I stand at the cash register, watching another news clip of Brendan punching the air. I am fortunately not in the video—the blogger was kind enough not to capture what I can only imagine was the dumbfounded expression on my face. Kate keeps texting me one-word messages as she watches the footage. (*Asshole! Idiot! Motherfucker!*) Her reaction when I called her earlier was a similar sort of spontaneous outpouring of expletives.

"Have you read the post yet?" Randy says, messing with his phone as he says it.

"Uh-uh," I say, my eyes still on the television. "Does it say anything beyond the obvious?"

"Well he mentions the doughnut muffins," Randy says, his thumb swiping away on his phone.

"What? The muffins?" I say, turning to him.

"Yeah," he says. "I can't believe that this has been live for three hours and you haven't read it. Hold on, let me find it." I look over his shoulder as he pulls up the article on the screen and hands me his phone. The post reads:

Hello, friends! Guess who was a fly on the wall when Brendan Berkshire, the two-timing Republican candidate caught earlier this week with his tongue down his assistant's throat, had a certifiable One Flew over the Cuckoo's Nest *moment in a local NoVa bakery?!?! This one is a good one, folks. Right up there with the clip of that dude throwing his shoe at former Prez Bush. Well worth a Howard Dean howl.*

The owner of the bakery is apparently Berkshire's estranged wife's best pal, and he appears to be begging for her forgiveness…

or something? For the record, the doughnut muffins in this place are in-cred-i-ble—well worth the trek out to Maple Hill even if you're not lucky enough to get a glimpse of a politician cracking under the weight of his own apparent stupidity. (I mean, would you cheat if you had a wife who looked like Kate Berkshire?)

I hand Randy his phone. "Well." I shrug. "I don't even know..."

"Yeah," he says, laughing. He appears to be enjoying this a little bit more than I would like.

"I think I've seen enough of this for one day," I say, reaching behind the counter for the remote to turn off the television.

"Aw, come on," Randy says.

"Randy, Kate is my best friend."

"Right," he says, like he's being reprimanded.

"Put on some music," I say, clicking off the TV. "We've wasted enough time on this."

CHAPTER TWENTY-ONE

When I arrive at Amy's a few days later to go for a walk, she's watching *The View*. I've decided to take the morning off, though I've already called the bakery twice this morning. It feels completely irresponsible to be away from work, but Jeannette and Randy practically threatened to quit if I didn't take a few hours for myself. The past few days have been crazy. I never in a zillion years could have predicted it, but the most bizarre thing has happened at work: Ever since Brendan's outburst made the news, my doughnut muffins have developed a bit of a following. Several customers have come in asking for "the thing that the guy wrote about on Politico." When I talked to Randy an hour ago, just after our usual commuter rush ended, he told me that even though he and Jeannette tripled the batch this morning, they were already nearly sold out. Last night, when I checked my voicemail, a PR person from a national firefighters' association called the shop asking for eight dozen for their annual convention next week and a local elementary school called asking for an order for an upcoming parents' meeting.

I walk circles around the living room while I wait for Amy to find her sneakers upstairs. It's the first time I've been to her place since I found out about her situation with Mike, and since I arrived, I've been scanning the place like a police detective, looking for clues I might've missed before I knew about what was going on. I keep waiting for something to jump out at me, some sign that I can shove into Amy's face that will convince her to get the hell out of here, but the place looks as normal as ever—Pottery Barn Kids catalog on the coffee table, laundry folded neatly in a basket next to the couch, Emma's plastic tea set stacked on top of the toy box in the corner. I hate to admit it, but I almost wish that Mike were doing more of the things that the websites I've read say that abusers do to their victims—not physically, of course, but maybe if he was being more paranoid and controlling about who she saw or where she went, it would be easier to get her to break free.

The women on *The View* are talking about—what else?—Kate. She released a public statement yesterday announcing that she's filing for a separation. It's the only solution, she says. She interrogated Brendan's body man—I can only imagine what that was like for the poor kid—and he insists that Stephanie was the only one. There weren't any high-priced hookers. There weren't any heartsick interns. Still, Kate says she'll never trust Brendan again. I gaze wearily at the television. "If you ask me, this Berkshire girl is an inspiration!" Joy Behar declares. "More politicians' wives could take a page from her book! Ya know, I think *she* should run for office!" The studio audience bursts into applause. I smirk.

For days, I've been avoiding calls from reporters requesting interviews about Brendan's meltdown. MSNBC has called daily and even filmed a spot in front of the bakery—I wouldn't let them come inside, even after they bought a couple dozen (you guessed it) doughnut muffins. The *New York Post* has been relentless, to the point that I told my employees not to pick up the phone if they see a Manhattan area code pop up on the caller ID. A junior reporter from a Washington tabloid comes in every day, orders a mocha, and lurks at a corner table waiting for something to happen like she's a member of the KGB. Kate keeps apologizing for the bother, as if she had anything to do with it. Brendan still won't stop calling her, but apparently she's the only one he's trying to talk to, because he hasn't been seen or heard from otherwise. The campaign released a statement saying that he's "dealing privately with his personal situation." I'm certain the low profile won't last long. For Brendan, staying out of the public eye is like trying to hold your breath underwater. There's only so much he can take before he'll pop back up, gasping for attention.

All of the news shows have dissected the same debate: Was Kate justified in giving Brendan that black eye? Matt Lauer asked a couple of pop psychologists about it on the *Today* show, Robin Roberts did a segment on *Good Morning America*, and Diane Sawyer did a piece about it on the evening news. "Does it count when the *woman's* the one who hits?" she'd said, one eyebrow cocked, a picture of a generic, distraught-looking couple in the little box over her left shoulder. Every time I saw one of the stories, I felt my stomach tighten. *Amy.* I can only imagine what she thinks watching all of this.

"Sorry!" she calls out, bounding down the stairs. She comes into the room and checks her watch. "How long do you have? I need to pick up Emma at preschool in about an hour. It was her turn for show-and-tell today and she decided to take one of Mike's old stethoscopes. How cute is that?"

"Adorable," I manage. I'm amazed—and terrified—by the way that she can bring up Mike's name so casually after confessing to me. "An hour is perfect," I say. "It will give me just enough time to get to work before lunch gets crazy." This morning, while I was conceivably doing the crossword in the paper but actually obsessing over my house loan payment, Larry tried unsuccessfully to convince me to come into the city to meet him for lunch. He even tried to sweeten the deal by telling me that he'd let me sneak into the museum's replica of Julia Child's kitchen. "I'll let you fondle the pots and pans," he'd joked. I'd laughed, too, but I was really thinking that I was awful for saying no. A better girlfriend would recognize that his work situation is tense right now and would accept his invitation in an effort to comfort him and give his day a little lift. A better girlfriend would also have told him about all these financial problems in the first place…I'm a terrible person.

Amy glances at the television and I notice the subtlest grimace as she listens to the hosts continue to opine about my oldest friend's marriage. "How's she doing?" Amy asks.

"You know Kate," I say. "Everything appears to be fine."

"I've left her a couple of messages and sent some flowers. Do you know if she got them?"

"She did," I say, leaving out how Kate had opened the card accompanying the long-stemmed yellow roses when I was at her place last week, read it, and tossed it onto the countertop, saying, "Little Miss Sunshine has a way of making me feel sick to my stomach." I'd picked up the card and read it: *Kate, I'm thinking about you every moment of every day! I'm always here for you! XOXOXO, Amy and family.* I was tempted to tell Kate about Amy and Mike right then but I decided against it. I couldn't upset her further.

"Mike and I saw her on the news the other night," Amy says.

"Yeah. Me, too." Kate's one public appearance was a brief shot on the local news, when a cameraman blocked her car as she was leaving her house. "I'm doing great," she said diplomatically as she smiled behind her oversized sunglasses, looking like a movie star off to a meeting with her agent. She seemed so at ease, with her elbow rested casually on the open car window, that it was as if the reporter was a neighbor who'd stopped her to compliment her yard. I can only imagine what Mike must've said when he saw it. He must be reveling in Kate's misfortune like his team just won the World Series.

"She looked so great," Amy says. "Is she really doing as well as she seems? I keep thinking about how horribly Brendan deceived her, with his trying to start a family and everything, too. I can't imagine a tougher situation."

You can't imagine a tougher situation? I think. *You? The one who's being hit by her husband?*

"Kate's bogged down by all of the details—the living arrangements, the meetings with lawyers," I say. "But honestly, Amy, she's doing well. She hated campaigning, as you know, and I think just being able to give that up has been a huge relief." I think for a moment before I continue. "I also think that being able to fully concentrate on herself has been really good for her," I add strategically, watching her lace up her sneakers. "There must have been more going on there than we realized, because I truly haven't seen her this happy in years."

Kate's actually been mainlining the contents of her and Brendan's wine cellar and calling me every night to give me her latest revelations about what an idiot Brendan is, but I'm lying a little bit for the sake of charity. I want—I can't believe I'm saying this—I want Kate to *inspire* Amy; to help her see why she needs to get the hell out of her marriage, or at least start to nudge her thoughts in that direction.

"Well that is so, so great!" Amy says, popping up from the couch. "Do you want a bottle of water to take with you? Speaking of water, have you ever tried that VitaminWater stuff? I bought some at Costco the other day. It's really good! Do you want one of those?" She walks toward the kitchen and I follow behind. While she's getting the bottles out of the fridge, I examine the to-do list on the counter that she's written in bubbly script: *"Make dentist appointments! Emma—swim lessons! Target—lightbulbs, M undershirts, freezer bags!"* There's a fresh-looking vase of daisies on the windowsill over the sink—maybe an apology from Mike for something he did? I shudder, thinking about it. My eyes wander to the frozen Stouffer's casserole defrosting in the sink.

"Don't judge me," Amy says, laughing, when she notices me looking at it.

"Never," I say, forcing a playful grin.

"Some nights, I'm just too tired to cook," she explains.

Why? I think. *Because of something Mike did? Because you're so distraught? Maybe you've been crying all day? Because your body is actually too physically and emotionally exhausted to handle cooking?* I take a deep breath, forcing myself to come back down to earth.

"I understand," I say. I start to offer her a sympathetic smile—maybe this is my opening—but she's already headed toward the front door, her ponytail bobbing behind her.

"You know, it's great that Kate is doing so well, but what about Brendan?" she says as we walk toward the foyer. "That thing at the bakery was pretty horrible. He must be under a serious amount of stress. He should talk to someone."

Walking behind her, there's a part of me that wants to grab her ponytail and spin her around and force her to look me in the eye and explain to me how it's reasonable for her to be concerned about Brendan's mental health but not her husband's—or her own.

"Well, I don't think there's been a whole lot of fallout for him, no matter how despondent he may have acted when he came to see me. Stephanie, the other woman, resigned the day the story broke and hightailed it back to the Midwest. The *Post* ran an online survey yesterday showing that Brendan still has plenty of support. Kate also said that the Republican Party is fully behind him so he'll have no problem continuing to campaign without her family's money."

Why are we wasting so much time talking about Brendan? I think. I came over here assuming we'd pick up where we'd left off at Finelli's. I need to find out more about where her head is about everything if I'm going to be able to help her. "Anyway, the other night—," I start, but then the phone in the kitchen rings. I'm closer so I jog back and grab the cordless off the counter. Before I hand it to Amy, I glance at the caller ID.

"It's Mike," I say. "Langley and Rutherford Internal Medicine." *Speak of the devil,* I think. *Literally.*

"Hey!" she says after she takes the phone from me. Her voice sounds like the wide smile on her face.

"Oh," she says and turns away from me, walking back into the kitchen. I follow right behind her.

"But—" She sighs and scratches her head.

"Okay." There's a long silence, during which she picks up a couple of nearly microscopic pieces of lint off the floor, straightens the dish towel hanging from the handle on the oven . . . and doesn't dare look at me. It's on purpose, I'm sure. *What did the prick say to her?*

"No, it's fine, I understand," she finally says. She clicks the phone off without saying good-bye.

"Sorry." The energy in the room has dropped like a storm is moving in. I swear, the room is actually darker. You can see it on Amy's face, like an internal dimmer switch has been dialed down. "You ready to go?" she says, picking at something in her eye, or pretending to.

"Is everything okay?"

Amy bites her lip. "Have you said anything to Kate about what I told you?"

"Of course not." The truth is that had everything not blown up with Brendan, I would have told her by now. While Kate might not be the best person to reach out to for heartfelt words of encouragement, she is perfect when you need someone to be honest about how you should handle a situation.

"What about Larry?"

I shake my head no. It's a wimpy attempt at a lie and we both know it.

"Remember how I told you that Mike was going to see a counselor? I made an appointment for him with a psychiatrist for this afternoon. A *great* one, Waverly. She specializes in . . ." She pauses, looking for the right words. "Mike's problem. She's written some groundbreaking research on helping men turn themselves around." She stops and throws her hands up into the air, and then shakes her head, exasperated. "Even *he* was excited about her when he read her bio!" she yells, looking up at the ceiling.

She walks to the counter next to the refrigerator, where a pile of mail sits unopened. She straightens it and then straightens it again. "But apparently he's changed his mind," she says quietly. "He says he's not going to go."

"He changed his mind about counseling?" I force myself to keep my voice steady. "Who does he think he—" I stop myself, remembering one of the tips I'd read on one of my websites: *Don't criticize the abuser's partner.*

Amy continues to rustle the mail. "Yeah, he said he just changed his mind." She straightens the pile a third time, angrily knocking it against the counter as she neatens the stack, and finally stuffs it into the basket on top of the counter.

"How do you feel about this?" I hate the earnest, touchy-feely sound of my voice, as if *I'm* the therapist. But I worry that if I tell her what I really think, I might just drive her away. The best thing is to just be supportive right now, I remind myself. She's probably already fully aware of my opinion.

When Amy turns to me, her bottom lip begins to quiver. "It's not okay," she says, her voice a tiny whisper, like she's talking to herself. "He has to see a counselor. We had a deal."

She walks across the room to the breakfast bar, hoists herself onto one of the wrought-iron barstools, and starts fiddling with the edge of a stack of St. Patrick's Day–themed paper napkins before she finally speaks.

"Everything has been so great," she says, making tiny tears in the napkin she's pulled off the top of the stack. "I mean, I know what you must think." She glances quickly at me. "I know you're worried. If it were you and Larry, I would be, too."

This would never happen to Larry and me, I think. But then the realization comes in a flash: Amy surely assumed the same thing about her relationship before it happened to her.

"Mike and I had this huge heart-to-heart a few weeks ago," she says, brushing the napkin shreds into a tiny mountain on the counter. "It was so great, like a time machine had taken us right back to the early days. It's been idyllic around here, Waverly. Nothing has happened." Her eyes flicker toward me. "For the first time in years, we're finally talking again. I mean, *really* talking. He knows what he's done." She pauses. "He apologizes every day." She pauses again. "I know that you must hate him."

Abhor him is more accurate.

"He's not what you think he is, Waverly. He's really not. And he's been proving it every day."

"Except today," I say carefully.

She exhales a slow and heavy burst of air as if she's a balloon that I've just popped. "We've been talking so much about our future," she says. "Just last night we were talking in bed about how much fun it would be to rent a place on the Outer Banks this summer. I sent my parents and my sisters an email about it this morning to see if they'd want to come. This weekend, we're going to drive into D.C. to take Emma to the zoo." She sighs again. "I just don't know what to do to convince him that he needs to see someone. It was so hard to get him to even consider it in the first place."

"Did he say anything about why he changed his mind today?" I ask. There are sirens going off in my brain, fire trucks roaring down the pathways between my ears. I want to scream a million different things at her (*Get out! How can you still love him?!*), so it kills me that I feel obligated to stick with these doughy, cautious questions.

She shakes her head. "He just said that he got too busy with patients and that he really doesn't think he needs the help anyway because he's realized how lucky he is to have a family like ours."

The way she says it is so sad, so lovelorn, that I somehow manage to simultaneously feel complete sorrow for her and absolute outrage that she could be so blinded by this . . . this . . . what do you even call him? He's not a man; I know that much.

She looks at her watch. "I'll figure it all out," she says resignedly. "You know what? I'm sorry. I'm going to have to skip our walk. I forgot about an errand that I need to do before I pick up Emma."

"An errand?" It worries me that she's suddenly changing our plans. It's not like her. None of this is like her.

"Amy, I'm starting to get really afraid for you," I confess. I have to say it. I know with all of my heart that her safety is at stake and I can't be so concerned about offending her that I put her at risk by keeping my mouth shut. "I'm here for you, you know," I say. "I'll do anything to help. Anything at all." It takes every ounce of my willpower not to start pleading with her.

Amy nods and smiles, a little too easily. Now that I know what's going on, I feel like I can infer so much more from her every move. Every smile is a sign that something is off. Every emphatic Amy-ism is just a clue that she's covering up. "I know you're here for me, Waverly," she says, in a way that's a little too lighthearted for me to feel good about.

"Anything you need," I say again. "Anything at all."

On my way to work I call Kate and tell her everything. I talk for fifteen minutes straight, with hardly an interruption from Kate save for the occasional gasp, which is evidence in and of itself that this is not just ordinary gossip, and somehow makes me feel better about spilling Amy's secret. It's obvious now that I'm not going to be able to help Amy on my own. I need her help.

"I don't quite know what to say," Kate says when I'm done. "You know that I've never been fond of Mike, but I never figured him for something like this. She really doesn't want to leave him?"

I rub at the crease that's appeared in the space between my eyebrows. "Kate, I think you should talk to her." I've pulled into the small gravel lot behind the bakery and turned off the car. Donovan is smoking outside the open back door. He sees me and flicks his

cigarette onto the ground, then rubs it out with his foot before piv-
oting to head back inside.

"You want *me* to talk to her?" Kate says. "What could I possibly
say to her? We've known each other for a long time but, Waverly,
come on. We don't really talk to each other anymore. Not like
that." She pauses for a beat. "We have nothing in common."

"I know you're not close but, Kate, come on. It's not like she's a
stranger. You have more in common than you might think."

"Oh, what?" Kate deadpans. "Because both of our marriages have
turned out to be disasters?" I hold the phone away from my ear.

"Kate, come on."

"What? Seriously, Wave. Why me?"

"Well, she didn't say as much, but she seems to think you have
it all figured out."

Kate laughs.

"She admires you, Kate."

"So because I've left Brendan you think I can talk her into doing
the same."

"Well, yes," I say, fiddling with a loose thread on the sleeve of
my coat. "Come on, Kate. We need to get her out of there."

"Why don't you call her family? She's so close to them. I'm surprised she hasn't talked to them about this."

"I thought about it, actually, but I think she'd just freak and
never talk to me again. And I don't want to scare her parents. I
wouldn't feel right telling them everything I just told you."

"Waverly, Jesus. How do you talk me into this shit?"

"Talk you into—? When have I ever talked you into anything?
When has *anyone* ever talked you into anything?" As soon as it's out
of my mouth and I hear the silence on the other end of the line, I
know what we're both thinking: Brendan talked her into plenty.

Kate sighs. "I'll think about it."

"Promise?"

"Jesus, Waverly."

"Okay, okay."

I rap my fingers against the steering wheel and check the time. I need to get into work. On the other end of the phone, I can hear water running, then the click-clack of Kate's heels across her hardwood floors.

"It is pretty shocking," Kate says, her voice softer. "I always thought they were just simple, you know, family people."

"Me, too," I say. "And I'm sure that Amy believed that most of all."

CHAPTER TWENTY-TWO

When lunch is over, I force myself into solitary confinement in my office and spend the next few hours counting money. My visit with Amy today has made me so edgy that I am actually, for once, looking forward to sitting down at my desk and getting lost in my work. Plus, I've deleted a record-breaking six voicemails from Gary in the past week, imploring me to pay my loan, along with two from my bank reminding me that payment's past due.

Once I get going, I discover, unbelievably, that the "incredible, superedible doughnut muffins," as Jeannette and Randy have started to call them, have brought my sales up a full thirty percent. *Thirty* percent. Because of muffins. For the past God-knows-how-long, I've been scheming to come up with innovative ways to make more money: the dinner delivery service, selling new products, the potential cookbook. Who could have predicted that the thing that would pull me out of this mess would be the muffins I've been selling since opening day?

I check my math five or six more times; never a bad idea, considering that numbers and I don't really get along. I can't believe what I'm seeing on my spreadsheets: If business continues like this for just a couple of weeks longer, I might actually be able to get my house loan back on track, pay the rent, and continue to pay my employees and all of my business costs. I still won't be able to pay myself—I have a feeling it's going to be a long while before I see a salary again, and I know I'll have to stick to a serious budget—but I just might be able to do this. The foreclosure risk would disappear. Alec would stop needling me about late rent checks. I tap out an excited drumbeat on my desk with my hands and look around my little closet of an office. I'm tempted to run out to the kitchen and tell Randy. I want to tell *someone*.

Larry's the person I should be telling. I get the teensiest, pinching pang of guilt: If I'd been honest with him about all of this, I could call him right now. But actually, the thought occurs to me, I can tell him everything now *and* explain how I fixed it, so it may in fact be a good thing that I've been so secretive…couldn't it? It's no sense getting caught up in my overanalysis, I reason. Not now, when for the first time in months, I actually have reason to be optimistic about my business. I wiggle my fingers and type off an email to the only person besides me who will appreciate my good news: Gary. Reading it over before I press "send," I feel amazing, like I've just balanced the federal budget. I giggle to myself, shaking my head. *Doughnut muffins.* The whole thing is ludicrous—and *wonderful.*

When I emerge from my office, Jeannette tells me that an event planner stopped in to order five dozen doughnut muffins for gift boxes for a wedding in Maryland next month. I walk to the front of the store, where Randy is chatting with a first-time customer who's happily scarfing a mini-cheesecake. I start to talk with them but then three hairdressers from the salon down the block stop in for doughnut muffins, and then a UPS guy comes in looking for one, and then an Alan Alda look-alike with his grandson. Around four o'clock, Randy and Jeannette and I talk over the to-dos for the following day and I decide to treat myself and take the rest of the afternoon off. In fact, I think I'll go home and surprise Larry with a nice dinner. I can't afford to buy the things I'd like to cook right now (short ribs…or, *oooh*, scallops), but I'm confident that I can make a damn fine meal out of the random scraps in my kitchen.

Right now, I'm confident about *everything*. I snag a bakery box of half a dozen doughnut muffins before I leave and practically sing good-bye to Randy as I walk out the door. Every business has its highs and lows, right? This was just a lesson I needed to learn.

Risotto is what I've come up with an hour later. Larry's always loved my risotto. It feels good to be outside of my own head, to be doing something for him for a change. I'm sautéing the spinach and mushrooms I had in the fridge and will add a can of white beans seasoned with a slab or three of bacon along with some rosemary from the plant I have out back. This will actually be quite nice. I grab my kitchen shears to head out for the rosemary when my phone rings. I pull it out of my back pocket, expecting to see the phone number for the bakery on the caller ID, but it's Amy.

"Hey, Ame," I say, cradling the phone on my shoulder as I open the back door.

"You're at home?" she says, sounding a little frantic.

"Yeah, I'm here. Is everything okay?"

"I'd gone to the bakery. I thought you'd be at work. Can I come over? I'm sort of just around the corner."

"Yes, of course," I say, suddenly feeling chilled. Something's wrong. I close the back door and walk back to the kitchen.

"I'll be right there," she says.

I click off the phone and clutch it to my chest. *What could this be about?* I rush to turn down the heat on the stove and hurry to the front of the house, where I watch from a window for Amy's minivan. But before I know it, I see her coming up the street, walking, with Emma in her arms. *Why is she walking? Where is her car?*

I open the door. "Everything okay?" I say, veiling my panic because of sweet Em.

Amy nods. There are tears in her eyes. "I parked down the street. I'm sorry to drop in on you like this."

"Amy, don't be sorry," I say. And then I notice that she's also carrying her giant monogrammed duffel bag—the one she carried on the plane to Florida—and it's packed full.

"Um," she says, noticing me looking at the bag as she gently sets Emma down. "Can we stay here tonight?"

"Of course," I say. "Of course!" *Is it wrong to be excited about this?* I pull her into a hug. "You can stay for as long as you need to," I whisper into her ear.

We take Emma into the living room and turn on Nickelodeon, and then we walk to the kitchen, where we can see her through the archway separating the rooms but talk privately.

"What happened?"

Amy sits down by the island and puts her head in her hands. Seconds later, her shoulders are shaking, and I realize that she's sobbing.

"Oh, Amy, it's okay," I say, wrapping my arms around her. "Everything is going to be just fine," I say.

"I just—ughhhh," she says, looking up at the ceiling and shaking her hands to get ahold of herself, as if she could shake the anxiety right out of her fingertips. "I'm so tired, Waverly. I'm so, so tired of all of this."

"I can't imagine," I say. "You're so strong, Amy. Just think of everything you've been through, and what you've survived."

She nods, nibbling her bottom lip. She looks almost childlike, sitting there hunched into herself.

"You don't deserve to be treated this way. No one deserves to be treated this way," I say. "What happened?"

"I just...when he told me that he didn't need the counseling...I kept thinking about it after you left and I just..." She shakes her head again.

"You don't have to explain it to me," I say. "I'm just glad you're here."

"He's going to know I'm here," she says.

I nod. "We can handle it. Larry will be home before long."

"Maybe he can move my car. I parked down the street, but maybe he could put it somewhere less detectable. I don't know why that seems like the right thing to do, but it just does."

"You don't have to explain anything to me."

"He'll probably come by here."

"What do you want us to do? Should we just not answer?"

"Maybe Larry should answer," she says. "He might be less angry if someone actually talks to him."

I nod. I don't have to question whether Larry can handle Mike. I don't even have to ask him whether he's willing to do it. I can rely on him for anything. How do I keep missing that?

Around six o'clock, we brace for Mike to start calling since he should be getting home from work at any moment. Larry's out moving the car and Amy and I are sitting around the coffee table with Emma, coloring with her and talking in code. Amy says she's been reading tons about "the issue." "It's been comforting to be able to look at it sort of objectively, almost like I was back in school, even though I'm sure it was a defense mechanism to approach it in such a clinical way. Whenever Emma naps, I'd 'study,'" she says.

"I don't know. I guess I just firmly believe that everyone deserves a second chance," she tells me, helping Emma color a picture of a bunny in her coloring book. She puts down her crayon and begins to pick at the chipping polish on her thumbnail.

I have to think hard about how to respond. "Amy, you deserve to be loved in the way that you love the people in your life. You're the most generous, kindhearted person I know. You can have more than this."

She just stares at me for a moment. It's hard to tell whether she agrees with me. "I'd bought him a stack of books on Amazon," she says. "The titles alone were hard to take—things like *Violent*

No More. I was so proud of him when he started reading them. A few Saturdays ago, I was out sweeping the front stoop and he came down from his office. I thought he'd been catching up on bills. He had one of the books in his hands and he had this excited look on his face that I haven't seen in years. 'You wouldn't believe all the stories in here from guys who sound just like me,' he said. He felt like he could've written the stories himself, and he said it gave him hope that he really could change. He was so optimistic, and he was working so hard, reading for a couple of hours every night before bed and even marking passages with a highlighter like he was studying for the MCAT again."

She stops and looks at Emma, who's happily singing to herself: "I'm bringing home my baby bumblebee. Won't my mommy be so proud of me?" Amy joins in for a few verses and Emma's face lights up.

"But then about a week ago, I noticed that he'd dropped everything," she says. I'm amazed at how she can shift her attention from me to Emma and then back to me so quickly, but then I realize that this is probably how she's survived the past three years. "He just stopped reading the books as if all of the time he'd spent had been nothing but a short-lived hobby he could easily abandon," she says. "Every night, I keep lying in bed, waiting to hear the sound of him lifting one of the books off of the table, but they just sit on the nightstand untouched. Instead, he flips through his *Sports Illustrated* or one of his medical journals. When I finally asked him about it a few nights ago, he told me he was just taking a break—he needed some time to let everything he's been learning sink in. 'This is intense stuff, Amy,' he'd said." She raises her eyebrows, resigned. "As if I wouldn't know."

I reach out and squeeze her wrist. I'm holding back tears. I can barely look at her.

"I don't know. Maybe I'm the one who should see someone," she says. "I thought about making myself an appointment earlier

today. He'd never have to know. I have a secret stash of cash in a
tampon box under my vanity. There's nearly nine hundred dollars.
I've skimmed it off of the grocery budget, collected whatever I've
found crumpled in a pocket while I did laundry."

Hearing this makes me so happy—she has actually thought
about getting away.

"I'm hungry, Mommy," Emma says.

"Oh, I'll get something for you, honey," I say, feeling my spine
crack as I pull myself up from my spot on the floor. "What would
you like? A banana? Some crackers? Dinner is almost ready."

As I'm walking to the kitchen, I hear Amy's phone ring. When
I turn to look at her, she nods at me. She holds the phone for a
minute—she's deciding whether to answer it, I can tell—and then
she presses a button to make the ring go silent and puts the phone
down on the couch behind her. "Emma," she says, running her
hand over her little girl's hair. "Emma, baby. Come give Mommy a
hug."

About an hour later, Amy's putting Emma to sleep upstairs. Larry
and I are sitting on the couch, where we're ostensibly watching the
college basketball game on the television, but I couldn't tell you
who's playing, much less what the score is. My head is spinning,
thinking about all of the scenarios that could play out tonight.
What if Mike goes absolutely nuts? What if he has a weapon? Amy's
phone keeps vibrating on the table in the corner. I asked her thirty
minutes (and countless calls) ago if she might just want to turn it
off, but she shook her head no. "I need to keep it on," she said, in a
way that didn't leave room for negotiating. Each time it stops ringing, she waits a few seconds, picks it up, checks the voicemail, and
puts it back down. When I ask if she's okay, she just nods.

∞

Finally, as we knew it would eventually, the doorbell rings. Larry looks at me, squeezes my knee, and gets up from the couch to get the door.

"Larry, do you really think we should answer?" I'd like to call the cops, if Amy would let me. She doesn't want to call the police until she thinks it through. I can't imagine that she hasn't *already* spent hours turning over her options, but I'm not about to debate her on this point. She's here.

"I'll just crack the door," he says.

From my spot on the couch, I have a perfect view of the foyer but I can't see the front door, which suits me fine. I'll get all that I need to see just watching Larry's side of the conversation, and I don't trust what I might do if I get face to face with Mike. Larry clears his throat as he unlatches the bolt. He keeps the chain lock in place.

"Where is she?" I hear.

"Hey, Mike," Larry says.

"Where's Amy?" he barks.

"Mike, listen," Larry says, his voice steady. "We're going to figure out a way to work this out, but you just can't see her right now, man. She needs some time." I know that he hates Mike with every drop of blood in his body and would probably love nothing more than to punch him right now, but he's as calm as if he were mediating an argument with his grandmother. His basic goodness fills me with simultaneous pride and shame that I've been the way that I've been with him.

"Hey, *man*," Mike says, mocking Larry. "I need to talk to my wife right this minute. Let me come in!"

"You don't need to do that right now," Larry says, gentle and firm. He shifts closer to the door—he's blocking Mike's view into the house.

"I don't think you understand—," Mike says. And just then, Amy comes down the stairs. She quickly glances at me and then walks to the door, putting her hand on Larry's back. "It's okay," she says.

I jump up. *No, it's not,* I think.

"Amy! Amy!" Mike yells when he hears her voice. I walk to the threshold between the living room and the foyer. I can feel my anxiety rising like a rash spreading over my skin.

"Amy, I can handle this for you," Larry says. "You don't have to talk to him."

"It's okay," she says. "I can do this."

Larry reluctantly steps aside. He comes to me and puts his arm around my shoulders. I grip his hand in mine. I wonder if Mike knows that I'm standing here. I can't bear to look at him. His voice changes the moment Amy appears in the doorway. "Ame, what are you doing?" he says sweetly, as if she's a child he's just caught playing in the flour bin.

"Mike," she ekes out. "I'm just—I'm really, really disappointed." She's crying now.

"Disappointed? How did I disappoint you?"

I dig my fingernails into Larry's hand and he hugs me tighter. *That bastard.* Listening to them, I realize that the dysfunction in their relationship goes far deeper than I imagined.

"We had an agreement about the counseling, Mike," she says, curling the fingers of one hand around the molding on the doorjamb.

"That's what this is about?" He laughs. "Oh, Amy, come on," he says.

"Mike, I need an explanation," she says, gathering herself. "It's hard for me to believe that you're committed to this if you're not going to get help."

From the way that he groans, I can tell that he's not taking her seriously. I grip Larry's arm—it's the only thing that's keeping me from flying to the door—and then I hear what he says next: "Listen, I know this sounds ridiculous, but when it comes right down to it, I'm a guy." He laughs. (He *laughs*!) "It's hard enough for me to talk about my problems, and if I'm going to talk to anyone about them, it's going to be to you."

"Larry, we have to stop this," I say, my voice shaking.

Amy is crying again. She almost looks like she's buying this.

"Amy, I promise you that I'm as committed as ever, but I want *you* to help me, not some stranger. You have the same credentials as these people. I remember when you were working, how good you were with those kids. Who could help me better than you?"

"But, Mike, you need to see someone who really knows this stuff," she says, her voice small. "Doctors who specialize in…it. You need counselors whose reference books aren't a stack of textbooks from the midnineties."

Or perhaps a counselor who isn't the direct recipient of your abuse, I think, my head now on Larry's chest. The even beat-beat of his heart is a sound as steady as a metronome. I hug him tighter, his shirt balled in my fists.

"Amy, I need you," he says. "You're my wife. The love of my life. The mother of our sweet, sweet girl. I know that we can get through this. Can't we? Can't we work through this together?"

I can taste the bile in the back of my throat. I can see now how he's playing her. Worse, I can see that she's under his spell.

"I need some time, Mike," she says.

He gasps. "Time for what?"

"I just need a little bit of time to think," she says.

"Do you love me, Amy? Do you really love me the way that a wife is supposed to love a husband?"

"Of course I do," she says. She's appeasing him now. "Of course, Mike. Of course."

I let go of Larry and step forward a bit. Her eyes dart toward me and then back to Mike.

"Just give me a little bit of time, okay?" she says, wiping her nose with the edge of her sleeve.

"But Amy—"

"Just a little bit of time," she says again, stepping back. She's starting to shake. Her voice is cracking.

"Amy, come on—" He's angrier now. I look over at Larry. He walks to the door and Amy, thank goodness, looks relieved to have his help.

"Mike, we're going to go now," Larry says, wedging himself between the two of them. "Why don't you take a little time to cool down now, okay?

"Larry, this is between—!"

"Mike, it's okay," Amy pleads, crying again. Larry is closing the door. I rush to Amy's side, and she collapses into me.

Early the next morning, Amy and I sit out back, sipping coffee on the stoop that leads down to my courtyard. Neither of us slept all night; I'm sure of it. I didn't even bother to go upstairs, opting instead to lie on the sofa under a quilt that Babci had made for me before I went off to college. I felt like I needed to stand vigil. And I'll admit that my worry had also bubbled over into actual fear. I dead-bolted the doors and turned on the alarm system for the first time in years. I wasn't putting anything past Mike. He'd continued to call Amy all evening until she finally, mercifully, decided to turn off her phone sometime around midnight.

At some point I did finally doze off, but the sleep was hardly restful—I had a horrendous nightmare. Amy and Mike were in their living room, watching *Jeopardy*. The dream started out just tepid and ordinary—Alex Trebek saying, "In August 2005 this 'Siberian Siren' became the first Russian ranked number one in women's tennis," and Amy responding, "Who is Maria Sharapova?" But it quickly turned ugly, even grotesque, to the point that now, sitting next to Amy and watching her drink from my mother's chipped NPR coffee mug, I can't help but see what my subconscious put her through. In the dream, she asked Mike if he wanted to play, because back when they were dating, they often cuddled on the couch in Amy's apartment and halfheartedly called out the answers while they zoned out at the end of the day. Mike responded by throwing the remote control down on the table, sending it skidding off of the side onto the floor.

And then it began: She started to plead that she missed him, and he responded by berating her—she was fucking stupid, an imbecile, a sad excuse for a woman.

Her head suddenly jerked backward, forced by his fist at the nape of her neck, a handful of her hair in his hand.

"Stand up," he said. His voice was even, like he was giving commands to the family dog.

It was as if I was her, feeling every merciless blow. She concentrated on sounds. If she listened to the sounds, it would help drown out the pain. The leather on her skin. Contestants buzzing in with their answers. *That's correct!*

Her leg.

Her back.

I woke up convulsing with sobs and worried that I'd woken the whole house and would have to explain the reason for it.

"Baby, don't pick any of those, okay? Just look at them," Amy calls to Emma.

Emma is sitting on the brick patio in sparkly purple children's sunglasses, running her fingers over the petals of the white pansies that I planted last fall. It's cool, and the brick is damp beneath my bare feet, but the air is bright and crisp and holds the promise of spring. It's going to be a pretty day.

Amy must be thinking the same thing because after she takes a sip from her coffee cup, she says that this time of year always makes her homesick. "In North Carolina, spring comes early and stays late," she says, holding the mug with both hands. "Here, there isn't the same assault of azalea blooms on every corner, daffodils and tulips suddenly poking up like fireworks around everyone's mailboxes," she says longingly. "I love that time in spring when every time you go outside in the late afternoon, you can smell someone firing up their grill."

I can tell that the thought gives her comfort, and her musing makes me think of my dad. On weekends during the summer between middle school and high school, when I should have been at sleepovers, prank-calling boys and playing "light as a feather, stiff as a board," Dad taught me how to grill on the old Weber in our backyard. Mom may have been the main cook in the family, but when the weather turned warm, there were few things my dad loved more than a barbecue. We grilled ribs and shrimp skewers, barbecued chicken and burgers. Mom would sit off to the side in one of our mesh lounge chairs, sipping a wine spritzer from a Solo cup while she pretended to read a magazine but mostly chided my dad whenever I got too close to the fire.

"A few weeks ago, we decided that we're not going home to my parents' house for Easter," Amy says. "It will be the first time I've ever missed it. Mike complained that he was just too exhausted from work to make the trip for a short weekend. You should have heard the disappointment in my mother's voice when I told her— and then, of course, as soon as I hung up the phone, she called my sisters, because Celia and Claire both called within twenty minutes. Mom said she'd made Emma a new Easter dress, with little cotton-tailed bunnies smocked along the neckline. My sisters were planning an Easter egg hunt for the kids. But Mike didn't want to go."

She drums her fingers along her coffee cup. I hear the beep of my next-door neighbor's car lock and see her race down her back stairs to her Volvo in the driveway behind her house. "I guess I might go now," she says. "I'd convinced myself that it was no big deal to miss it and that I needed to make some memories in my own home. I thought that if Mom and Dad knew we were having trouble, they'd tell me that that's what I needed to do. Stay home and focus on my own family."

I'd met Amy's parents enough times over the years to know that they were the type of couple you might see featured in one of those magazine stories about what makes marriage last, the two of them posed with their arms around each other's baby-boomer-sized waists. Her parents were sweetly, uncommonly romantic; the kind of Hallmark card couple that it was hard to fathom could exist in the twenty-first century. Amy told me once that they still hold hands in the car and raise their glasses to toast each other when they go out to dinner. They set a high standard. Thinking about it, I realize that this might be part of why Amy's kept her abuse a secret for so long.

"Ame, when are you going to call your mom and tell her what's going on?" I ask.

She sighs in a way that confirms my new theory. "You know, I've thought all along that I could handle this on my own if I just made my family my priority. I thought that bearing this one secret was the right thing to do, because it would all resolve itself soon enough. It would be just a little blip in our history, a hiccup. I know that sounds crazy."

Yes, it absolutely does, but nothing surprises me anymore—that's what I want to tell her.

"You know, my biggest nightmare, next to something happening to Emma, is failing at marriage," Amy says. "Lately, things haven't been so bad that I worried that Mike would fall into his old habits, but I have found it harder and harder to convince myself that things are as they should be. We eat dinner in near silence, talking to Emma instead of to each other. It made me think of when I was in middle school, and my girlfriends and I would make crib notes of conversation topics before we called the boys we liked. I've felt—for

years, really—that I need a cheat sheet to figure out how to talk to
my own husband. The other night at dinner, when Emma stopped
eating, she looked up at us and said, 'All finished!' My first thought
was, 'Yup, you said it.'"

"But Amy, this isn't about failing at marriage. This is about
telling the people who love you. The people who really and truly
have your best interests at heart and can help you get out of this."

"I know, I know," she says. "It's just hard. My dad..." Her voice
trails off.

"I can only imagine." I think of my own father, who was fortu-
nate to have such a late bloomer for a daughter that he never had
to deal with boyfriends, but it still didn't stop him from making
thinly veiled comments about how traumatic it would be when the
time came.

"The thing that's hard to explain is how much I still love
him...how sentimental I can still get," she says. "His doctor's-
office-antiseptic scent...I've always joked that it's like wooden
tongue depressors and cotton. And he's addicted to Altoids. I can't
have one without thinking of him." I think of Larry, who's as familiar to me as my own reflection in the mirror. Despite all of my
anxiety over where we're headed, he's still everything I know about
home. I can't imagine what Amy must feel.

"It was right after Florida when he had a sort of breakdown and
apologized for everything," she says, lowering her voice as Emma
skips toward us and asks for the sippy cup on the steps by Amy's
feet. "I was doing dishes, and he'd just come home from a run,
and I heard him making these sniffling, grunting sounds behind
me. I thought he was just making the usual annoying phlegmy gurgling sounds that he always makes when he stretches after a run,
but when I looked over my shoulder at him, he was sitting on the
floor against the refrigerator with his head between his knees, crying. I've only seen him cry once—ever. It was the night after he
lost his first patient, a twelve-year-old boy who'd been hit by a car

while he was riding his bike. He hadn't cried at our wedding. He hadn't even cried when Emma was born. He just started saying he was sorry, over and over again. He said he'd never meant to hurt me. It was the first time he'd ever shown remorse for any of it.

"I'd spent so much time wondering if this apology would ever actually happen. I thought about it while I flipped through coupons at the grocery store, while I squirted baby shampoo into my hand during Emma's baths, while I sat between you and Kate in restaurants. Now that it was happening, I was stunned silent. Even more than the revenge fantasy, what I'd always wanted was for everything to just magically fade away. I prayed for amnesia. The thing is, my husband's not a villain, but a broken man who is very, very sick. He has an illness, and I'm the person who vowed, 'in sickness and in health.'

"We sat in silence for a long time, Mike crying, me studying him. Later that night, when we talked everything out, there were a hundred things that I wanted to ask him: What makes you do it? Why do you do it? How do you feel when you're doing it? Are you really sorry? Why are you sorry now? But it was impossible to tell how he'd react, and I worried that if I asked the wrong thing, it would be over. Anyway, that was the night that he decided to go to counseling." She pauses for a moment. "It's embarrassing to admit this stuff to you. Larry's so great. You must be horrified by all of this. Your relationship is perfect."

"Not exactly," I say. It takes me a moment to decide whether to go further—is it completely inappropriate to complain about my problems to Amy or would it make her feel better to talk about something other than her ordeal? Hearing her describe the details of what she's been through brings it into full relief. It's tragic. There's no other word for it.

"What do you mean?" She looks at me over her coffee mug.

"I don't want to burden you with my junk," I say. "Not right now."

"No, please, tell me." She laughs. "Make me feel a little better about myself."

I study her for a minute, just to be sure. "Okay," I say, taking a deep breath. "I've had some real problems with the bakery." I look over my shoulder toward the back door. Larry's inside getting ready for work.

"You have?" she says, surprised.

"Yeah. Money problems," I say.

"How bad?"

I take a gulp. "A lot of debt. I stopped taking a salary around the time we went to Florida. My rent on the building is consistently late. And until yesterday, I thought I was going to default on my home loan, which means I would have risked losing the house." I've wondered several times over the past few months whether coming clean would feel like a relief, but it unfortunately doesn't. Telling the truth hurts.

"Oh my God, Waverly. I had no idea. Here I am, eating up all of your time with my problems, and you're dealing with plenty on your own!"

"Please, don't you dare apologize!" I interrupt.

"Larry must at least be a huge support."

"He probably would be, if I told him."

"Larry doesn't know?" she says. "Why haven't you told him, Waverly?"

I take a deep breath. Why? *Why, why, why?* "I thought I could handle it on my own. I still think I can, actually."

"Sounds familiar," Amy says. She looks at me and laughs. It's a "what the hell is wrong with us?" laugh. *What the hell is wrong with us?*

I smile back at her. "At this point, I've kept it secret for so long that I feel like it's such a deception, like I've dug such a deep hole that there's just no good way to tell him. I don't know how he'll react when he finds out how dishonest I've been. I'm scared I'll lose him."

"But, Waverly, if your house was at risk…He could help. He should really know. And you'd feel so much better."

"I know, I know." I watch Emma hopscotch across the patio.

"Don't be so hard on yourself," she says. "You're so independent, and I admire you for it, but you never take anyone's help. You can't go through the world alone, Waverly. You know that, right?"

"Why are we talking about me? Are you going to charge me at the end of the hour?" I joke, aware that I'm also deflecting her question.

"Seriously, Waverly. You need to talk to him. Larry will be understanding."

"That's the problem!" I whine. "Why can't I see that? I mean, I *know* that. I think. But I feel like I invent problems in our relationship, almost like I'm trying to sabotage it."

"Maybe you are," she says.

"But why would I do that?"

She shrugs. "Maybe you don't feel worthy of his love or something?"

I raise an eyebrow, considering it. I suppose I do take some sort of comfort in the identity I've created for myself—like if Kate's the beautiful one and Amy's the sweet one and I'm the sad, orphaned fuck-up, I can keep my expectations low and shirk off any real, adult responsibility. *Good move, Waverly,* I think. Look at where that's led you…

I put my hand over Amy's and squeeze it. "Well, things have actually picked up a little bit, so I can tell him soon, once I know for sure that the house is okay," I say. I fill her in on Brendan's unintended influence on my business.

"I'm so glad that things are turning around," she says. I know that she's legitimately happy for me—Amy always is—but I can tell from the distracted way she looks at me when she says it that she's wondering about her own fate.

Despite everything, I'm sure she still wants the perfect family life she'd been building with Mike. I can see it as clearly as if the symbols appear in a cartoon thought bubble over her head: an old-fashioned pram with another baby gurgling happily inside, family nights with board games and popcorn, photo albums packed with years upon years of memories. But just look at the amount of dysfunction she's willing to put up with to keep the dream intact. It's like she's held on to a certain identity for so long that it doesn't even occur to her to want something else. And then it hits me: *Is that what I've done, too?*

Emma gets up from her froggy crouch and toddles toward us. Amy licks her thumb and rubs a smudge off of her cheek. "Come here, Emma," I say, hooking my hands under her armpits and pulling her onto my lap. Her hair and hands are sticky from the doughnut muffin she ate this morning.

"I'll make a deal with you," I say to Amy, squinting at her. The sun is gloriously bright all of a sudden. "Promise me that you'll talk to your mother—or at least to one of your sisters—and I'll come clean with Larry."

She wrinkles her nose, considering my proposition. "I'll promise you this," she says, holding her hand to her brow to shade her eyes when she turns to look at me. "I'll think about it."

CHAPTER TWENTY-THREE

Later that afternoon, as I'm walking up Kate's front walk and admiring the flowers that her gardener must have put in since I was here the other day, I leave a message for Amy to find out how she's doing, though what I really want to know is whether she's called her mother yet. When I talked to her an hour ago, she said that she and Emma might go to Old Town to walk around for a while. I worried about leaving her at the house alone, but she insisted that she would be fine and that she had no intention of opening the door. Larry offered to stay home, too, but she wouldn't have it. So when I got in the car to head to the bakery, I sent a quick text to my neighbor across the street. She's a freelance magazine writer whose desk is positioned right under her front window, where she keeps tabs on all of the action in the neighborhood, because she's always posting persnickety messages on the neighborhood Listserv about who's not cleaning up after their dog and who's left their outside lights on all day. I asked her to send me a message if she saw anything weird in front of my house. I doubt she's taken her eyes off my door all morning.

When I drove up Kate's long driveway, there were a couple of black SUVs parked by the house, and when I reach the front door, it's wide open. I step inside and walk back toward the kitchen, calling Kate's name. As I pass Brendan's office, I notice a couple of twentysomething guys loading files into cardboard boxes. They're debating health care. Typical Washington nerds.

Kate's standing in the threshold of the French doors that lead from her kitchen to her back patio. On the kitchen table next to her is what must be the remnants of her lunch: half a wedge of Brie, a handful of crackers, an almost empty jar of olives.

"Hey," she says when she sees me. She's wearing a men's oxford shirt with the sleeves rolled up and a pair of jeans. Her hair's knotted back and she doesn't have on any makeup. She's breathtaking. Even after all of these years, it can still sneak up on me.

"How's Amy doing?" she asks. I'd filled her in earlier this morning.

"Fine," I say, grabbing the jar of olives. "I called to check on her on my way over and she said everything was cool. No sign of Mike, which is great. Can I have one of these?" I hold up the jar.

"At your own risk. They're of questionable age," she says. "I was starving when I realized I had no food in the house, so this is what I went with."

I poke my finger into the jar to fish out an olive. "So, those guys," I say, nodding back toward the hallway.

"Brendan's staffers. They're packing up the rest of his office. They got everything else out yesterday." She's not her usual firecracker self, I notice. She turns back toward the open doors, her arms crossed over her chest like she's cold.

"I was just standing here trying to remember why Brendan and I bought this house," she says wistfully.

I walk over and stand next to her, gazing out at the backyard. The pool is on the right, and behind it, a softly sloping hill of lush green grass leads to a gazebo that will be covered in blooming wisteria within the next few weeks. I remember Kate asking me what the plant was last spring, and when I teased her for not knowing the names of the things growing in her own backyard, she rolled her eyes and said something about how she just writes a check and leaves the rest to the gardener. At the time, I was spiraling into my money issues, and I remember thinking—only half bitterly—that Kate should fire her gardener and hire me.

"Do you know that in the two years that we've lived in this house, we've *never* been in the pool?" she says now. "We never once had a party here. Never once had breakfast or read the paper under the gazebo." She shakes her head. "The backyard is just another facade, totally meaningless. I've basically lived here by myself—Brendan's always been working...or doing who knows what else," she adds under her breath. "Six thousand square feet for one person. A house like this was meant for crowds of people, maybe children even." She glances at me. "Noise. Life." She shakes her head.

I look at her, perplexed. She's been so steely since Brendan's affair went public, and I wonder what's made her so suddenly contemplative.

Her phone rings and she walks to the kitchen counter to grab it. "Ugh." She rolls her eyes after she looks at the caller ID. "My mother. She won't stop calling. 'I'm imploring you to reconsider,'" she says, mimicking Evelyn's snooty-snoot way of speaking. "'You're making a mockery of yourself, Katherine. What will you do now?'" She slides the still-ringing phone across the counter.

"I'm thinking about a safari. Botswana," she says. "I haven't been since I was a teenager, but there are these amazing guides you can hire to take you to all of the best reserves. Want to join me?" She raises her eyebrows.

Huh? Before I can answer—*no, Kate, I can't fly off to Africa on a whim*—one of Brendan's staffers comes into the kitchen. "Excuse me. Mrs. Berkshire? We're just about done," he says somberly, cowering a little. I know that campaign underlings are made to do all sorts of demeaning work beyond the usual coffee fetching, but this must be horribly awkward.

"Fine," she says, hardly glancing at him, and then she turns back to me, leaving him standing there, unsure what to do. "What was I saying?" she says to me.

African safari, I think. "I can't remember," I say, noticing the staffer scuttle away out of the corner of my eye. I don't want to get into a conversation about why I can't go on a luxury vacation right now.

"Thank God they're leaving," she says once he's left the room. "They've been stomping around here for two days as if they were a hazmat team who'd come to clean up a chemical spill." We hear the front door close. "I want to make sure they got everything. Come on." I follow her down the dark, cavernous hall. She's barefooted, so the only sound as we walk is the squeak-squeak of my sneakers. I never realized how empty this place could feel. How lonesome.

Brendan's office smells faintly of his occasional cigars. Of all the rooms in Kate's house, this is the only one I've never been in before. The walls are oak paneled. The carpet is golf-club green. I feel uptight just standing here. Kate immediately walks to the far wall, where a portrait hangs of her and Brendan. I recognize it as their official campaign portrait. They're on their side porch, standing behind the railing where an American flag had been hung. Her hands are clasped at her waist. His right palm is on her shoulder. They look trustworthy, openhearted. You'd love for them to be your next-door neighbors. She hoists it off the wall and puts it on the floor behind Brendan's desk, positioning it so that the photo's turned inward. "Enough of that," she says. She goes about opening and closing the empty drawers, the file cabinets. "Looks like they got everything," she says. She looks at me and nods efficiently. "Okay," she says. We stand there staring at each other.

"Are you okay?" I say, looking at her suspiciously.

She nods unconvincingly. "It's just…" She shrugs.

"It's all happened kind of fast," I say.

"Yeah," she says. "Yeah, it has." She sits down on the green carpet and crosses her legs. I follow suit.

"Brendan's called me six times today," she says. "I'm keeping count. It's like I'm going through a high school breakup." I think back to Kate's high school breakups. Her romances were not of the *Sweet Valley High* variety—instead of football game pep rallies and prom night wine coolers, Kate's dates took her to the Inn at Little Washington and wooed her with gin martinis.

"What does he say when he calls?"

"I refuse to talk to him and he won't leave messages. I don't want to hear his voice. I don't want to see him. When we signed the separation papers at the lawyer's office yesterday—he insisted we do it in person, together, which was ridiculous—he just kept saying over and over again that he wished we could work it out."

"Do you wish you could work it out?"

"No. I don't know. I don't know what the hell I want." It's probably the first time this statement has ever come out of Kate's mouth, and it's unsettling to hear. Judging from the troubled look on her face, she feels the same way.

"Well, welcome to the club. I don't think I've ever known," I say, trying to make her feel better. *What do I want?* It could be the tagline for my life. The words tick at me all day long, like somebody flicking a finger against the side of my head: *What do I want? What do I want?*

She smirks at me. "Please."

"Do you miss him?"

She thinks about it for a minute. "I've missed him for a long time. I realized that yesterday, sitting in that conference room. I studied his face while he was signing the papers, and it was as if he was some strange sort of mirage, a figment of my imagination. I looked at him and thought, 'Who *is* this person?' But then I come back here and the silence is so horrible. It's so bad that I almost pine for the sound of the reporters outside. I think I'm going to put my house on the market."

"Where would you go?"

She shrugs. "I liked living in Georgetown when we were first married."

Who wouldn't have? I think. They lived in Brendan's four-thousand-square-foot show palace near the French embassy. The *Washingtonian* ran a feature about it.

"Or there's always my parents' apartment at the Ritz." She sighs, as if it's a fate worse than living in a trailer park.

Thankfully, before I'm able to examine the predicament of Kate's having several homes to choose from while I can barely hang on to my one, my phone rings. *Maybe Amy,* I think. I pull it out of my front pocket. "It's the bakery," I say. "Give me a sec."

"Hey-eyyyy!" Randy says excitedly. "Do you have a second?"

"Yeah, yeah," I say. "I'm headed back over there in a minute."

"Are you sitting down?" he says. I can actually feel him smiling.

"On the floor actually," I say, running my hand along the carpet. "What is it?"

"We got a visit this morning from a reporter."

"Oh, Jesus." *Is this Brendan thing ever going to die?*

"No, no, no. Not like that. Well, sort of not like that," Randy says.

"Okay. Tell me."

"The reporter was from the *New York Times*. They want to do a story, Waverly. Well, they *are* doing a story—about the bakery. Well, it's actually kind of about Brendan. But about the bakery, too. And the muffins."

"What?" My heart starts to flutter the way that it did when I ran my numbers the other day. "What do you mean?"

"The reporter said that she's writing a story for the front page of the Sunday Styles section. It will be below the fold, but still, it's the front page. Of Sunday Styles. In the *New York Times*. She said—I made sure to remember it exactly—she said it's a 'tongue-in-cheek yet thoughtful look at landmarks from political scandals—'"

"Oh, great," I moan. I glance at Kate. She has that far-off look on her face that she had when I arrived. This time I'm grateful for it. I don't want her hearing this.

"No, no, no. It will be good, Waverly. She said it will just be a couple of paragraphs about Maggie's—she said she wants to include it because it's timely—and that she'll include the address and is mentioning the muffins."

"I just don't want it to come off the wrong way," I say, carefully choosing my words so as not to pique Kate's interest.

"Waverly, think about it," Randy moans. "Even if it did—which it won't—it's the fucking *New York Times*. Do you know how many bakeries in this country—in this *zip code*—would kill to be in the *New York Times*?"

"You're right, you're right," I say, a smile spreading on my face despite my best efforts. "You're right."

"Get ready, girl," Randy says. "You're about to become famous."

"Ugh, doubt that," I say. "I'll see you in a bit."

"So what was that about?" Kate says.

I look at her, sitting with her legs folded underneath her. *How to do this?* It had crossed my mind, when I was working in my office the other day, that it is kind of fucked-up that the success that's eluded me for so long is coming out of Kate's breakup. But then I saw the numbers and, well...I take a gulp and tell her. About everything. There's a part of me that knows that I'm telling her because it might distract from the fact that Brendan was my unwitting publicity tool, but it's amazing how easy it is to just confess everything after I've already done it once this morning, when I told Amy. Maybe this means that telling Larry won't be so bad after all. It's doubtful, but maybe if I keep telling myself that, it will give me the courage to go ahead and do it.

"Well, I'm glad that things are turning around for you," she says curtly when I'm finished. There isn't an ounce of sympathy in her voice. She scratches her nose and then hops up and brushes off her hands.

"Kate."

"No, no," she says sharply. "I'm glad we could help."

Ouch.

Aside from when I was opening the bakery, I've never talked to Kate about money. Not like this. Why would I? It would be like trying to talk to someone in a foreign language. I routinely spend hours sitting at my desk, chewing on a pencil and typing on my calculator until I'm woozy from all of the numbers. Kate, meanwhile, probably never bothers to look at her account balances. Why would she, when getting money out of the bank must be like getting a glass of water out of a faucet; you don't have to think about where it comes from because there's a seemingly unlimited supply somewhere.

"Kate, please don't be angry. I know that this is weird…all of it…If I could change the way that it's happened, I would."

She nods, unimpressed.

"It's not as if people come in asking about Brendan. His name doesn't even come up. They just want the muffins. And it's not as if I'm milking the opportunity by selling T-shirts with Brendan's face on them or something. I've turned reporters away. I've been completely passive about the whole thing. It just happened."

She raises her eyebrows and nods. "Yup. But you're not unhappy about it."

"Kate, please. You don't understand what it's been like…"

She laughs. "No, I don't. I guess I've been too busy watching my marriage implode."

"Kate, that's not fair." I'm suddenly sweltering; it must be two hundred degrees in here. I pull off the cardigan I'm wearing over my T-shirt and take a deep breath. "I can call the reporter and tell her to take me out of the article."

She rolls her eyes. "No, don't. I mean, what's one more piece of bad publicity?" She puts her hands on her head, closes her eyes, and takes a deep, long breath. "You know what? Don't worry about it," she says, her voice tired. "If it will help you keep Maggie's going, it's fine."

"But, Kate—"

"Really, Waverly. It's fine."

When I get to work a little while later, Randy and Jeannette greet me with applause. "Stop, stop," I say, shaking my head. I feel tremendously conflicted about this now.

"I gave the reporter your email address," Randy says. "She said she'd be in touch with questions."

I check to make sure that nothing's burning, literally or figuratively, and that all of the customers out front are happy, and then I head back into my office. I slump into my swivel chair and click open my email. There it is: tternkin@nytimes.com. Her email is short and sweet:

Ms. Brown,

Sorry to miss you today. The article will appear in Sunday's paper. I don't know that we'll have room, but if we can fit it, would you be up for giving us the muffin recipe? (Great, by the way, I had one when I was there earlier.) Any questions, shoot me an email.

I type out a reply with the recipe and ask whether it's possible for her to send me a preview of the story before it runs. I start to explain that I'm a good friend of Kate Berkshire's and that I'm sensitive to how she and Brendan are perceived, but then I delete it. If she's read any of the press about Brendan's outburst, then she already knows that I'm Kate's friend. I hit "send" and swivel absentmindedly in my chair for a few minutes. I want to be excited about this, but I keep picturing the look on Kate's face when I told her. There's a part of me that's angry at her for not being more understanding about the difficulty of my situation, but then I try to imagine what it's like to be in her shoes. Her perfect snow globe of an existence has been shattered. As much as she pretends like leaving Brendan is an easy decision, it has to be horrible. I guess I'll just have to cross my fingers and hope for the best with the article.

I pick up the phone to call Larry to tell him about the story. Now that I've confessed my money situation to Amy and Kate, I have to come clean with him. Today's Thursday—I tell myself I'll do it before the article comes out on Sunday. I start to dial his number, but then I change my mind—I should check on Amy to see how she's doing at the house.

"I was just about to call you," she says when she answers.

My heart leaps. "Is everything okay?" I ask anxiously.

"It's fine, it's fine," she says. "I'm actually...well, I'm actually at home."

"Oh." *Why does she sound so strange?*

"Yes, at home."

"Oh, wait. You mean *your* home?" I say.

"Yeah."

"Wait—But Amy—Are you just picking up some stuff? Is Mike there? Have you called your mom?" Though I've stopped swiveling in my chair, I feel like I'm spinning.

"No, no. I just—I had to come home," she says. "I called Mike this morning and we talked. We're working it out."

"What?" I feel like the floor's just dropped beneath me.

"It's hard to explain. I can't just leave, Waverly. He's my husband."

"He's your husband who beats you," I say. Fuck what the websites say about not criticizing the abuser—someone needs to get through to her! My heart is pounding like someone is banging a drum inside my chest. A thousand drums. "Amy, I'm sorry, but you're doing the wrong thing here. He's going to hurt you again. It's not safe there. You have to get out of that house. Think of what it's doing to Emma."

She gasps. "What it's doing to Emma?" she says. "Do you actually think I haven't thought about that, Waverly? How dare you."

Fuck. I need to be the person she can lean on right now. If she pulls away from me, I might never get her back. "I'm sorry, Amy. I'm really sorry. I'm just really, really worried about you. He's going to hit you again, Amy. You know he is."

"Waverly, this is my home. I know how you feel about Mike—I see the way that you grit your teeth when his name comes up—and I understand it. If the tables were turned and this had happened to you, I would feel the same way. But I know my husband like nobody else does and I know his commitment to getting better, despite what's happened over the past several days. We had a long talk this morning and he's agreed to do the counseling. He knows now how important this is to me. Staying at your place made him realize it."

"So you never intended to leave? This was just a way to get his attention?"

She's quiet for a moment. "I have to look forward, Waverly. I have to be optimistic. My husband is not a monster. He's the same man I fell for all of those years ago and he's sick. He was abused himself. I know that he can be the guy he once was. He wants to be that, Waverly. He says as much."

Over the years, I've come to discover that there are lots of people who find Amy's particular brand of optimism to be an inherent sign of dim-wittedness. I've seen the patronizing way that strangers sometimes respond to her when they first meet her. Yes, her eager enthusiasm can be morning-show-host annoying, and, yes, she is more apt to want to talk about her latest get at Target than the state of the economy, but she isn't stupid. That's what's so frustrating about this. The problem is that Amy is a fixer—she takes care of everyone around her and always has, trying to make life "just right," as if it's as easy as rubbing a stain out of the carpet. Hell, she made a career out of it. It's one of the reasons why I love her, but now it's as if she's willing to sacrifice herself just to make her marriage work.

"Listen," she says. "I know that you want me to be like Kate, to make a clean break and move on. But I'm sorry; I'm not like her— I have an actual, real marriage that's based on love. I can't abandon it like it's a bad party I'm desperate to leave."

"Amy, I know how difficult this must be for you," I say, trying a different tactic. "And I understand how much you love Mike," I manage, though the words stick in my throat. "But I am really, really worried about your safety. What if you and Mike made an agreement that you would stay with me temporarily, while you guys work on things?"

"Waverly, I have to be here at home to help him."

"But Amy…"

"This is my home, Waverly. I have to be here. I know you don't understand it, but this is where I belong."

I slump down, dropping my head on to my desk. "Oh, Amy, I don't feel good about this. You deserve so much more than this."

"I know that," she says. "And I'm going to get what I need here, at home. That's exactly what I'm fighting for."

I hang up reluctantly when she says that she has to go, and try to get absorbed in clearing out my email inbox. Then I start shuffling papers on my desk. Then I straighten the cookbooks on my book-shelf. I don't know what to do with myself. I don't want to call Larry now. Kate's pissed at me. Amy's…I don't know. I feel like I've failed all of the important people in my life.

I open my desk drawer to find a thumbtack so that I can hang next week's schedule on the bulletin board outside my office, and as I'm fishing through the mess of junk, an old bottle of perfume comes rolling out from the back of the drawer. I'd totally forgot-ten that I had this. It's one of those roller-ball-style bottles, and it's

L'Air du Temps. My mother's fragrance. I bought it years ago on a whim, when I was at the mall, shopping for Christmas presents with Amy.

I open up the bottle and rub the fragrance on the insides of my wrists. God, it's like aromatherapy. *Mom.* Ages ago, when I was in my midtwenties and still teaching, Larry and I took advantage of a President's Day holiday and drove south to a vineyard near Charlottesville. We found a spot at the table in the tasting room, and as I slid into my chair, I immediately noticed that the woman next to me was wearing my mother's perfume. I remember trying to concentrate on the sommelier's dissertation about Virginia wines, but my eyes were welling up with tears. I eventually just had to leave the room. Too many memories were closing in on me: how we would wave at each other by curling one finger as she was closing my door after she tucked me in at night, how she loudly sang along whenever a Linda Ronstadt song came on the radio, how she'd play with my hair when we watched made-for-TV movies together.

I realize that I'm absentmindedly twirling my hair, thinking about it, when Larry calls. I don't pick up. I *can't* pick up. The only person I need right now is my mom, and she's not here.

CHAPTER TWENTY-FOUR

It's just two paragraphs. One. Two. But in the six hours since the Sunday *Times* hit the stands, I have had more phone calls and seen more customers than I have in years. We expected an uptick in business, of course, but not like this, and certainly not at least until Monday. I mean, who reads about a muffin in the paper and then runs right out to buy one? A lot of people, apparently, because at one point this morning, I nearly had a line out the door.

Jeannette gives me a quick squeeze as she rushes past me, where I'm—yep—making another batch. Randy keeps high-fiving me. I never told him the extent of my business issues—I worried he'd quit—but given his level of excitement over this, he must've known more than I thought. Looking back, I realize that it would have been impossible for him not to know that I was having serious problems, what with the phone calls from my lender, my accountant, my idiot landlord.

I'm just about to start filling muffin tins when Larry walks in, carrying a stack of newspapers. "I think it's safe to say that business is booming!" he says to the room. Jeannette lets out a little "yee haw" as she hurries back out to the front of the store.

"This is incredible," Larry says to me.

"Isn't it crazy?" I say, grabbing the paper off the top of the stack. *And aren't I crazy?* I think to myself. I still haven't told Larry anything. When I got all psyched up to do it a few nights ago, even rehearsing my speech in the kitchen beforehand, he walked in from

work and told me that Kyle had been fired that day. The good news
is that it means that Larry's job is probably safe. The bad news is
that his good friend and colleague is out of work. He was so upset about the situation that I couldn't bear to load him down more
with my confession.

Okay, I used it as an excuse.

Larry leans over my shoulder as I find the Style section and read
the article again. I've already almost memorized it:

*Just outside of D.C., in picturesque Maple Hill, Virginia, is
Maggie's, the bakery where Brendan Berkshire, the leading candidate for the Virginia governorship, recently had an emotional
breakdown that was caught on video and that many D.C. Dems
are happily calling the moment when his campaign jumped the
shark—we'll know for sure in the June primaries. But the real
sensation is this cozy bakery, where owner Waverly Brown turns
out homey baked goods, sweets, and breakfast and lunch dishes
seven days a week.*

*The item of the moment is her doughnut muffin, a gooey
piece of goodness that customers are scrambling for ever since the
Politico blogger who first published the Berkshire scene mentioned
that he was eating one when he shot the footage. It's cinnamon
and spice and everything nice...something that lots of people
might say you don't see enough of in this town.*

"It's pretty good, huh?" I say to Larry, studying the slightly grainy,
postage-stamp-sized photo of the bakery's facade. There wasn't
room for my recipe, but it's just as well. The main thing is that the
writer didn't mention Kate; I've studied all four sentences over and
over, and I can't find a single thing for her to get pissed off about.

"It's fantastic," he says, softly patting my back. "I'm so proud of
you."

"I can't believe this place!" I say, peeking out to see the crowd that's gathered in front of the cash register. "We may as well have put a sign out front advertising free money."

Larry laughs and shakes his head. "Those damn muffins. I mean, they're good—don't get me wrong—but you've been selling them for years."

"I know!" I laugh. "It's ridiculous."

"Do you want me to stick around and help out?" Back when I first opened, Larry would often pinch-hit when I was short on staff or got into a jam.

"It's okay. It's Donovan's day off, but Randy called him earlier and he said he'd come in. Let me walk you out, though." I ask Jeannette if she can finish the batch that I'm working on, and then take Larry up to the front of the store. We weave our way through the mass of people as we go, and I thank the regulars who spot me and shout congratulatory sentiments or give me a thumbs-up from across the room.

We're nearly to the front door when a familiar voice calls my name. "Waverly! Waverly, over here!"

I turn and see Gary, my accountant, dressed in exercise gear and holding a coffee and a muffin.

Hmmm.

"Larry! Hey, man! I haven't seen you in years!" Gary says. I actually hired Gary after Larry met him playing flag football in a local league. They do that sort of half handshake, half slapping-each-other-five thing that men do. My heart is beating double-time. Larry doesn't exactly know about how much time Gary and I have spent together lately.

Before I can think of a way to steer the conversation so that Gary doesn't rat on me, he nudges me with the hand that's holding his coffee and says, "Waverly, congratulations! I'd say that if business keeps up like this, you won't have a thing to worry about with that house loan."

I feel Larry's head snap toward me.

Damn it, Gary.

He must realize what he's just done, because his eyes widen and the next thing I know, he's nodding good-bye and telling Larry that they should grab a beer sometime as he hurries away from us.

"House loan?" Larry says.

It's like a force field just went up between us. I can't look at him. I can't, I can't.

"Waverly."

I feel like a child. I *am* a child.

Ten, twenty seconds pass.

I take a deep breath. "Let's go back to my office and talk."

He has his fingers steepled, watching me explain. It's a gesture he never makes. He looks too serious. Too brooding. Not like himself at all. Right now I need laid-back Larry. Hands-behind-his-head, leaned-back-in-his-chair Larry. Feet-tapping-out-some-old-classic-rock-tune Larry.

I've told him about everything and he hasn't said a word. In fact, he's hardly moved. "I kept thinking that if I could just get a handle on things, then you would never have to worry about any of it," I say, coming to a close. I force myself to smile, but I can tell by the way that it feels that it's an unconvincing one. "And now, everything looks like it's going to work out! So there really wasn't any need for you to know. Plus, you had all of that stuff going on with *your* work. I didn't want to burden you with any of this."

I stand there for what seems like a year, shuffling my feet from side to side and playing with the edge of my dishrag, which I've pulled out of my back pocket. Randy is right. It really is like my security blanket.

"How much credit card debt is there?" Larry says.

Oh God. That's the first thing he has to say? After everything I just told him?

I look down at my feet. "About twenty-seven thousand dollars."

"Twenty-seven?" Larry gasps.

"Well, it's not like I racked it up because I was out buying new handbags!" I yelp. "It was all for business costs. Believe it or not, running this place is expensive."

"Believe it or not," Larry says, mocking me. "I understand that. I grew up one of seven kids, with parents who ran a hardware store, Waverly. Do you think I don't know what it's like to own your own business?" He runs his hands through his hair and looks at me. "I know it's not easy, but Jesus, why didn't you say anything? We could have lost our house?"

"No. I don't think so. Not now. I'll be able to get caught up on the loan," I say.

"Holy shit," he says, remembering something. "Is this why the cable got cut off when you were in Florida?"

I close my eyes. "Yes." *Damn it.* "But I'm handling everything now. Things like that won't happen again."

"Waverly, that's what you're not getting here—whether or not you can handle it isn't what I'm concerned about. What really bothers me is that you didn't think you needed to tell me. Shit, you can't be honest with me after ten years, Waverly?"

I feel like I'm an inch tall. Less than that. I feel smaller than whatever is smaller than a flea. I feel like nothing. "I'm sorry," I say. "I don't know why..." I shake my head.

"I could've helped you."

"I didn't want your help."

"You needed it."

I turn away from him. He's right. I know he's right. "I'm sorry."

"Stop saying you're sorry, Waverly," he says. "Tell me why you lied to me."

I almost never notice the noise at work—the banging of pots and pans, the whirring motor of my mixer, the faint din of the customers in front, dishes hitting the sink, faucets running, my younger employees cackling to each other, Jeannette singing, Randy laughing and calling out orders. Now, in the quiet, in the vibrating hum of this moment where I need to have an answer, I feel like I can pick each individual sound out of the cacophonous roar that accompanies me every day. I turn back around to face him. He's staring at me, waiting.

"I wanted to be able to handle it myself."

"That's not an answer. Why did you lie to me?"

"Because I wanted to be able to handle it myself!" I shriek. "Because I felt like a fucking loser, Larry! Because I was ashamed of myself. I *am* ashamed of myself!"

"I just don't understand that at all. You're hardly the first business owner to have a bad year. I don't know what it has to do with why you lied to me. I should be the person you confide in, Waverly. That's what I'm here for."

"I know."

"I don't think you do," he says. He gets up from my desk. "This is bad."

Over the past year, when I've pictured what it would be like if and when Larry found out about all of this, I've assumed that he would be furious. There would be screaming and finger-pointing, doors slamming, marching out the door. But this—his quiet disappointment—is worse. I knew he would be angry with me, but it stupidly never occurred to me that he would feel so let down.

"Larry, I just didn't want you to know that I couldn't do this myself," I say softly. "You know how much pride I take in my work. I didn't want to have to ask for help."

He taps his fingers along the edge of my desk before he speaks. "That's the thing, though, Waverly. There's nothing wrong with asking for help. Needing someone doesn't make you weak. I thought you knew that."

"I'm sorry," I say again.

"Maybe this is why you've been focusing so much on Amy and

Kate," he says. He's not even looking at me. He's picked up a pencil off of my desk and is twirling it in one hand. It drops, he picks
it back up. Over and over.

"What do you mean?" I say.

Finally, he looks at me. "Maybe you've been obsessing about
your friends not so much because you want to help them but because you want to avoid your own problems."

I rear back, shocked that he could say such a thing, but before
I can think of how to respond, he stands and heads for the door. I
know deep down that to some extent, he's probably right.

"You should get back out there," he says, digging his keys out of
his pocket. He brushes past me and shouts good-bye to Randy.

I stand in the threshold of my office for several minutes after
the screen door that he left through has sprung shut, watching the
messy commotion of the kitchen. Then I wipe my hands on my rag
and head back out to the front of the store, where music is playing
and everyone is high on sugar, and it's all because of me.

I wedge myself behind the cash register, telling Jeannette that I'll
take it from here. "How can I help you?" I say to the next person in
line.

CHAPTER TWENTY-FIVE

A week later, I'm sitting in the diner where Amy and I have agreed to meet for lunch. I haven't seen her since she spent the night, and our phone calls have been stunted, to say the least. She doesn't call me now—I only call her—and every time I ask her how she's doing, she says in an uncharacteristically clipped way that she's fine, and then she asks me how work is going, and then the next thing you know, she's hanging up, saying she has to run off somewhere. I'm starting to understand, on many levels, how frustrating it is to worry over someone who doesn't want your help.

This is a standing date, something that makes Amy's no-show status especially suspect. Every spring, I take a week off from work and we kick off my vacation with lunch at Paulsen's, a rusty old soda shop that has been on Main Street since the 1940s. Amy always spends the first ten minutes of every lunch chiding me for never actually going anywhere during my time off. I can hear her now: "You don't have kids! Please, on behalf of all of us who do, *go somewhere*! Brazil, Ireland . . . hell, at least go to Miami—somewhere where you can stay out all night and sleep all day." She can't understand how much I look forward to just sticking around the house with no agenda. I catch up on my cookbook reading and revisit favorite recipes. If I feel like it, I eat fried chicken for breakfast, don't brush my teeth until noon, and watch *Seinfeld* reruns after my afternoon nap. It's just puttering around, but at the end of the week,

I'm convinced that I feel better than I ever could if I spent the week blowing my retirement fund on five-star spa treatments, something that Kate once tried to convince me to do.

For obvious reasons, this year is not one in which I should be taking a vacation, even if it's just to laze around the house. When I mentioned to Amy on the phone a few days ago that I was skipping this year's break, I asked if she would still meet me for lunch. I knew that I was guilting her into it, but I need to see her to know she's okay.

I lean forward in my stool to get another look at the line of people snaking out the front door of the diner. Still no sign of Amy. I turn my phone over in my hand to check the time. I've been waiting almost twenty minutes and I've called her four times. My heart feels like it's beating a little faster with each minute that passes. Is she late because she's just late? Is she standing me up because she's irritated with me? Or is it something worse?

The woman sitting next to me at the counter is maybe twenty. The color that she's chosen to dye her yellow-blond hair reminds me of the banana cream pie that I sell in the summertime. She's engrossed in an *Us Weekly* story about a B-movie actress explaining "How I Finally Lost the Weight!" I hesitate before interrupting her.

"Um, excuse me." I lean toward her. She's just taken a huge gulp of chocolate milk shake and she smiles sheepishly, holding up one finger while she swallows.

"I'm sorry." I wince sweetly. "But could I ask your opinion? How many times would you call a friend who's supposed to meet you for lunch before you accept that you've been stood up?"

"Ohhh," the girl says, looking up at the ceiling while she yanks under her shirt at her bra strap. "Um, I guess it depends on the friend? How well do you know…him?" She raises her eyebrows and leans in conspiratorially. "How many times have you called?"

"Four."

She cringes. "I don't think he's coming," she says, like she's breaking bad news.

"Oh, it's not a date," I correct her.

She nods at me, a pitying, sympathizing, "we can both pretend that it's not a date if that will make you feel better" kind of nod.

"Really, it's just my girlfriend," I say. I don't know why I feel compelled to explain myself to a kid; a kid who will eventually hopefully learn that she doesn't need to wear so much eyeliner. "She's been going through a tough time," I continue. "And the last time that she didn't show up somewhere it was because something bad happened, so I'm just worried that—" The girl's eyes are glazing over. "Never mind. I'm sorry I interrupted you."

"It's okay." She shrugs and touches her hand to my arm. Her fake nails are as cold and hard as coins. "We've all been there." She nods gravely.

I nod back. It isn't worth it to try to convince her that I'm telling the truth. I look down at my phone and will it to ring. It's 12:36. I'll give Amy until 12:40 to walk into the crowded restaurant, and if she doesn't, I will drive to her house.

I consider calling Larry or Kate to ask their opinion, but I don't want to bother Kate, who has enough on her mind, and Larry's not really an option. When I got home from the bakery on the night after my confession, buzzed from two glasses of champagne from the bottle that the staff had surprised me with, I'd slipped into bed next to him and crumpled against his side, waking him with my sobs that I was sorry. "You need to decide what you want," he said. He didn't put his arm around me to comfort me. He didn't even turn over.

"I'm so sorry that I disappointed you," I gulped out, wiping my nose with my fist.

"Stop worrying about how you might have disappointed me, Waverly," he said with a clarity that made it immediately obvious that he actually hadn't been sleeping at all when I crawled into bed.

"What you need to figure out is what you even want from me. Because if you can't confide in me, if you don't need me, than I don't know what I'm doing here."

"I love you," I said.

"Figure it out," he replied.

I've been tiptoeing around him since. Work has been so busy that I've been using it as an excuse to stay away from the house and avoid the big sit-down that I know we need to have. On the rare occasions that we've both been home and awake, our interaction has consisted of nothing but small talk—how was your day and blah, blah, blah. He doesn't want to talk to me. I've made a point to mention the progress I've been making on my bills ("Made a payment to the house lender today…I think I might be able to get my rent check in early next month…"), as if it might make up for my mistakes.

I take a sip of my soda and peer toward the front door again, where the amoeba of hungry lunch-goers seems to have doubled. They stand in an unorganized mass along the wall, their eyes darting from table to table, looking for almost-empty plates, wallets being pulled out of pockets, any sign that they might get seated soon. Business obviously isn't hurting here, I think, wishing that I could stand up and announce to the crowd that they ought to try the excellent bakery down the road that was mentioned in the *New York Times* last Sunday.

The waitress behind the counter passes by, locking her eyes on me and then looking at the laminated menu she slapped in front of me when I sat down. I know that look—it's the "if you're not going to order, make room for someone who will" look. I flip the menu over to scan the entrees. A BLT had been on my mind all morning, but now the thought of it makes my stomach turn. *We had said 12:15, hadn't we?*

I look at my phone again: 12:39. Close enough.

I slide a few dollars across the counter to pay for my soda and hop off of the stool, avoiding my neighbor's sympathetic smile and the waitress's eye roll as I turn to walk out the door.

Amy will never forgive me for freaking out if it's just a simple misunderstanding. On the drive over, I call her twice more, bringing the tally up to six calls in thirty minutes. God, I hope that that's all that this is, a simple misunderstanding.

When I arrive at her house, I stand on the concrete landing of her front porch and jingle my keys in my fist, trying to stop the loop of horror scenes that have been rolling through my mind ever since I left the diner. I ring the doorbell three times. Nobody answers. *Please, God, just let her be okay.*

I try to peer through the sheer curtains that line the windows on either side of the door but I can't make anything out. I turn and look at the houses across the street. All of the garage doors are closed. There are no cars in the driveways. A soggy stack of newspapers, as limp as wilted lettuce, lies piled at the end of one of them. I could be turning naked cartwheels across Amy's front lawn and nobody would notice. Maybe this kind of quiet is the very reason why some people move to neighborhoods like this, but to me, it's eerie. The houses look so flawless from the outside; hedges trimmed so carefully that it's as if they've all been given the same standard, military-issue buzz cuts, the front doors gussied up with wreaths and welcome mats. I wonder who Amy's neighbors are; what they do, where they're from, how they spend their evenings when they return home at the end of the day—what they think of the young family across the street.

I'm just about to give up and walk around the house to the backyard, where I might be able to get a better view inside from the sliding glass door beside the kitchen, when I hear a noise on the other side of the door, like the doorknob jangling.

"Amy?" I knock excitedly on the door. "Ame, is that you?" I try to look through the windows again but still can't make anything out. The doorknob jiggles again from the inside of the house. "Amy?"

"I can't open," a small voice says from the other side of the door. *Emma!*

"Emma, honey? Is that you?" My heartbeat quickens, a tap-tap-tap that matches the impatient rhythm of my fist knocking against the door.

The doorknob jiggles again.

"Emma? It's Waverly."

"Aunt Wave-uh-lee?" Emma squeaks.

"Emma, where's your mommy? Is your mommy there?" I wait for a reply. *One-Mississippi, two-Mississippi, three-Mississippi,* I count, trying to keep myself calm so that I won't frighten her. "Emma, sweetie? Is your daddy there? Are you by yourself? Is there a grown-up there who can open the door?"

"Mommy's upstairs," the girl says. Relief floods over me as if it's been dumped on my head from a bucket over the door. Dammit, Amy. Did she just forget? I punch the doorbell several times in a row. "Emma, can you get your mommy to come to the door?"

"Mommy?"

"Yes, honey. Get your mommy to come to the door. Can you do that?"

"No!"

Shit. This is definitely not the time to play games. "Emma, come on. Now, get your mommy."

"No. Mommy's sleeping."

I freeze with my hand on the doorknob. Sleeping? While Emma's awake? No way. That alone tells me that my intuition is dead-on. Something's wrong. I step back and lift the doormat, hoping to find a spare key, and then do the same with the potted plants on either side of the door. No luck. I dial Amy's home number on my cell phone and hear the muffled ring inside the house.

"Emma, can you unlock the door?"

"It's locked," Emma says.

"Is there a key, honey?"

"A key?" She sounds genuinely confused. I can't waste time trying to explain to her.

"Emma, honey, you stay right there, okay? I'm going to go around to the back of the house and try to come inside that way." I run and unlatch the back gate, nearly tripping over a coiled hose as I make my way around to the porch steps, where I leap over them to get to the sliding glass door.

Fuck, also locked! I cup my hands around my eyes and squint through the sliding glass door. The kitchen is immaculate again, napkins neatly snug in their holder in the center of the kitchen table, apples and oranges stacked in a blue bowl on the counter. *What the hell is going on?* I bang on the door, calling for Emma.

"Emma!" I pound my fist. "Emma, come on, it's Waverly." I watch through the window and Emma finally turns the corner into the kitchen, clutching a ratty stuffed bunny. "Honey," I kneel down so that we are eye to eye through the thick-paned glass. "Tell me, can you wake your mommy up?"

"Mommy's upstairs," the little girl says, holding one palm up like she's a tiny cocktail waitress holding an invisible tray. "I told you, she's sleeping."

"Okay, honey. Can you wake her up for me?" I pull my phone out of my pocket and dial the home number again, hoping the sound will wake Amy.

"She's night-night upstairs."

"Emma, are you okay?"

The little girl stares back at me, holding her bunny and rubbing one of the tattered ears between her thumb and forefinger. This isn't right. Emma should be at preschool and Amy should be sitting across from me at Paulsen's, halfway through the tuna melt she always stuffs with potato chips.

I look out at the yard, and then to the identical, desolate, treeless backyards of the neighbors, tapping my fingers against my chin. *Am I crazy to do this?* Before I can talk myself out of it, I dial the three numbers—911. I hit "send." Emma stands silently watching me on the other side of the door, so close to the glass that her tiny potbelly almost touches it. I force myself to smile at her. I wave, bending my fingers at the knuckles, and she waves back.

"Nine-one-one. What's your emergency?"

"Uh," I start. I hold the phone with my right hand and shake my left one at my side, trying to work out my nerves. "It's my friend. I'm outside her house and I'm worried that something has happened to her. Her daughter, she's three, she's just standing on the other side of the locked door, telling me her mother's asleep."

"Do you hear noises? Is there anything else that gives you reason to believe that something has happened to your friend inside the house?"

Even the 911 operator makes me feel like I'm overreacting. "Yes, I have reason to believe that something has happened to her."

"Please continue."

I close my eyes. "I know that there's a history of physical abuse in her home."

"What's the address? We'll send someone out."

I give the operator the information and then shove the phone back into my pocket. "Emma, honey, hold on," I say. "People are going to be here to open the door any minute."

When the policeman pulls up in front of the house and gets out of the car, the first thing I think is that he looks like a teenager dressed in an officer's costume. I need someone serious, somebody with experience, not some kid who looks like he drives around all day telling fart jokes over his two-way radio. "You're the woman who called?" he says, slamming the door of his cruiser and walking up the driveway.

"Yes." I wring my hands to keep them from trembling. "My friend's daughter is inside and she says her mom's upstairs asleep but I think something's wrong."

He stops halfway up the driveway and flips open a notebook, where he starts writing down notes—*slowly*. "And you told the operator that you believe that there's a history of abuse in the home?" He doesn't look up when he says it, just continues his methodical, careful scratching.

"Yes, my friend has told me that her husband abuses her. Or abused her, I guess."

He keeps writing and then taps the end of his pen against his notebook, as if he's trying to find the right word before he continues. "Which one?" he says, looking up at me.

"What?" I say, confused.

"Abuses her or abused her? You said both."

"Oh." Despite the baby face, he's wearing a badge and has a gun holstered to his waist, both of which intimidate me, as I'm certain they're supposed to. I force myself to hold his gaze, reminding myself that I have to get this right for Amy. "She told me that he stopped but to be honest, I don't believe her."

He starts writing again. "Okay," he finally says. He puts his notebook in his front shirt pocket and walks up to the house.

"Her daughter is on the other side of the door," I say, walking close behind him. I don't want him to scare her. He knocks and rings the doorbell twice.

"Her little girl, Emma, she's right on the other side of the door," I say again over his shoulder. "Or she was just a minute ago."

He tries to peer into the windows as I had before he arrived. "There's noth—," I start.

He knocks again, this time louder. "Police!" he shouts. "This is the police!"

I hear Emma whine from behind the door.

"Emma, honey?" I step forward and press my ear to the door, ignoring the look that I can feel the officer giving me. "Emma, honey?"

Nothing.

"Emma, baby, come on, say something," I say again.

I look at the officer. "She must have gone somewhere. I don't hear her."

The officer turns from me and pinches his mouth with his thumb and forefinger. He's apparently trying to determine what to do next. Why doesn't he just force the door open, break a window—something?

"Emma!" I bang loudly on the door. "Isn't there something else you can do?" I say to him.

He keeps staring off into the distance, ignoring me.

"Emma!" I say again.

Finally, he turns to me and says, "I'm not supposed to enter a home without reason, but since there appears to be a child in the house alone—"

"She's not in the house alone. She said her mother was sleeping."

He nods but it's not a nod of recognition. He obviously just wants me to shut up. "I'm going to call for backup," he says and heads back to his car.

After an agonizing and awkward amount of time that is probably just a few minutes but feels like a lifetime, during which I continue to bang on the front door and peer inside all of the first-floor windows while the cop sits in his car texting his friends or doing God knows what, another police cruiser finally shows up. This officer is a relief. He's older, with basset-hound jowls and the kind of posture that suggests a military background. He is both far more senior and far more capable than the guy I've been dealing with. He takes a tool out of his trunk and while I stand on the front walk, the two of them ram it against the door. I pray that Emma isn't just on the other side. When it finally swings open, I want to sprint into the house. The younger cop lets the door fall all the way open before he takes a step inside, a move that looks so choreographed that I think he must practice it in front of the mirror at home. I wonder, despondently, if this is the first time he's ever done this.

When the other cop enters the house, I start to follow behind them. "No, I'm sorry, ma'am," he says, putting his arm out to stop me. "I need you to stay outside, just in case."

I slump against the doorjamb, defeated. *Just in case of what?* My adrenaline is pumping so hard that I feel nauseous. My eyes fall on the table in Amy's foyer, her keys in a dish on top of it, a picture of Emma covered in cake from her first birthday. It's become a horribly windy afternoon, and I brush my hair away from my face, the wind echoing a low, hollow moan that I can feel in my ears. I try to concentrate on the sound of the officers chuffing their way up the stairs.

"This is the police," one says. "Is everything okay in here? I'm here to help."

Where is Emma? "Emma?" I call out. "Emma, it's Aunt Waverly."

Before I have a second to consider going in to look for her, I hear the thump-thump-thump of footsteps rushing down the stairs. I lean into the doorway. "You say that her daughter is in here somewhere?" the older policeman says, his expression and posture now even more charged.

"Yes, yes!" I shout. *Something is wrong. Oh God. What's wrong?* "She was talking to me from the other side of the door! Just a minute ago!"

"Okay," he says. He pulls a phone out of his holster and presses a button before speaking into it. "This is Officer Dillard. I'm at 42 Green Leaf Court. I'm going to need an ambulance."

Ambulance.

I grab at the wall to keep from falling to the ground and claw toward the officer with my other hand. "Oh God, what's wrong?" I scream, my voice vibrating with fear. "Oh no, oh God, please tell me she's okay!"

He puts his hand over where I'd grabbed his forearm and gently peels me off of him. "Is there someone you can call?" he says.

Larry, who by a stroke of luck is working from home today to finish up a paper for a journal submission, pulls up to the house less than five minutes after the ambulance. I'm sitting in the front yard, holding Emma in my lap on the damp ground. She'd been in her room, hiding behind a mound of stuffed animals in a corner, and she hasn't said a word to me since the officer brought her out of the house.

Larry jogs toward us. "What's the latest?" he says to me in a low voice, glancing at Emma as he says it.

"They haven't told me anything yet," I say, winding a section of Emma's hair between my fingers. "The paramedics got here and went into the house with the police officers and then they came back out and got a stretcher." I feel dizzy, like I've just been spinning in circles, like when my mom and I used to twirl in the yard together when I was a kid. I kiss the top of Emma's head.

"The police?"

"All inside." A third car had come along with the ambulance.

Larry gets up and walks toward the house, craning to try to see inside without getting too close to the front door. I hear a car in the distance and pray that it isn't headed toward us. I can't imagine what could happen—what I'd do—if Mike shows up now. But he wouldn't, would he? He couldn't. Not since I'm certain he has something to do with this. The car I'd heard—a truck from a lawn-care company—passes by the turn into the cul-de-sac. I hug Emma closer. I haven't seen any of Amy's neighbors. If anyone's home, they've apparently decided that they can get a better show from behind their curtains. I scan the windows, looking.

Larry walks back and kneels down next to me. "Have they called anyone else? Asked you any other questions?" He twiddles his thumbs in the same way that he does when he worries over his laptop when he works at home. I reach for him and curl my arm around the sleeve of his fleece jacket. He sits beside me, puts his arm around my shoulders, and gently pinches Emma's upper arm, smiling at her.

I tell him that the younger police officer took a statement from me. He didn't want to know anything but the basics—my name and age, how long I'd known Amy and Mike. When he asked me to confirm that I said that there was a history of abuse in their home and I started to answer, he cut me off and told me that he just needed a statement that I said that there was a history. Nothing else. Before I could convince him to let me tell him more, he turned and walked back into the house.

My eyes are fixed on the open front door. "No one's said a word to me. The police officer brought Emma out after he talked to me," I say. I rub her back softly. She's pulling at the grass and lining up the blades in neat rows on my leg.

"No one's called Mike?" Larry says quietly into my ear, so closely that it tickles.

I shake my head, and he pulls me closer.

CHAPTER TWENTY-SIX

Larry and I are singing with Emma, trying to remember the words to "Mockingbird," when they finally bring Amy out of the house. The paramedics hold tight to each side of her stretcher with the grim, dutiful expressions of pallbearers. I lose control when I see her, forgetting that I'd promised myself just a few minutes earlier that no matter what, I would stay calm for Emma.

I sprint toward Amy, stumbling awkwardly, my legs as weak as twigs. I scream her name and her head falls in my direction. She's barely conscious. She squints at me as if she can't exactly place me. Her stare is as dim as pond water.

She's wearing the same paint-splattered, fraying UNC sweatshirt that she's had for as long as I've known her, and probably longer. I've seen her in it a million times. The memories flash by me, sharp and quick, like in one of those flip books I loved as a kid: eating takeout and watching *Will and Grace* in our apartments after work, taking a lasagna to her house on the day that she brought Emma home, painting furniture together in the bakery before it opened, a few weeks ago when she was limping.

Her mouth gapes open like it froze midsentence. When I get closer, squeezing myself as close as I can between one of the paramedics and the stretcher, I notice the mottled, black skin around her right eye and the blood crusted around her nostrils, her eyes, her mouth. There's a sheet over her lower half that flaps in the wind, and when it balloons up, I can see that she is bare from the waist down. Her thigh is covered in a sickening swirl of bruises: black, purple, and red, a hideous rainbow of colors. There are other marks along her neck, all yellowed at the edges, like paper left out in the sun.

"Is she going to be okay?" I scream out, to anyone who will answer.

"We found her like this in her bed," says a voice behind me. I turn. It's the young police officer that'd first arrived after my 911 call.

"Tell me more. What else?"

"She's not totally with it, confused really, so she may have some sort of brain injury." He says it as casually as if he's describing the plays in a football game.

I scramble toward the ambulance and grab the back of one of the paramedic's jackets. "I'm coming with you," I say.

"I'm sorry, ma'am," he says. "We can't let you. You're going to have to follow behind."

I'm frantic. I turn to where I was sitting with Larry and Emma and see that he already has her in his car. I run to the passenger-side door he's already opened for me.

On the ride to the hospital, the ambulance's siren screaming in front of us like a wailing animal, I hold tight to Emma in the backseat. It's hard to tell how much she understands, but my guess is that it's more than we think. Back at Amy's house, while we were waiting on the paramedics to bring Amy out, I'd told her that her mommy was sick and that those nice people were just going to give her some medicine to help her feel better. There was nothing childlike about the somber way that she nodded, nor the way that she simply turned back to playing with the grass without asking any other questions. It made me suspect that she'd already witnessed more than anyone should ever have to, much less a three-year-old.

In the rearview mirror, I catch Larry's eye and he smiles at me but it's the kind of worried, closed-lip smile that people offer when they have nothing else to give. I saw it plenty in the weeks after my parents died and never wanted to see it again.

The siren screeches, its menace filling my ears as we careen over the wooded ribbon of the highway hugging the Potomac. I grip the underside of my seat with my free hand, bracing myself as if I'm sitting in a raft and plunging down the river that rages just beyond us.

I've been to Georgetown Hospital once since my parents died. Just once, when Emma was born. It took every ounce of my will to hold it together during our thirty-minute visit, to smile and coo over the baby as I was meant to instead of hurl myself out the window like I wanted to. There is far too much to remember here, and it all comes rushing back the moment I step out of Larry's car and into the glaringly bright hallway of the ER. I see the check-in counter where I once stood, asking how to find my parents, and the crowded waiting area that reminds me of a bus depot. One of the paramedics tells me that Amy's been taken to the trauma bay and that a doctor will come and find me.

Larry's taken Emma back to our house, and for twenty minutes, I stand alone near the nurse's station in the main treatment area. Two barrel-chested surgeons in scrubs and caps stare me down as they hurry past me before disappearing into one of the curtained rooms along the periphery. A nurse looks over the high counter that separates the nurse's station from the rest of the room and asks me if I need anything. I'm clearly in the way but I'm not going anywhere. The nurse points me toward the waiting room but I cut her off; I know where it is. I know its nubby upholstery and the sweet-rotten snack-machine smell. I know the cafeteria, the coffee shop, and this very nurse's station, where you're met with openhearted sympathy or sheer annoyance depending on who's on duty. In two months it will be the sixteenth anniversary of my parents' death and it's still too soon to be back here. I didn't need to see any of this again. Ever.

I stand in my spot as if there is an *X* taped onto the floor beneath me. When the doctor finds me, I'm relieved that I don't recognize her. I'd dreaded that it would be somebody who'd cared for my parents. She's rosy and plump, with a sensible short haircut and a mauve turtleneck underneath her scrubs. She looks like a woman who might run a church preschool. She smiles kindly and extends her hand to introduce herself. Her name is Dr. Meyer. She points me toward an alcove where we can talk.

Dr. Meyer leans against the wall and slowly sways back and forth against it as if she's scratching an itch on her back. The casual gesture might put me off if not for the thoughtful cadence of her voice and the way that her eyes hold mine despite the constant blur of people blazing past us in the hall every few seconds. I lean back against the wall behind me.

"Your friend has suffered from an epidural hematoma," she says. "It's a brain injury that affects the middle meningeal artery, which is one of the arteries that supplies blood to the brain. The hematoma, or blood mass, forms on the outside of the dura, which you can think of as the protective layer that covers the brain." She cups her right hand into a C shape and makes an arc, back and forth, to clarify her explanation. "She's in surgery, where our neurology team is working to remove the mass."

I stare at a smudge on the wall behind her head, waiting for her words to settle into place. "Is she going to be okay?" I sputter. My mouth feels like I've been chewing on sawdust.

"These hematomas are traumatic injuries, meaning that they result from some sort of blow to the head. Sometimes from car accidents, sometimes from an altercation of some sort." I can tell from the way that she says it that this is not the first time she's given this speech. "I know that it must have been frightening when you saw her. She seemed confused? Not lucid?"

When I nod, the movement feels severe enough to make me topple over. I try a few deep breaths. The doctor keeps talking. I lean my head back on the wall behind me and shift my weight more sturdily toward my feet.

"Her recovery depends on how long it's been since the injury occurred. Usually sufferers have a lucid period immediately following the trauma and then they quickly decline. Did you talk to her at all today? Did she complain about being tired? Having a headache?"

"I didn't talk to her today." I messed around online when I first got into the bakery, reading the online comments about the *Times* article. I made myself a cappuccino. I talked to Randy about a chocolate hazelnut torte recipe I read in *Food & Wine* the night before. I called the farmer who supplies my eggs. Meanwhile, Amy... I shake off the thought and try to refocus on the doctor.

"The good news is that, with these kinds of injuries, a full recovery is very possible if the patient gets into surgery quickly enough."

"And if they don't? What if it's been too long?" I put my hands to my mouth, crossing my fingers over each other.

The doctor reaches out and squeezes my shoulder.

"What? What does that mean?" I remember this now: the not knowing, the feeling that you are the only one in the hospital who isn't in on something.

"It will be another few hours before we know how this is going to go," she says. "Is there somebody who can come be with you? Somebody whom I can call?"

I shake my head impatiently. "Wait a second. What if it's been too long? What if she can't recover?"

"Let's not focus on the what-ifs right now," she says. "So far, the surgery is progressing in the way that it should. Let's focus on that. Are you sure I can't call somebody for you?"

"I can do it," I say.

The doctor reaches forward to pat my arm and I flinch. She notices and takes a step back. "Okay," she says. "I'll be in touch as soon as I have some more news."

I slump back against the wall and slide down to the floor. I watch Dr. Meyer weave her way through the crowded mass of people and stretchers and wheelchairs like she is an expert skier traversing a well-known slope. When she disappears behind a pair of doors, I take a deep breath and dig my hand into the front pocket of my jeans for my phone.

"A listing in Chapel Hill, North Carolina," I say when the operator comes on. "Davis and Margaret Lane." I swallow against the web of phlegm in the back of my throat. "Yes, it's a residence."

CHAPTER TWENTY-SEVEN

I can't just sit here and wait. It will be four hours before Amy's family can get here, and probably more with traffic. When Amy's mother picked up the phone, probably expecting that it would be one of her daughters, a neighbor, a telemarketer, I stammered that Amy had been in an accident and that they needed to get here as soon as they could. It's a head injury, I'd told her, and when she asked where Mike was and I said I didn't know, and that Emma was safe at my house, that was all she needed to hear before she said they were getting in the car and hung up the phone. She wasn't hysterical, as I'd feared. She didn't ask any other questions. In fact, when I pressed the "end" button on my phone, I almost felt as if she'd been expecting and dreading this call.

I don't feel right leaving Amy alone, but I can't stay here. I need to do something. I call Kate and ask her to come to the hospital. When she arrives, there are tears in her eyes. "I'll call you if anything happens," she says, pressing her keys into my hands because my car is still in Amy's driveway. "Go." She nods. "*Go.*"

I park Kate's car in front of the Maple Hill police department. It's dusk, usually my favorite time of day, but today it feels ominous and angry, a reminder that I don't need. I zip my jacket against the wind as I walk toward the precinct and shove my hands in my pockets, twisting the scraps of soggy tissue inside. Dr. Meyer couldn't tell me how long it would be before Amy would speak, or if she ever would. This is my chance to speak for her, and I pray that I will be able to say everything that needs to be said.

The police department is right in the middle of town, smack in the center of the bull's-eye if you were to look at an aerial map of the city I've lived in all my life. Yet standing frozen in front of the entrance, I realize that I've never really noticed it until now. There is a refurbished old-fashioned movie theater around the corner that Larry drags me to occasionally to see the classic westerns they sometimes play, and a frame shop at the end of the block where I'd had some of my grandmother's recipes framed for my office a couple of years ago. How nearsighted has my life been that I've never noticed the cavalry of police cruisers lined up like dominoes in front of the building, or the proud flagpole in a patch of grass in the middle of the circular drive, with the Virginia state flag flapping loudly in the wind? It strikes me that if somebody came into the bakery, sweaty and gasping for breath and screaming for the address of the nearest police station, it would have taken me a minute to remember exactly where this place is. It is so strange what you don't notice until you absolutely have to. It is so odd what you can completely pass over.

The precinct is quieter than I imagined it would be, a stark contrast to the hustle of the emergency room I've just left. The officer at the front counter is studying something on his computer. "I'd like to talk to somebody about my friend Amy Rutherford," I start, my voice not nearly as authoritative as it had sounded in my head when I'd practiced on the way over. "Your officers found her in her house this afternoon. I'm Waverly Brown. I gave a statement."

"Rutherford?" the officer repeats, wrinkling his brow. He scratches the side of his face. His skin is pockmarked and he needs to shave. "Hold on a minute."

He stands and disappears behind the closed door on the other side of the counter.

I wait, shuffling my feet against the sparkly-flecked linoleum floor. A door down the hall to my left opens and the wind rushes in.

"This is ridiculous!" a voice shouts.

I turn toward the door.

Mike!

He is a good thirty feet away from me, handcuffed between two cops. The moment I hear his voice, I want to throw myself down the hall and hurt him as badly as I possibly can. I want him to suffer. But because I'm here for Amy, I force myself to stand still. It's like trying to ignore a magnetic pull, like I'm on the losing end of an invisible game of tug-of-war, but I make myself stand frozen. I have to keep my composure. I am here for Amy.

"Hey!" he yells, trying to get my attention. "Waverly!"

I can't help myself—I turn again to look. He's craning his neck toward me like a dog trying to escape his leash. He may as well be exactly that; my heart is racing as if a rabid pit bull's careening toward me. When his eyes meet mine, it's not like it used to be; I don't feel the sort of mild dislike I used to feel in his presence, the slightly aggravated confusion over what Amy sees in him. Now I see pure evil.

"Waverly! Come on...Waverly!" I grip the counter in front of me—I'm shaking with rage. It's obvious that I hear him. I'm the only person in the dim hallway. Thankfully, just before my anger's about to bubble over, they disappear behind a door.

"Ma'am?" I hadn't noticed that the officer I'd spoken with had returned.

"I'm sorry," I say, loosening my grip on the counter. I'm breathless.

"Ma'am, our report says that you gave a statement on the scene." He must have missed this when I said it on the way in.

"Yes, but there's more I need to say. Can I talk to somebody?

Add to my statement?" I look down the hall. "That was her husband I just saw. In the handcuffs."

"We're handling everything. Someone will call you if we need more." He taps the end of his pen impatiently against the counter.

I grab it and he lurches back. I need to do this for Amy. "I'm sorry," I say, looking deep into his eyes. "But I must see someone. Please. *Please.*"

He rolls his eyes and turns back again. "Give me a minute," he says. "I'll see if there's someone around."

The interrogation room is as cold as the walk-in refrigerator at the bakery, and the folding metal chair that the police officer across the table asked me to sit in—she actually sort of pointed her hand toward it when we entered the room—is creaky and rusting along its gray edges, the seating equivalent of an old dented can of peas.

Every time I shift in my seat, a high-pitched screech erupts from under one of the legs of the chair. After the third or fourth time it happens, the most bizarre thought pops into my head: it's the kind of coffin-creaking-open noise that plays right before the opening beats of "Thriller." I think of Jenny Ryan, my childhood next-door neighbor, and how the two of us would spend hours in her living room trying to learn the choreography, pausing and rewinding the tape of the video over and over again on her family's Betamax. The memory leads me to another one—Amy—dancing on the roof deck of this pubby sort of sports bar that we used to go to in Adams Morgan when we were in our twenties. She would always pull me toward her, bopping her head: "Come on, Waverly! Who cares if no one else is dancing! You'll never see these people again!" I always wrestled myself away from her, more content to stand against the railing, nurse my beer, and watch. The handful of times when Amy was able to persuade me to dance with her were always at the end of the night, in the safe confines of our across-the-hall apartments, music blaring through our open doors, our upstairs neighbors screaming at us to shut up and go to sleep. I wish now that I'd never turned her down.

The policewoman sitting across from me—Lieutenant Dillon, her black-and-white plastic badge says—doesn't flinch as I recite every detail about what I know about Amy and Mike's relationship. I try to remember everything that I can, to toss out every shoddy scrap of information that comes to me, but the lieutenant doesn't make it easy for me. I tell her about the injuries I've seen. I give her a near-verbatim account of what Amy told me that night at Finelli's. I explain how Mike skipped counseling and how he belittled her in front of us. I tell her that it was just ten days ago when Amy came to me with a bag under her arm and said that she was leaving him.

She doesn't give me any indication that I'm telling her too much or too little or the right thing or the wrong thing. Worse, she doesn't offer any reason to believe that she is sorry for what's happened to Amy. I want to believe that she has to be this unemotional to do her job—that we are all the better off for it—but even when I tell her about the welts on Amy's back and the things that Mike said to her, she looks at me as vacantly as if I've been reciting the items on a Chinese takeout menu. She just keeps scribbling and scribbling on the yellow legal pad in front of her, her head bent so deeply that I can see the oily white of her scalp along her part, which is so straight that it looks like she measured it against a ruler. What is it about the police officers in this town that they take such copious notes? I pause to take a breath and think of what else I can tell her. The only sound in the room is the damn chair and the scratch, scratch, scratch of Lieutenant Dillon's pen against the paper.

"So what is he being charged with?" I ask.

"I can't give you any of that information, Ms. Brown," the woman says, her head still bent. Even though she is clear across the table, I can smell the sour scent of her coffee breath along with the mint that has failed to cover it up. "So you say that she said that they were working things out? Do you have any reason to think that they *weren't* working things out?"

I shoot forward in my chair. *Has this soulless bitch been listening to me at all?*

"Yes," I say, trying to keep my voice steady. "I mean, I don't have specific, concrete reasons. I just—She said that this had been going on for years, and when I was around him lately, he always seemed so angry, and like I said, she said that he had decided not to seek help, which I didn't think was a very good sign, and she didn't either. She was ready to leave him, and then she changed her mind. He scared her. She lived in fear of him. Really, I think he brainwashed her." I shake my head at her, disbelieving. "And, let's see," I say, my voice rising. "She's in critical condition now because he practically beat her to death." Tears start to roll down my cheeks. I squint my eyes, trying to stop them.

The officer looks up at me, her head still bent toward the table.

"I'm sorry." I shake my head at her, my palms turned up toward the dank, gray ceiling. "I guess I'm the kind of person who believes that if somebody's an abuser, he doesn't just suddenly stop one day and turn into a wonderful husband. I mean, she *told* me that he hit her. She *told* me it had been happening for three years. I've seen the bruises."

"But you don't have anything specific you can tell me about *recent* abuse?"

"It was barely over a month ago when I saw the bruises!"

"But nothing since then?"

I rub my hands over my face and wish that when I pull them away—*I don't want to pull them away*—I will be magically transported somewhere else and none of this will have happened. I'll be on a beach on the north shore of Oahu or in a bar in Amsterdam, anywhere but here.

I blink the room back into focus. "No, I guess she hasn't told me anything about specific incidents since that one that I already told you about," I finally answer her. I chew on my lip, trying to think of any other details. Then it hits me—my diary. "I don't know how helpful this would be, because it just repeats everything I've told you, but I keep a diary. And even though I haven't written anything in it about Amy recently, I did make notes after she told me specific things." I point to the legal pad on the table. "All of the stuff I told you," I repeat.

"What kind of notes?" The officer shifts forward in her seat. *Could she actually be interested?*

"Well, I don't keep a detailed diary," I say. "I mean, I don't write entries that are pages and pages. Just sentences scribbled here and there, like, *'February 3, dinner at Italian restaurant. Amy told me about Mike hitting her.'*"

Dillon nods and scribbles some more notes. I swear that I'll see that blue ink for days after this. "But it's dated? You mark the entries with dates?"

"Yes."

"Okay, that's good. That's really good."

I nod back at her. *Finally, something.*

"I think that's it for now," she says, her eyes following the back-and-forth of her pen over her pad as she reviews her notes. She reaches into her pocket to fish out a business card. "Call me if you think of anything else."

I reach out to take it, but she slaps it on the table like a blackjack dealer. She starts to stand.

"Wait," I say over the screech of the chair as I stand. "What happens next?"

"He'll be charged." She's fumbling with her ballpoint pen, trying to get it to stay tucked behind her ear.

"Charged with what?" I say.

"We'll be in touch if we need anything else from you," she says, reaching for the doorknob.

"But wait! Charged with what?" I say.

She shakes her head—a disallowing, end-of-story shake. "We'll be in touch."

I get in the car to call Larry and check on Emma. Larry tells me that they stopped at the grocery store on the way home, where he bought a frozen pizza for dinner and supplies to make ice cream sundaes. They've just come in from playing in the backyard. He says that Emma is now busily stacking the coins that they dumped out of the fish bowl where Larry puts his spare change.

"Are you okay?" he says.

I shake my head no and then realize that he can't see me. "It's not good, Lare," I manage. "How am I going to explain to her parents...?"

"She's so lucky to have you, hon. We all are."

It's the first time that any tenderness has passed between us since our fight, and I want to be able to tell him that it helps, and that I'm so thankful for him, but the past few hours have me so shaken that I shouldn't even be behind the wheel of a car, much less trying to string coherent sentences together. "Thank you," I say. "For everything. Tell Emma that her grandparents and her aunts will be here soon."

When I get back to the hospital, Kate is in the waiting room, on the phone with her lawyer. "Still nothing," she mouths. I sit down next to her, and she wraps an arm around me. I fold myself into her and rest my head on her shoulder. She squeezes my arm. "It's going to be all right," she says, and I close my eyes, thankful, for once, for her unshakeable conviction.

The people around me are like ghosts, changing shape every few hours. First, an elderly woman and her adult children talk in hushed whispers about her husband's—their father's—heart attack. Then a husky, bearded man in carpenter's pants, who paces in circles while he growls on his phone to his insurance company. Then a young married couple who don't utter a single word to each other during the entire ninety minutes that they sit across from us, but hold each other's hands so hard that I can see the whites of their knuckles.

I stare past the images on the flat screen across the room— Pat Sajak and Vanna White, a sitcom with an endlessly repetitive laugh track, the teaser for the eleven o'clock news. There could be a breaking news report about a medieval mob of club-wielding maniacs about to storm the hospital and it wouldn't faze me. I can't move. My mind is stuck on one image that replays itself over and over again like a skipping record: Amy, her head cracked open on an operating table. And the very real possibility that none of this might have happened had I called somebody, done *something*, when Amy first told me what was going on in her home. She kept saying that everything was fine. I never should have believed her.

I force myself off of the scratchy couch in the waiting room only after Amy's mother calls from the parking area outside. I wait for them in the hallway, and when they appear behind a janitor wielding a floor buffer, I realize that I haven't seen them in at least a year. My nerves start to make my insides turn like something is crawling around in my stomach.

Amy's mother leads the four of them like a majorette in a very somber marching band, her shoulder-length silver hair the same color as her silk blouse and flapping behind her like wings. Amy's sisters, Celia and Claire, in lockstep just behind their mother's left shoulder, are holding hands. They look so much like Amy that it's as if they are a pair of paper dolls whose third has been torn away from them. Celia, with her pregnant belly, looks so much like Amy did when she was expecting. Amy's father follows behind them, taking one step for every two of theirs, as if by moving slowly enough he might never have to confront the situation. Even though I have seen him only a handful of times since Amy's wedding— we chatted about fly fishing at one of Emma's birthday parties, and about his mother's biscuits when Amy brought them to visit the bakery—I feel like I can sense everything that he's thinking just by watching him walk toward me. His slumped shoulders and angry, anxious fists look just like what I'm feeling inside.

When Amy's mother sees me, she rushes toward me and hugs me hard, as if by holding me she might reach through to Amy. I know there is no way to comfort her, and I bite hard on the inside of my cheek to keep myself from breaking down.

"Waverly, how did this happen?" Claire says, her voice warbling. "I just don't understand how this happened," she says again.

The four of them are looking at me wide-eyed. Now I have to tell them what put Amy here, and it occurs to me, standing across from them in the goddamn hospital, that if I'd just been brave enough to call them when Amy first told me—instead of letting her convince me that she was "fine, just fine"—it would be a whole hell of a lot easier to explain what I am about to now.

"How long has it been happening?" Margaret suddenly says, her eyes narrowing. She puts her palm to her chest and takes a deep breath, pursing her lips before she continues. "He's been hitting her for a while, hasn't he?"

It is so hard to look at them that I feel like I have weights attached to my eyelids, but when I finally do, I can tell that they've been talking about this very possibility and that they might not be surprised by anything I'm about to say after all. They have the determined look of people with a plan, and it comforts me somehow. How long have they known? Did it only occur to them tonight when I called, or have they been speculating for longer, all of them wishing away the same anxious thoughts that I've been battling?

"Yes," is all I can get out. "She told me several weeks ago."

Margaret steps forward and wraps her thin, graceful hands around my arms. She pulls me toward her and looks at me with the kind of compassionate steadiness I haven't seen since I gazed into my own mother's eyes. "Tell us everything you know," she says.

I look down the long hallway toward the room where Amy is fighting for her life. Then I clear my throat and start talking.

CHAPTER TWENTY-EIGHT

Around six the next morning, Larry brings Emma to the hospital and picks up Amy's two sisters and me, and we drop the three of them off at the Holiday Inn near the hospital. Amy is in the surgical intensive care unit, or SICU, and we won't know how successful her surgery was until after her sedation wears off.

"How are you doing?" he says as soon as they're out of the car, putting his hand on my knee as he slowly pulls away from the entrance. When I open my mouth to speak, I burst into tears. He veers left, pulling into the parking lot in front of the hotel, and shuts off the engine. I bend forward, my head in my knees, and sob so hard that I nearly vomit. I don't think I've ever cried like this, not even when my parents died, when I'd wail in the shower so that Babci wouldn't hear me. Everything I've been holding in overtakes me, and no matter how many times Larry purrs that it will be okay, no matter how gently he rubs my back, I feel like I'm falling deeper and deeper. When I eventually catch my breath, I keep my head locked in my lap and listen to the soft murmur of the newscaster reporting the weather on NPR. "Clear blue skies and lots of sunshine," he says.

Larry puts his hand on the back of my head and softly runs his fingers through my hair. "How did it go with her family?" he asks.

I tell him that it was every bit as horrendous as I'd imagined it would be. I trudged through each detail with the same candidness

as when I'd given my statement to the police. It was almost easier that way—to just spit it all out like a confession, which, in a
way, it felt like it was. As I pushed through, I watched the kalei-
doscopic way that their faces shifted from shock to worry to anger
and to fear. They hadn't actually known anything. "She kept as-
suring me that they were working it out," I'd finished, not able to
look at them when I said it. Nothing could have sounded more
ridiculous. I keep replaying the scene in my head, as if by forcing myself to relive the humiliation, I might be able to somehow
change things.

Larry has a morning meeting, so he starts the car and we head
home. It's rush hour, and even though we're headed away from
the city, this is D.C. The traffic on the Beltway is hardly moving.
Neither of us says much. I wonder if he's still angry with me. We
inch down the highway, the green exit signs flipping by slowly,
and I people watch, trying to lose myself: an Indian woman in a
business suit driving a Saab, sipping a venti-something out of the
telltale cup; four carpoolers, all men around my age, laughing rau-
cously; a couple staring vacantly out the windshield, bored or tired
or both. Everyone looks so normal. So responsible in their trudge
toward work. So well-adjusted. So fine. A week ago, I might have
envied these strangers, projecting my vision of their perfect lives
onto them. *How nice that she can buy a giant coffee like that every day
and not worry about her budget,* I might have thought, looking at
that woman. *How lucky for those guys to be able to ride to work each
day and laugh. How sweet that that couple gets to start and end their
day together.* But now—now I just see nightmares: That woman
needs her giant coffee because she was up all night worrying about
her impending divorce. Those men are all laughing to make up for
the fact that they know their department at work is about to be cut.
That couple isn't speaking because he hit her before they left for the
office. I glance at Larry, then grab his hand.

He squeezes back.

I look out the window, at the driver passing by on the right. He's handsome. Navy suit. Singing along to something. Where is Mike?

When I get inside the house, I see what Larry's left for me on the kitchen counter: An old box of Unisom that he must've dug out of the shoebox of medicine that we keep in the linen closet. Next to it, there's a note: *"Get some sleep. Will call you after mtg. I love you."*

I walk to the living room and collapse into one of the faded floral armchairs I inherited from my grandmother. I can see myself in the mirror on the wall across the room. I look like I've plunged my fingers into an ashtray and wiped wide swaths of ash under each eye. The whites of my eyes are fissured with red, like the fragile insides of an old china teacup. I look just as I should.

I trace my finger along the pattern in the upholstery and wonder when Kate will get here. Shortly after Amy's family arrived last night, she left the hospital, saying that she'd text in the morning and come by. I could tell that she felt like she was intruding. She chatted briefly with Amy's mom, offering to call one of the doctors her family knows.

I touch my fingertips to the swollen pads under my eyes. I'm so puffy from crying that I can feel my eyelids when I blink. I remember a Sunday afternoon years and years ago—I must have been fifteen or sixteen—when my mother and I got in a fight about something. I can't even remember what it was now. I came to Babci's and sat in this very room and bawled my eyes out. She brought me a bag of frozen peas from the kitchen to bring down the swelling. I'd asked her if I could come live with her and she'd laughed. "Maybe someday," she'd said. I can't believe that I almost let myself lose this place.

There's a black-and-white picture in a frame on the table next to me. I'm probably around ten or eleven, at the beach with Mom and Dad. My swimsuit has a rainbow running diagonally across the front like a sash, and I'm kneeling in the sand at the edge of the water. Mom is on one side of me, deeply tanned, with a rare cigarette in one hand. Dad is on the other, in a faded T-shirt, cutoffs, and what looks to be the very first pair of Nike sneakers ever made. Our smiles are identical, wide and spontaneous, like we're all laughing at the same joke.

The doorbell rings.

"How is she?" Kate says when I answer.

"No news yet. Margaret said she'd call as soon as she could."

She drops her bag on the worn Oriental rug and holds her arms out to me. She's dressed in expensive-looking jeans and snakeskin cowboy boots, like she's on her way to a hoedown at the Four Seasons. I wrap my arms around her. She smells powdery and perfumey like a department store makeup counter.

We walk to the living room, plopping down on either end of the couch. I hug a throw pillow to my chest. Kate does the same. It occurs to me that we've sat just like this, on this very sofa, countless times over the course of our friendship: in high school when Babci would have us over for Polish tea cookies; after my parents died, on Thanksgiving and Christmas Day, stuffed from the feasts that Babci and I cooked together; and now, this.

"How's her family?" Kate says.

"About how you would expect." I rake my hands through my hair. "Her father didn't say a word the whole time I was there." After I'd finished telling them what I knew, he'd turned away from us, breaking away from our huddle like he was quitting the team, and retreated to a chair in the corner of the waiting room, where he sat with his head in his hands until the doctor came to give us an update.

"And what about Mike? I still can't believe you saw him at the police station."

"The police came to the hospital and talked to Amy's family. He's being charged with something called 'malicious wounding' because her injuries are so severe. It's like an attempted murder charge. He could get serious jail time."

"Good. How serious?"

"Five to twenty years."

"Well, that's good!" Kate's face lights up. "Isn't that good?"

I shrug. "To be honest, I can't think positively about much of anything until I know that Amy's okay. And the police were quick to explain that even with a known history of abuse and what Amy's just been through, Mike could plead not guilty when the charges are read against him today. And he could hire a good defense lawyer and be out on bond as early as this afternoon."

Kate's jaw drops. "That's the most asinine thing I've ever heard." She pinches her bottom lip between her thumb and forefinger, thinking. "I can call someone," she says.

"We really can't do anything until Amy wakes up. Until we know—"

"Yeah," she interrupts before I have to say more.

For several minutes, we're both lost in thought. I can't stop imagining Amy in that hospital bed, and every time I remember what put her there, the thought sneaking through the back door of my brain like an uninvited guest, my heart leaps as if I'm just learning it again for the first time. I'll never get used to this. I'll never, ever get used to this.

Kate starts tapping her boot angrily against the coffee table. "It's just unbelievable," she says, her voice exploding into the room. "That this could happen to Amy. To someone like us."

"Happens every day, Kate." I'm tired. I'm mentally done. The past twenty-four hours is catching up with me.

She shrugs. "Not to women like Amy. Not the doctor's wife. The preschool mom. The potluck organizer in the cul-de-sac."

"You know, you're wrong about that, though," I say, dipping my head back on the chair and studying the pattern of a water stain on the ceiling. "It's women like us…it's women not at all like us. It's anyone. It's everyone. It's women in bad neighborhoods with alcoholic boyfriends and it's pop stars and movie stars, too."

"Yeah, but would you ever have expected this? Dr. and Mrs. Michael Rutherford?"

"No." I shake my head. "No." I shake it again. "I mean, it had been going on for years before it ever crossed my mind. The whole thing completely bewilders me. I think it always will."

Kate pulls herself up from the collection of throw pillows on the couch and pushes her shoulders back. "Well, it seems like this is the year of surprises." She chuckles, not really meaning it.

"Kate, how are you *really* doing? Aside from the jokes."

"How am I doing?" Kate raps her fingertips against her cheek, considering the question. "I guess I should have expected it. That's what I think."

"That's ridiculous," I say. "I certainly never thought that Brendan, or anyone, could do this to you. When people looked at the two of you, they saw this picture-perfect example of everything we're supposed to want: You're both gorgeous, well educated, poised, wealthy. And I say that because I've done my fair share of envying, too."

"Oh, please," she rolls her eyes.

"Well, I have," I say, locking my eyes on her so that she knows just how serious I am. "Your life always seemed so easy, Kate. You have to know that. Meanwhile, mine…"

She sighs. "I know what you're saying. You don't have to say anything else."

"I guess the bottom line is this," I say. "I don't think anyone ever expected that this would happen to you." I pause for a moment, weighing whether to say it. "Including you."

Kate crosses her arms over her chest and sinks back on the couch. She gazes across the room, her mind far off somewhere, and rolls her tongue against the inside of her cheek.

"Maybe I shouldn't have said that," I venture. "But you know? If there's one thing that this situation with Amy has taught me it's that it's stupid for us to just sit quietly by while we watch each other suffer. You seem good, Kate; you really do. I don't know anyone with your backbone, with your strength. But are you *really* okay?"

Kate looks at me. "I've told you. I got rid of the excess baggage and I'm moving on." She smiles wide, her eyes crinkling as she does it. "Life is good."

I raise my eyebrows. "Really?" I say. "I am your oldest friend in the world—in fact, let's be honest; I'm your only true friend. And you're going to give me a T-shirt slogan to explain how you're feeling about your husband's infidelity?"

She tilts her head to the side and considers me, slack jawed. I can't tell whether she's about to get up and walk out or finally start talking. "Okay, the truth," she says, slapping her palms against her thighs and sitting back up.

I smile at her.

"The truth is that I feel like an asshole. For not seeing it sooner, of course, and for not catching him before it got out the way that it did. But, more than anything, for being a part of the whole charade in the first place." She rubs her hands over her eyes. "I knew what I was getting into with Brendan. I've spent a lot of time thinking about it over the past few weeks, wandering around alone in that big stupid house, and I don't know why I ever did it. He was everything I've always hated about my life. All of that showiness. The dinner parties with people you can't stand to socialize with but feel you have to, the life dominated by what the newspaper writes about you. God, I felt like a fucking fraud every time I stepped up to a podium." She daintily presses her pinky to each tear duct. "I don't know how it happened, Waverly. I've always been so sure that I wouldn't grow up to be like my mother, and yet, the second I met Brendan, I just completely abandoned myself. When I was traveling all of the time, I was so in love with my life, but I hated the way that my mother constantly told me to grow up and settle down. And then..." She glances at me. "It's embarrassing to admit."

"What?"

"Well on one side, I had my mother telling me that the vagabond sort of life I was leading was childish. Then on the other, I had you and Amy, both coupled off. I guess I felt like settling down was the only option. And I wasn't getting any younger."

"Brendan was familiar," I say. "It was what you knew. It's easy to see why it happened."

Kate nods. "Why didn't you stop me?" she cracks.

"Because you said you loved him, Kate."

"I did," she says. "I do." She's quiet for a moment. "And you know, in the beginning, he really did seem to love *me*, without all of the..." She waves her hand in the air. "You know."

"He loves you. He's an idiot for doing what he did to you, but I don't doubt that he loves you."

She nods.

"I called him," she says. "Last night when I left the hospital."

"You did?"

"Yeah." She hugs her knees to her chest. "After everything with Amy, being in the hospital yesterday...I guess I just decided that it was time to call a truce." She shakes her head. "It suddenly seemed very silly to not even talk to him."

"So how did it go?"

"Not horribly, actually," she says. "I told him about Amy and he's just as horrified by it as the rest of us. And surprised. We started talking about us, of course, and he said that despite my decision, he's really grateful for the marriage that we had, especially in light of what I'd just told him. He said that he's thankful for what I've done for us, which was nice for him to acknowledge, finally. He said that he was sorry that he hadn't paid closer attention. He thought that I was happy."

"I thought you were, too. I mean, you complained a lot, but I thought you were basically happy."

"Well, what were you supposed to think? How could I not have been happy? When the *Washington Post* is running stories in the Metro section every other day about how fabulous you are, and the people who surround you all day are essentially paid to kiss your ass, I don't think many people would see it as a hardship. And that's what I kept telling myself: 'Kate, you're supposed to be happy. You're supposed to be grateful for all of this.' Meanwhile, Brendan and I had gotten to the point where we hardly spoke to each other unless it was about work, or about his wanting children—and even that wasn't so much a talk as it was him trying to convince me in the ten seconds that I let pass before I would just tell him no again. If I'm getting really honest about it"—she stops and points a teasing finger at me— "*and I guess you're making me get really honest about it*—I was so resentful of him for putting me through the campaign even though he never had to strong-arm me into it. I was the one who told him to go for it, who quit my job, who just forgot about myself." She purses her lips. "And, well, he forgot about me, too. Frankly, I can't blame him. When it comes right down to it, I was wholeheartedly living up to the image. It was what I thought that I was supposed to want."

She pauses, and I see a thoughtful, ponderous look in her eyes that I've never seen in our decades of friendship. "I still love him. I really do. But I feel like something's happening to me, like some layers have been peeled off of me or something. Does that make sense? With Brendan gone—well, with the campaign gone—I get to be *myself* again. I don't think that ever could have happened if we kept going the way we were going. Why is it so hard for us to just be ourselves? To just be honest about what we want?" I can see her thinking it through.

"I don't know." My mind flashes to Larry and all of the hours I've spent worrying over our relationship.

"So what are you going to do?" I ask her. "You're certain you're ready to leave him?"

"I don't know what I want anymore," she says, throwing her hands up into the air. "But the funny thing is, it's kind of a relief."

We sit silently for another moment. This is one of the great gifts of old friendship; to quietly sit in a room together. I listen to the screech and crunch of a garbage truck on the street outside.

"You know what's strange about all of this?" Kate says.

"Hmmm?"

"I've frankly always been a little bit jealous of Amy."

"Really?" Now, *this* is honesty.

"I know what I used to say." Kate shakes her head. "And I'm not saying any of this because of what's happened to her. I'm really not. But I've always envied her. That's my dirty little secret. She always seemed so simple, you know? Simple in the best possible way, and so happy without having to strive for all of this extraneous crap. I mean, my mother trained me to worry about such inane things—reputation, social standing. Amy never had to worry about that stuff. She just had—" She stops herself. "Well, she *seemed* to have exactly what she wanted. The sweet house, the family life."

"She definitely did," I say, nodding.

"It's kind of ironic, then, isn't it?" Kate says.

"What?"

"Well, Amy and I both *seemed* to have a lot of things, and it turns out that neither of us really had much of anything."

"I always thought that you both had it all figured out," I say.

"Oh, please," Kate says. "You're the most steady of the three of us. You're the rock."

I gasp. "That's the most ridiculous thing I've ever heard."

"It's true!" she says, but then she must be able to tell from the way that I've gotten up to rearrange the magazines and tchotchkes on the coffee table that I'm not in the mood to talk about myself. She points at my cell phone sitting on top of Larry's latest issue of *The Journal of American History*. "No word from anyone yet?"

I pick it up and look at the screen to make sure. "No, nothing."

"Then in the meantime," Kate says, leaning toward me, "we should do what Amy needs us to do most."

"What's that?" I say.

"Figure out what we're going to do about Mike." She gets up and walks across the room to pick up her purse, rifles through it, and pulls out a small leather diary. "I happen to know a really great lawyer."

CHAPTER TWENTY-NINE

Later in the day, I thumb through a mass of cardigans on the sale rack at the J.Crew in Georgetown Park, trying to distract myself. After Kate took me to pick up my car, which was still in front of Amy's house from the day before, I came home and fell into a heavy, much-needed sleep. Three hours later, I woke with a jolt and checked my phone—no calls except for one missed one from Randy. I spent ten minutes pacing from room to room before I decided that my restlessness would only lead to more useless wallowing, so I went ahead and drove into Georgetown, so that I'm at least near the hospital when Margaret's call finally comes in.

Behind me in the store, a college-age Asian woman is holding a tiny pair of jeans up to her childlike waist, asking her friend's opinion. Next to me, a woman swipes furiously through the corduroys, digging for her size. I feel myself seething; it's almost like I can hear my anger ratcheting up, like climbing a ladder. How can these women just be going about their day while one of my best friends lies down the street with her head cracked open like Humpty Dumpty's? It's as if there's a force field around me that divides our realities: On the outside, it's swirls of springtime and the smell of the sun in the air. But inside, here where I stand, it's darkness, damp cold, and the kind of piercing quiet that makes you want to scream. As the minutes pass without word from Margaret, I feel increasingly uncomfortable in a relentless and awful way, like my body is trying to turn itself inside out. I wander toward a bin of hair accessories, pick up a tortoiseshell barrette, examine it halfheartedly, and toss it back in. Then it hits me: This horrible, "nobody knows what's happening to me" feeling must have been exactly how Amy felt, all the time.

Twenty minutes later, just after I've pushed a lid onto a paper cup of exorbitantly priced coffee at Dean & Deluca, my phone finally rings. I look at the area code: 919. *Yes!* Finally.

"Margaret?" I don't bother with hello.

"Waverly, she's awake."

"And?"

"It will be a while before we know for certain. She's still groggy from the surgery, and the doctors say she'll need to be monitored very closely over the next several hours to make sure that everything continues to progress in the way that they want it to, but...oh, Waverly." Her voice breaks. "They're very optimistic!"

If not for the steaming cup of coffee in my hand, I'd leap with joy.

"She wants to see you," Margaret says. "Get here as soon as you can."

Amy's skin looks gray and chalky, like cement dust has been applied to it with a powder puff. Her head has been shaved and is covered in a turban of gauze and medical tape. The topography of her body underneath the bed linens looks childlike and frail. A tangle of tubes and wires weaves from her head and arms and chest to the IVs and monitors gathered behind her bed like watchmen. I cup my hands over my mouth, trying to keep the tears in as I rush toward her. "Can I hug you?" I say, squeaking out the words.

"Yeah, yeah, of course," Amy says, a tired smile spreading across her face. I cautiously put my arms around her and press the side of my face to Amy's, giving her a soft peck on the cheek before I let go. Her family is outside, giving the two of us some time.

I sit on the edge of a vinyl chair next to the bed and slide it closer to her, and then shift to avoid a bright beam of sunlight that's escaped through the vertical blinds.

"You can close those blinds if you want to," Amy says.

I shake my head and carefully place my hand on her arm. I just want to touch her, to hold her hand or put my palm to her cheek; to confirm that she's really lying here awake and alive, to prove that she's going to be okay.

Amy turns her head against the pillow and gazes drowsily at me.

"How do you feel?" I ask. It's the only place to start.

"Mmm," Amy says, thinking about it. She attempts to shrug. I look at the IV tube coming out of her hand. It reminds me of visiting her in the hospital on the morning after Emma was born. There was a crowd of family in the room and nurses bustled in and out. Animated, happy conversation whirled around the room—"the baby came so fast, Amy was so brave, did you see the size of Emma's little feet?" Now it's just the two of us, the room silent except for the static beep-beep of the machine monitoring her heart rate.

"I feel achy," Amy says. "Like I haven't used my body in a very long time...kind of like when I started running again after Emma was born. Isn't that strange?"

I squeeze her arm.

"Nothing hurts, exactly, it's just...I'm very tired."

I nod, squeeze her arm again. *Thank God, she's alive.*

"They drilled a hole in my skull. I have titanium plates now." She chuckles, thinking of something. "When I was a kid, I begged mom to let me cut my hair like Cyndi Lauper's. You know, like on the cover of the album with 'Girls Just Wanna Have Fun.' I guess I finally got my wish." She smiles, a flash of the old Amy. Then her voice dips: "I'm dying to see Emma."

"I'm sure you are. When can you?"

"Now," she says. "But I told them to wait. I need to figure out what to say to her. Claire is keeping her at the hotel. Thanks for helping with all of that, by the way."

I nod. "Amy, you know that you can talk to me...about any of this," I say. I feel like every time I say it, it becomes less effective; a watered-down mantra that she doesn't want to hear.

"I know," Amy says. She fumbles to grasp for my hand.

Unlike my relationship with Kate, my friendship with Amy is punctuated by physical affection. It's her nature, and became mine with her. We press our hands against each other's arms when we speak, swoop the hair out of each other's eyes, pick lint off each other's sweaters, and hug hello and good-bye even when the interval between the two is mere minutes, but I can't remember ever holding Amy's hand. It feels light and damp, like a child's.

"I'm okay," Amy says.

I swallow against the gob of phlegm pressing against the back of my throat and squeeze my hand tighter around Amy's.

"I am. I'm okay." She gazes down toward the end of the bed. From where I sit, it's hard to tell whether she's closed her eyes.

"You know, I'm alive," she finally says. When she looks up at me, she has tears in her eyes. I brush one from my cheek. "I'll just be happy when I can get out of here. Start to get past this."

I nod, thinking about all of the things that Amy will have to endure once she gets out. It's not like there will be a "Welcome Home" party with a banner hanging across her living room and balloons tied to the mailbox. Flowers somehow don't even seem appropriate. Will she even want to go back to that house? Will she even stay in Virginia? "You know you can stay with me if you need to," I say. "While you get everything figured out."

She doesn't say anything.

"What happened?" I say, spitting it out before I waver any longer about whether to ask.

Amy gazes back at me. Then, this time, she squeezes my hand. "I'm going to be fine."

"Have you talked to the police? About what you're going to do?"

Amy nods. "A little while ago."

"I heard about the arrest," I say, deciding that it's better at this point not to tell Amy that I'd seen Mike at the police station. "What's the next step? Will there be a hearing, or...?"

"Oh." An almost undetectable scowl flashes across her face, as quickly as a bird zipping past the window. "I'm hoping not."

I frown. "What then?" Did he admit to doing this? Is he going to quietly cooperate? Will he go straight to jail?" There are so many questions I want to ask.

Amy shifts under the sheets. "I don't want him to go to jail," she says, her voice so quiet that I'm not sure that I've heard her right.

"Wait," I say. "What?"

"If it was up to me, the charges would be dropped." Amy slides her hand out of mine. She runs her fingers over the gauze that wraps across her forehead, almost analyzing it in the way that she touches it, as if she's reading braille.

"Oh, so then is he just cooperating...or something?" I'm completely confused.

Amy closes her eyes and tries to shake her head, a barely perceptible wag. "No, no. It's nothing like that, Waverly. I don't want to get police, lawyers, all of that stuff..." She purses her lips like she's disgusted. "This woman called me a few hours ago. I swear it was within minutes after I woke up, before I even had a chance to talk to my parents. She was some sort of advocate assigned to me by the state. I don't know."

"Amy, slow down, okay?" I can see the anxiety taking over her face. It probably isn't good for her. "Now, who was this woman who called? Take your time."

"An advocate." She glances up at me. "A..." She sighs. "A domestic violence advocate."

I nod.

"She explained to me what Mike was being charged with and when I told her that I didn't want him to be charged with anything, she said that it wasn't up to me. Can you *believe* that? She said that because it's a criminal case, the state will prosecute him regardless of whether I want to be involved. She said that it's standard."

"But I don't understand." I reach out for her. "You don't want him to be charged?" Maybe this is all too much for her right now. Maybe she isn't thinking straight. Surely it will take a while for her to recover from the injury and the surgery alone, much less all of the psychological consequences of how it happened in the first place. Maybe we shouldn't be talking about it.

"I'm not leaving him, Waverly. He needs help."

I pull my hand back from the bed as if I've just been burned. *Did I hear that right?* "Wait." I grip the metal armrests on my chair. "What?"

"I'm not leaving him."

"Uh, uh—," I stammer. "Have you talked to your family about this?"

"That's just it, Waverly," she says. "Mike's my family. Emma's my family."

I'm stunned. There's no other word for it. Looking at her lying in the bed, I realize that I am looking at the shell of the woman I used to know. Is Amy still in there somewhere? What kind of spell would have to be cast to bring her back? *Could* she be brought back? I don't know what to feel. I am desperate, furious, heartbroken, afraid. I want to scream at her that she is out of her mind. *He almost killed you!* I want to yell. *He* will *kill you!*

When I finally figure out something to say, the words come out tightly coiled and controlled. I am trying not to lose my composure. "Amy, I think that this is affecting Emma. I really think it's harming her," I say. I know it's a cheap shot, invoking her daughter, but I'm desperate.

She looks at me. "Waverly, that's part of the reason why I know that we have to figure this out. For Emma."

Has he really whittled her down to this? "Amy," I plead. My heartbeat feels like a whirring windup toy inside my chest. "Honey, just look. Look at what he did to you, Amy."

"I know. I'm not stupid, Waverly. I know," she says. "But he's sick. This is proof that he needs me more than ever."

"Amy, why don't you think about this? You don't have to make any decisions right away. You've been through so much."

"Waverly," she says. "He's already pleaded not guilty. His lawyer called me a little while ago and took a statement from me about my intentions to stay with him. With that, and with his clean record, he should be out on bond later today. Once I'm home, we'll deal with the trial and what to do about getting his charge reduced. I know that you don't understand this, but this is my marriage. This is what I have to do. I'm not a child. I know what I'm doing."

I look into the deep brown of Amy's eyes and search for some remnant of the woman I used to know. Somebody out in the hallway laughs. It seems gruesomely appropriate.

Amy reaches her hand out to me, stretching from her shoulder and wiggling her fingers for me to grab it. I look at her hand, and then, reluctant and heartbroken, I clasp mine to it.

CHAPTER THIRTY

What is it, Waverly?" Margaret's face goes pale when she sees me. As she stands, her copy of *Good Housekeeping* falls from her lap onto the floor.

"She's staying," I say before I can think better of it. Amy's father makes a sound I've never heard before; an awful, guttural, wounded animal kind of moan. He flees the room before I can react, almost knocking into me as he escapes into the hallway. I should've taken some time to think. Margaret follows behind him, then Celia. I stand there, hopeless, while the other people in the waiting room play with their phones and flip through their magazines, pretending not to have heard me.

I sit for an hour, getting up every five or ten minutes to peer down the hall to Amy's room, as if by staring long and hard enough, I might be able to see through the closed door to what's happening inside. Please let her family talk some sense into her. If she won't even listen to them, then I'll know for certain that we're beyond rock bottom.

I get up for another door check and Margaret is walking toward me down the hall. The door to Amy's room is closing behind her—Celia and her dad are still in there. "Let's go get a coffee," Margaret says, wrapping her long silver cardigan tightly around herself.

She says nothing as we walk down the hallway, wait for the elevator, and head toward the cafeteria. Walking behind her after we exit, I notice that she and Amy have the same bouncy stride.

We pass a couple of doctors on our way into the cafeteria. "Thank you!" Margaret smiles at them as they hold the door open for us. She sounds so cheerful. It's as if a doctor just told her, *We got all of the tumor out and the lymph nodes are clear!* or *It's a healthy baby boy!* I'm awestruck by the way that she can pretend like she hasn't just received the kind of news that could knock a person off of the trajectory of her life forever. I think of my own mother, whose state of mind at any given moment was transparent and always available for public consumption. She talked too loudly in restaurants and movie theaters and didn't care who heard her, barreled through crowds, knocked things off of tables without noticing. My father said that she moved through life like a linebacker. Being with other people's mothers always makes me miss my own a little more than usual. I can't help but compare.

We sit. Margaret dumps two creamers and two sugars into her coffee. "Amy always jokes that I like my coffee like dessert," she says. She taps the plastic stirrer against the edge of the paper cup and then sets it neatly on a napkin to her right.

"*Waverly*," Margaret says slowly, as if she's feeling the sound of my name on her lips for the first time. She looks across the vast room. We're not the only somber pair sharing coffee.

"I just want to know where my little girl's gone," she says quietly. "Ever since I got your call I have not been able to stop wondering what I could have done to contribute to this. Did I not show her how to stand up for herself? Did I not teach her self-respect, and how to make others respect her?" She says *others* like it's a dirty word. I know what it implies. "You know how we women are, or, I don't know…" She runs the tips of her fingers over her lips, thinking. "Maybe I'm too old-fashioned. I always pushed our girls to have good manners, to treat people well. Now I'm wondering about all of the things I should've been teaching them instead of reprimanding them for not getting their thank-you notes out fast enough or worrying over what they wore to school." She shakes her head. "Girls," she says, almost like she's lamenting the word.

"Margaret, you can't blame yourself for this," I say. "You're a wonderful mother. Amy always says so. She's said that if she can do half the job with Emma that you did with her and Celia and Claire, then she'll know that she used her life well. More than once, she's told me about how you used to sit together at the kitchen table and talk after school while she did her homework. It's obvious that it's a wonderful memory for her."

"Thank you," Margaret says. Her hand shakes as she raises her cup to her lips. "Davis says that we should hire somebody to investigate him, to see if there's anything else in his past that might help put him away. As difficult as this is on all of us, I think it's the worst for Davis...to be a father and to have another man treat your little girl this way. It's awful, Waverly."

I grab a sugar packet off of the stack on the table and start turning it in my hand. "How did you know?" I ask, thinking of what she said when they arrived. "Did you know?"

"Well, I never suspected anything like this," she says. "Never. If I'd known that this was going on, I would have been up here a long time ago."

I wince. *Why didn't I say something?*

"Mike was a little stoic, but he was always polite to us," she says. "I wondered about his background and why we never heard more about his mother, but I thought he was just private. I wasn't thrilled with the way that he treated Amy the last few times I saw him. He seemed to criticize her, and I thought that if he was doing it in front of us, then it must be worse in private. But I never thought that something like this could happen, not until you called. And then it was strange: I called Celia immediately after I talked to you, and right away, she said, 'He did it.' It too easily made sense. Do you understand what I mean? It was like I'd known it subconsciously, like my body had intuited it before my brain could, because I wasn't as surprised as I should have been."

"I'm so sorry that I didn't tell you." I can't look at her as I say it. "I should have called you."

"No, no. Don't feel sorry. I understand why you didn't."

"No, I should have," I say. "It was silly of me to think that I was being loyal to her by keeping her secret." I take a tiny sip of my coffee and then push the cup aside. My stomach is churning with acid. I haven't eaten anything in well over twenty-four hours. Cafeteria coffee is the last thing I need.

"Waverly, what should we do?" Margaret says. When I look up at her I can see how frightened she is. This is not the same woman who'd gathered her family around her a day earlier like a general leading her army into the battle of their lives. Now she just looks empty.

"I don't know," I say, my voice breaking. "There has to be something." Trying to form a conscious thought is beginning to exhaust me. My emotions are ricocheting from one extreme to the other. My worry is so deep that I want to yank Amy out of that hospital bed and take her somewhere where she'll find herself again. I love her so much. But at the same time I'm so frustrated with her that I almost wish I didn't know her at all. I guess, in a way, I don't.

"There has to be something we can do," Margaret says again. It's as if we think that something will come to us if we just keep repeating it over and over. She crumples one of her napkins and wipes her nose efficiently. She clears her throat. "We just have to." She looks across the table at me. "Because if we don't..."

"I know." I nod solemnly. "If we don't."

A family sits down next to us—a mom and dad and two little boys. The mother sets down the tray in the center of the table and the boys attack, grabbing for a plastic-wrapped honey bun, a bottle of juice, a paper container of French fries. The mother and the father each tap their straws on the table to rip the paper wrappers, neither of them noticing that they're moving in sync. Margaret and I both watch them.

"Tell me what's happening with you," she says when she turns back to me.

"Me?"

She glances back at the family. "It might be nice to talk about something else," she says.

Oh, of course, I think. She doesn't want these people to hear about Amy.

"Well," I say. "There's a lot to catch up on." I tell her about the business and the money and then, finally, Larry. And when I get to that part, she does something I never would have expected: She laughs.

"What?" I say.

"Oh, I'm sorry, honey. It's just…" She puts her hand to her mouth and shakes her head, still giggling. "It's just that you're missing the point."

"I don't understand."

She laughs again. "I don't mean to be patronizing, hon. I'm sorry." She takes a breath and swallows, gathering herself. "Do you know that Davis and I have been married for forty-four years? We got engaged the day after our high school graduation. We'd known each other all of our lives. We grew up just around the corner from each other, went to the same school, the same church—but I didn't know him in the sense that you're talking about. I wasn't 'sure' about him. I'm *still* not. He could leave me tomorrow for that cute redheaded nurse who's working with Amy." She laughs. It's good to see her laugh. "But that's all part of the fun. You grow together and apart; you make mistakes and you solve them. And with each year that passes, you learn more—about yourself and about each other—and hopefully love each other more, too, despite all of the things you've done wrong. That's unconditional love. Real, true, can't-be-replicated love."

"Yeah," I say, a little breathless. "I don't know why I never thought of it that way."

"Try not to worry so much," she says, reaching across the table and patting my arm. "Things work out." She looks at me, realizing the irony of what she's just said. "We can only hope, right?"

I nod. "I guess that's all we can do."

When we get back to the waiting room, Davis tells us that there's no update. He and Celia talked with Amy until she got drowsy and then left to let her sleep. I say good-bye. I need to check in with work, even if it's just to quickly pop in and make sure everything's running smoothly.

As I'm turning to go, I see Margaret and Davis embrace. I can't imagine what they're feeling. They must've dreamt so much for their daughters—graduations and weddings, grandchildren, the simple hope that they would be happy. What's happened to Amy must be crushing.

I think of my parents, whose constant mantra was, "We just want you to be happy." Growing up, it was a blessing and a curse. On the one hand, I loved knowing that I didn't have the kind of parents who expected me to become a lawyer or go to a certain school, but I also occasionally wished that they'd give me more guidance. Neither of them offered an opinion when it came to my future. They didn't care what I wore or worry over whom I hung around with. I'm certain that if they were alive now and I went to them with questions about my business or my relationship, they'd say what they always had: "We just want you to be happy."

Listening to Margaret talk, I realized that I've been trying too hard to make that happen. My parents didn't give me an ultimatum. It wasn't "be happy or else." But even before they died, I looked at it that way. I suppose it's partly because I'm an only child. I always felt I was their one shot, so I had to get everything right. When they said, "We just want you to be happy," I didn't feel relief or comfort. What entered my mind was one relentless, aggressive, forever question: *How? How? How?*

My entire adult life, I've been struggling so hard searching for this sort of higher, enlightened perfection. But really, after talking to Margaret and watching her and Davis together, I realize that all I need to do to make my parents proud—to make myself happy— is to stop second-guessing my blessings, stop thinking that the grass is always greener, and know how lucky I am to have my particular messed-up, mucked-up life. I learned when Mom and Dad died that life is precious, but instead of using that lesson to be grateful for every extra day I get, I've been trying to mold my life into some superfantastic, errorless masterpiece. I realize now that all they really wanted for me was to have my own one-of-a-kind life. I ought to start embracing it.

Outside, I find my car and slump into the front seat. Before I put my key in the ignition, I grab my phone and punch out a text to Larry: *I love you.*

Just as I'm about to shift into reverse, my phone buzzes back. *I love you, too,* his message reads. *Come home.*

CHAPTER THIRTY-ONE

Two weeks later, I am sitting with one of my customers, chatting about whether the red velvet cupcake trend is here to stay, when I feel my cell phone vibrate in my front pocket. "I'm sorry, I need to take this," I say, pushing myself up from the table. It's Margaret, calling with her daily update. I hit the "answer" button on my phone with one hand while I clear an empty coffee mug from a nearby table with the other. "Hey, Margaret," I say, dropping the dish in the plastic tub just inside the door of the kitchen. "How's she doing today?"

Amy left the hospital five days ago with a strong prognosis. It looks like she will fully recover, though her doctors stress that she needs to get ample rest over the next few weeks while her body recovers. How she's going to relax, I have no idea. Ever since she announced she was going home to Mike, her family and I have been a revolving door of worry, each of us taking turns auditioning our point of view on the matter at her bedside:

Her father: "Good men—men worth sticking it out for—don't do this. He should be in jail, Amy. Why can't you see that?"

Claire: "He'll do it again, Amy."

Celia: "Deep down, you know he will, Amy."

Her mother: "If you're so intent on working it out, why don't you at least live with us while you do it? We're worried about your safety, honey."

Me, wringing my hands like an old woman: "Let him go to counseling first, like you'd planned, and then go back to him... think of Emma... talk to Kate... stay with Larry and me."

All of us: "Why can't you see what he's doing to you?"

Despite our protests, she's back at home with Mike, who, unbelievably, has been left almost fully responsible for her care. When she told her mother that this was what she wanted and that the decision was final, Margaret tried to get her to speak with one of the hospital psychiatrists, but she wouldn't have it. There's nothing any of us can do. So she's home, being nursed back to health by the man who nearly killed her.

Her sisters had to go back to North Carolina to their families, but Margaret and Davis refuse to leave D.C. They're at a Marriott behind a shopping center around the corner from Amy's subdivision. Every morning, Margaret goes to Amy's for a visit, takes Emma out to play, and calls me afterward with a report. She has not seen Mike. Amy refuses to let their paths cross, and it's probably better that way. Her father, who's reticent as it is, is so destroyed by what's happened to the most ebullient of his three daughters that he doesn't speak at all when I see him. Margaret says he spends most of his time in their hotel room, making calls and doing research about ways that they might be able to legally force Mike out of their lives once and for all.

But there's really nothing that any of us can do. Mike pled not guilty the day after he was arrested, was released a few hours later, and because of Amy's statement, the lack of evidence, and his clean record, the charges have been reduced to simple domestic battery instead of malicious wounding. It's unlikely that he'll go to jail at all. Instead, he'll get "one year suspended," which means that he'll occasionally have to meet with a parole officer. He may as well have been caught speeding or stealing a pack of gum, and it's nothing short of appalling that he's free to do as he pleases. After everything that's happened, I fear what that might be.

On the day that Amy left the hospital, I watched as a couple of nurses placed her in her father's car as carefully as if she was a piece of antique furniture. Amy promised me, looking out from the dim backseat, that she would be in touch. "Call you tomorrow," she said, smiling as if this was one of our usual good-byes, as if we'd just met for breakfast or gone for a jog.

Of course, she hasn't called. I knew when she said it that she wouldn't.

Now I worry whether I'll ever hear my friend's voice again. Amy knew that I'd talked to the police. I told her about my conversation with Lieutenant Dillon and how I'd given her my diary entries. I wanted Amy to see how serious this was. I pleaded with her to think about what she was doing. Every day, I call her cell phone and leave another message asking her to call me back, but she doesn't. I've called the home phone, too, but on the one occasion that somebody actually answered, it was Mike, his "hello" as chipper as if he'd just popped up to grab the phone during a family game of Monopoly. I threw the phone down as if I'd just been stung. As much as I worry about Amy, I couldn't bring myself to speak to him.

I hardly sleep. At night, my mind reels with horrible projections about what Amy is bound to face before long. The grout on our bathroom tile is cleaner than it's ever been. The kitchen cabinets have been alphabetically organized. Larry begs me to come to bed, but I don't bother. When Kate called me close to midnight last night and heard my mixer whirring in the background—I was making lemon icebox cookies—she implored me to just get in the car and go to Amy's. She even offered to pick me up and come along.

But I can't bring myself to do it. Everything else I've tried has proved useless. Why would this be any different?

"So it's just the same as yesterday," Margaret says, sighing heavily. "I guess he went out to pick up some groceries while I was there. Sooner or later, he's going to run out of errands to do. He's going to have to face us."

"It's telling that Amy's so insistent on keeping you apart," I say.

"And it's frightening," Margaret says. "You know he's the one controlling everything, like she's his puppet. I can't imagine what he says to her."

"I don't even want to think about it," I say. "How's Emma?"

"She's with me right now. We're at the playground in the neighborhood. Swinging."

I start to ask her whether Amy's said anything about me, but I stop myself. Margaret knows that I call her every day, and neither of us can make sense of why she won't speak to me. Margaret believes that she's displaced her anger. She won't let herself be mad at Mike so she's made me the enemy—or he has. I'm the one who told her family and went to the police.

We hang on the line, both of us wishing that there was more to say, but as the days snap by, it's becoming more and more obvious that we're helpless. Until Amy changes her mind, there's nothing that we can do. I say good-bye and tell her that I'll look forward to talking with her tomorrow.

Jeannette must've been waiting for me to get off the phone because when I step out of my office, she's waiting for me. "What is it? Is something wrong?" I say, scanning the kitchen behind me.

"Everything's fine." She laughs. "God, you're paranoid." She has no idea. I've told Randy what happened but not anyone else on staff—I need work to be immaculate, a refuge from the rest of my life. "You actually got a really interesting phone call."

She hands me a slip of paper. Her handwriting is like Larry's, the letters so tiny that I have to hold the paper up close to read it. *Mark*

Brinson, the Butterman Catalog." And then a number with an area code I don't recognize. "He said to call him today, if you can."

"Is this, like, the real Butterman Catalog?" I ask.

"Yeah, the fruit baskets. My mom always got the catalogs. She sent Christmas gifts from it every year."

"Mine, too." I remember the catalog sitting dog-eared on the kitchen counter, my mom's ever-present can of Tab nearby.

I call the number from my cell as I step out the back door into the parking lot behind the bakery. With the ovens going, it gets obscenely hot in the kitchen and I need some relief, not that I'm going to get much outside today. It's fully spring, but for the past several days, it's felt like July. I keep overhearing customers make jokes about global warming and, from some of them, snickers about the bullheaded Republicans who don't believe in it. Typical D.C., where even a simple conversation about the weather can quickly become political.

"Mark Brinson," the voice on the end of the line says.

"Hi, it's Waverly Brown returning your call," I say.

"Waverly! Thanks for getting back to me so quickly. How are things in the nation's capital?"

Ugh. He has an overenthusiastic salesman's voice. I'm immediately turned off.

"Good, good. Where are you calling from?"

"Oregon. Portland, Oregon. Ever been?"

"No, I never have."

"Well, it's beautiful. You should come see us. Maybe after this conversation, you will!"

"I'm curious why you called me. That's for sure."

"Are you familiar with our company, Ms. Brown?"

"It's Waverly. And yeah, I know the catalog."

"Well we're more than just the catalog," he says. "We have dozens of stores across the country. We've been in business since the 1930s."

"That's impressive," I say. "So what do you want with a punk like me?" *Seriously,* I think.

"Ms. Brown, I have a cousin in D.C. She's a triathlete, like me. Ever done a triathlon, Ms. Brown?"

"It's Waverly," I say again, more impatiently this time. "I run some but I'm not much of an athlete. I just don't have time with my business, which I assume has something to do with why you called?"

"Lots of great running trails in your area," he says.

I throw my head back. *Come on. Get to the point, already!*

"I was out there a few months ago, visiting my cousin. We're training for an Ironman together."

"That's an accomplishment."

"Yes, the training's intense. Well the reason why I'm calling"—*finally!*—"is because when I was there a few weeks ago, my cousin and I had just finished a long bike ride and she took me by your bakery. I had one of your famous doughnut muffins. Let me tell you, after a two-hour ride, it really hit the spot. You're really talented."

"Thank you," I say.

"And then, wouldn't you know it, I was on the plane home the next day, thumbing through the Sunday *New York Times,* when I saw the article about you. What a coup that must have been for you! And well deserved!"

"Thanks so much," I say, starting to like him a little more. I can feel myself smiling.

"It got me thinking, and so I called the bakery a couple of weeks ago and had a couple dozen shipped out here. Do you recall? I had them shipped to my personal address."

I have a vague recollection of Randy telling me about something like this, but it must have happened around the same time that Amy was in the hospital because I can't totally remember, and I should. We've had a handful of people, usually past customers who've left the area, call once or twice asking for shipments of a particular favorite goodie, but it certainly doesn't happen frequently enough that I wouldn't notice. "I do, I remember," I lie. "How did you like them? They survived the trip, I hope?"

"They were fantastic, but the truth is that they weren't for me. My job is to find new products for our mail-order business. And I'm calling because we'd like to start offering our customers your muffins. We want to be in business with you, Ms. Brown."

I stop pacing around the parking lot and fall back against Randy's Jetta, which is parked in the spot next to my car.

"We can work out the details later, but I wanted to start with this introductory call to introduce myself and find out whether this is something that even interests you. Does this interest you?"

"Yeah," I gasp. "It definitely interests me!" I know that I probably shouldn't sound so eager, but I can't help it. My muffins being sold nationwide? I don't want to get ahead of myself, but I could pay off the house loan in full. I could buy the bakery space from that nitwit Alec. I wouldn't feel nauseous every time I got a bill in the mail. Larry and I could even take a vacation together. Or, hell, just go out for a nice dinner.

"Well, that's great. That's great that you're interested. I'm going to put together some information for you and we'll chat more over the next few days. Does that sound good?"

"That sounds fantastic," I say.

After I've given him my email address and thanked him a dozen more times, I hang up and turn a celebratory twirl. I fall back on the warm hood of my old rusted-up Subaru and shield my eyes from the sun with one hand while I call Larry with the other.

"Hellooo," he says. I hear a baseball game on the television in the background.

"Guess what?" I can't believe what I'm about to say. "I have some good news."

CHAPTER THIRTY-TWO

A few nights later, Kate, Larry, and I are standing at the island in my kitchen, hovering over a giant bowl of linguine. "Family style," Larry says, laughing, spearing his fork into the food. When I poured the pasta into the bowl on the island, Kate and Larry charged, Larry handing Kate a fork from the silver canister where we keep them on the counter. We ended up not bothering with bowls. "I think more pepper," I say through a forkful. "You think more pepper?"

"Sure," Kate says, her mouth also full.

I grab the grinder off of the counter behind me and turn a few twists over the bowl. Kate begins to tell us about the trip she's thinking about taking over Memorial Day—to India.

"Is this some sort of *Eat, Pray, Love* thing?" Larry jokes.

Kate holds her fork over her head and makes a motion like she's going to stab him. Only Larry can get away with that kind of sarcasm with her. Anyone else would be walking backward out the door by now, hands up in defense, saying they didn't mean any harm.

"Actually, Brendan and I met for dinner yesterday," she says.

I put my fork down. "Dinner? Yesterday?" I look at my watch. "Um, how many hours has it been since then and you're just now telling me?"

"Well, you've been so busy becoming a national superstar that I didn't want to bother you with it."

"Please." I roll my eyes. The deal with the catalog is going to go through and it's all happening very quickly. The muffins will appear in next month's issue. A photographer and food stylist are coming out at the end of the week to take photos of me and the muffins. I've made an appointment with Kate's hairdresser; you'd think I was getting a root canal, I'm so anxious about it. Mark Brinson says we're shooting for ten thousand orders this first go-round. *Ten thousand orders.* I don't know whether I'll ever be able to wrap my head around that number.

My first check, a signing bonus, is in the mail. Earlier today, I got online and moved some money around to cover next month's loan payment. My house is officially safe. It was a relief to see the zero balance on the loan after I was done, but I didn't exactly jump up and down like a sweepstakes winner. It was more like the kind of relief you feel when you're driving and you swerve to avoid getting in an accident that would have been your fault. You tell yourself you'll pay closer attention from here on out.

"So? How was dinner?" Larry says. This is the good aspect of Larry having never made friends with any of my friends' significant others. He can participate in girl talk.

"Well," Kate says, pausing to swallow her bite. "He was actually available for dinner. That's the first thing. A few months ago, I don't think that Brendan would have stopped working even if his own mother died."

I feel myself tense up. Even all these years later, I still feel it when someone mentions a parent dying.

"So where did you go?" I say.

"Of course you ask about the restaurant first," she teases. "Restaurant Nora." It's one of our mutual favorites. I haven't been in years, with the budget and all.

"Did anyone bother you?" Larry says. "I mean, the two of you together, in public."

"Not a one," she says, smiling. Brendan and Kate became old

news a few weeks ago, when pictures surfaced of two Miss USA contestants smoking pot in an Atlantic City hotel room before the pageant. Miss Vermont and Miss Idaho, apparently. Kate joked that Brendan probably bought them the drugs and hired the photographer.

"So? How was it?" I ask.

"It was good. You know, it was actually kind of nice. Strange, being together like that. He's been staying on Capitol Hill. An apartment."

"Are you having second thoughts?" I ask.

She shrugs and glances at Larry.

He notices. "You girls need me to leave so you can really pick this thing apart?" he says.

"No, no," Kate says. "No. I haven't made any decisions. I don't know what I'm thinking. I don't know what I'll do. It was nice, though, even to just sit together, and even though it was awkward. I wonder when I'll be able to look at him without seeing those photos of him with her."

"I'm sure," I say. "But it's a start. If that's what you want—a start."

The doorbell rings. Larry and I look at each other and shrug. "I'll get it," he says, putting down his fork and wiping his hands on his jeans.

After he's left the kitchen, I look at Kate and say, "So? What else?"

But before she can answer, Larry calls, "Hon, come here."

Walking down the hallway toward the front door, the first thing I see is pink. And then, like a gear slowly turning, the source of the salmony color registers in my brain: Amy's pink trench coat. She's standing with Larry, in sweatpants, her coat, and a baseball cap that only partially covers the bandages around her head. Emma's standing beside her, her arms stretched high to show Larry the stuffed penguin she's holding. Both of them look tiny next to his burly heft.

"I've been calling," I say. I don't know why it's the first thing out of my mouth.

She presses her lips together and lowers her eyes toward Emma, smoothing her hand over her little girl's hair. "I'm not supposed to be driving." She tugs on her hat. "I didn't get your calls."

I nod. Kate walks up behind me. "Amy," she gasps.

Amy scans the room anxiously, and then her eyes finally rest on me. "I need your help," she says, her voice breaking.

I have to lock my knees to keep from crumpling onto the floor with relief. "Okay," I say. "Anything at all."

Amy just nods, not needing to say more.

Twenty minutes later, we decide that Margaret and Davis should pick up Emma and take her to the hotel. She'll be safer there. She doesn't need to be hanging around here while we figure out what we're going to do. Amy's on the phone with her mother, giving her directions to my house. She's pacing my living room, circling around the coffee table as if she's following the lines of an invisible toy train track. She looks so frail beneath the oversized sweatpants and sweatshirt she wears, her head a turban of gauze beneath the hat. I want to tell her to sit down, to rest, but I'm scared that anything I might say will be the wrong thing that sends her back out the door.

"No, there's nothing to be scared of, Mom." She scowls into the phone. "I have to stay here because I have to deal with this now. Going down to North Carolina would just prolong everything. No, no, he doesn't know that I've left."

The doorbell rings and it's as if its gentle chimes are an air raid signal. Larry and I leap from our spots on the couch. *What if it's*

Mike? There's a rolling ache in my gut as I peek out of the curtains, but I can't make anything out. I go to the door.

"Oh, Jesus," I say, relieved when I peek through the peephole. I twist open the brass lock on the heavy wooden door. "It's just my neighbor." The nosy freelance writer.

We chat for a minute and hardly more—she sweetly stopped by to congratulate me on the *Times* article, making me feel guilty for wanting to slam the door in her face—and I turn back toward the living room. Kate is tapping her foot impatiently and playing with one of the bangles on her wrist as she waits for Amy to get off the phone. I go to the kitchen to refill Amy's glass of water. She's off by the time I'm back.

"Please sit down, Amy," I say. "I'm sure you shouldn't be moving around like this."

As she moves to sit on the couch, Kate and I both rush to help her. She stops us. "I'm fine," she says.

We're all quiet for a moment. I sit down across from her, on the floor, resting an elbow on the coffee table.

"My mom didn't say, 'I told you so,' at least," she says sullenly. Another minute passes. "It's hard to believe that the bogeyman we're guarding ourselves from is my husband."

Kate and I look at each other. Larry slips quietly from the room, knowing that the three of us need this time together, and goes to check on Emma, who's coloring in the kitchen.

"Do you know that he once drove four hours to North Carolina after a thirty-six-hour hospital shift to pick up barbecue from my favorite place back home just because I'd mentioned that I was desperate for some?" She starts to cry. I jump up from my spot on the floor to sit next to her.

"You're going to be okay," Kate says, scooting down the couch until she's next to her. "Everything's going to be fine," she assures her again.

Amy nods. The look on her face is a yearning one, like she wishes that Kate's certainty could somehow transfer through the air between them and land on her, like a costume she could jump into.

Amy rubs her palms over her thighs. "I was in bed," she starts. "Emma was curled up next to me, in the crook of my arm. We were watching *The Little Mermaid*. Claire bought it for her while I was in the hospital. Ever since I got home, Emma seems to spend most of every day either asking to watch Ariel and Prince Eric or singing the songs from the movie. I didn't mind—I've loved just snuggling up with her. Part of me was starting to get resentful that I'd eventually have to get out of bed.

"Mike was downstairs making dinner. He said earlier today that he was actually thinking about taking a leave from work to take care of me. And, he said—" She pauses to look at me. "To take care of himself. I know you'll never believe me, but he's really been incredible. Three times a day, he carries up trays of food. Cereal or toast in the morning, lunches of soup and cookies that Emma says are from her, ginger ale in one of the crystal wineglasses we got as a wedding present. While I lay upstairs with Emma, I could hear him doing the dishes, pushing the vacuum, opening and closing the washing machine door. I know that nobody else understands what an effort he's making, but I can. I decided that that's all that mattered."

I'll never understand how she can speak sympathetically about him, I think, watching her. It's as if she's a puzzle I'll never figure out, as if she's something I've never seen before.

"It's not as if I didn't know this would be hard," she says. "Believe me, over the past few weeks I've felt like everything I've learned in my thirty-five years of life, every moral truth, every hard-won lesson, has just flitted away. I've hardly let myself think about the specifics of what I have to deal with going forward, except for when Mike came into the bedroom to talk about his case or give me updates from his calls with his lawyer. I didn't want to deal with it. Not yet. Not until I had at least a few more days of cuddling with my baby girl and watching the happy way that she stretched her little body against mine as if she was still a part of it."

I think of the way that Emma had acted after the police brought her out of their house, and how while she was sitting with me in their front yard, she seemed so aware, almost wise, in the way that the commotion around her didn't faze her. I twirled my fingers around her cider-colored curls, watched her doughy fingers pick at the grass, and thought that it was like she was waiting for all of the adults around her to figure out what she already knew. She knew too much.

"Mike said that everything was much more likely to work in our favor if I testified on his behalf," she says.

Our favor, I think.

"He wanted me to say that he was taking some sort of medication and that he was also drinking when everything happened. He said it would be easy to come up with a story about a drug that would make him hallucinate at the wrong dosage." She looks at me. "He said that whatever you told the police wouldn't hold up as long as I said it wasn't true."

He's pure evil, I think to myself.

"The truth is that he was drunk when he put me in the hospital, and he never drinks, hardly ever, except for a beer here and there. And I felt like I was a broken record, with the way I was pushing him so hard to see a counselor. How many times had he told me that I'd be more help to him than a stranger? I wanted to have the same faith in myself that he seemed to. I wanted us to be able to do this at home, together. As a family. As a husband and wife. I actually don't remember what happened a few weeks ago. Not exactly. I know it was early in the morning and I kept hitting the snooze alarm. He yanked me out of bed and said something about how it was my fault he'd overslept."

Kate and I look at each other.

"When I was in the hospital, he called me the evening after he got out on bond. He was so happy when I told him that I was coming home. He told me how strong I was, and how thankful he was to have me to show him what true strength was all about. He said he needed to learn from me. And then—the look on his face when he saw me after Mom and Dad brought me home showed how sorry he was. He started shaking, and then sobbing, and then he stumbled onto the bed next to me and begged for my forgiveness. I remember I rubbed his back, trying to comfort him. I kept thinking, *For better or for worse, in sickness and in health.* I kept thinking that he was far sicker than I was, worse off than I could ever be. I thought that he needed me. But then today…" She shakes her head. "Oh Lord. Today."

"What happened?" I say, my voice barely a whisper.

"Well, the phone started to ring again. Emma and I were watching the movie. She was playing with the bandage on my arm where my IV had been inserted, drawing shapes on it with her fingertip. She kept saying how much fun she was having."

Tears spring to her eyes.

"Suddenly, Mike barged into the room. Both Emma and I jumped, and then, before I could figure out what was happening, he threw the cordless phone at the wall behind us like he was aiming for us. His eyes were…the way that they get. He started screaming: 'Your fucking friends and your fucking family need to stop calling here!'"

Oh God. It wasn't me—I hadn't called today—but it still makes me feel awful.

"He had never done this in front of Emma before. I could feel her tensed up against me. She was scared to death. He was saying ridiculous things. About how I hadn't explained to everybody that he could take care of me. About how I had no faith in him, just like his mother. I grasped Emma's hand under the covers and she squeezed back hard. I tried to get him to stop. I kept looking at Emma to try to signal to him that he couldn't do this in front of her. He said, 'It amazes me how incredibly stupid you are.' Emma turned herself toward me so slightly that Mike couldn't notice, but I could feel it. Every muscle in her little body was trembling. And then…" She shakes her head and takes a deep breath. I look worriedly at Kate.

"It was so…just crazy. You know that I hate that word, but that's what it was," she says. "He took the teddy bear off of the bed that Mom gave me in the hospital. Emma picked it out for me one day while she and Claire were at Target. He asked me where I got it, like he was accusing me of something. I told him that Emma gave it to me. He started screaming: 'Emma got you this? Our three-year-old? She went to the store? Drove there herself? With her money?' He was shaking the stuffed animal at us and his voice was getting louder. It was absurd. He started calling me other names, saying I was a stupid whore…And then, out of nowhere, Emma peeled away from me. Her tiny voice pierced the air. She started screaming, 'Daddy, no!' and swinging at him, grabbing for the teddy bear. She was lunging for him, up on the bed in her cupcake-print pajamas with the blueberry stain on the front, screaming for him to stop." She gasps. "And somehow he did. He left the room, as if he'd never been there at all."

"We sat there listening as he left the house. I pictured Mike leaving. I've watched him from the window so many times before that I could imagine every move. I asked Emma if she was okay, kissing the top of her head over and over again, like I was stamping her. Do you know what she said?"

Kate and I both shake our heads, stunned at everything we've heard.

"She said, 'I want to watch my movie, Mommy.' I turned it back on and watched her, noticing the way her eyebrows subtly twitched with the action on the TV screen. Now I have no doubt that Emma's understood what's been going on for far longer than I ever could have imagined. Or maybe I was just in denial.

"I can't blame anyone but myself for that. I swear, I feel like I just took my little girl and sat her on a raft and pushed her off of the shoreline, waving good-bye while I watched her drift, stuck and helpless. Say what you will about the beatings not being my fault, but it was my choice to keep Emma in that house and pretend that nothing was wrong. I realized a few hours ago that I can't do it for another second. We were supposed to be a family. That's what kept me at home with him. But I'm realizing now that that place was nothing like a home, and we were as far from a family as anything I can imagine. I need to rescue Emma. And if I'm so far gone that I could do this to my daughter, then a tiny part of me also recognizes—finally, I guess—that I need to save myself."

I wrap my arms around her. "Oh, Amy." Her name stumbles out of my mouth.

"I'm so sorry," she moans.

Kate embraces her from the other side.

"No, no, there's nothing to be sorry about," I whisper. "Nothing at all to be sorry about."

"You're going to be okay," Kate says. She grasps my hand behind Amy's back.

"We're going to figure this out," I say. "Everything's going to be fine."

CHAPTER THIRTY-THREE

Amy had brought several plastic shopping bags to our house. She says that when she was in the midst of leaving, moving as quickly as she could and yanking things at random as if she was participating in a timed scavenger hunt, she had a strange realization: This was the answer to the "What would you take with you if your house was on fire?" question. This was the fire. And even though it's been only three days since she left, she's discovering now that leaving—the physical act of getting up and walking out the door—is the easiest part. "It's everything that happens before and after you cross over the threshold that could kill you," she says.

It isn't the way she'd imagined it. In her lowest moments, like on the somber, silent mornings she'd spend dotting concealer over the marks his knuckles had left on her temple, she'd crafted a mental list of the things she would need to take with her should she ever decide to leave: the numbers for their bank accounts, her passport, Emma's birth certificate, their social security cards, Emma's medical records, her address book, the folders from her old job and the few she kept from college, the locket her mother gave her on her sixteenth birthday, the charm bracelet she started when she was pregnant with Emma, the cameo her grandmother left for her, Emma's baby book, photos from her twenties, her high school yearbook. Emma's favorite toys—the worn Elmo doll, a cheap teddy bear from the drugstore that had become her favorite despite its scratchy fur, *The Very Hungry Caterpillar*. Her wedding album. She didn't know why, but her wedding album. As she was racing around the house, wondering whether Mike was going to come in and catch her, she realized that this was not the big production she'd envisioned, with a U-Haul van backed up to the garage while Mike was at work. "When Emma found me in the kitchen stuffing my phone charger into my bag and asked what I was doing, I told her that we were going to stay at Aunt Waverly's for a little while. The smile that came across her face was all the confirmation I needed to know that I was doing the right thing," she says.

We're pulling into Amy's driveway.

Even though it seems like Amy's been on the phone with the police ever since she showed up at my house, and they fully support what we're about to do, I've driven here reluctantly. I thought that we should at least have somebody accompany us, but Amy insists that it's unnecessary. Nobody's seen or heard from Mike—not the police, who came by the house after Amy's initial call to let them know that she wanted to move forward with prosecuting Mike; not the neighbors; not his coworkers; and most frightening of all, not even Amy. In a way, it's almost worse that he's just vanished, because it's impossible to guess what he might be plotting or where he might be. Amy wants to take out a restraining order—it's the first step of many to protect herself—but the police can't serve him with the paperwork if they can't find him.

Kate's car pulls up behind ours. It's an unusually cold May morning. Steam escapes from our mouths as we get out of the cars and greet each other.

"So what are we going to do if he's here?" Kate says, glancing over at the house.

Amy shakes her head. "He's not going to be here. The sheriff's office has been twice to try to serve him with the papers."

We decide to enter the house through the utility door on the side of the garage. We can check to see if his car is here and make a quick escape if it is. Amy unlocks the door and pushes it open. "Not here," she says.

"Thank God," Kate and I say simultaneously. The three of us walk through the darkened, empty garage—first Amy, then me, then Kate—to the door that leads into the house, and then into the kitchen.

It's difficult to explain what I feel when we step inside and Amy turns on the light, but I have to grab Amy's shoulders from behind, and I don't know whether it's to steady her or brace myself. The house has been ransacked. Every dinner plate and drinking glass has been smashed onto the kitchen floor. The contents of the refrigerator—gallons of milk and juice, leftover dinners, containers of ketchup and jam and mustard—have been thrown against the cabinets. The room is saturated with the smell of rotting food.

"Oh dear God," Kate whispers behind me.

Amy doesn't say a word. She steps methodically over the piles of broken glass and trash and mess and walks into the living room. I follow behind her.

"Be careful, Amy," I say. She should be recuperating in bed. We're all worried about her recovery, but she's insistent on pushing forward. Larry and I theorized last night that she's acting this way because it's the only way she'll survive. She has to be purposeful if she's going to get through this without falling apart.

Every picture in the living room has been smashed. The TV is pulled away from the wall. The couch cushions are strewn across the floor.

"Let's go upstairs," Amy says.

We follow behind her. No one says a word. The only sound is our footsteps up the creaky staircase. In her bedroom, she finds the contents of her jewelry box on the floor, along with most of her clothing. The bathrooms and guest room are equally destroyed.

The only room that remains untouched is Emma's. We breathe a collective sigh of relief when we discover it.

They use the spare bedroom as an office. Amy sits down at the desk and opens the drawer where they keep the checkbooks for their various accounts. Everything's gone.

"I need to check something online," she says. I stand behind her as she goes to click on the computer.

"Unbelievable," she says, tapping the mouse repeatedly. "The Internet's out." She picks up the phone on the corner of the desk and tries it. "The phone's out, too."

"Can I use yours?" she asks me. Yesterday, when she tried to use her cell, she discovered that she had no service. She'd said that Mike probably did it. Now we're all sure of it.

Kate and I watch as she calls information for the number for her bank, then starts punching keys, occasionally muttering words like "accounts" and "check balances" as she moves through the automated menu. Then she hangs up, hands me the phone, and bends her head to her knees.

"He took everything," she says through her hands. "All of the accounts are empty."

She begins to cry. To be honest, it's a relief. She's hardly shown any emotion since that first night at my house.

"How did this happen?" she says through her tears. "How did this happen to me?"

I want so badly to be able to give her an answer. This never should have happened to her. Not Amy. Not when this—a home, a family—was all she ever wanted.

Over the next hour, Kate and I stand around, quite helplessly, while Amy goes room by room, trying to determine what she wants to bring with her. In her bedroom, she puts a couple of stacks of clothes into a bag. In the bathroom, she opens and closes drawers, ultimately taking nothing. When she gets to Emma's room she sits on the floor and begins flipping through the pile of books in a basket next to her bed. It's horrible to watch her, cross-legged on Emma's sunny yellow quilt, like she's a girl herself.

I stand in the threshold of the door, still wishing I knew what to say. Kate's been back in Amy's bathroom, picking up the smashed eye shadow boxes and powder compacts that Mike destroyed. She walks up behind me and puts a hand on my shoulder.

"I mean, what do I do now?" Amy says, tossing aside Emma's *Guess How Much I Love You.* "Do I pull Emma out of school? Do I hire a moving company? Who takes what? What if he doesn't pay the mortgage? How do I go about selling the house?"

Kate rushes to her before I do. "Listen, listen," she coos, sitting down next to Amy. "I know that the particulars of our situations are different, but it was just a few weeks ago that I sat in my bedroom doing this very same thing. Except, well, I was the one who'd trashed the room," she jokes.

Amy actually smiles. It's barely a grin, but it's a smile. I walk across the room and sit down on the floor in front of them.

"I think that the first thing you ought to do is talk to someone," Kate says. "I had Waverly. She's pretty good."

I gently nudge her foot with mine.

"You don't need to figure out any of this logistical stuff yet," Kate says. "That's all going to take care of itself."

"It's just that this was my home. My family."

"I know, Amy. I know," Kate says. I watch her pull Amy toward her. Amy puts her head on Kate's shoulder and starts to cry. I have never seen Kate so tender.

"I don't know what I'm doing. What am I doing going through all of this stuff? What am I hoping to find?" she says.

"I know. It's awful," Kate says again. "I know you can't look at it this way now, and I know that it's horrifying to see everything you know fall apart, but I promise you that it's ultimately a good thing."

"Everything I know and everything I have is broken."

"That's the beauty of it, though," Kate says. "I know it's hard to see, but that's really the most wonderful thing about all of this. I know that our situations are so, so different, Amy. I understand that. But I have this sense of relief now that I think you'll also experience. It's not easy—I'm not going to lie to you. I often feel sad, but I feel *right*. Does that make sense?"

Amy doesn't say anything.

"The one thing that I can tell you," Kate continues, "is that now, when I wake up in the morning and look in the mirror, I feel like I see myself again, not this…" She circles her hand in front of her face. "Not this image of what I'm *supposed to* be. I'm learning who I really am, I guess, or I'm coming back to her. And I think you will, too." Kate grabs Amy's hand. "You're going to get through this," she says.

"Well, I know that I was trying hard to hold on to what I wanted to be; that's for sure," Amy says. "Or what I thought I *needed* to be. To be happy."

"That's exactly it," Kate says. "But you've told the truth now, and that's the hardest part. That's what I'm learning. You have to be honest with yourself about what you really want, who you really are, and what's best for you. Once you've done that…" She shrugs.

"Yes, except"—Amy chews on her bottom lip—"where do I go from here?"

"Wherever you want," Kate says. "Now you get to go wherever you want."

Amy rubs her eyes and looks over at me. "Hey," she says, reaching for me. "Thank you. For everything."

"Don't," I say. "It's what you would have done. It's *less* than what you would've done."

"That's not true at all," Amy says. She looks around the room. "Let's get out of here," she finally says. "I don't want to be here anymore."

As we walk down the stairs and through the house to the door, each of us holding a bag or two of the things Amy's chosen to carry into her new life, I think, looking around at the mess, that before I knew what was happening with Amy, I thought of her home as such a haven. That was the way that she made it look, and I always compared: *Would I ever have a family like hers? Would I get the white picket fence, too?* But now I know better. I know because in our own particular ways, we all did the same thing: faked it. Amy pretended that she had a happy family. Kate embraced a role that wasn't right for her. I lied to everyone who's important to me, thinking all the while that I could never be happy until everything was perfect.

Later that night, Amy relents and takes a sleeping pill. Emma's still at the hotel with her grandparents, and Larry is upstairs getting ready for bed. I walk to the back door in the kitchen and bolt the dead bolts. I check the lock on the window over the kitchen sink. It's not that I believe that Mike is bound to show up, exactly. It's just that I want to be ready in case he does. It's like that old superstition about carrying an umbrella so that it won't rain. If I take all of the proper precautions, maybe he'll stay away.

A few minutes later, after I've finished the dishes, Larry finds me scrubbing at the sludge that has built up on the stove top.

"Hey," he says, kissing the top of my head. "Want some help?"

I shake my head. I can see the faint outline of his reflection in the tile backsplash. He needs a haircut, as usual. He's wearing his ancient Ramones T-shirt.

"She's lucky to have you guys," he says, kissing the top of my head again and rubbing his hands lightly over my back.

I nod and stop scrubbing, and then turn to him. "Thanks for everything you've done to help," I say, wrapping my arms around him. "With Emma. With everything."

"Of course," he says.

Of course, I repeat to myself.

Earlier in the day, after my third and final attempt to try to get Amy to eat something, she said something that's been on my mind since. She was standing on the threshold between the kitchen and the living room, watching Larry sing "The Itsy Bitsy Spider" with Emma.

"He'll be a great dad someday, you know," she said, taking a sip of the cup of tea I'd forced into her hands. "When you both finally realize that you were made to be a family."

I didn't know what to say considering the circumstances, so I didn't say anything. I walked to where Amy stood and looked over her shoulder at Larry, who was now folding a hat out of the Sports section. Emma giggled and reached for it, dancing around him impatiently.

Now I wrap my arms tighter around Larry's waist, dropping my sponge on the floor behind him. As I nestle against his chest, my mind drifts to being at Amy's house and watching the way that Kate comforted Amy today. Amy must have been surprised by it, and it reminds me of when my parents died, and how people I hardly knew did the most wonderful things, like dropping meals off unannounced, or writing to tell me about some heartfelt memory they had about one of them. A lesson I'd learned then is starting to work its way back to me: I need to hold on to the people who care for me, because the next time I fall—and there will be a next time; there always will—they'll be the ones to help me through.

It seems so silly, looking back now, that I kept my problems a secret from the people who cared for me most. Isn't it easier, I realize now, to just let things be? And, I think, my fingers laced behind Larry's back, to hold on to a good and true thing when you have it? I need him just as he is. *Now.* I need to be just who I am. *Now.* Someday—hopefully a long time in the future—I may have to let him go, just like I did with my parents. But in the meantime, I should celebrate. Because what I have is a lot.

CHAPTER THIRTY-FOUR

Last night, after I finally collapsed into bed, I dreamt that it was summertime. I was in my childhood bedroom, sitting in the center of my twin bed, which was pushed against a wall under a window. I rested my elbows on the window ledge and dragged a bumpy trail across the window's screen with my fingernail. I was wearing one of the gauzy white nightgowns that Babci made for me at the start of every summer, and it was damp in the spot between my shoulder blades, where my hair was wet from the shower and combed into thick, seal-slick strands.

Sitting with my nose nearly pressed to the screen, I could smell summer in the air; that distinct, indelible scent that the sun leaves on the street after radiating onto the concrete all day. I could hear the television down the hall—a laugh track, my parents watching *Johnny Carson*. I pictured my mother curled into a corner of the couch and drinking a soda out of a plastic tumbler. She'd have a forgotten needlepoint on her legs, which would be tanned from her weekend tennis. My dad would be in the chair next to her, contentedly twiddling his thumbs while he watched Johnny banter with Ed McMahon.

There was nothing to be afraid of here; that's what I felt gazing out of my bedroom window at the peaceful street that I grew up on. It was quiet and dark, with a thousand shadows where dangerous things could lurk, but I wasn't scared. Not even a little bit. This was home. As predictable as a calendar.

Then suddenly it was as if a curtain was pulled, and my adult self, sitting in my childhood bed, realized that I could still have that security, because it—my parents—were still deep down inside of me, and always would be, no matter how many mistakes I made. I pulled my faded Holly Hobbie sheets up to my chest, heard the chirping crickets outside my window, and knew that this peace—this optimistic, childlike certainty—was going to lead me now. I didn't need to waste another minute worrying. It wasn't too late. I could hold on to everything I'd learned over the past year—all of the problems with work and my money, all of the tragedy—and life would still be quite good. The sun always rises.

I still feel it, two hours after getting out of bed. I'm brushing my teeth to get the stale coffee taste out of my mouth even though I know I'm minutes from another cup. Downstairs, I can hear Emma's cartoon. Amy and Larry are chatting with Amy's parents—about the weather. What a beautiful thing, to chat about the weather. There's no talk of Mike, who's on all of our minds nevertheless, and probably will be for a long while. There's no sense of, "What should we do?" For now, in this moment, it's just eight a.m. A Thursday morning. Let it be.

The doorbell rings. It's Kate, who insists on accompanying me to my hair appointment before the catalog photo shoot later today. I put my toothbrush in the holder next to Larry's and then hang my towel over his on the crowded hook on the back of the door. I glance in the mirror, decide I look fine, and then I go downstairs, where my family is waiting for me.

ACKNOWLEDGMENTS

I am immensely grateful to my agent, Katherine Fausset, for her unparalleled wisdom and enthusiasm for this book, and to my editor, Emily Griffin, for her insightful, expert work. Thank you for making this experience such an enjoyable one.

Thanks also to Eileen Chetti, Erica Warren, and the rest of the team at Grand Central. Matthew Crowley, Susan Laubach, Jason Sulham, Rita Anita, Claudia Ybarra, Michael Johnson, and Chris Reisenger were generous with their professional expertise and helped me keep my facts straight. Jessica Crowley, Jay Lewis, and Peter Kusek read early drafts and provided valuable feedback.

The National Domestic Violence Hotline connected me with several women who bravely shared their stories with me. Thank you so much for your candid honesty. My respect for you is boundless.

Most of all, to my family: Thanks for making me feel like the luckiest girl alive. You're everything.

READING GROUP GUIDE

AUTHOR'S NOTE

This story started with a rumor. Years ago, I'd heard whispers that someone I knew was being hit by her partner. For a variety of good reasons, I never believed it, and I still don't. But the questions surrounding it stuck with me: what if it were true, after all, and what if I'd sat idly by while someone I knew was in crisis? Yet I also wondered—and I'm ashamed to admit it, because it feels like a horribly lazy and selfish way to be—*How much could I have really helped?* The question nagged at me: when is deciding that something's "not your business" irresponsible and when, conversely, is it the only choice? How much, really, can you insert yourself into someone else's troubled relationship?

These are the questions I was working with when I began the first draft of this novel. The story grew from there, of course. While it's still very much a story about how women's friendships influence our love relationships and vice versa, it ultimately became a story about the way that we compare ourselves to each other, even to our closest friends, and about the images that we both create for ourselves and project onto people's lives. I don't believe that Waverly's an inherently jealous person, and yet her life is consumed by the comparisons she makes and the feeling that she doesn't quite measure up. Even though she's aware, as we all are, that the grass isn't *actually* any greener next door—she knows that Kate doesn't really have it all, and she knows that Amy and Mike don't have a perfect family—she still can't help but feel like she's the only person on earth who's flawed, and her shame about this runs deep enough to almost cost her every good thing she's created for herself.

This feels to me like an instinctively female problem, and even after spending hundreds of hours thinking about this story while I sat at my desk, or ate dinner, or went for a run, or nursed my two babies, I still can't put my finger on why. Do we compare ourselves to each other because we feel, on some level, like we're expected to have it all—Kate's beauty and wealth, Amy's dedication to motherhood and family, Waverly's independent spirit? Does it start in middle school with appearances, and if so does the ante slowly ratchet up from "Why is she already wearing a bra and I'm not?" to "Why is she getting married, or having kids, or getting promoted, and I'm not?" Maybe it's just human nature, but we all know what the deeper question is when we play this game with ourselves: What's wrong with *me*?

The answer is "nothing," of course. There's a decent amount of Waverly in me—for many years during my teens and twenties, I was a class-A perfectionist who actually believed that if every area of my life wasn't scrubbed to a flawless shine, then I was failing at life. It was exhausting. But I've come to believe that it's our imperfections that make us and, ultimately, connect us. It doesn't do any of us any good to pretend we have it all figured out. I frankly like a person a whole lot more when she welcomes me into her messy house, wipes sandwich crumbs off the table before she sets a drink in front of me, and tells me a story about whatever real-deal, nittygritty monster she's wrestling with that day. Don't you?

I'm a person who loves quotes, and I recently came across this one from Theodore Roosevelt that sums all of this up pretty perfectly. I've come to think of it as the mission statement for this book: "Comparison is the thief of joy." Or, as a wise friend once told me: Don't look left. Don't look right. Be yourself.

QUESTIONS FOR FURTHER DISCUSSION

1. At its heart, *How Lucky You Are* is a novel about friendship. Do you have just a few close friends, like Waverly does, or do you rely on a much larger circle?

2. In what ways does Kate fit your stereotype of a politician's wife? In what ways does she defy the stereotype?

3. Have you ever had a friend with Amy's sort of optimism and willingness to see the best in people? Or, have you been that person?

4. Kate and Waverly both make comments throughout the novel about growing up in the Washington, D.C. area. How much does where you come from influence your personality?

5. As Waverly's financial situation worsens, she finds herself less and less able to take a hard look at her finances. Do you think this is a common response to a crisis?

6. Waverly says that she doesn't care whether she and Larry ever marry. Do you believe her? Do you think it's possible to have a lifelong commitment without marriage?

7. In one of the novel's most heartbreaking moments, Waverly catches herself wishing that Amy's injuries might be ever so slightly worse so that she'd realize she needed to leave Mike.

Have you ever wished for something awful in the service of the greater good?

8. Gore Vidal once said, "Every time a friend succeeds, I die a little." Does this statement apply to any of the characters in the book? Why or why not?

9. Waverly spends so much time looking at others' lives from the outside, imagining that their exterior order is connected to inner peace. Do you find that this is actually true more often than not?

10. On a related note, Amy and Kate both have perfectly clean and organized homes—albeit on quite different scales—while Waverly lives with more disorder. What do we learn about or project onto people from seeing the inside and outside of their homes?

11. During their conversation in the hospital cafeteria, Amy's mother tells Waverly that you can never have absolute certainty about a relationship's future. Do you believe that to be true?

12. In that same conversation, Amy's mother worries whether she concentrated too much on raising "nice girls." Is too much pressure put on girls and women to be nice? Do women seem weaker if they're perceived as agreeable and optimistic?

13. At one point early in the novel, Waverly tells us about losing her parents and says that she doesn't need to pay a therapist to tell her what she already knows. What sort of emotional transitions and breakthroughs has she made by the novel's end? How many are driven by external events versus internal changes?

14. What do you think happens after the novel's final pages? Do you think that Mike is gone for good? Do you see a future for Kate and Brendan? Will Waverly and Larry ever marry or start a family?